Music by My Bedside

OTHER WORKS IN DALKEY ARCHIVE PRESS'S
TURKISH LITERATURE SERIES

Farewell: A Mansion in Occupied Istanbul
Ayşe Kulin

Music by
My Bedside

Kürşat Başar

Translated by Çiğdem Aksoy Fromm

Dalkey Archive Press
Champaign | London | Dublin

Originally published in Turkish as *Başucumda müzik* by İş bankası Kültür Yay, Istanbul, 2003.

A catalog record for this book is available from the Library of Congress.
ISBN 978-1-56478-815-3

This book has been supported by the Ministry of Culture and Tourism of Turkey in the framework of the TEDA project

In cooperation with Barbaros Altug and Everest Yayınları

Partially funded by a grant from the Illinois Arts Council, a state agency.

www.dalkeyarchive.com

Cover: design and composition by Mikhail Iliatov

Printed on permanent/durable acid-free paper and bound in the United States of America

I can't sleep without music by my bedside.

Ever since I was a kid.

An old love song is always playing on that little music box, stirring up unforgettable images of days long past.

Memory's so strange!

Without warning, images come to life, their colors grow palpable, pulling you into the realm of the past, as if you were stuck in a broken time machine. The images and their dates jumble together. You can't tell which scent pairs with which memory. Perhaps you know instinctively which of them is precious; and sometimes, while the intricate mechanism of recollection is whirling you around, the images flow by, gliding across the windowpanes of a speeding train. Suddenly, a single memory glitters, catching your eye for a moment, and at that very instant you yearn, more than you've ever yearned for anything, to return to that image, to that one and only feeling, which has gone unnoticed.

Some people don't have a home.

I've spent my life moving from place to place—in ephemeral homes, hotel rooms, guesthouses, and on the road. I can no longer recall all those places, in countless corners of the world.

They say recapturing the past is pleasing. No, not at all.

Though they may compel us to smile at first, memories fade away when we reach for them, and regardless of our actions, they plunge us into sorrow.

I have never been attached to my belongings. Nor do I care to collect mementos.

Most often, I refrain from engraving mental pictures in my mind. Yet, all is in vain! Have not all those images stowed away for a lifetime hunted me down until this very day?

Since my childhood, I have always wondered about the recording mechanism of the human mind. Images, colors, faces, scenery, photographs, houses, roads, clothes, scents, sounds, and feelings all register in my memory with unfathomable speed. So the next time you chance upon something or someone—a spitting image—you remember . . .

Time after time, I stroll through the sophisticated, ever-growing, gargantuan archives of my mind and lose myself in a myriad of swirling concentric circles. Wishing to catch and recall a particular memory, an emotion, or a moment bygone, I find myself engulfed in an utterly different time and place. I wonder how I happen to find myself by the seaside, inhaling the scents of an unexpected spring just as I was listening to the half-destroyed records of a conversation that took place in the rooms of my childhood.

Nowadays, space travel is possible. However, setting off on a journey in time is only possible if our destination is the unknown cities of our memory, traveling through our inner selves.

Space travel . . .

Even in the recent past, these two words were still evocative of the mysterious world of tales.

For us ordinary people, unimaginable secrets concealed themselves beyond the borders of our world. New worlds of our infinite imagination. Strange creatures that would suddenly appear before us in some unknown corner of the universe. Trepidation. Exhilaration.

The dreams of the unknown.

That unequaled feeling of having demolished your own borders to dive into the obscurity of a boundless universe.

Who could know what there was to find? What would happen when the first human set foot on the surface of the moon? Did the creatures who watched us—and probably visited our world secretly—live in an adjacent universe?

Would it be enough to traverse the borders of the Earth to discover the mystery of life?

We waited anxiously.

Then they went there. Flaring rockets were sent into the darkness of outer space one after another. Then, one day, we saw them walk on the ashen surface of the moon, jumping up and down on the craters like children. We saw it all. Was it not incredible? Honestly. Something we had heard of only in fairy tales, comic books or films had come true in the blink of an eye. They were there, and we were watching them from our living rooms. They romped in the wilderness, among the craters, like burlesque puppets hopping about in an absolute terra nova. They went there, but at the cost of our dreams, which perished. Neither the unforeseen creatures nor the faraway lands that responded to our clandestine messages existed from then on. The closer we got to the universe, the farther it slipped away and faded into the distance. The endless void deepened as it slowly engulfed us. We returned to Earth after we put out our flags on top of a wrinkled-faced planet, as if we were small children desiring to prove ourselves. That was it. Colorful pieces of fabric swaying in the wind on the moonscape, on a lonesome planet. Traces of childish pride inscribed on a limitless sky.

If there were someone watching us, he must have roared with laughter at our ludicrous feat.

So much has run its course. Things unattended in the routine of everyday life. So many disasters, wars, and inventions that reached us through the stark headlines of the daily paper. An unceasing evolution has passed us by, unglorified.

The world must have grown up just as we did and was left bereft of its charm.

Because we saw ourselves from there, from afar, from those strange places, we realized we were but a speck of dust in eternity.

Merely a speck of dust in the vast universe.

Did we really understand?

I have been told the same thing over and over since I was a little girl: "Accept reality!"

Yeah, but why accept the kind of reality that makes me miserable?

Think what you like, but I am fond of lies. Fantasies, dreams, and harmless lies.

If someone idles away her years in such a house like this, dwelling on nothing but reality, all that is left to do is to wonder why life takes so long to end. And you cannot help getting bored.

Besides, who can say that the lively play of fantasy is not truly life itself?

No sooner than I put my head on my pillow and hear the same music again, I can arrange all those incomprehensible coincidences and believe that all is destiny, a farfetched narrative, our predetermined fate from the day we were born.

So who knows, maybe that is the way it was.

Remembering is tiresome. However, if you manage not to forget anything, carry with you all the time everything that has receded into the past—images, details, faces, scents, and voices—you no longer have to recall them because they stay with you forever.

They are neither memories nor the indistinct, threadbare pieces of your lost life; nor are they faded photographs that can be revived or tampered with anymore. They are life itself, keeping pace with you with every new day.

Some things are never forgotten—like someone you miss, someone you remember even when he is with you, by your side.

Therefore, as I recline here on these summer afternoons, I can tell myself this curious story, each time with a new beginning.

Despite all its confusion and perplexity, isolation, sadness, pain of separation, hopeful expectations, loneliness, and unspeakable longing, it seems to me the most delightful story in the world.

I will certainly tell this tale in various ways, and each time I unfold it, I will add new things that I had failed to notice before, but what difference does it make . . . ?

Here, on this spring morning, far away in the city of light, I suddenly wake up in a small hotel room with the rays of the sun and hear that song—the song that I will never forget. I feel as if it comes through my dreams.

I feel as if the dream I am having still goes on; yes, just like now, I am unable to tell whether I am dreaming or awake. I rush to the window and open it. The cool morning breeze caresses my face, and I see a blind man playing that melody on his accordion in front of the door.

How many years have passed since then? Forty? More? Never mind! A blind man is playing "Everything Has Disappeared But You." I am unaware that from then on I will mix up everything and not be able to tell truth from fantasy. I watch in surprise as the street musician plays our song.

How many of us realize that an unexpected coincidence is in fact a magical sign, like those encountered by a young hero in a tale, leading him to embark on an entirely new adventure?

What a strange coincidence that music is. My heart beats madly, as if I have done something wrong. As if some expected and long-awaited good news has arrived. As if I have suddenly become naked in front of a crowd.

Then someone knocks at my door, and it sinks in that this is not a coincidence. Young men in hotel uniforms carry in roses of all colors—roses with long stems. The small hotel room is soon packed with red, white, yellow, pink, purple, and orange roses. The blind musician keeps on playing the old song:

I am not separated from you,
not even for a moment,
even if you are far, far away.
Everything brings you to me,
Scents, sounds, voices.
My eyes do not see,
I have forgotten all that I know
Except for your face,
Even if you are far, far away.

Instantly the song I have never forgotten touches somewhere deep inside of me. The melody fills me with joy, it makes me happy, but it also makes me cry with sorrow.

As I try to remember the lyrics, I smell the fragrant roses.

His handwriting appears inside a bunch of roses: "When you receive these flowers, you'll hear the song you and I promised never to forget. Distances do not mean much for us. If we have a true bond between us, like you said we have, listen to that beautiful song, which I believe reflects our genuine bond. Let it bring me to you, just as it has brought you to me. I don't know what's going through your mind now, but you should know that wherever you go, I'll find you. Some coincidences are nothing but destiny. Tell me, who can change destiny?"

I know his letter by heart.

Like everything else he has written. Like all of our meetings. All dates, places, and phone calls.

Women do not forget.

And really, what are coincidences but fate, or unexpected gifts that life gives us out of the blue?

What we cannot know or will never understand is the reason our destiny is the way it is. Instead of taking us somewhere entirely different, why does an obscure detail, an unexpected surprise, or a small trick of fate thrust us somewhere we don't expect? We cannot know how a few short seconds can affect one's entire life.

What an odd game!

Everyone has to learn the same game over and over again, making the same mistakes and protecting himself. Nobody can say he knows the game perfectly or can teach someone else how to play it.

Standing on the sidelines to learn the game by watching others play is out of question. Even as a spectator, you are still in the game. You have no other choice except to become part of the game, in one way or another.

But can't we at least pause at a certain point and change our role?

Is this only about courage, or when you think you are in control of the coincidences, do they in fact control you?

We start with absolutely no knowledge and learn all the rules on our own. If we knew that each step we take will determine an unknown future which will materialize years from now, we couldn't survive.

Isn't this unfair?

You have to participate in a game in which you cannot even decide whom to play with or whom to compete against, knowing that it is your one and only chance to play it. Repetition is not allowed.

If only we could have one more chance. If only we could change a decision we made at a milestone in our life and start over again.

I know, it doesn't work that way.

Now I'm traveling from one memory to another.

Come. Join me!

If you asked me what was the one thing that determined my destiny, I'd tell you it was that song.

Yes, a song that was playing in my dream.

If you have ever told someone, "everything has disappeared from my life but you," or if you have ever felt this way in your heart, you surely know that it makes you feel as if you have sprouted wings. And it is terrifying.

You would give everything to forget all and send that feeling into oblivion with a single touch of a magic wand, but—how strange—even if that were possible, you could not bring yourself to part with it.

The helplessness of suddenly realizing that your inner self, which you thought would always do as you tell it, has begun to act crazily, like an unleashed rebellious child. The astonishment of realizing that you are unable to deal with it. And the inexorable allure of that adventure which has brought you to a matchless state of ecstasy you could find nowhere else.

I know a few languages, but none contain words that could describe this feeling.

Wait a minute! That broken time machine is now hurling me back into the past, carrying me to one of those ordinary childhood moments which truly, yet unexpectedly, determine the course of your life, although the very same piece of memory had somehow seemed unimportant when you lived thatactual moment.

I now go to that winter morning when a cold distant sun hung sulking in the sky.

To Ankara, when I was fourteen.

Does childhood make cities seem more beautiful in memories than they actually are?

Or is it that we destroy and devastate cities as time goes by?

Later, each time I visited Ankara, I only saw an ugly, worn out place packed with clumsy buildings. A city that had lost its beautiful sunny mornings forever.

Tedious, oppressive, drab apartment complexes had replaced those spacious boulevards of my childhood, the bright orderly buildings, wide public squares, sunny hills, and lovely homes with pretty gardens.

Perhaps the steppes were rejecting the untimely siege that had begun through the symbols of a new civilization, which we believed were magnificent.

Later, each time I saw the shantytowns, the ramshackle, jerry-built structures, and the impoverished inhabitants next to the old homes near the castle, I couldn't help wondering if that was all we had succeeded in achieving over so many years in the capital city of hopes.

Now, that cold mausoleum on Rasattepe—the symbol of this city—gives me nothing but a deep feeling of gloom.

I wish that instead of following the tradition of the Pharaohs, who sought eternal life after death, we had protected the warm, modest home of our national leader, the place where he had lived when he was filled with the hope of building a new country. This would have made life, rather than death, the symbol of this city. I also wish we had believed that many others like him could have grown up in all of these homes.

No, I don't adore Ankara anymore. Besides, I haven't been there for years.

I tell you, when you are a child, you see things differently.

Maybe it is not the city but my weary eyes that make me think even the spring sun has changed. Maybe that mist which seems to cover the people is not real but just a film over my eyes.

This is not the same city where I raced my bike, leaving our small house with a garden, nor the one where I sometimes slid on my school bag on the sloping streets that are now lined with giant buildings with glass façades and big hotels.

I wish I could have saved the images of Ankara of my childhood to revisit again and again, not allowing new images to replace them.

Unfortunately, this is how our memory works. As time goes by, memory blurs and become vague. Images, sounds, and voices are superimposed, replacing each other. No wonder when I spend my time at home, I catch myself humming some worthless refrain from one of the contemporary songs they keep playing on TV nowadays instead of the beautiful melodies of the past.

What can you do? It's not only one's own face in the mirror that grows old.

Those serene summer afternoons when Ayla and I played in the garden are somewhere just here.

Nobody told us back then that those days would grow distant when we tried to recall them, that memories would be lost quickly, and that we wouldn't be able to replace them with anything as pure, beautiful, happy or comforting.

No, they never warned us.

I can hear my mother's voice calling us for afternoon tea. The wonderful smell of the warm walnut pastries and apple cookies reach all the way here.

We will go in now, and the tranquil atmosphere of the dim hallway—something that is perhaps only found in old houses—will surround us. We will make ourselves comfortable on the armchairs covered with old, dirty upholstery and wait for our tea.

When was that? Ayla had come in with a book in her hand again. She had said, "Do you remember years ago when you showed me a poem in a magazine and said that the author would be a great poet one day?

"How can I remember that?" I replied. "Is he a great poet now?"

She laughed. "I don't know. Find out for yourself. Here's his new book. I enjoyed it very much."

I read the book that night. Somewhere, it said, "Childhood is something like the sky / it does not go anywhere."

It is true. Childhood does not go anywhere. It is always there.

Everywhere we go, it tags along, as if holding our hand.

Ayla has those pictures. I used to tell her, "Don't show these photos to anyone. Anyone who sees them will not want to marry you!" Yet, she wouldn't listen.

In the pictures, we both look like boys. Our hair is tousled. We have bruises everywhere. We are dressed in plaid pants or overalls, and we're either climbing on something or jumping from a tree.

It's strange, but most of those scars are still with me. Today, when I look at my knees, elbows, or feet, I say, yes this is the one that happened when I fell out of the tree while picking mulberries with Ayla, or this happened when I fell off my bike that morning. The traces of my own little history, like chapter headings.

If I had been told that I could stop at a certain moment in my life and stay there forever, I would have chosen one of two moments.

The first is when I was rocking in the swing hanging from the branches of a tree in the garden of my childhood.

The other is the day I first kissed the man I loved more than anyone in my whole life.

In those times, I didn't realize that a feeling which finds you suddenly at some distinct point in your life in an unexplainable way stays with you forever.

During that most wonderful kiss of my life, I felt the same excitement and joy I had while rocking on a swing. Perhaps at that moment, I realized that I had found again what I had been seeking for years without even being aware of it.

In all those books, films, and songs we were told about love.

And in ancients scrolls, legends, tales, and drawings engraved on walls, too.

Even people who do not go through adventures that involve a mysterious feeling that drags you along were carried away by the excitement of love and felt as if they were in a totally different realm.

Some have even written books, carried out experiments, or tried to define this feeling through scientific equations.

Many strived to write the common language of falling in love.

In fact, it is quite simple: you are in love if you feel as if you're rocking on a swing when you kiss someone.

You see, I am unable to arrange my thoughts and am struggling to tell you this without confusing you.

It is as though I've entered the attic of a haunted house, packed with old, dusty furniture. I rummage through everything I happen to come across, bewildered, like a small child who picks up something, opens and plays with it, only to immediately pick up something else—something that attracts his attention more.

A box, cast aside and forgotten; a broken wooden horse with its red paint scraped off; a wooden puppet (the one whose nose gets longer when he lies); a bunch of old letters—who knows what lines they contain—tightly bound by an old piece of ribbon; photographs of people whose names I can hardly remember; dusty books; dolls with missing legs; broken alarm clocks; tin boxes; cracked ceramic trinkets whose polish is worn away . . .

Isn't this the oldest thing I remember from my childhood: my brother's steel train set painted in red and green? I used to admire how smoke blew from the locomotive as it moved along the rails. At the station, a woman dressed in a coat and a hat and carrying a chic handbag, a man in uniform—the stationmaster perhaps—and a few passengers holding their suitcases were waiting. A door on the train opened, and someone got out. When the train left again, it switched to another track, leading to either a bridge or a tunnel. It was my brother, in his short brown overalls and suspenders that never stayed in their place, who did all of this by moving the rails spread across the floor and by pulling various levers. I was stretched out on our old Erzurum carpet with its intricate and colorful design, with my head between my hands and my elbows on the floor. I kept telling my brother, "Come on, let the whistle blow, let the smoke come out."

The music begins when the crank of the old phonograph is turned, carrying me away as if I have suddenly come across an ex-love.

Did I say "ex-love?" I do not have an ex-love. I only have one love.

Among all of the pieces of furniture, I find a red bicycle with its paint scraped away and its metal parts rusted. I wipe off the dust and manage to ring the bell. I get on the bike and let myself loose in time. Suddenly, I am racing downhill at full speed.

On a matchless winter day.

In Ankara, when I was fourteen.

On a cool, happy morning of my carefree days.

The slope goes down to the road where our home is located. I used to climb all the way up, huffing and puffing, and then come down like the wind, scared and with beating heart, yet enjoying every moment. (Many years later, I saw a film in which a little boy riding his bicycle as fast as I used to, took off and flew over the clouds. I felt exactly the same thing on that slope.)

As I speed down the hill as usual, I see my brother at the corner of the road. He is talking to a tall man I have never seen before.

I am wearing a big cap so that my hair does not fly in the wind. My father's cap. (I usually throw away everything, but it seems I had not been able to let go of that cap. Recently, I found it at home, hidden in a corner. I couldn't decide whether I should be happy or sad. I just sat there and cried, with the cap on my lap.)

Clouds are moving high above in the sky. White round clouds that make me think I could climb up on them and float far away, to distant unknown lands.

In the blink of an eye, I reach where my brother and the tall man are standing. Frightened that I will hit them, I quickly turn the bike and plunge to the ground.

As I stand up, trying to tidy myself, my brother laughs and says to the man, "And this is my little sister." I blush and stare at the ground.

The man looks like an actor. His slightly graying sideburns are in pleasing harmony with his dark blue eyes. He's wearing a khaki brown jacket with a leather collar. Underneath, he has a thick turtleneck sweater. I lift my head to look at him. His eyes glow in the wintry light. I can't tell whether they are harsh or soft, or if they are looking at me or far into the distance. He turns to my brother and says with a mocking smile, "Your little sister is a bit mischievous, it seems."

Is it funny that the first word I heard from him was about my "mischievousness"?

Well, that was how it happened.

Who would have known?

As we were walking home, I said to my brother, "What a cold man!"

"Cold?" he laughed. "Mr. Fuat? What do you know! All the women in Ankara are in love with him."

I remember that the same night, in the dark, I thought about him as I slowly fell asleep.

I fantasized that one day I would suddenly appear in front of him, and he would be surprised and not know how to react when I told him that I was that boyish, mischievous girl who had not caught even a bit of his attention in the past.

My beauty would astonish him, and he would be unable to decide what to do or how to act.

If you wonder whether I really fantasized that, let me tell you the truth: I did, imagining it like a movie in my mind's eye. The scene is still vivid in my memory.

However, the strange thing was not a fourteen-year-old girl's daydreaming, but what was to happen afterwards.

I pulled the blanket all the way over my head.

So, he is the man with whom all the women are in love?

But of course, this was just a dream to last a single night. It was nothing more than a young girl's fantasy no one knew about, a tale she wrote, or a film she created in her own mind.

Now we should put the pieces in their places and draw back a little so that we can see the whole picture better.

During my school years, my father used to tell me that I "walked on air." My friends were always amazed at the things I did. It was true that I was walking on air. I still do the same. All I lacked was a couple of wings. I really don't understand why I didn't care a bit about all the rules people thought important and tried hard to comply with.

I have always admired the heroines in novels who do things others can't. If you don't do what others cannot, you can't be a heroine in the first place, can you? You can only be one of those people who read about the life of a heroine in a book.

But no, I was sure I wanted to be one those women: someone who does not read about another's life and daydreams, but is the heroine of an adventure who can make her dreams come true.

I thought so when I was just a little girl. Since the nights I imagined those dreams.

Can a human change his destiny? I decided to create my own destiny. That's why I did things no one thought I would. I tried to build a future for myself that I desired. Maybe everything has happened just because of this. Sometimes I suspect it. Maybe that great power I challenged wanted to tell me that only He was capable of determining human destiny.

In fact, life was difficult.

I realized this much later. Had I known it earlier, would I have been so hasty in starting a new life for myself?

I was a senior in high school. One day, when I came home from school, my mother told me, "Your Aunt Süheyla will visit us tomorrow. She'll have another family with her. I've heard that their son works for the Ministry of Foreign Affairs. He has been appointed to a diplomatic position in America. I think he saw you outside one day."

"What do you mean? Will he ask me to marry him?" I was shocked.

"Yes, but if you ask my opinion, I'm not in favor of it. Besides, I wouldn't want you to go so far away. Nevertheless, we cannot ask them not to visit. Let them come. We can ask for time to think and then send them a negative answer in the proper way."

"I won't marry anyone. Why should I? How could you come up with such a strange idea?" I was furious.

"My dear, nobody's telling you to get married, but this is the way things happen. You have grown up, and you have to get used to the fact that people will ask for your hand in marriage."

"I'll never get used to it!"

A world map signed by İsmet İnönü was hanging on my wall. A big, old map. My father had given it to me. I went to my room and looked at it. America . . . so far away . . . like a dream . . . across the ocean . . . the country of stars. How do you get there? How can you cross such a long distance?

"How? By boat, of course!" said my brother.

"I bet it lasts too long. I'd immediately get seasick."

"Hey, I think you are willing to get married but you're putting on an act! I will never hand over my dear sister to a stranger, let alone allow her to go to the other end of the world."

"Are you kidding? I only asked because I was curious. What on earth would I do there with a total stranger? Think of it! Besides, did you forget that I'm going to enroll in Türk Kuşu to become a pilot? I'll soar in the sky in my plane and fly over you while you're riding your horse."

"That sounds more like you. I wouldn't believe my eyes if I saw you cooking in the kitchen."

"God forbid!"

The lights in our house were always on. They still are, even today. Wherever I live, the rooms are always filled with light. Perhaps this habit was born out of the distress and darkness of the war years.

"What is this again? The whole house is like a torchlight procession!" my mother always grumbled, yet my father never turned the lights off.

When all the lights in the house are on, I go back to those days. I feel as if I have always been there with my parents and my brother, with whom I continuously joked, and I feel that I'm not alone.

I'm scared of loneliness.

I cannot sleep when the lights are off.

I have never wanted to be left alone. But here I am, in solitude. I feel isolated even when surrounded by many people. All alone, I turn on all the lights in the house and spend my time like that, day and night. Life is like this: if you're afraid of loneliness, be good to everyone and do everything others tell you to; otherwise, they will leave you by yourself.

All the lights were on again. My brother made fun of my long, embroidered dress.

"Look at our little one! She's turned into a lady without our noticing. Those high-heeled shoes suit you. If only you could walk properly in them!"

Standing in front of the mirror, I scrutinized myself. My hair, combed and made pretty, covered my shoulders. My mother had applied some of her mascara to my eyelashes. My long red dress, with a collar and buttoned in the front, had a fabulous fine texture.

When my mother entered the room, she could not turn her gaze away from me. Our eyes met in the mirror.

"My dear girl, did you really grow up so fast! We haven't realized how you have grown and blossomed!" Tears filled her eyes, and she was silent. My mother cried almost about everything. I don't.

When my father saw me, I blushed and looked down. He held my hand and had me turn around. "Look at my little tigress," he said. "She has become a young woman. I feel as if I have already lost you"

That evening, we all laughed about my pretty, doll-like appearance.

Later, Turgut told me, "When I stepped into your house that evening and saw you, I was dumbfounded. I was expecting to see a European-looking, scrawny girl wearing pants and a cap, and when I saw such a beauty, my heart skipped a beat."

Yet, when I saw him, my heart did not beat faster.

I only remember having thought what a nice, deep voice he had and how well he spoke. I told my brother, "He talks like a radio announcer."

Most of the time, he kept his head down. Our eyes didn't even meet, or maybe only once. Then I went to another room, and with my brother who had followed me, listened to the guests in the living room. "As you know, our aim in coming here tonight is . . ."

"Idiot, he's drinking salty coffee with pleasure!" We giggled and ran inside.

Later, Turgut said, "Of course I realized you had put salt in my coffee, but I liked that you did something so naughty."

No one thought I would assent to such a marriage arrangement. The subject wasn't even discussed at home for many days. Then other people, some acquaintances, tried to intercede. People whom my father greatly respected paid visits to us.

Ayla made me describe the whole procedure in detail. My mother scolded us a couple of times as we discussed the same subject, and we had a good time laughing.

Ayla was always saying, "We are not so foolish as to marry. I couldn't stand some guy telling me what to do. I'll do whatever I want. I'll earn money and spend it myself. That's it!"

She and I used to have so many dreams. First, we would travel throughout Anatolia. Then we would discover the world. As my father said, we would surpass all men and achieve the greatest success.

Then, one evening my father wanted to talk to me. As usual, all the lights in the living room were on. "Sit down, young lady," he said, and I took a seat in one of the heavy brown velvet armchairs.

He was drinking tea from a small delicate glass and eating dried raisins, as usual. He took a sip, placed his glass in the saucer, and leaned back in his chair.

"My dear daughter, you saw that young lad. Tell me what you think. I know what answer I would give, but I'd like your opinion."

My brother was reading the newspaper. My mother joined us, holding a plate full of apples.

I was perched on my seat. When I had to talk about something serious with my father, I was never able to look directly into his eyes. So as usual, I gazed at the floor.

"I've made my decision," I said.

The living room lights, mixed with our images, reflected on the window panes. I looked out the window into the distance.

"And?" said my father.

"I'm going to get married," I replied.

The plate dropped from my mother's hands, and the green and red apples rolled across the floor. My brother jumped up, throwing down his newspaper. A look of shock spread across my father's face.

"What are you saying?" My mother stammered. "This girl of ours is teasing us."

"No, I'm not," I said. "I want to get married."

"She's nuts. She has gone crazy!" shouted my brother.

"Wait a minute," my father interjected, trying to calm them down. Then he turned to me, "This is nothing to joke about. I did not give the matter much consideration because I thought you weren't interested. I asked you for the sake of custom since we have to give them an answer. So what do you say? Do you really want to marry him?"

His voice was cracked. He was at a loss as to what to say.

"Yes, I want to marry him. I've made my decision."

My mother began to cry.

They knew that when I said I would do something, I always did it.

"This is all your fault," my mother began to reproach my father.

"Are you really going to let her go to the other end of the world?" my brother exclaimed. "With a man she doesn't even know! Say something, Mother . . ." He stopped speaking when my father motioned for him to keep silent.

"She is not going anywhere now. Let's stop this discussion and sleep on it. We'll talk again tomorrow. It's late."

I thought I should not think about the matter anymore. I had reached a decision. It was over.

If you think about something too long, you cannot do anything in the end.

My brother was angry with me. Before going to bed, he came to my room, stared at me through the door, and said, "I thought you were intelligent. What happened to 'becoming a pilot'? Like a peasant girl, you're going to marry the first guy who shows interest in you. Good for you!"

My mother also came to my room. She stroked my hair and talked for a long time. "You're so young," she said. "You have no idea about housework or managing a household. You don't even know that young man. We won't be around. You'll be far away. Somewhere you don't even know. This is no game. What if you're unhappy or bored. What will you do then? Other people won't put up with your moodiness or pamper you like we do. Both of you would be upset then! Oh, God! Why did I let them come? It's all my fault. On the other hand, he looks like a nice, friendly young man, but . . ."

My mother! My dear mother! I found out much later that mothers can realize certain truths immediately. He was just like you described him, Mother: a nice and friendly man.

But what can a woman in whom storms break and tempests roar do with a nice, friendly man?

In those days, however, I did not recognize or understand this.

When Ayla heard my decision, she was speechless. She didn't know what to say. She couldn't believe it. "I knew you were a bit crazy, but I wasn't aware that you were insane!" she finally exclaimed. "Why don't you also give birth to five children so that you can all play together?" She thought that I was having a good time fooling everyone and that I would change my mind in a couple of days.

When my brother couldn't succeed in changing my mind by mockery, he tried a different method. "They should at least meet each other a few times, go out for dinner, and see if they can get along or not," he nagged my mother. "I can't believe it! You're saying nothing, as if that fellow is a rarity. He's just an employee of the Ministry of Foreign Affairs. What's the hurry? My sister is certainly out of her senses, but what about you?"

In the end, Turgut, my brother, and I went out for dinner.

Turgut told us stories. He described how our life in the States would be. He talked about great men and great events. The world was being reconstructed there, and we would take our place in that new world. It would be an excellent opportunity for me. I would be able to improve my English, read, and meet new people. This would be beneficial for our future. He spoke about everything in great detail. I didn't say much. At first, my brother was rather distant, but then he joined in the conversation. Eventually, the two of them seemed to like and understand each other.

I don't know if my brother's opinion was changed by that dinner, but at least he stopped objecting.

For days, many people visited us. My mother and my aunts welcomed the guests, and while appearing to be happy about the "favorable event," they kept whispering and murmuring to each other when alone and didn't cease complaining.

I remember the evening I accepted the marriage offer. I had told myself that I wasn't a girl who would spend time in silly romances, watch a man's changing moods and try to attribute meanings to them, worry if he would call or not, wonder if he still loved me, brood over something he said, or carry a handkerchief wet with tears. I convinced myself that it was better not to marry someone I loved passionately but someone who loved and admired me.

How strange! I must have gotten those ideas from the novels I used to read back then.

Oh, those pitiful people who consider themselves intelligent and think that they will be able to create their own fate, which, in fact, they do not even believe in.

As I lay wide awake on my bed in the dark, I thought that I was about to go to a distant land where I would be able to do everything I wanted and that I would be very happy. Hadn't my brother always said, "You do not suit this place. You're very young now, but when you grow older, people will not smile and chuckle at the things you do and the way you behave. Beware."

I wonder why I decided to say "yes"—an answer that even surprised my suitor—when my peers were patiently waiting for their "prince on a white horse," like in the novels they read.

Who wouldn't be amazed to see such an intractable, rebellious, frivolous girl get married to her first suitor, without even holding his hand, and accept accompanying him to the other side of the world?

Even I can't believe it when I look back and think.

Everything happened in a hurry.

Not even a special wedding gown was sewn for me. A tailor called Hatice cut up an old wedding gown belonging to one of my aunts and sewed the pieces into a dress fitting my measurements. We prepared a tiara of flowers for my head. My mother placed the flowers one by one. As she looked at me in the mirror while stringing the fresh flowers, she kept crying. Ayla tried to act strong, restraining her tears, but as I said good-bye, she hugged me and began sobbing. What I had done began to sink in at that moment. Perhaps I wouldn't see them for a long time. I wouldn't be near my best friend, my brother, my mother—and my father, who tried hard to look strong, doing his best to conceal his teary eyes, unable to believe that his daughter was about to fly away.

I confess that I clenched my jaw, and fists too. With a plastic smile on my face, I kept talking nonsense, telling people things like "we'll see each other soon" or "I'll see you in no time."

Everyone was saying I looked like a beautiful doll. Funny, since my mother had bought a giant doll dressed in a wedding gown and given it to me as a present to take along. Ayla was carrying the doll around, not letting go of it even for an instant. (That doll, with her fixed smile and bead-like eyes, followed me everywhere I went. She has stayed with me all this time. There she is now, sitting in the corner. Her wedding gown is a bit dirty after so many years.)

After the wedding ceremony, attended by only a few guests, we went directly to my in-laws' home. Upon entering their house, I was overcome by a sudden discomfort and gloom. "What have I done?" I thought, and my eyes filled with tears. I was on the verge of crying. Had it been possible I would have run back home. All I wanted at that moment was to be in my own room, in my own bed, cuddled under my own quilt and to wake up in the morning to my old life.

I got up from the armchair I had collapsed into and went to the bathroom to wash my face. With great difficulty, I resisted fleeing.

Soon we were shown to our bedroom. My mother-in-law brought a few towels, pajamas, and a pair of slippers. Then she closed the door and walked away.

We—a timid young couple—were all alone in front of the big double bed.

That confident, lighthearted young man with a European air was no longer beside me; a helpless, tongue-tied young lad stood next to me, unsure of what to say or do. I couldn't believe my situation. We sat there without uttering a word for at least half an hour. He perched on the foot of the bed, and I sat on an armchair. He continually poured water into a glass from the pitcher on the night table, gulped it down, and asked every now and then if I wanted some too. The pitcher was soon empty. Eventually, he said, "Okay. Why don't you take off your wedding gown and let's go to bed. We have to leave early tomorrow."

Blood rushed to my face.

What an odd tradition! I had never undressed next to anyone. Not even my brother had seen me in my nightgown. How could I go to bed with a total stranger? I was furious and broke out in a sweat. "Mr. Turgut," I said sternly. "Go out and smoke a cigarette. I'll change and get into bed. Then you can come in. Understood?"

Although taken aback by my authoritarian tone, he laughed. "Yes, ma'am," he said and left the room.

I quickly took off my wedding gown and put on that foolish-looking ruffled nightgown. I jumped into the bed and pulled up the heavy hand-embroidered quilt.

I had thought I would stay awake out of excitement, but in fact, I dozed off before he returned to the room. He did not have the heart to wake me up. So, we both went to bed and fell asleep without doing anything else. Thankfully, we were to set off at dawn.

First, we traveled to London. For the first time in my life, I was in a foreign country. Eveything was brand new. I felt both free and caged at the same time. It is hard to describe. I enjoyed seeing new things and places, strolling around like a grown-up woman; yet, at the same time, I missed the people I had left behind and felt depressed because I realized that this was not a holiday but the beginning of a long new life.

We went sightseeing and shopping. Turgut enjoyed choosing clothes for me. This gave him the chance to buy me what he wanted me to wear. A proper little lady. A young, European woman. Neither feminine nor childish. For him, everything in life had to comply with norms. Everything had to be according to the rules. Nothing could be extreme.

We visited museums and castles. We took walks along the river. Turgut kept telling me romantic things. He spoke about films and novels and even recited poetry, acting as if we were two sweethearts desperately in love. His voice was impressive and very soft. Even when one did not pay attention to the content of his words, listening to his voice was enjoyable. One evening, we went out to dinner. Just the two of us. Candles were lit. Wine was served. I had put on makeup and my prettiest blue dress.

"Look," he said, "everyone's watching us."

Turgut was truly happy about that.

Everyone really did look at us—wherever we went. Maybe they thought I was too young. Whatever I wore, I looked like a young girl. As soon as people learned we were newlyweds, they took interest in us. In shops, they gave us presents; in restaurants, they offered us drinks; and in cafés, they wanted to chat with us.

But I was not in love with Turgut. In fact, he was not in love with me either. Why would someone fall in love with a kid whom he had seen from a distance?

The stories of love and romance did not last long. He was not convincing, and I did not enjoy hearing them.

Turgut had dreams of his own. He wanted to develop strong connections in America. He would prove his worth and capability and be promoted. He would learn another language. We would wait for a few years to have a child.

Before we had left Turkey, Turgut and my father had had a talk. My father had asked him to make sure that I continued my education. Now Turgut told me I could at least attend a language school.

He was a good soul. He wanted me to be happy. He believed that by conforming to the rules and through mutual respect, a couple could look forward to the future and be happy. He believed that a life could be constructed in this way. In reality, he had so few expectations that there was no reason he could not be happy with any woman.

One evening before we went for abroad, my mother had struggled to tell me something. When she couldn't do it, she had told my aunt to tell me. My aunt, in a rather indirect way, said that one did not always find what she wished for in marriage and that if that happened in my case, I would eventually get used to it.

At that time, I hadn't understood what she meant.

Our home in the United States was in a suburban town full of beautiful two-storey houses surrounded by greenery.

The neighborhood was so green that in the first few days I was amazed that there could be so many trees in a city. One could even see squirrels scampering about.

For some incomprehensible reason, everyone is fond of America. I'm not. I wonder if this dislike has something to do with the fact that I spent the first years of my marriage there and that I had suddenly found myself all alone in an entirely different world.

Turgut always came up with new things to try to make me happy. He invited Turkish people to our home, organized the kind of weekend picnics Americans are crazy about, or took me to different places and events, from drive-ins to boat races.

Bored to death, I played all sorts of sports: bowling, tennis, anything. I went to a language school. I mowed the lawn at home. I drove around town in a convertible. Everyone thought I was American. I dressed like an American, and I acted like an American. In a short time, I even began talking like an American. I made friends with everyone, from neighbors to blond girls with bobs.

Everyone envied us. All those women, who tried hard to be attractive for their husbands and gave birth to one child after another, kept saying how they admired us and what an exemplary couple we were.

They were surprised that a girl—from somewhere like ancient Egypt, they thought—was like them. They kept on making me tell them about Turkey and listened in awe as if I were talking about a land that had long disappeared.

What I remember most vividly, I suppose, is the drive-in movie theaters. Turgut's biggest hobbies were cars and comic books. As soon as we arrived in the United States, he bought a second-hand car from someone who was leaving the embassy: a dark green, plump convertible. It was a huge car. I used to struggle to open the doors. It had snow-white leather seats, a wooden steering wheel, and white tires. Turgut adored it. Every Saturday, he spent hours washing and polishing it in front of our house. Only after that could we go for a ride.

On summer nights, as we sat in the car, watching a movie at the drive-in, I would wrap a shawl around my shoulders and lose myself in dreams. We must have watched an amazing number of films, but if you asked me, I wouldn't be able to remember even one of them in much detail.

Later, when we were alone at home in the evening, I would either take a seat in front of the television or pick up a book and make myself comfortable in an armchair.

We did not talk much. Days went by in the same way, as if this were the normal way to lead a married life. Turgut seemed content. On the other hand, I guess few women at that time had the slightest thought of asking their husbands, "Do you think we're happy?"

Life was like that: get a two-storey house with a garden, have children, go on a picnic with your new car on the weekends, attend evening parties where the women played bridge and the men watched a game on TV or discussed politics. The kids would grow up, get married, and the number of framed photographs on the shelves, sideboards, and coffee table would increase. When you got old, you would expect the children to celebrate New Year's Eve at your place, sit with your grandchildren on your lap, and hope that they would be consoled with a few fond memories at your funeral, which, hopefully, would be memorable.

This was how the families on TV lived. Beautiful young mothers, who waited for their husbands at home and tried to be close friends with their children, told us that a small world in a small house could be the most beautiful planet in the universe.

What else did you expect it to be like?

Turgut worked zealously and enthusiastically. He constantly told me about our future life—how he wanted his life to be.

We would have children. (two were enough.) Perhaps we would have to spend a few years in a distant and rather undesirable country, but it had to be. After that, we would return to Ankara. From then on, things would be easier. Besides being able to save a lot of money, we would be assigned to European capitals.

He made a great start to his career as a diplomat. Even at night, he read about history and studied. Although he was not interested, he bought books about art history, attended the opera and ballet, and began to learn a third language.

Diplomats were genial, intelligent people who never revealed their personal opinion, no matter what subject was discussed.

The luncheons and dinners had to be in accordance with certain unwritten but well-understood rules. There were specific ways to give compliments, and diplomats' wives were responsible for choosing presents that would be sent to Turkey, as well as welcoming visitors from abroad and showing them around.

I was not very adept at any of these tasks.

Thankfully, I was still considered too young, so no one really minded.

Even when I said the wrong things at the wrong time, people smiled at Turgut as if to say, "Don't worry. We know that she's still a child. Soon, she will understand and get used to these things."

Once Fuat told me, "Sometimes I forget that you're just a child, but I'm still amazed how you can say such things and do whatever you wish even at this age."

They have always wondered. Bewildered. All of them . . .

All my life, I have heard the gossip that followed me. Wherever I went, I noticed how everyone suddenly stopped talking as soon as I stepped into the room.

Wasn't it the same even at school? Everyone tried hard to get on well with me, yet they still adopted a hands-off attitude. I never had a close friend except Ayla. Was that because I always said things openly instead of gossiping or saying things behind people's backs? Maybe it was because it was impossible to determine the course of my actions.

There was another thing they could not comprehend: some

people build their lives as they will. Others make do just with talking about the lives of others.

I didn't want to waste my life talking about the lives of other people.

So I let them talk about mine.

Would they respect me because I was devoted to my husband? Or because I did not break the rules? Was I supposed to live my life as they wanted, so that they would not talk behind my back and spread their repulsive gossip?

Of course I couldn't do that, and I didn't even care.

Why should I care about what people think of me, especially when I don't find them worthy?

It doesn't matter one bit to me!

Even as a child, I pitied such people. I used to secretly watch my mother's friends who came to our house for tea parties. I always felt sorry for those women, who had nothing to talk about except their husbands and the lives of people they had never met.

They were the kind of people who did not say what they really thought but what others wanted to hear.

I often used to tell myself I would never ever be like them, even if they knocked me down.

And I did not become like them.

To tell the honest truth, I fought against myself in those days.

I had no one to tell me what to do. I was at the beginning of a new life, and it did not have a user's manual. What had to be done was obvious. What's more, it was the same for everyone.

Each of us was one of those ordinary women: volunteers who promised to make a comfortable home so that our husbands would be successful and buy us more.

If you didn't question too much, watched what others were doing, and followed the right example, the same system continued onas if it were a secret scroll transferred from one to another.

But that kind of life bored me to death.

After Turgut went to bed, I used to lie on the big sofa in the living room and read novels that transported me to different worlds. After watching a film, I used to live in that film for many days.

It almost felt as if a different person dwelled inside of me: that good old friend of mine. The friend inside my mind who had talked to me when I was a child, shared my lonely moments, come with me wherever I went, shared my happiness and sadness, known when my heart was broken when no one else did, and given me advice. My imaginary friend had grown up, too, but stayed with me.

Most of you have known such a friend. The friend in you who shared your deepest secrets. Yet, one day you discovered that your friend, your confidant, had gone away quietly and secretly, without even leaving a letter of farewell, as if she had known that she had to go.

What can I say? My friend didn't leave me.

My friend is still here, by my side, sitting in that chair across from me and laughing about my situation.

Strange, but after a while, I began to confuse our identities: who's she and who am I?

I used to wake up one day thinking life was beautiful with all the small things that were part of it.

When I woke up the next day, I thought I had made a real mess of my life and hated myself for being like one of those women stuck in their small worlds.

We were still at the beginning of everything, a whole life that would be spent in the same way. Slowly but surely, joy would fade away, and all the new images would age and wear out.

Sometimes I would think I had married a very nice person and that even though we were not having a great romance like in the movies or in novels, such romances always ended in disaster. Real life consisted of the framed photographs of children.

Then, unbearable anguish would overwhelm me, and I would ponder the impossible prospect of spending my whole life with a man who had no idea about who I was and would never understand even a tiny bit of what I thought or felt.

I had once seen a machine at the hospital. When the thin line on the screen no longer moved, people understood the patient had died.

I felt the same way. Our machine neither emitted a sound nor indicated the slightest stir.

Our life was a straight, thin line.

How bizarre! We often do not tell the most noteworthy things to the ones we love, and when we finally do, they cannot hear us anymore.

Some mornings one wakes up with a strange feeling of distress for no reason at all. Something obscure, a vague uneasy feeling, a kind of worry eats your heart, yet you do not know why.

It was such a morning. A cold morning in March. In the garden next door, children wearing colorful hats were dressing a giant snowman with a long red scarf with tassels. They stuck a carrot in the middle of its face. I listened to their merry giggles as they threw snowballs at each other and rolled on the snow-covered ground. Peggy Lee was singing on the radio: "There's a small hotel with a wishing well. I wish that we were there together. Not a sign of people. Who wants people." I was sitting back comfortably and sipping my morning tea on a light yellow armchair with a strange elongated form. We had bought it from the big furniture store that had recently opened on the outskirts of town, but Turgut had somehow come not to like this piece of furniture.

A photo of Audrey Hepburn receiving an award was on the first page of the daily paper. She had been given it for her role in that film where she played the part of a princess who fooled all the news reporters in Rome, strolled alone on the streets, and met a journalist.

The paper also reported on the cancerous effect of cigarettes, as well as that the tobacco companies objected to this news.

It was a morning in March.

The doorbell rang just as I was scrutinizing Audrey's necklace.

As soon as I saw Turgut on our doorstep, I sensed that something was wrong.

"I've just received some news. Your father has fallen ill and been hospitalized. But don't worry, he's okay."

It was obvious he was lying, but I wanted to believe him. He had already made arrangements for me to fly to Turkey early the next day.

That odd distress in the morning, the way my heart had been clenched, was apparently not irrelevant.

When I arrived in Ankara, my brother picked me up at the airport, and we went directly to the hospital. On the way there, he told me my father was temporarily unconscious but was expected to regain consciousness any time. Everything had happened late at night, without warning.

When we got to the hospital, my mother cried for a long while, embracing me tightly. My father was all alone in a room, lying on a bed. A silent, white, plain room.

Like a helpless child, he lay there with his eyes closed, his long white eyebrows curling upward, his luxuriant gray hair spread out on the pillow. His face was very pale.

I stood beside his bed and held his hand. I waited for him to open his eyes, to chat with me like in the old days, or at least to smile with his eyes. In fact, I wanted nothing more than to hear him say my name.

Nights passed. And mornings, too.

In that cold, gloomy hospital room—purgatory opening to the land of the dead—I watched that old man waste away, day by day. Sitting there and holding his hand only made me realize that all was in vain and that we were in desperate straits against this relentless blow of life.

It was unbelievable. I couldn't understand. Even though I lived far away and did not see him, I had never thought my father would leave us all alone and go away. I believed he would stay with us forever. He would remain intact as the pillar of our home who ensured the order of our lives.

I had never seen him become ill, complain, or get tired and rest at home.

My father had always been the same. Like a rock. He had always been a lively, strong, healthy man, with a deep, loud voice, who was active all the time.

It was a nightmare to watch him lie there without stirring, without even moving his eyelids, as if he were cross with all of us. I felt like screaming, but I couldn't make a sound. I wanted to wake up from that nightmarish sleep, fluttering like a bird.

I would wake up and they would tell me it had all been a bad dream. Everything would return to its usual course. I would get out of bed and start a brand new day full of happiness and joy, hastening to tell everyone about my nightmare.

I wish it had happened like that: just like in a bad dream.

People came and left. They stuck needles into his feet and hands and studied those machines that we watched too, hoping they would give us good news any moment. In the end, all people said was, "Where there's life, there's hope."

During those long days and nights, I found out there is but one very short moment between life and death, a moment we can never perceive.

That unknown moment would come one day and this promenade would end. That was all that would happen.

I wished so much that he would wake up suddenly, just for a short while, say his last words like in films, and that we could tell each other the things we had not been able to say in a lifetime.

A few hours before I had arrived, he had still been able to speak. He had asked about me and reproached my mother, saying, "Didn't I tell you we shouldn't have sent her so far away?"

After that, he had not uttered a single word.

My mother told this to everyone who came to visit.

"Oh, God," I thought, "Why? Why did you withhold those few things from me and my father? Why didn't you let him stay conscious for a few more hours? Why didn't you let him know that his dear daughter came and that she is there by his side?"

I was confused. I was scared. I was helpless.

I was unhappy as I had never been before.

You find yourself suddenly in ruins. You had been in a happy home all together, laughing with joy, and a tremor of a few seconds smashes to pieces that secure life you thought would last forever. The ground slides from under your feet as if moved by an earthquake.

We placed the bright flowers I had brought into a vase on the night table next to his bed. I looked at those flowers and imagined that I would lie in a similar bed one day, while people waited for me to open my eyes. I had no idea when that time would come.

No one knew.

As my father lay in his bed without the slightest movement, we knew nothing. We didn't even know if he knew what had happened to him, where he was, if he felt pain, or heard us. Nothing.

Maybe he was having a dream and was in utter confusion, unable to decide which direction to take. Perhaps he was just standing there in his dream, without knowing which of the roads in front of him he should choose. Or, maybe he was roaming around comfortably in his dream, as if he had found his real home in a garden that looked surprisingly familiar to him.

In the end, he left us late one night.

He left before I could say anything to him, before I could look in his eyes for the last time, and before he let us beg him to come back.

If there's a moment in life that truly determines our lives, mine was when I kept vigil over him, half asleep and half awake.

During those hours, the uselessness of the life I was trying to establish dawned upon me.

I realized that nothing in this world is safe and secure. We are cast about by the whirlpool of life that is stronger than each of us, and one day, unexpectedly, we are flung out. In my mind, I gave up.

I gave up everything.

We are on a spinning merry-go-round. We either spend those few short moments lost in bliss, or we choose to spend them in vain, asking ourselves why we keep spinning.

I chose the first option.

Without even being aware of my choice.

I had held my father's hand and told him I'd never leave him again, yet he had left me and gone far away. I learned that we could not keep someone with us for a lifetime just by holding onto his hand tightly.

I wish the reason for my trip to Turkey had been to see my mother and brother and share so many wonderful stories and memories.

We had not seen each other for such a long time, and I had many things to tell them.

Another country, the people I had met, my school, my marriage, programs on television, the drive-in cinema, giant shopping malls.

We were not able to talk about any of this. At such a period in our lives, the details of a distant life on the other side of the ocean, the new home I had decorated myself with modern furniture, the neighborhood where all the grass was cut to the same height, the squirrels, the convertible, and the photos of the trips we had taken were suddenly unimportant.

The presents I had specially selected for my father (sports shoes one could not find in Turkey, and carefully selected books), gloves and hats for my mother, boots for horseback riding and the latest music records for my brother.

I had imagined how happy they would be when I gave them their presents. I had missed them so much that I had constructed and played a beautiful picture of happiness as we met again in my mind over and over. I imagined how we would all sit in our living room with all the lights on, surrounded with enough food to feed an army, talking about the good old days. I would tell them about all the delicious dishes I was able to cook and would ask for new recipes.

Yet, when we returned home, and my mother, my brother and I were finally alone late at night after all the relatives, acquaintances, and neighbors had left, after having listened to all the talk about my father and what a special man he was, and after there were no more tears left to cry, we could not find much to speak about, even if we had wished to.

My brother gathered and organized our father's documents and all the odds and ends in his drawer. My father had glued photographs of my brother and me taken at almost every age into a notebook, putting dates and short notes next to them to remind himself of those days.

After a rainy funeral, days full of pain and confusion, and nights passed praying and chanting for the deceased, I left my mother and brother again without even being able to embrace them in joy and happiness.

I was shattered, as if something inside me had cracked. Subdued, as if I had grown up suddenly.

A few weeks later, when the first rays of the sun appeared, heralding the end of the freezing, gloomy winter that had imprisoned us at home, we went on a trip to the Midwest.

I guess our friends had organized this trip since they thought I needed a change and that I was no longer a laughing, joking childish young women but a taciturn, distant person who stopped talking in the middle of a sentence, gazed vacantly, and whose eyes filled with tears at any moment.

As the whole group, we crowded into our cars and followed each other.

We drove on newly constructed, broad, well-organized highways.

We saw new houses spread everywhere. We gazed at modern districts of small identical homes with gardens.

New type of restaurants to gobble food . . . drive-in cinemas everywhere, one after the other . . . motels advertised with flashing signs . . . oil wells . . . bicycles, new-generation family cars loaded with tents, golf clubs . . . solitude in a vast land extending as far as the eye could see.

Finally, when we arrived at a small town, we found it decorated with flags. As we walked along the road with houses lining both sides, we remarked that the flags gave the town a holiday spirit.

A flag was placed by the door of each small house within a garden. The greenery and the immaculate nature of this small town almost invited one to spend a whole life there.

We felt as if we had entered a town in one of those American films that opened with beautiful music, making it clear from the beginning that the story would have a happy ending. We waited for "Mr. Smith" to pop out from somewhere with a broad smile on his face and solve all our problems.

Then, all of a sudden, we realized that photographs were hanging in each window—pictures of young soldiers.

They were not celebrating a holiday here.

In this town, a son from almost every home had failed to return.

At once, that joyful, bright spring day turned into a gloomy winter evening. That dream-like town, which made one happy to be alive, disappeared.

What we had mistaken for holiday spirit was, in fact, commemoration of unforgettable pain.

I had thought they had won the war somewhere, far away. I had forgotten that no one can win a war.

Those kids who looked like heroes in their framed photographs embellished with Purple Hearts, those smiling kids, had suddenly died one day in a foreign country. They had not said good-bye to their parents, to their childhood, to their girlfriends or fiancées, to their schools, and their ordinary everyday lives because they had been shot by a bullet fired from the gun of some other kid they didn't know, who had perhaps left his own life and family behind to go to war.

Far away from home.

Years had passed, but every spring the town was still decorated with flags to commemorate the day those boys had been wished a safe journey, and the photographs and medals were placed in the windows of every home, where a silent acrid pain would prevail forever.

On that spring day, when a wonderful outing had turned into an unexpected shock, I asked myself which moment of happiness could ever veil the deep anguish of those mothers.

In those years, everyone used to go around with babies in their arms, and everything was arranged to accommodate families with many children.

Everyone we knew asked us when we would have our first child. People who did not have a child within the first few years of marriage were considered strange.

This thought, which had excited me now and then, turned to fear as I passed by those houses decorated with flags and photographs.

Tell me: what happiness that came from living with the children whose pictures now hung on those window was worth endless pain?

The war had passed right through my childhood, like a storm that horrifies you even when you are in a sheltered and secure home. I don't remember much, except what my father used to tell us now and then, and that we often had to turn off all the lights in the house.

Later, I happened to meet a woman in London, who was only a couple of years older than I was.

She told me that one day she and the other Jewish people were brought to one of those death camps where they were stripped naked, and she explained what they felt at the terrifying moment when they expected gas from the shower heads to fill the room.

In those horrifying minutes, they expected death instantly.

Then, all of a sudden, water instead of gas poured from the showers. Sheer fortune. Unexpected luck had saved them from the incredible nightmare that had cost the lives of millions.

She was only a little girl when they were picked up and put into trains where they shivered in the cold: they knew they were being taken to their death. She was talking about the years I used to play hopscotch in our backyard. Maybe it had happened on one of those tranquil spring days in Ankara, on one of those afternoons when my mother had called me into the house, combed my hair, and given me cookies and tea. Or perhaps I was in Kandilli, enjoying the warm summer days at my grandmother's house, when that girl set off on her bitter journey, trembling in a train that passed somewhere just a few hundred miles away from where I was.

That is how it was.

Just a few hundred miles.

Just a few hours away.

You just can't comprehend what really happened even when you see the traces of those mass graves, watch those films, or read those books.

When we were in the United States, the diary of a young girl was published.

The diary of a girl who managed to hide with her family in a house in Amsterdam for two years, but who was eventually caught, sent to a concentration camp, and about whom nothing was ever heard again.

I read that book and studied the girl's smiling face.

I read what she wrote in a tiny den where she lived for two long years without getting any fresh air, what she felt and experienced day by day, and how she grew up while sharing a whole life in her diary.

I was not able to discern the truth when I saw the faces of mothers and fathers in that town decorated with flags, but only years later, when I sat opposite that woman in the café and listened to her story as she gulped down her cream-filled cake.

The human being is the only creature capable of genocide.

As she told me her story, with tears rolling down her cheeks every now and then, I listened in rage and bitterness, mortified and remorseful, promising myself that I would never forget how this woman—who was my age but looked different by light-years—was still able to cling to life.

Thank God that I had not been busy with collecting memories, making photo albums, or carrying all the petty stuff that I had accumulated over the years.

If I had created a photo album, perhaps most of the photos would have shown me packing my suitcases.

Whether because of packing up, being dragged from one place to another or, as my mother says, of having rushed even at the time of my birth, I was not able to become a real part of this world.

We, the images and I (what does it matter anyway), have passed each other by.

Yet, that morning, when I put the beautiful new dolls for the neighbors (there were even small closets and tiny tea cups for a dollhouse), the small things I had bought for my mother, my brother Nihat, and

Ayla, and my records into my suitcase, I remember that the radio announced the Russians had made a bomb that was stronger than the atom bomb. I can still visualize that day. I walk on the wet autumn leaves in the garden and step into the car. As the car moves, I turn back and look at the charming house I'm leaving behind.

We were returning to Ankara. I was overcome by an incomprehensible sense of excitement. Turgut was surprised. "Let's see how you'll get used to Ankara again, after such a long time," he said.

"Let us in fact see how people in Ankara will get used to me!" I answered, chuckling.

He and I always had an invisible, unmentioned wall between us. Neither of us attempted to break down that wall. Strange, but we succeeded in living like two not-so-close friends sharing a house.

He was one of those people who managed not to show any sign of emotion.

For him, life was a simple mechanism that was predetermined, confined, and clearly defined by rules.

Great happiness, joy, excitement, and non-conforming acts had no place in his life.

Maybe that is why he didn't experience great disappointments, frustrations or destruction.

Who knows, maybe his way is the right way. I confess that sometimes when I found myself swirled into maelstroms, I secretly envied his way of constructing a life.

Life was a duty for him. Responsibilities towards everyone had to be fulfilled, work had to have priority above everything else, a certain distance had to be kept in relationships with other people, all rules had to be followed, and in his little free time, he had to do things to develop himself.

For him, even having fun was a duty to be fulfilled.

Acting on impulse and knocking at someone's door one evening without planning beforehand, seeing someone you miss, going somewhere you have never been and spending the whole night there . . .

No, none of these things were acceptable to him. Waking up on the weekends, mowing the grass, dusting the books and placing them in their exact place on the shelves, organizing the drawers, tearing scrap paper first into four and then into eight exact pieces and then throwing them in the garbage can, separating the clothes that had to be taken to the dry cleaner, washing the car, strolling in the afternoon, shopping, visiting places that had to be seen, and going to the cinema and the theater were all arranged according to a fixed program.

I used to watch in amazement as he wrote the greeting cards that had his name printed with his beautiful handwriting and carefully placed them one by one into envelopes long before each religious holiday and New Year's Eve.

He did not call his mother on impulse all those years he spent away from her. The exact day and the time to call his mother was set: every week on Friday.

His biggest interests were cars and comic books, which he read as enthusiastically as a little kid, whenever he wasn't busy improving himself by learning Mandarin Chinese, practicing the flute, or attending the opera.

He also read health magazines and books on technology, paid attention to his diet, smoked once in a blue moon, and limited himself to one glass of alcohol at cocktail parties or receptions.

I'm sure that he didn't put on a wrinkled shirt even once in his life.

If he had, he would probably have been the unhappiest person on earth.

Many years later, one evening, for the first (and perhaps the last) time, he went out of the protective cocoon of order he had woven around himself. He always walked with his head up, but now he lurched and, raising his voice, said, "Do you think I don't know about the exciting things other people experience or that I lack their emotions? I know all about them, of course, but such things ruin one's life. I've known what I've wanted since I was a child. Because of that, I've done everything according to a plan. Happiness is not beyond mountains, or in a paradise you reach after having great adventures. Happiness is right here, beside you . . . in your own home. If you can't recognize it here, how are you going to find some obscure happiness somewhere else? Go then. Go and find it."

He was right. He was one of those people who knew what they wanted. He didn't want to live a wild life but to stand securely at the exact place that he could call his own.

It was true that he desired to build up his life the way he wanted it. Knowing that he would be satisfied with the happiness right beside him, he did not want to grow unhappy by dreaming of things he had never seen or had. However, he had made the wrong decision for the life he wanted to establish.

"The only thing that makes me sad is not being able to make a place for myself in the life you have planned," I replied. "I wish I could be a part of it. I wish I were more like you. Please forgive me. I did not choose anything myself, even when I thought I was the one who chose."

It really was like that.

I would have also liked to live as if gliding on a tranquil sea on a warm, calm, late spring day.

Peace. Some choose to have peace. A life far away from ups and downs, pulsations, expectations, frustrations, fear, and worry. A life protected from all danger.

I don't remember when, but once I was in a village in Bolu on a summer afternoon and saw an old man sitting in front of his home under the crimson sky, staring into the empty distance.

When I greeted him and asked what he was doing, he said, "I'm waiting, dear girl."

"What are you waiting for?"

He turned his gaze away from empty space and looked at me. Surprised by my question, he said, "What could I be waiting for? For the day to end of course!"

The word "peace" always reminds me of that old man sitting there, waiting for the day to end.

That old man who had reduced his life to a simple moment of staring into space.

Perhaps I would have also liked to be a person who did not care what happened either right beside her or farther away than she could know. Thus, I thought that staring into space, observing the ever-changing crimson sky was much more fulfilling than anything else. Maybe.

But I wasn't able to be someone like that.

Unforeseen storms ruled my life. It is true that there was a harbor I could take refuge in, and I did take shelter in it. Yet, what could I do? I realized each time that those storms attracted me instead of frightening me, calling me into that unknown realm, where I was unable to forget the excitement of being hurled in this or that direction by the wind.

That is why each time I packed my suitcases, the excitement and joy of beginning my life all over again overwhelmed me, rather than the calmness of a person who feels she is entering a new stage in her orderly life.

Some people have a single life. They call this being honest. A life whose each and every detail is known. It must be like living in a bell jar. What a foolish thing to do! What a big lie!

It is, indeed, a lie because none of us is living in a globe, under glass. I wonder what we would find in our memory if we opened it without fear. So many things that have nothing to do with our words or our appearance. Even we would be bewildered.

How foolish! Because why should one want to be held captive in a single life?

Some people search after the truth for a lifetime, while some create their own truth and believe in it.

As far as I'm concerned, only cowards believe life must be lived within the boundaries of a small world and according to the rules of their own world. What's more, they also judge others, in every century, by the rules that are different in each section of the world map painted with a different color.

Isn't that glamorous scene in a ballroom illuminated by crystal chandeliers and full of beautiful, charming women in shimmering gowns, which rustle as they dance with handsome men, the center point of many tales and young girls' dreams?

This is the perfect picture of life, consisting of only the best aspects and omitting all the rest—the unhappiness, poverty, pain, ailments, distress, and wickedness. Naturally, this picture is fleeting. A short moment, a snapshot in time.

An unforgettable waltz inevitably accompanies that picture. When the young lady enters the ballroom after so many days of excitement and hours of preparation, gently picking up the fluffy skirt sweeping the floor as she takes small steps, all eyes turn to look at her. It is a unique moment.

A moment of glory.

This was the picture, down to the minutest detail, that would be engraved in my memory one night in the ballroom of the most famous hotel in Ankara.

As I walked on to the shiny floor bathed in light, I knew that everyone in the room stopped for a moment and turned to look at me. I held my skirt gently and took small, serene steps toward the center of the room.

How can I ever forget that evening gown made of ivory taffeta leaving my shoulders bare? It circled my waist tightly and billowed all the way to my feet. I wore long gloves of the same color, which covered my arms. A gossamer thin shawl covered my shoulders. I had a necklace of emeralds, with a matching set of earrings. My lips were painted bright red. Although my hair was made into a bun, some locks spilled down the sides of my face.

But what caused that incomprehensible clenching in my heart or the odd swelling in my chest? It was not just because of the attention all the important guests showed to a young girl walking under the crystal lights as if she were a film star.

It was also not because of that same young girl's excitement about returning to this city years later—this time as a young woman—and showing off her breathtaking beauty, which everyone would truly admire.

That princess expected someone to take her hand, pull her away from the brilliant lights and the colorful dream illuminating her, and say, "You don't know what you want, but I do. You don't even know what you're dreaming of, but I do, and I will make it come true. Hold my hand, close your eyes, and come with me without question."

He would be the prince who appeared in tales, riding a white horse, the kind of handsome hero we see in films, or the perfect dream we give up one day, thinking that all is, unfortunately, a lie: life was different, and that dream was a fairytale.

Nowadays, I know that films emphasize this truth from the first scene. Dreams have long been lost, and we have accepted it as a fact. There is no longer a hero who will grasp the princess's hand and take her through the realm of stars to his humble home surrounded by wildflowers and tell her that from that day on, every new day will begin with joy and bliss.

What happened to those heroes?

What happened to all those men who always kept their word, who succeeded in returning from war, who put enemies to the sword with the power of knowing that someone was waiting for them faithfully, who overcame the greatest of difficulties inspired by the dream of their lovers, and who, when you looked into their eyes, made you melt away?

So does everyone feel better that way? Do they eat their popcorn and then go back to their boring homes saying, "Look, it was all a lie. There are no tales and no heroes. We're all the same, and life is hard. No one can be happy with a single kiss alone."

I don't know. I don't know why we have to give up that hero who touches that ramshackle hut with a magic wand and turns it into the most magnificent castle in the world…

In those days, the heroes in films used to possess the power to change the world, to take unhappy princesses on dreamy nights, and enter upon an adventure about which neither of them knew.

None of us thought about what would happen at the end of those adventures.

For we knew that he always kept his word, and if—with his hand on her hair—the gloomy expression of the princess was replaced with a gleaming heartfelt smile, the ramshackle hut would sooner or later turn into a glamorous castle.

We were sure that when someone like that came and took our hand to take us away, we wouldn't care where we were headed.

We knew that in a magical place at a magical moment, a single magical kiss could bring someone back to life.

There, on that brilliant Ankara evening, as I was shaking hands with people, smiling at them, and humbly accepting the compliments, I knew he would come.

That hero.

It sounds impossible, but he really came.

Now, as I think back, I ask myself whether it had not always been so? Whenever I called him inside my mind, didn't he always come out of the blue? Didn't he always find me, or appear suddenly in front of me in the most unexpected places or at the most unexpected moments?

Does it sound strange to you? Well, to me, too.

I really didn't know that I was waiting for someone, but what I hoped for was something that you usually put back on the dusty shelves of your archive of special memories that you never share with anyone although it captures you for a moment before it is soon forgotten.

One of those innumerable moments that do not become real, but only flash in your mind and are lost to oblivion in no time.

It had to be like that.

But when I raised my head, I saw him in front of me. He had extended his hand, inviting me for a dance with that matchless smile of his.

When I found myself in his arms, dancing among other couples and rotating under the huge crystal chandelier, I suddenly remembered the day I had first met him and had been carried away by my imagination. I felt as if I were in that dream.

How is it possible for someone to build castles in the air and one day find out that her dream had come true?

At such an unexpected moment, when I least hoped for it, when the feelings I had not first recognized but then remembered, when I was in that film-like setting.

I was turning and twirling in his arms. I was dizzy. I looked into his eyes. I wasn't able to hear what he said. I was so small compared to him that I wasn't dancing but flying in his arms.

At the end, drawing closer to my ear, he whispered, "Young lady, may I ask you at exactly what time your carriage will turn into a pumpkin?"

I must have had a stupid smile on my face. I felt my cheeks flush. He asked again, probably thinking I hadn't understood.

"So you don't remember me," I said without looking into his eyes.

He was surprised.

"Remember you? I'm sure I haven't seen you before. I never would have forgotten you."

"So it's about time that I transform back into Cinderella," I said.

The dance was over. Before he could say anything to me and before the orchestra began playing a new tune, I rushed to where my brother was standing.

But he followed me and said to my brother, "Nihat, it seems you know the answer to a secret. Tell me, who is this young lady?"

Nihat laughed, "She's my little sister. Didn't you recognize her? She's the one who rode straight into us on her bike."

Fuat appraised me in amazement.

"Unbelievable! Are you that little kid?" he said.

"Yes," I said, "but you didn't let me . . ."

He broke into loud laughter and lifted me up in the air. With my feet off the ground, I was unable to do anything but watch him laugh and turn me around in his arms. Chuckling, he said, "Who would expect that small, mischievous child to grow into a beautiful princess?"

And of course the whole ballroom was watching.

Then a woman on the stage began to sing that song. Was that also a coincidence when this special song started to play in the background?

Violetta's song. In Turkish, it meant: "The woman who was led astray . . ."

Isn't it always the same?

Don't we suddenly wake up when we're having a wonderful dream?

As soon as my feet touched the ground again, I noticed a beautiful brunette, dressed in a dark blue silk dress, wearing a glittering pearl necklace, and with her long hair in a bun, staring at me with a strange expression on her face. She was much older than I was, yet she looked younger than her age. I immediately understood who she was.

This was the first time I saw her.

I didn't know what to do. Like a child, unwilling to wake up, I kept on standing there with my cheeks on fire. All the people and their humming voices had disappeared for me for a moment, and although I tried to immerse myself in the atmosphere again, I couldn't.

On that evening in Ankara, I tried hard to wake up from the most unexpected dream I was having in a sparkling room.

He immediately grabbed his wife's hand, pulling her toward himself before he introduced us to each other in a loud voice that everyone could hear.

"Maide, come, look at her. She's Nihat's little sister. The first time I saw her, she was a kid this tall . . . riding a bike."

I extended my hand, and she touched my fingers limply, as if unwilling to take my hand in full. I was not able to look her in the eye.

"Well, she certainly still is a child," she said, smiling courteously.

The ladies with her glanced at each other and giggled.

A waiter wearing white gloves offered us drinks from his tray. Everyone picked up one of the tall glasses.

"To everyone's health," Fuat said, and we all raised our glasses in a toast.

Then he told the story of our first amusing encounter.

How I had been riding my bike while he and my brother were talking, and how I couldn't manage to stop it and fell off. The whole story. Nihat supported him with details every now and then.

Everyone seemed to listen with interest.

I was surprised at the fact that he remembered everything.

He had remembered, but for him, it was a mere coincidence. He had remembered, yet he would not have known what I had dreamed on the night after our first meeting.

He was jolly, like an uncle who happened to meet his little niece after a long time.

Thankfully, he kept talking and no one expected me to say anything. Otherwise, I would have surely talked nonsense. Just like everyone else around me, my eyes were fixed on him.

His hair had begun receding on the sides of his head and had turned slightly grayer since I had last seen him. He seemed older than he was in his black swallow-tailed coat and white shirt.

Turgut had watched everything from a distance before joining us and facing a bombardment of questions

"It seems our young diplomat has won the heart of our little one.

How do you like being here after living in the States? What are you going to do? Where are you going to live? Maide, we'll meet them often from now on, won't we? We're expecting you for dinner next week. No excuses!"

Surprised at Fuat's informal friendliness, Turgut tried his best to answer every question, but no one seemed to pay attention to him.

When Fuat spoke with endless ardor and enthusiasm, no one usually knew what to say or do.

He talked with such ease that even I would have thought he knew me intimately since my childhood, and that he was a close family friend.

All I wanted was to leave that room as soon as possible, go away and cherish the secret moment I had experienced a few minutes ago before it was spoiled.

I wish it were possible!

Fortunately, a few minutes later the Prime Minister, surrounded by a group of people, entered the ballroom, and the whole crowd stirred to make room for him, giving him all their attention. Our small group scattered when Fuat asked permission to go in that direction.

Later, he told me, "I came back and looked for you to introduce you to the Prime Minister but you had disappeared."

"What could I have done," I replied, "My carriage turned into a pumpkin."

Yes, that was him. The man whom all the women loved!

He had danced madly with me. I had let myself go in his arms, and as I whirled around the room with him—or when my world had whirled around—I had forgotten everything: who I was, where I was, and what was going on.

Years after our first encounter, when I entered that ballroom with the vague feeling that I would meet someone I hadn't known before, someone had touched my shoulder, and the world had begun to spin in a totally different way.

That was how it all began.

Who could have imagined that an innocent childhood dream would take me to the present day?

To the present day, I said. To the present day, but after going through so much . . .

Our days in the capital began like this.

Like a dream.

Of course, not much time was required for me to get used to our new life.

In the beginning, we couldn't decide what to do. Finding a house we liked didn't look easy. After searching around for a couple of days, we decided the best thing to do was to settle in a hotel first.

Looking for a house in the dead of winter and lodging at my mother's or my mother-in-law's home didn't suit me.

Turgut thought that we would not be staying in Ankara for long. He said I would spend most of my time with my mother anyway and that it was not reasonable to establish a home now that we would leave again soon.

In fact, he preferred to be away. He was not happy that we had returned. Yet, on the other hand, this was the right place to be closer to the ones "at the top" and to build up strong connections with influential people.

We stayed at the most famous hotel in Ankara. State officials met there to talk about important matters. In truth, the future of the country was taking shape at this hotel. It was also where I attended the balls that made me feel like a princess.

At lunchtime, the men came to the hotel, and we all ate together at a big table, drank our coffee, and chatted for an hour or two.

Fuat liked those crowded tables. He enjoyed seeing everyone at the same time, teasing the younger people, paying compliments to the ladies, and asking the waiters about the special dishes prepared for him every day.

I was his latest favorite.

He used to turn to me unexpectedly and say, "Tell me young lady, did you read all the newspapers from top to bottom today?"

When a new book or film was mentioned, he was always interested in my opinion.

I was fortunate that everyone still regarded me as a child. I said exactly what I thought. I criticized the government, and found fault in many things but it was always met with a smile and passed over easily, just as the opinions of small children are accepted in a somewhat mocking manner.

The men were formal with each other, but the wives were able to voice their thoughts more easily.

Who knows, maybe this "tactlessness" of mine, as Turgut defined it, was seen as spoiled behavior because of having lived in America.

Only Fuat used to kid me about what I said, insisted on asking questions, and led passionate discussions to refute my arguments.

I felt that he wasn't happy about all that was going on in the country and about being in the center of it. Sometimes when he opposed my opinions and almost got cross with me, he would suddenly gaze into the distance, and I would think that he really didn't believe what he claimed.

61

Frankly, I did not want to discuss political matters with him in depth.

How boring were the luncheons he didn't attend because of more important matters.

Every morning when I woke up, I sat in front of the mirror and tried to decide what to wear that day.

Toward midday, an inexplicable excitement would begin to swell inside me. Sometimes I would take off what I had been wearing and look for something else to put on.

I didn't have anything else to do. In the morning I had breakfast downstairs and then visited my mother or met with Ayla. Then I returned to the hotel and read the newspapers and the magazines in the tea room. After that, I went to my room to get dressed for lunch.

At exactly quarter past twelve Turgut arrived. We went down together for lunch. Every day, as we descended the stairs covered with a red carpet, I would play a game I had made up. At each step, I would tell myself, "He's going to come" or "He's not going to come." As I put my foot on the last step, I would rejoice if it turned out to be a "He's going to come" step.

When we entered the dining hall, I would check whether my little game had predicted the truth or not.

It was actually Fuat who had started the luncheon tradition. In this way, all his colleagues and team members could be together at lunchtime.

Sometimes when someone complained jokingly, he used to say, "It's so hard to curry favor with you people. I'm having you eat the best dishes in Ankara and you still complain."

He always came alone, although the wives of the others joined us now and then.

The invitation he had extended to us that night at the ball—when his eyes were fixed on his wife—never took place. It wasn't even mentioned again. We did not visit them at their home, and his wife Maide never joined us at the hotel. I only came across her occasionally at receptions.

Maide was a tall woman with long chestnut-colored hair and slightly slanted eyes. Everyone praised her elegance, her beautiful pronunciation, the way she spoke Turkish softly without the slightest mistake, her stylish outfits, and how graceful she was.

However, she was distant to everyone, even her husband. No matter how close you get to some people, you still cannot ask them a question out of the blue or tell them an ordinary joke. You don't even know why you feel that way. Maide was one of those people.

Sometimes the ladies had afternoon tea at the hotel.

We drank tea, made small talk, and even played card games.

I know it sounds like a strange way of life for a young woman in her early twenties.

But this was how our days passed. No one did anything substantial, and no one thought about it.

Some of the women expected their husbands to be assigned to a foreign country, and some of them had just come back from abroad. We shared memories, our experiences in other lands, and the new and interesting things we had encountered. Most of all, however, we discussed how underdeveloped our country was. As soon as the gossip about one subject was finished, chitchat about another began.

"I know you're bored to death, but please put up with it and be patient just a little longer," Turgut often said, thinking I was blasé. "Soon the new assignments will be discussed." He just couldn't understand why I was not bored with the luncheons I had to attend with people much older than myself, the receptions and parties in the evenings, and with having to live in one room in a hotel.

Someone who didn't even know me very well would definitely

know that I wouldn't stay at that hotel for more than three days in a row.

My mother attributed it to the fact that I had "finally settled down," but my brother insisting on mocking me by saying, "Let's wait and see. There's something more to it than we know."

Ayla had still not got used to my being a married woman, and when she invited me out in the evenings, she usually forgot about Turgut. If the three of us went out together, she sulked and got bored. Once Turgut said, "That friend of yours seems to resent our marriage."

I had never liked going around in a group. I don't like family visits either. Since Turgut was aware of this, he did not insist. He let me meet Ayla and my mother on my own, and to please him in return, I attended some receptions with him, though not often.

Each time I met Fuat, I played the same game. He was unaware of it, of course. I used to try to guess the hidden meaning of the things he told me, his smile, or his jokes.

Then I would laugh at myself. It was obvious that he wasn't interested in me. He joked with everyone. He flirted with all women. He paid compliments to all the ladies.

Sometimes I heard him say to another woman, "What a nice outfit you have, it surely becomes to you. My eyes were dazzled as soon as you came in."

Later, when he asked me a simple question, he wouldn't understand why I gave him such a short and sharp answer.

Fool!

Once he did not come for three days in a row.

I knew he was in the city.

When he came on the fourth day, I didn't go down for lunch, saying that I was ill.

This was the game I played—a childish game that he wasn't aware of.

It really was childish.

Then something happened.

On the day when I feigned illness and didn't join the group for lunch, Fuat returned to the hotel in the afternoon. He was alone.

I was in the tearoom, in full make-up, sipping tea and reading a book.

It was evident that I wasn't ill.

I didn't know what to do when I saw him all of a sudden in front of me.

It was not his habit to come to the hotel in the afternoon.

"Good for you. You recovered quite fast," he said smiling. "I thought of paying a visit to our little patient."

He sat down and made himself comfortable. I blushed and mumbled something.

He ordered a coffee and lit a cigarette, remaining silent while staring into my eyes. His gaze seemed to pass right through me. His thoughts were probably wandering. His legs were crossed, and he kept swinging one of his feet up and down.

He picked up my book and said, "Do you like Hüseyin Rahmi?"

"Yes," I replied. "I read his books especially when I'm depressed. He makes me laugh. I laugh, and at the same time, I feel sad."

"You feel sad? Why?"

"So many years have passed since he wrote these books but not much has changed, has it?"

"Life doesn't change that easily," Fuat replied. "But maybe this proves the craft of a writer."

"Yes," I said. "In this book, he ridicules columnists and journalists in such a way that I almost fainted with laughter!"

"Why don't you lend it to me so that I can have a good time too.

I need to read such a book these days."

"You know what," I said, "when he died, they found many gloves and hats in his home, which he had knitted himself. He used to worry about what would happen to his cats after he died."

"Novelists are strange people," he said. "If they weren't, they wouldn't try to create new worlds to escape to.

"Don't say that too loud and anger the novelists. What kind of novels do you like?"

Fuat thought for a while, and then replied, "I guess I like those that resemble an attic."

"An attic?"

"Yes," he continued. "In complete disarray and full of things scattered everywhere. Like a magical attic. When you read, you lose yourself in it. In all the stuff there, you find some things that suit you. Eventually, you realize that disorder and confusion are in fact complete and in accord."

He drew on his cigarette. "Aren't our lives like that, too?"

"I don't know," I said, "perhaps you're right."

I was limp and helpless, trembling out of nervousness. All the waiters were looking at us. I tried not to talk much, but at the same time talked incessantly. Every word I said rang sharply in my ears as soon as it was out of my mouth, as if I had said something stupid, and to make up for it, I said something else again.

Finally, he finished his coffee, extinguished his cigarette, leaned a little forward in his chair, put my book on his lap, and whispered, "Young lady, I knew you weren't ill."

Immediately I relaxed. He hadn't been so close to me since the day we had danced. Unable to look into his eyes from such a short distance, I looked at the floor.

"Have you come all the way here just to tell me that?"

He stood up, and as he left, said, "No. I came here to see you."

There was nothing odd in what he said, but I froze, as if he had just told me the greatest secret ever.

He left as quickly as he had come.

Things did not end there.

After that day, Fuat often came to the hotel in the afternoon, and if he saw me there, he sat with me. We chatted about this and that and drank tea. Although neither of us voiced it, we had a secret deal that these meetings were to take place at hours when no one else would be there but the two of us. We never agreed on a time to get together, and neither of us knew whether the other would be waiting. Still, we managed to meet.

What did we talk about? Mostly books and films rather than daily events. Sometimes he told me about his childhood and his school years. I had the habit of reading foreign newspapers and magazines. He was interested in what they contained and often asked me to save articles that attracted my attention. This became my special concern. Two scientists in Cambridge had discovered the secret code of human beings. They claimed that each one of us had a unique inner written formula. No one had the same code. After deciphering these codes one day, it would be possible to find cures for all diseases and the secret of longer life.

Satellites were sent to outer space. In a university, scientists had invented a machine that translated brain waves. Soon, it might even be possible to watch our own dreams like a movie.

We talked about such things. Sometimes the subject of men and women came up. We talked about marriage and relationships, comparing the situation in Turkey with those in other countries, as if this topic had nothing to do with us.

In the end, it didn't matter what we spoke about. What mattered was that he came and sat with me.

As time went by, an unexpected friendship and sympathy grew

between us. We were able to discuss many things that we couldn't talk about with others.

It didn't take long for the gossip to start.

The strange thing was that it wasn't my husband, who was under my very nose, but my mother, who rarely left home, who said one day, "I've been hearing about some inappropriate behavior. What's going on?"

For the first time, I realized what I had been doing and the direction I had taken.

I could not confess the truth, even to myself.

"Come on, Mom," I answered. "People need to gossip. He's old enough to be my father. He jokes with everyone. He just considers me a kid and spends more time talking with me than with others. That's all."

Was that not all?

Is it just me who thinks like this, or is it true that we often show more interest in the lives of others than in our own?

Who knows, maybe it's because we think our lives lack vivacity and color.

In those days, I came to realize that people were talking about us in their small worlds. They had found a brand new subject, something different to talk about. If you think this disturbed me, you're wrong. To the contrary, I enjoyed it.

Because nothing was happening as they imagined.

I liked the fact that they were talking about a film in which I was playing the main role, while their lives began with humdrum mornings and ended in humdrum evenings.

They were my audience. No matter what they said about me, I was the star, whose role they would give anything to have for themselves.

It was indeed childish, but I enjoyed it all the same. I was amused by the way conversations were interrupted and everyone turned to look at me when I entered a room, the way some people ignored me, pretending not to notice that I was there, and how others tried to engage me in small talk, as if making an effort to act normal.

I continued to play my game, and new people joined in constantly.

What child wouldn't enjoy having others take for real the game he had been playing by himself in his dark room and joining him in playing it?

Besides, just as an American author had once said, "Old maids sweeten their tea with scandal."

I sometimes felt like telling Fuat about the gossip, but even though I tried, I couldn't bring myself to talk about it to him.

I was aware that he was playing his own game.

At first I didn't understand but later I was sure.

He used to get carried away for a moment while looking into my eyes, and then acquire the airs of a man who was chatting with his best friend.

I was aware but not sure yet.

That is why I wanted to tell him.

One day, as we were talking about this and that, I suddenly wanted to ask at the most unexpected moment: "Do you know that everyone is talking about us? Haven't you realized that?" Or, I wanted to say: "It would be better if you did not come here alone from now on. People are attributing different meanings to your visits."

But just as I was about to tell him, I changed my mind.

Perhaps I was scared that if I did, I would spoil the game.

I disappeared for a few days. I visited my mother, went shopping, and met with Ayla. I also sat in my room and did something I had long neglected: I wrote postcards and letters to my friends in America.

Actually, I didn't care much about putting an end to the gossip. All I wanted was to provoke him.

But when we met again like foolish high school kids, we continued from where we had stopped, as if it was normal that I had disappeared from sight for so many days.

One afternoon we were sitting face to face and sipping our tea as usual. All of a sudden, he said, "I'm going into politics."

"I know," I responded.

He waited for me to continue, but I didn't.

"Aren't you going to say anything?"

"Are you asking for my opinion? If so, I don't think politics suit you."

He seemed taken aback. He must have thought I wouldn't be that direct.

"So you think politics is not my thing. But there's so much to be done. If we don't do it, who will?"

He probably thought I would support his view enthusiastically.

"Besides," he added, "aren't you the one who is always criticizing what's going on. How can someone change his country just by sitting and complaining?"

He looked annoyed. He stood up, poured a glass of water and sat down again. He was lost in thought. "We all have our own destiny as well as our duty," he said.

"I wish you luck," I said.

While everyone congratulated and encouraged him, my opposition was a little out of place. Later that evening, I asked myself why I always said whatever came to my mind.

Maybe I was afraid that if he entered politics, I would be able to see him less often.

Naturally, he didn't listen to me.

An outsider to the world of politics, he was appointed to a top position on the Prime Minister's order. Everyone talked about it.

Already, some supported him and others criticized him behind his back.

In a way he resembled me: someone who talked and acted on impulse, who wanted things to happen immediately, who didn't listen to others when he decided to do something, and who could offend even those closest to him . . .

Such people make enemies quickly. People who are not used to taking orders, people who do not swallow their words, and the ones who do not like being an ordinary man in the street will always have to cope with hostility.

For me, politics was not for people who wanted to do something for the benefit of the country but for those who were interested in their own benefits, who played games, and who were ready to risk all to achieve their personal agendas. I have never believed that politicians can do anything good.

Besides, just a little farther from here, people had already begun to discuss different things in their homes. The brilliant days of the government were slowly fading. The dreams everyone had about a new time, a growing country, and a happy future were wearing out. Now, in a state of fatigue, people no longer appreciated the new people who came to power, realizing that nothing had changed the way they had expected.

By degrees, he became one of the people at the top and watched the view self-confidently from high above, enjoying what he saw.

He no longer took pains to discover what was going on below his level.

But when I went a few streets away from our hotel to visit my mother, talk with my brother, or read the papers, I could see that things were not going well.

Later, when we were able to talk about these things, he told me, "You're still so young. You think the world is a nice place. It has always been so. Whoever climbs to the top thinks the view is wonderful, feels pleased and content, and forgets that it's all transitory. Things have always been this way, but we still want to climb to the top."

Do we really want that?

I didn't. I never have.

I've never understood why the ones at top fail to see the view as it is.

Lost in thought, he looked at me and said, "Who knows, maybe there, from the summit, everything is so far away in the distance. Maybe that's why it looks beautiful."

His confidence in his knowledge and insight, the well-conceived answers he gave in an easy-going manner, which I had pondered deeply, and his calm expression free of doubt always convinced me I was wrong.

At least at that moment.

I had to understand. He was like that. He was one of those people whom others watched in curiosity, who had to climb up his path with consistent effort, who constantly gave orders to others, who told about life, and who tried to build a life with his own hands.

According to him, there was so much to be done and the only reason things were not accomplished correctly was that cowards and lazy people held power. I guess, in those days, he truly believed he could change things and accomplish the ideas he had always had in mind but which, for some reason or another, he had not been able to implement until that day.

Leaders are such people. But I sometimes wonder whether

leaders really believe they can change things and make life better or if they try to prove to themselves their self-confidence. I'm not really sure.

As the election results were celebrated with balls, we packed our suitcases, getting ready to set off for our new destination.

Thankfully, the election brought to an end our afternoon meetings, as well as the gossip.

Anyway, everyone was busy discussing the new government and the debates surrounding it.

I must confess, in the beginning I felt lonely and scared. It must have been then that I realized the game which had amused me, and made me forget how lonely I was, had taken a dangerous route.

At first, I often went down to the tearoom in the afternoon, wondering if he would show up. I opened a book or magazine but ended up reading the same page over and over, waiting for him to appear. Everyone else came through that damned door except him.

He was touring the country before the election in those days. He addressed the public. He did not have time for me.

Slowly, I abandoned all the crazy thoughts that had taken root in my mind and repeated to myself that it was time to put an end to this silly game.

My addiction to cigarettes, which I still cannot end, is from those days.

But it didn't take long for those days to come to an end.

One way or another, Turgut had managed to be assigned abroad just as he had wished. He was unhappy about being in Turkey and wanted to leave as soon as possible. At night, when we were alone, he constantly talked about his wish to leave. Anyhow, we were leading a temporary life in Ankara. We had spent months in a hotel room with open suitcases, taking our meals outside and waiting for news of his new appointment to arrive anytime.

Eventually, the long-awaited news came, and we got ready to set off for the city of mist.

I didn't attend the reception held the day before we left, saying I wanted to spend my last evening with my mother and brother.

Fuat had not only won the elections but also been appointed as a minister in the new government. I didn't congratulate him on his success.

I do not remember now whether I had wanted to punish him in my own way or felt that meeting him again would be the beginning of an unexpected disaster.

At dinner with my mother, my brother, Ayla, and Turgut's family, we talked about the good old days, my father, and the future that awaited us. We talked and laughed about the first evening Turgut had visited my parents' home.

My mother blushed as she said, "Did you really put salt into his coffee? I swear I had no idea you did such a thing!"

"I noticed it," Turgut said, "but what could I do? Besides I liked her mischievousness and drank it without saying a word."

My mother had cooked all my favorite dishes and insisted that we finish them.

She was happy that we weren't going too far.

Unable to conceal his happiness at leaving Ankara, Turgut said to Nihat, "We're going at the right time. There are the elections, and the fight never ends. I hope it goes smoothly for you all!"

Once again, I would have to begin a life in a new place and among people I didn't know. I was both excited and distressed.

"What can we do?" Turgut remarked. "This is our life. Just when we're getting used to a place, we have to pack our things and move somewhere else."

All the lights in this house were on for the first time since my father's death. It was also the first time since his passing that laughter dominated the place. At the same time, it would be the last.

My mother and brother were leaving Ankara too. They had decided to settle in Istanbul at my grandmother's home. After my father's death, my mother did not want to stay in the family house. Even entering the living room, where we used to spend time as a family, upset her. My grandmother had passed away, and her house in Istanbul was vacant.

Since my brother did not want to leave our mother alone, he found a job in a company belonging to a friend in Istanbul.

"One traveler is enough in a family. Besides, I don't like traveling," he said, stressing how much he had missed Istanbul. And I encouraged them, saying, "What on earth do people like about Ankara anyway! Istanbul is a much better place to live. You've made the best decision."

The following week, Ayla was going to participate in an archaeological excavation in Anatolia. She was very excited, and during our time together in Ankara, she had constantly talked about it, looking forward to her journey back in time, after having read so many books. She would work with renowned archaeologists, and it was a sign of success on her part that they had chosen an inexperienced young woman like her. Her father had retired, so she had also decided to live in Istanbul year round.

That evening when we all sat together and enjoyed dinner for the last time in that house was a milestone marking the beginning of a new life for each of us.

A brand new period in our lives full of novel, unknown things.

I remember that my mother hugged me as we were leaving and cried, "You're leaving again. I spend my days longing for you. I wish I had not let you marry a diplomat." Then she gave me a prayer written on a piece of paper placed in a small leather case for me to carry wherever I went. I also recall that my heart fluttered like a bird, and I wanted to have a brief last look at the hotel ballroom.

I didn't do it, of course.

Besides, the ball was already over when we got to the hotel.

I hung the prayer my mother gave me around my neck and went to bed.

We set off early the next day.

Maybe the reason we often fail to understand people and are sometimes surprised by them in the most unexpected ways is because we forget they have many different facets and we are satisfied with the image they present as a whole.

Don't we usually forget about the different aspects of our own character and get stuck in false self-conceptions?

We struggle for a long time to create a form others will like and approve of, a perfect design and unity out of the chaos, that shapeless pulp, in ourselves.

Like an endless civil war.

Time passes, altering our identity, taking it captive, changing it by force, and creating an entirely new being.

In the end, naturally, you never know who has won.

It seems that I did not run the chance of abandoning even the smallest pieces that form me. Unaware, I preferred to live with the crowd and multiplicity inside of me.

Did I do so because I couldn't bring myself to give anything up?

Or because I believed life couldn't be restricted, or that it shouldn't be limited by hiding in a room or following a preconceived path?

Or maybe just because of coincidences.

I don't know.

All I know is that I was confronted continuously with new sides of myself and was surprised each time.

It has always hurt me that the game of life can be played only once, and that in spite of our lack of experience, we are not given a second chance.

Isn't this unjust?

Don't you think that making a choice at every fork in the road, choosing one direction and foregoing the other (without knowing what would have happened had we gone in the other direction); abandoning some people; not going to the right but to the left after thinking, or just listening to our inner voice (in reality, the voice of others); and determining our whole life as a result of all those ordinary choices is just nonsense?

It probably was the second year after we left Ankara.

I remember very well that summer morning in the living room of the two-storey red brick house from which I could hear the sound of the mounted policemen passing by.

I was reading a magazine article about people who claimed they had been abducted by aliens and taken on a strange journey of light, which they could not remember.

I remember it very well.

The front cover of the magazine was illustrated with a photograph of Marilyn Monroe. Underneath, a caption read: "The unhappiest beauty of all times!"

I read the long article that began with the question, "Have aliens really arrived?"

Such subjects have always excited me.

I don't care whether they're true or not.

Some people claimed that they were surrounded by a bright light and weren't able to see anything. They related that they felt as if they were in a very long, restful sleep, or a dream they wished would never end. They also said they were hurled with incredible speed for hours through a corridor of bluish, bright light in the sky, as if caught in a radiant whirlwind. They heard a sound which resembled the deafening screech of sirens. Soon, however, everything slowly calmed down, the storm ended, and they found themselves in a silent, tranquil void.

Sometimes when you wake up, you know you have had a wonderful dream and feel blissful, but you cannot remember or recount it. That is exactly how they felt.

A young woman said she had thought she was dead but wasn't frightened. On the contrary, she remembered having abandoned herself with ease.

These people were asked various questions.

The article included photos of scientists, authors, and psychiatrists who had investigated this strange phenomenon. One doctor discussed the reasons why people make up such stories. The scientists explained why it wasn't possible for human beings to travel in space like that. They talked about confusing imagination with fact.

How bored I was with those idiots!

I tossed the magazine away.

I'd do anything to experience such an extraordinary thing.

I envy those people who have opened a window in their

humdrum, unhappy, empty lives and lost themselves in a dream no one had before when they looked at an undefined cluster of light in the night sky.

Just like primitive people.

I would love to be one of those who see things for the first time, who have the joy of facing something new, and who are the first to step on terra nova—an undiscovered island or a boundless continent of ice.

I am fed up with cities built centuries ago, streets that millions trampled before me, the shared memory of humankind, and glamorous structures of bricks laid on top of the other.

They are all know-it-alls! Everyone knows about everything!

I'm sick and tired of the wretchedness of this arrogant civilization!

If we were able to put together all that we have learned in thousands of years, it would fit into a small box when compared to what we have not discovered. Yet, no one is aware of this fact.

In one of her letters, Ayla had written, "People think it bizarre that I spend months on a forlorn excavation far away from everyone. Honestly, I sometimes doubt myself, too. But there's not even the smallest piece of land that can still be discovered on this earth. At least I can find the door to a tomb deep inside the earth after digging for months. After thousands of years, I can be the first one to stand in front of that tomb, at the gate of that lost land. Time has passed. I can stand at the threshold of one time and open the door to another. The moment of opening that door is worth everything."

That was it! How nicely she had put it.

Wasn't this all I ever wanted throughout my childhood, no, throughout my whole life?

Standing in one time and opening the door to another.

Opening a door to a realm of things beyond our knowledge, in a land of the obscure and the undefined. You open the door when you're too frightened to realize you are overwhelmed by fear and emerge into an entirely different world—a world where you have no idea what you will encounter or in which direction you will be pulled.

I know that such things remain in childhood.

Childhood has an end. Everything we see for the first time is taught to us. Everything soon becomes familiar. Even the new things we see are comprehended by comparison with past experiences. As years pass, we get accustomed to everything, and it all becomes common. Familiar and well-known. Familiar and ordinary. Familiar and harmless. Familiar and a part of us.

This is the kind of world we try to establish: a world in which we think we'll be protected from all threats.

Childhood ends, doesn't it? Childhood ends, and all of the different children in us grow up, or perhaps they go away. Along that long road, at every curve and every fork, we silently desert them one by one, unaware of what we are doing. In the end, we are left all alone.

Only one person remains from all those different children.

Why isn't it possible to hold each one of them by the hand and continue to walk on the path together?

As I sat and looked through magazines that morning, these thoughts crossed my mind.

I was wholly absorbed in what I read, unaware it was midday already. The sound of the doorbell brought me to my senses.

I hadn't tidied up the house after breakfast. Newspapers and magazines were scattered about. My teacup was still on the breakfast table. Dressed in my rose-colored housecoat, I put my hair up before I went to answer the door. At this time of the day, it could only be the postman.

I opened the door and for a moment stood there petrified.

As if they had agreed beforehand, there they were standing at my doorstep in suits of same color and with the same hats on their heads.

The two of them. Those two men who have determined my life.

I stood there motionless, utterly bewildered, as if aliens had come to take me away to infinity.

"I'm sorry I couldn't let you know earlier," Turgut apologized, "but when I met Mr. Fuat so unexpectedly, I couldn't let him go. We thought the three of us could have lunch together."

"But why didn't you call me! Look at me! Welcome, welcome! Come in!" I mumbled. Suddenly, I had turned into a young girl who came across her platonic love and discovered that in reality, everyone knew about her secret passion.

"I'm sorry, it's our fault," Fuat said immediately. "I told him but he wouldn't listen. We have disturbed you. Please pardon our impoliteness."

"Please! Please come in and make yourself at home. I'll be right back," I said and ran to the bedroom.

I closed the bedroom door and leaned back against it. My heart, pounding madly, skipped a beat.

I sat in front of the mirror, put on make-up with shaking hands, and then took everything out of my wardrobe, struggling to decide what to wear.

After a few unsuccessful trials, I managed to gather my hair in a bun, put on my pearl earrings, and from all the blouses, skirts and pants I had thrown onto the bed, I chose a dark green and light brown plaid dress with a white collar and belted at the waist.

I turned around and inspected the image in the mirror. I powdered my face. Now I looked exactly like a high school girl going out for the afternoon.

Turgut and Fuat were standing in the hallway, waiting for me to join them. I picked up my handbag, and we left.

It was a hot day, but you could feel that autumn was on its way. A chauffeur in a uniform and a hat held the door for us, and we got in the car. Turgut and I sat on one large single seat, and Fuat sat facing us.

As we turned to get to the square, we found ourselves in the middle of a demonstration.

The crowd, accompanied by mounted policemen, was protesting for the rights of black people. "Stop slavery!" was written across their signs.

While we sat in the car, waiting for the demonstrators, shouting slogans, to pass, Fuat did something unexpected. "Come," he said, and got out of the car. At a loss for words, we followed him. He pushed the policemen in front of us to get to the front and took the arms of the protesters in the front row. We suddenly found ourselves shouting slogans with them. Turgut was nervous. "Let's hope no one takes a picture of us. It would be a disaster."

But Fuat didn't care. Marching in the front row, he was screaming, "Slavery must end! Give people their rights!"

Later, at lunch, he told us the story of the senseless killing of a black child by white men a few weeks ago. He also told us about Ankara and that he still had not become used to being at the center of politics.

Our eyes met just once. Most of the time, he talked to Turgut, giving him advice like an older brother. Soon, the Cyprus issue arose. Fuat took out an old hardcover copy of *Othello* and read with his perfect English some parts he had underlined, but I felt as if neither of them wanted to delve into that subject in my presence.

Honestly, I did not care what Fuat talked about as long as he continued to speak. One could listen to him for ages. He talked with such enthusiasm, using long intricate sentences and phrases embellished with a tone that was sometimes full of ardor and other times calm and withdrawn, making you think he was reading lines from a book.

We were sitting at a table next to the window. The restaurant was crowded. With the hum of voices in the background, we listened intently to every word he said. After coffee, he took a cigarette out of a silver case with his long elegant fingers, lit it, and stopped abruptly for a single moment to stare at me. Then he turned his eyes to look off in the distance, as if he were no longer in that room. A melancholy song was playing. It was probably Doris Day, singing "Secret Love".

That momentary lapse into silence when he lost himself in thought was one of the first special moments I recorded about him in my memory.

Then he opened the newspaper on the table. "Look at that!" he exclaimed. "There's a concert at the museum at four o'clock." Turgut glanced at his watch uneasily. "No, no, don't worry," Fuat continued. "You go back to work. I'll go there by myself. Besides, I'm leaving in the evening."

He knew, of course, that we wouldn't let him go there alone and that I would have to accompany him.

Much later, he told me laughing, "I wonder how it occurred to me to take a look at the paper that day."

We walked to the museum, and I took his arm as we climbed the stairs to the entrance. I pretended to be hosting an important guest as usual, but the truth was different. At the same time, I felt like a brash high school girl who was arm in arm with a man much older than herself. Whatever I did, no matter how much I spoke, I couldn't stop my heart from beating madly. In my mind, I sang to myself that melody without a break.

We entered the museum, bought our tickets, and began to walk around the ground floor. The concert would not start for more than an hour.

As soon as we passed through a huge door, entered the great hall, and saw that painting facing us, I realized what was happening to me.

It was as if someone had placed the painting there to tell me, "Don't you really understand what is happening to you?"

A plump child with wings hovered above the clouds in the sky with a bow in his hand. The cherub had an odd smile on his face, and he resembled a mischievous kid who expected to be punished.

The arrow he shot traveled all the way through the colors, clouds, and forests in the painting and pierced my heart.

It was so real that I even felt an abrupt pain in my chest.

I regained my senses when Fuat said, "He doesn't look like the god of love but a small child. Don't you think he looks rather innocent?"

Innocent?

"I don't know," I replied. "He looks as if he's shooting arrows just to make mischief."

Fuat laughed. "But isn't love a mischievous thing?"

I suddenly recalled that day years ago. The morning in Ankara when we had first met. Wasn't that the same thing he had told me then? "Your little sister is a little mischievous, I suppose."

Surely, he didn't remember that.

Standing in that huge, empty hall under the high ceiling decorated with paintings from hundreds of years ago, we stood transfixed by that splendid painting.

I stood there like a small girl who was confused about feelings she couldn't define and did not know what to do. Let me tell you, at that moment I wanted time to stand still and stay there forever.

Our identities, our attachments, the time and the place were obliterated. I almost felt as if I were the woman from the past in the painting, who secretly met her lover among the trees, and whose long skirt could be heard rustling from where I stood. If I closed my eyes, I thought, I would be able to walk into that painting and along the same path into a new life and replace her.

In fact, I now know why that plump little angel was laughing so mischievously. I also know that at that very moment, I entered another path inside of me and set off for an unknown period in time beyond my control.

To an unknown time.

To an unknown destination.

Don't we think that we are very different from all the people that we pass on the street as we wander about with an arrow thrust into our heart, certain that we are on cloud nine?

Until we feel the penetrating pain of the arrow.

(When that long-awaited phone call does not come. When that letter fails to arrive. When those eyes are somehow not able to look into yours for the first time. Or a totally different word is uttered instead of that which was expected.)

At that moment, I had none of this in mind. Words poured from my mouth as I talked non-stop to mask my excitement. We visited other halls, and the same child, that angel, always appeared suddenly in different paintings, with the same sweet smile and glittering eyes.

With those eyes, the angel said, "You thought you could escape, but you can't."

If our heart clenches for no reason and then begins to pound, we run to a doctor.

Yet we are not frightened when we feel dizzy, our heart skips a beat, or we become short of breath when our eyes happen to meet those of someone we don't even know.

Curious.

It suddenly occurred to me: If there were really life far away in those stars flickering like tiny lights in the night sky, and if one day, someone from one of those distant worlds came here, to this museum, what would he think about all these paintings?

A bearded man with a crown of thorns on his head and nailed by his feet and hands to a plank, a naked man and a naked woman (accompanied by a snake!) picking an apple from a tree, a plump, winged child with a bow and arrow, smiling constantly from above the clouds . . .

Pain, sins, and love?

Faith and lack of faith?

Torture, solitude, and relief?

Being punished, being punished, being punished?

Perhaps he would not be able to attribute a meaning to any of these.

I said this to him, too. He laughed and said, "Our life does appear simple, doesn't it?"

"It is simple, and it never changes," I replied.

We went upstairs, took two empty seats on one of the wooden benches, and sat among the audience under the huge dome.

Who knows, maybe all those things, all the surprising coincidences and the wonderful music that suddenly started to play in that place where nobody knew us—among those paintings, the depictions of scenes from holy books, myths of The Creation, great wars, destruction, and the illustrated stories of great love affairs—was a little too much for a young woman with a secret love story.

Fuat leaned toward me and whispered something in my ear. I

felt dizzy. I was in a dream, and what he had said didn't matter. I was just hoping that moment would never end; I wanted to remain forever in that state of overwhelming inebriation.

He bent forward, looked at my face, and smiled, realizing I hadn't understood what he had said.

Again, I felt his lips and his breath close to my ear. This time, I heard what he said.

"I came here for you. Since the day you left, you've been on my mind. I'm not able to spend another day without being near you. I'm ready to take all risks. Would you consider getting divorced and marrying me?"

This is exactly what he said.

The music played with instruments of past centuries, that enchanting music played in a place that had been built hundreds of years ago, was at its most lyrical. It made you restless. It gave you wings. I was dizzy. My hands were locked together on my knees. My face was flushed, and my lips were dry. I wasn't there. I didn't know where I was, as if someone was stepping out of my body and leaving me. Eventually, with a deep, stern voice, I managed to say, "You must have lost your mind."

Those weren't the words I wanted to tell him, but what else could I have said?

I had once watched a film in Ankara about a girl from a poor neighborhood on the outskirts of the city who said and did whatever she wanted without hesitating. (Was it Filiz Akın or Fatma Girik who acted in the lead role?) I would have given the world to be like her then.

Dream and reality had mixed together. My fantasies had suddenly become reality without warning.

Until that day, he had always addressed me formally, but now he said "you" in the most informal way, and his first sentence had been "Will you marry me?"

Unbelievable!

This is what happens when you travel fearlessly between fantasy and reality.

All of a sudden, the magical unity had shattered, and in my mind I heard the voices of a thousand beings speaking in chorus again.

I had to settle it now, once and for all.

I would never see him again.

Maybe I had to be calm and take this like one of his usual jokes or games.

Or perhaps I should remain silent and allow time for things to settle.

A swarm of sentences were being constructed and deconstructed at the same time, one after the other.

As we rode in the cab, he said, "Please forgive me for being so abrupt. I've been torturing myself for months as to how I should tell you. I wanted to write a letter, but I couldn't. I wanted to call you, I couldn't. All I could do was come here. I made up some excuse to be here and came. So that I could tell you. That's all."

I continued to sulk.

In fact, I wanted to laugh out loud.

But I was frightened in a way I hadn't expected.

I was trying to overcome all the voices saying different things in my mind.

This was a game I had been playing on my own, and he was the hero of my game. Now, all at once, he had decided to become part of the game. He wanted to play the game together. But it was a perilous game. It had not crossed my mind, not even once, that the game would one day turn to reality.

"It's impossible," I said. "You're married. You have a child. Don't you care about your family and your position? Besides, I'm also married. Let's stop it here and now and forget everything that's been said today."

I couldn't believe I had expressed these thoughts in well-arranged sentences. My voice echoed in the cab. I was speaking with tight lips and clenched teeth, scared that the cab driver could understand what we were talking about.

"I don't care about my job, position, or anything else," he insisted. "If you cannot reach what your heart desires, what else matters?"

Can one take whatever his heart desires? I wish it had been possible.

Then, suddenly, he said, "Forget about other people and tell me what's really on your mind . . . what you truly wish."

I looked outside through the car window, trying to keep my eyes from meeting his. How could I tell him what I really wanted or how I really felt. I didn't even have the courage to confess it to myself. Was he aware of how I struggled to stop what I dreamed of?

"What's on my mind?" I said eventually. "What goes through my mind? You are joking with me."

He took my face in his hands and turned it toward himself. I blushed again and tried to look away.

"You know very well when I joke and when I tell the truth." His voice was soft and gentle. It sounded like the voice of another person speaking in the distance.

A few minutes ago I was ready to sacrifice all I had just to stay by his side forever, but now, I felt like a caged animal and wanted to get out of the cab as soon as possible. I wanted to shut myself in my room and be alone.

I said, "This is my fault. I cannot forgive myself." I was aware I was talking nonsense, as if somebody else were dictating my words.

"If there's someone who cannot be forgiven, it's me," he replied quickly. "But I really don't care. Come with me, and I'll go wherever in the world you want to go. I'll give up everything."

At that moment, I realized I was dealing with a kid.

No, he wasn't lying.

If you could have looked into his eyes, if you had been in my shoes, you would have understood.

For a moment, I thought the cab would not stop but go all the way to the airport, and that we would get on a plane, fly away, and begin a new life together somewhere else.

Could it have been possible?

If we had succeeded in forgetting about everyone else, our pasts, the consequences facing us, all our responsibilities, and opening the door of the dream had gone on that unexpected journey, would everything have changed?

And it was there: The door in the fairy tale—the door that would open when you pronounced the magic words was right beside me. It was the door of a cab speeding through the streets of London.

I knew what the magical words were. They were there, on the tip of my tongue. If I said them and opened that door, I would probably achieve what many people have desired in vain for hundreds of years.

I wished for everything to turn into a movie all at once and that we could begin a life of our own wherever we wanted.

We could go to a faraway island, meet new people, and spend our days and nights as we wished, not according to other people's desires. As far away as possible. For as long as it lasted.

What did it matter if it were as short as a film? Couldn't we have fit everything in? Couldn't we have built a life, every moment of which we would cherish till the end of our days? In place of all those boring meetings, those hours passed in vain, those days when we wanted to say things but couldn't and met people we pretended to like, and those nights full of self-pity when you put your head on the pillow and wondered if your whole life was destined to be spent in such a colorless way.

I wished that we had no secrets between us and that we could tell each other everything, even the things that could make us angry, things we would be scared to hear, and the things one might be afraid to confess even to himself. We would be naked and stripped of our identities, constructed over the years brick by brick, that we would no longer be two separate human beings. We could then pass without fear and trepidation through the gates that opened before us, one after the other, and enter those secret corridors without thinking about what awaited us.

I felt odd. I felt that we could find something that only belonged to us and would bring us together. Something even we weren't aware of, something granted to just the two of us. Two separate parts of something that would reveal the joy of life only if united.

Otherwise, could I feel so close to a man I only knew occasionally? I felt closer to him than I had ever felt to any other person.

As he waited for me to give him an answer, these thoughts dominated my mind. Not in well-arranged or well-thought-out sentences, though. I was mixed up, but I believed something would emerge from me and change the direction of both the cab and our lives, and that I wouldn't be able to stop it.

I would not worry about anything and just tell him, "Hold my hand and let's go." Then we would go far, far away.

This was what I truly wanted to do.

Yet I couldn't bring myself to do it.

All I did was to say with an icy voice, "Please, let us close this subject. I consider it one of your jokes. Let it remain a joke, a big joke."

Maybe, if I had managed to be brave enough for once in my life, everything would have changed despite all odds. Not only for the two of us, but for everyone.

So it began like that.

With separation.

With us separating even before we united.

I looked at him through the window. He paused for a moment and then changed his mind, hurrying toward his hotel.

His hat on his head, with the wrinkled back of his thin summer jacket . . . stooping, his shoulders fallen . . . disappearing in the heavy mist descending slowly.

That blurred image is still in my memory like a photograph.

It was to be repeated so many times.

As he left . . . always when he left.

Time passed.

Whenever I went out, my feet guided me there, to the same museum. I don't recall how many times I entered that hall where the cherubs waited for me. The women in uniform who sat on small stools and read their books must have thought I had a mysterious bond with that painting.

I wonder how many times I stood there, in front of it, asking myself whether it had all been a dream.

Undoubtedly, it had been a dream.

The daydream of a young woman.

She wasn't aware of what she had done.

Even if she were, what would have changed?

Impossible things . . .

In those days, I read books about impossible things. Diaries written hundreds of years ago. Feverish lines from love letters. The way lives were wasted by waiting in desperation and lost in the anguish of an impossible love.

In any case, what is lived cannot be put on paper.

Films with the same theme were playing those days, of women who went through forbidden loves, secret affairs, emotional tides that would make one shudder. Dangerous liaisons. No one found such things strange or unacceptable as they were regarded in the past.

Though not considered strange, those films always had unhappy endings.

As I walked on the streets alone, I often caught myself smiling, and then I regained my senses. The crowds passing me by were like inanimate objects. Feeling as if I didn't exist, I gave myself over to imagination. I crossed into a different world and made believe everything was possible there.

In the meantime, I wondered why he had not called, though many days had passed since he left.

I must confess I woke up to every new day with the hope of hearing from him.

Like before the luncheons, I expected him to suddenly appear and join us.

I was reluctant to leave the house in case I missed a possible call. Yet, it was also unbearable to stay home.

You couldn't imagine the daydreams I indulged in.

Had I been too harsh with him? Maybe I had embarrassed him by reacting too sharply to what he had told me with such difficulty. Perhaps.

I told myself repeatedly that since he had given up so soon and so easily his feelings must have been a lie.

Could he have really thought I was altogether indifferent to him?

Maybe he suffered greatly and desired to call me but couldn't find a way. But why didn't he at least send a postcard? But what if Turgut happened to see it? He definitely was afraid of that possibility. But what could happen if he just sent a simple card, a few lines to extend his thanks and so on.

I usually regained my self-control and convinced myself I had done the right thing. He must have come to his senses as soon as he arrived at his hotel; now, he was waiting for time to help fade that childish dream.

He was a grownup. He must have understood what he had done was utter nonsense and been glad that his moment of madness had been warded off rather harmlessly.

On the other hand, how could I know that he didn't court other women in the same way, hoping to lead them astray?

No matter what I told myself, I still desired to live that single incomparable moment one more time. I was willing to be content with one call, a single letter, some news, anything that would revive it.

One day I almost called him after standing by the telephone and biting my nails. I was planning to introduce myself with a fake name.

Turgut was not aware of anything, but he thought I was bored at home. Every now and then we attended parties. We tried to go and visit places at the weekend, but when his workload increased, he began to bring work home as well. Perhaps one gets used to leading a mediocre life among mediocre things. You don't feel the need to question yourself when you don't have any expectations.

I was so lonely.

The postman delivered letters all the time: from my family and my friends, but none from him.

Nothing came from him, but I received a postcard from Ayla that delighted me. That crazy girl! She had sent a postcard with a picture of a fertility god, without an envelope of course! "I'm bored to death with these stupid gods who think they will stay in their tombs forever. What's more, I have missed you so much! Leyla Gencer is singing *Madame Butterfly*. Get some tickets so that we can go and see it together. I'll be there next week."

That's the way she was. She knew about what was happening at the other end of the world, even if she were hundred meters below ground.

I was overcome by joy, as if she was going to enter the door at that moment. I immediately prepared her room. I was planning to try to convince her to stay with us for a while.

I made all the arrangements: the places we would visit, the restaurants we would go to, as well as the theaters and the concerts.

On the day of her arrival, I was getting ready to go and pick her up at the airport when the bell suddenly began to ring madly. I put on my housecoat and hurried to the door. Ayla rushed in with her suitcase and an envelope in her hand. We hugged each other like little kids. Tears rolled down my cheeks.

"Hey, what's going on?" she said. "Don't scare me. Why are you crying! Did you think I would journey to the center of the earth and never come back? Don't worry. Nothing will happen to me. Look at me. I'm safe and sound!"

She gave me the envelope after we sat down to drink tea. "I found this at the door. It's for you."

I took the envelope and tore its corner. The handwriting on it was not familiar.

Believe it or not, Ayla had entered my house with the letter I had been waiting for so long.

When I noticed that the letter was from him, I blushed. Excusing myself, I rushed to my bedroom and closed the door. It was a short letter written in a formal tone: "Dear Madam, first of all, please accept my apologies for not having extended my heartfelt thanks for your kind hospitality sooner. As you know, I had to go on many trips. All those places were very boring. Fortunately, the angels were always beside me. Looking forward to seeing you again soon. With best regards . . ."

He had put his initials like a seal at the end of the letter.

That was all he had written.

I'm not sure if anyone else who read it would get any meaning out of it, but I did. I understood that he had not forgotten anything. That he still cherished the memory of that day. That what I had told him had not changed his feelings for me. He had written, "The angels were always beside me."

I hid the letter and went back to Ayla.

Can a few lines written in black ink with a quivering pen change the colors of the world or the light of life so suddenly?

That day, I learned they could.

Are words that powerful?

Words are really powerful.

Lives are rubbed out, things done are forgotten. Only words remain from countless moments that are impossible to be remembered, from the undefined feelings one has in everyday life, and from a whole lifetime that is renewed, replaced, and refreshed and that finally leaves its worn out images in the past.

As Ayla told me about the story of a mysterious ancient city she had found, wasn't she conveying the words inscribed on ancient tablets?

Kings in the past who praised themselves, who tried to leave an unforgettable name to a future civilization, and who wished a woman who opened that door thousands of years later to read about their lives had ordered those tablets to be written.

What had they expected? Had they realized the immortality they strove for was inherent in those scribbled letters?

Immortality is neither beyond the mountains in the elixir of mysterious water-flowers, nor in the glory of stone monuments that challenge the ages.

Monuments do not speak. Statues cannot quote a real story. Everything translated from one language to another and transferred from generation to generation through the legends of long dead witnesses is doomed to alter and spoil.

Only words on a clay tablet, a piece of papyrus, fabric or paper can resist merciless time and transport you to remote places, if immortality is ever possible.

As you see, the words of a king who thought he was the ruler of heaven and earth had reached a woman with a ponytail who spoke an entirely different language, thousands of years later. In her hands, the whole story was slowly transformed from the code of an incomprehensible language into a new form everyone could understand.

What the ruler of heaven and earth, forgotten for thousands of years, strove to proclaim to an obscure future had come to light again and been cleaned of dust through a series of coincidences.

Wouldn't it be nice if the mysterious texts concealed in human beings, and not just the writings left by great kings or terrible emperors, could be discovered and decoded after having remained hidden for thousands of years?

But most of us depart this world with things unsaid, don't we?

Even the ones who think they know us the most do not know us well, in truth.

Yes. Words are powerful.

If there is a path into a woman's heart, believe me, it passes through words.

Moreover, that path itself is covered with words.

Nothing can turn a woman's head more than well-arranged words.

Just like the way incantations open the doors in tales.

Or did you forget about Cyrano?

Words were the reason I had been seduced by him. Words that no one but he could arrange in that special way. Something had started the ball rolling in Ankara when we chatted about this and that. Without even being aware of it . . .

Later, letters consisting of carefully drafted sentences would follow.

Once he wrote to me: "For a very long time, I thought my life had already turned into a hazy, chilly autumn. When I saw you, I suddenly woke up to a sunny morning. Now, wherever I go in this world, my days are always sunny and bright regardless of the season, because I think of you (no, I didn't express it correctly; it is because your face and your smile are always by my side). I wonder if you are aware you have changed the way the world shines for me?"

If you knew how I counted the days to receive those letters, you would probably laugh.

But don't laugh, please.

Nowadays, no one cares about letters or postcards. They send each other short messages with their cell phones.

They talk to each other with phones that can transfer their images.

Yet, nothing can replace words.

When that special person says something, which everyone has been telling each other for centuries, your life suddenly takes on a different look.

Those lines I memorized still put me on cloud nine.

When I strolled with Ayla on the streets of London, smoked cigarettes on the banks of the river, or ran with her on the wet leaves in the park like small children . . . when we got on the merry-go-round and screamed with joy at the fairground that had recently opened . . . when we looked for a warm café, arm-in-arm with our collars all the way up to protect ourselves against the biting cold . . . when we chatted, watching the passersby on the street and the double-decker buses through the windows covered with condensation . . .

I had a secret, and I couldn't keep it from Ayla.

Finally, as we sipped our tea at a café, everything poured out of my mouth. The museum . . . the little angels . . . the music of past centuries . . . and all he had told me.

Opening her eyes wide as always, she listened to me in silence.

"You must have lost your mind," she said later.

"That is exactly what I said," I replied. She was about to continue but I motioned for her to stop. "But," I continued, "please don't tell me anything bad."

She giggled. "What shall I do then, tell you what you want to hear? You have always liked people who told you things you wanted to hear. Alright. As you wish. Whatever I say won't matter anyway. Whatever will be, will be."

She knew. She knew well that life ridiculed even the most powerful emperors and the fools who believed they were gods but could at most achieve becoming a mummy that turned to dust as soon as their plundered tombs were opened.

Whatever will be will be.

I confess, I was still unable to take anything seriously. I still saw everything as a game. He and I were involved in an "impossible flirtation." It was something that added spice and zest to my life, which had become worn rather early. It enabled me to take joy in songs, streets, and words again. That was all.

This was such a curious feeling. I felt as if my mind had suddenly expanded, absorbing even the minutest detail of everything around me with insatiable desire.

I felt I could perceive not only things in the open but also beyond them. I smelled the fragrance of the flowers behind a garden wall as I passed by. My eyes filled with tears when I tried to think how an old and exhausted woman who tried to make way for herself in the crowd felt. I wanted to touch everything and everyone, unable to stand still because of the inexpressible joy overwhelming me.

I felt as if all those ordinary love songs I had heard so many times were sung for me. Each of them had figurative meanings.

"Look here! Are you in love or what?" Ayla asked. "No good can come from this. Don't go too far. This is no child's game!"

"Did you say love? You can't be serious! How did you come up with such an idea? It's my fault I told you about this."

"Are you kidding? Just pray no one else recognizes it. It's so obvious!"

I hung my head in shame. Was she right? I tried to remember if I had told her about our first encounter years ago. Upon realizing that I had not, I blushed.

If she knew about that moment, she would definitely be afraid.

She only knew about the dance at the ball and the conversations we had at the hotel, just like everyone else.

Although Ayla frowned in worry, she was still taking it as a joke.

Who could take all these things seriously at such a moment?

Dances, angels, coincidences . . . Everything truly resembled the pieces of a jigsaw puzzle.

"Let's take a walk," Ayla said. "I didn't come here to chat. If they allow a child to get married, this is what's bound to happen. She still plays games!"

How much I had missed her good spirits . . . her easy-going approach even at the most poignant moment . . . the confidence of knowing she was always there for me.

As a poet had once said: "Everything disappears but true friend-ship."

Her face had tanned during the summer and turned swarthy. I saw lines at the corners of her big black eyes. If she kept on living like this, she would soon look older than her age. She had never taken good care of herself.

Girls that were just a few years younger than us were twirling hoops around their waists. That was a new amusement in those days. A group of men and women mounted on horses passed them by.

While we were walking on the riverbank, a sudden, strong wind blew, causing the dry leaves on the ground, as well as our skirts, to fly up. As we tried to run while holding our skirts down, we both screamed and burst out laughing. Everyone looked at us, but it didn't bother us a bit.

A wind had hurled us into the garden of childhood again. Suddenly.

In the evening, when the three of us went out for dinner, Turgut told me he would be going to Geneva for a few days the following morning. "Fortunately, Ayla is here. You won't be alone," he said.

I know it's insanity to attribute a special meaning to every little thing, but what can I do? When I look back and remember, everything seems to have been arranged by a mysterious hand.

Ayla looked at me with an evasive smile.

She had not believed me when I had decided to get married. Then, after meeting Turgut, she had opposed me harshly. For her, Turgut was a like a book that you somehow start reading and finish just for the sake of having read it. "Besides," she had said, "when you read such books, you always expect something interesting to happen but nothing does."

"You have always been cruel."

"Have I? You should also be cruel especially when your life is at stake!"

She just didn't understand how it was possible for me to accept such a marriage.

"You can definitely do whatever you want. But only for the sake of something that's worth it!" she said angrily. "Not just to have a stupid, supine husband."

She never inquired about Turgut or referred to our marriage in her letters. It was as though she and I, the best of friends, were separated from each other not because of my marriage but because we lived in cities far away from each other.

Turgut wasn't fond of her either. It would be out of the question for a man, who already found me much too tactless, to like Ayla, who loudly voiced whatever crossed her mind.

But with his usual politeness, he asked her questions about the excavation and pretended to be interested in what she said. In fact, he did listen to what she explained. He liked being informed about everything.

The next evening, we went to see *Madame Butterfly*. Gentlemen in formal dark suits, ladies in chic evening gowns and glittering jewels, and ushers that looked as if they had come from a past era in their red outfits and powdered wigs . . .

As we entered the building next to the royal coach through the crowd lined up on both sides, watching the people arrive, we felt we also had our share of the great public admiration for the great Turkish opera singer.

Our seats were in the middle of the auditorium. I guess we were the youngest and the plainest people in the audience.

Before the lights went out, a gentleman with a moustache and dressed in a black suit approached us and gave me a small package. "Welcome," he said, "this is for you." He left as quickly as he had appeared. I suddenly felt as if we were two characters in a spy movie.

Stunned, I looked at the package. "Open it," Ayla whispered. I obeyed. There were two fans in the package—black, graceful, and embellished with the figures of birds and flowers. There was also a note written on a small piece of paper.

"Do you know that in olden times, ladies used to go everywhere with a fan in their hand. If you held the fan in your right hand and covered your face, it meant 'follow me.' But if you did the same thing with the fan in your left hand, it meant 'leave me alone.' If you opened the fan and held it in front of your chest, it meant 'I'm in love.' Enjoy it."

Under the note, a big and shapeless "F" appeared as always: his signature.

At that moment, the lights faded, the curtain raised, and the music began. I was too confused to watch the opera. I sensed Ayla watching me out of the corner of her eye, yet I pretended not to notice.

How had I not seen him? For sure, he was not alone. Was his wife with him? If she were, could he have sent me the package? Maybe he had handed it to the man beforehand. Or maybe he wasn't there at all and had sent it with somebody else. No, that didn't make sense. If he weren't there now, how would he know where we sat? If he didn't know, how would he have prepared the gift? I was in utter confusion. He had probably come earlier and found out that we would be at the opera too, with no one else with us. He must have gone mad, I told myself. What he had done was insane!

Ayla grasped my arm, whispering, "You're killing me with curiosity. What is it that you have there?"

"Nothing. Just two fans. Here, one's for you."

"I can see they're fans. But where did they come from? Who sent them? What's in the note?"

"Note? What note? Oh, nothing important. It's like a glossary of fans."

"A glossary of fans?"

"Yes. It mentions all the things you can do with a fan . . . what it all means, and so on."

"Bravo! The world is falling apart, but the gentleman is busy with a glossary of fans. And they call me a nut! What are you looking at?"

"I saw him! He's there! There, in the front row, toward the left. No, don't stare! They'll see us!"

"They'll see us? Do you think he cares?"

We had to stop talking when someone told us to keep quiet.

Then we listened to that beautiful but mournful voice.

She sang:

"You pleased me from the first moment I saw you/ and you said things I've not heard before/ now I'm happy/ oh, so happy."

The man replied:

"Give me your dear little hands so that I may kiss them/ My Butterfly!/ How aptly you were named/ delicate butterfly . . ."

Her voice charmed us, touching everyone in the room deep in the soul.

"Across the sea it is said, when a man catches a butterfly/ he'll pierce her poor little body with a pin and then fix her in a glass case."

The man answered:

"There is a little truth in that/ but do you know why?/ It is so she cannot escape . . ."

Soon happiness, a house full of colorful flowers, and joyous songs slowly turned into the endless wait of a sorrowful woman. Into a life that depended on the cannon-shots from a ship expected to arrive in a distant harbor.

We were soon immersed in the magic of the vivid and bright costumes, the scenery made of transparent paper flowers covering the whole stage like a garden, the lights, and the shadows.

In the end, when she sang her farewell song to her baby: "look for the last time upon your mother's face/so that some trace will remain"—we were no longer able to hold back our tears.

Not only us but everyone.

As the curtain fell, the entire audience jumped up from their seats. We all applauded frantically. The young woman's pain had plunged into our hearts, especially with the last song, and we also felt excited and proud of the loud applause Leyla Gencer was receiving. We felt as if we were being praised, too. Ayla hugged me and kissed my cheek. You could hear people shouting, "Bravo! Bravo!" A curtain of tears veiled my eyes, causing me to see the stage through a glass stained with teardrops. It was incredible.

I can't remember how long we applauded, until our hands hurt, or how many times the curtain opened and closed.

Then, suddenly, I saw him. He was looking at me. The fan was in my right hand. If I held it in front of my face, it would mean I wanted him to follow me. It was truly an enchanting moment. I would not hold the fan like that. I took it into my left hand. I thought

I saw a smile on his face for a brief moment. Then I opened the fan and covered my face.

I was restless at home that night. I didn't want to take off my dress decorated with pearls around the collar and a fluffy tulle skirt. It had been an unforgettable evening. Everyone in the glittering hall had been overcome by emotion, with the glamorous colors of the garments, and the spell of the music. But what about me? As if all those things were not enough, Fuat had showed up. The unexpected gift, that strange note, and the glossary of fans.

I kept thinking, "That man is crazy. Really crazy."

He wasn't lying. He was truly in love with me. Evidently, what I had told him in the cab had gone in one ear and out the other. Using the opera as an excuse, he had come here in no time flat. Would he call me? He knew Turgut was away of course. Would he do that? I wouldn't be surprised.

Is it possible to explain my elation?

To get just a little closer to an indescribable beauty you have never seen before and to slightly touch it, to get just a little bit closer and caress it gently, like a timid novice.

That was all there was to it.

But even that—to become closer, to touch it—was enough to put me up in the clouds.

Would I have wanted him by my side? Would I have wished to be with him, talk to him by the fire until the first light of morning, discuss the "real story" we had not talked about before, and listen to what he would tell me about his life, his childhood, the moments that caused him to act in such a mad way, the day he had first worn a tie, what he did when he ran away from school, or when he completed his military service? Then, only then, I would ask him to confess all that was in his heart, to shatter the wall between us and tell me all there was to be said or left unsaid, while pouring out his true feelings without any barriers between us.

Would I have wanted this?

I don't know. Perhaps I hadn't asked myself this question back then. Just a touch from a distance, the encounter of the eyes, the helpless expression of his face as I held the fan in front of my face, the way I couldn't look him in the eyes (did he really understand what I wanted to say?), the way he stood there stunned, unable to move, how he talked to people in the crowd in desperation (maybe he really thought he should stop this game), how he probably thought I would turn around and look at him before we left (he must have expected me to turn to look, but I didn't, of course). That song is still in my ears. That instant chill I felt all over as he passed me by.

It is true I felt such things then. Fantastic feelings. Nothing that is real can replace them.

We arrived home. I wanted to do strange things such as dancing and spinning around and getting lost in a whirlpool. I was intoxicated and mesmerized, and those feelings felt new to me.

I knew he wouldn't be able to leave the people he was with. The ambassador was giving a reception. They would go to his residence and then return to their hotel together late at night.

Ayla and I sat for hours and chatted. When the first hours of the morning arrived, we were still talking about the good old days. Our eyes were filled with tears at one moment, and we laughed and giggled at another, just like in our childhood.

We talked about the mysterious codes she had been struggling to solve for many months, the book she planned to write, the ancient city that would come to light entirely in a few years, and the unsurpassed journey she had made to the magical time of unknown lands.

Both of us were aware that our minds were on something else.

But my dearest friend didn't question me further, and I didn't tell her anything else.

We both realized that the situation had extended beyond the boundaries of a game. Maybe that's why we remained silent, in order not to give voice to the concern rooted deeply in both of us.

Upon waking up after a bad sleep and a dark, tangled dream, I was not tired but happy and excited.

That fan and the short note had suddenly separated me from everyone else on earth, transforming me into a brand new person. I suppose I had not drawn a lesson from that pathetic love story we had watched the previous night.

I could not avoid looking at the phone.

While we were drinking coffee after breakfast, it rang. It was almost midday. I ran to answer it, trying hard to sound normal. I was scared I wouldn't be able to speak. Unfortunately, it was Turgut, and I learned from him that the call I was waiting for would not come.

He informed me about unpleasant events in Istanbul. People had taken to the streets, shops had been looted, and martial law had been declared. According to his description, the city was in shambles.

It was not difficult to understand why Fuat had returned abruptly.

"I'll be home soon," said Turgut. "We'll go out to dinner together."

Ayla was curious, noticing the sour look on my face.

I told her.

She laughed.

"Even history is against you," she said.

That was a phrase said merely for the sake of saying it. One of her usual jokes.

Who would have dwelled on it?

Yes. History.

In a way, the whole world had begun to fight in those days. The only result being that, after millions of people died, everyone tried harder to make more arms. Every day the newspapers wrote about new, more powerful bombs. We were assailed with news about new wars and struggles around the world. Kings were overthrown, dictators were replaced, the police and the public clashed, bombs exploded, and people died.

It was mass madness.

That year, every single place from Cyprus to Algeria, and from Suez to Hungary turned into a battlefield.

Crowds carrying placards filled the public squares. They screamed, "We don't want war!" They were protesting against the wars in remote countries that their nations were engaged in and the bombs their countries produced. Yet, no one listened to them.

Wherever I went, that song played: "*Que sera, sera*." Just like Ayla said, "Whatever will be, will be!"

It really was like that. One didn't know what time would bring. Just like a small child doesn't know what the future will bring to him, how could one know where this bizarre world was heading, what a simple street protest would cause, and that a lunatic who shot his gun somewhere, some time, for no comprehensible reason would lead humanity into endless war?

In Budapest, people climbed on tanks and pounded their fists on them. News about boycotts and marches from Istanbul to Ankara was broadcast.

However, people here discussed why Monroe had married the writer with glasses. I'll never forget a photograph of Marilyn that was taken at that time, with a voluminous book in her hand: *Ulysses*, Joyce's incomprehensible novel. Was this the photographer's trick, or a way to express that the famous blond was not stupid after all?

Grace Kelly had married, too. The dream in the movies had become real. She and the prince stood hand in hand on the palace balcony and smiled to the public. She was a dreamlike beauty in her wedding gown complete with a long bridal veil.

No one had time to fuss over the pains of others.

The newspapers wrote a few lines about the people who died and sometimes published a photo of a child that might upset the readers for a few minutes.

When the news arrived from Istanbul, I asked Ayla, "What's going on? Has the whole world gone mad? Why does everyone want to kill each other?"

"Who knows," she replied, "maybe we don't see the world as a place worth living in. Why else would we sacrifice everything for thousands of years just to invent weapons to destroy humanity?"

Ayla left a few days after our night at the opera. Before leaving, she told me, "I would like to ask you to pull yourself together, but I wonder if it will be of any use."

"You're really making a mountain out of a molehill," I replied. "I'm bored here. Don't I have the right to a little fun? Don't exaggerate things!"

It's difficult to explain. But that was really what I kept telling myself. One part of me knew I was taking things a little too seriously, but another part still thought everything was a harmless game.

On one hand, I waited to hear from him, and on the other, I consoled myself by saying, "Of course he's aware this is just a secret game between us, he's a grownup, and he's certainly not serious." Yet, at the same time, I was annoyed and upset that he didn't call.

I even planned how I would treat him the next time we met. He would learn his lesson. That gentleman thought he could cozy up to me like that and then disappear, thinking I would sit here and wait for him!

I didn't wait for him!

Then I realized I had ignored all the signals.

Perhaps he had given it all up. How could a man insist when the woman he approached refused to give him the green light?

How stupid I had been! I had held the fan in front of my face. The man had traveled all the way here. Twice. He discovered all the possibilities of seeing me, tried so hard, and had to tell many lies perhaps. In return, he had to put up with my grim exterior.

Oh! All right, but could he be that foolish? How could he have expected me to open the fan all the way and tell him "I love you, follow me" as if I were a high school girl.

So, like a high school girl, I was tense and moody.

Days passed without knowing what I waited for or what I should do.

I had a double life. One life I kept hidden inside of me, and no one had a clue about it. It was as if I was my own confidant. I kept talking to myself as if I were pouring my heart out to someone else.

Sometimes I gave myself advice, and sometimes I gave up and allowed myself to do whatever I wanted.

Was that insane? Not at all! In truth, I was aware of everything that had been going on. I did desire him. Unbelievably so. More than I had desired anyone.

When I was a young girl, I had suddenly become a married woman. I had no idea that when you truly desire someone frightening things could happen in your body.

Maybe I suspected it, but I didn't understand it. Yet now I know that pretentious words are useless. It's almost impossible to stop that secret shudder that embraces your entire being, causing you to fear that your soul is about to leave your body.

It was only after I met him that I had begun buying feminine clothes. Even if we didn't meet, I dressed up for him and sat in front of my dressing table every morning.

You know why? Because it's not important what one goes through. What counts is how you feel.

I felt as if I shared everything I experienced with him.

But I was afraid it would all turn into reality. Everything would be spoiled then. The excitement would turn to anxiety. I would begin to live like a criminal afraid of being caught. I would feel remorse.

Since I was aware of these consequences, I was content with the daydream I had fostered on my own.

If he had not taken a step toward me, everything would have remained like it had started, and when I recalled it many years later, my body wouldn't shudder, but I would probably feel the shadow of a shudder. Doesn't everyone have such a memory of something buried deep inside of him, without having actually experienced it.

What is innocence?

Weren't the colors swirling around me those days the excitement of rediscovering the world, as if I could read it in another language, and was that feeling, like a gift given to me, which took my feet off the ground, innocent?

If this mutual game that included deceit continued, and if it proceeded to a kiss, which took my breath away even when imagining it, would all these secret gifts become soiled?

Ayla wrote a letter to me after her return to Turkey. As if forecasting what would happen, she tried to warn me and prevent some things from happening.

"My Dear Friend,

"I was utterly bewildered when I left the solitary days of a forgotten time and suddenly came to you and the center of the world. Upon returning to that great solitude after those joyful days we spent together, a deep gloom has descended on me. One always asks oneself where they belong. In the small world they have created for themselves, in some corner, they spend a lifetime, forgetting its numberless missed and lost fragments. Do you remember you once told me that you travel the world and I travel in time. I cannot forget how my mother had cried when I entered the university to study archaeology, saying, "What a pity! My girl will become a grave digger." She wasn't wrong.

"Do you think we will discover the center of the Earth while I'm digging and you're traveling?

"I was happy to see you joyful and excited for the first time in years, but I also felt scared. You can probably guess how I struggled many nights to keep words from flowing and not to say too much of what I thought. Besides, would it have mattered if I had said those things, especially since you have never listened to what I or any other person said?

"Here, at night, a biting wind blows as if it's singing an obscure melody. In a few days, we will have packed up our things. The rain has already begun falling. I have to go back to Istanbul and work among my books and papers so that I can understand who is who in an old-time mystery and find out what all those characters are trying to tell us, like a detective who gathers all the clues to unravel a murder mystery. It looks difficult, but in fact, it's like solving a puzzle. Then there's a congress in Venice in the spring, but for me, it's going to be like a holiday. I wish you could come, too. How nice it would be.

"I have a big fear coiling up deep inside of me. I am scared this childish game of yours, this impossible dream, will bring you distress. When you come across something you don't know, you can sometimes forget about everything. Sometimes withdrawal is the best way.

"Next week, I'll be going back home. I'll give you a call. A big kiss for you."

Oh, my dearest friend! How clumsy she is when she says things she doesn't believe.

She had asked whether we would be able to discover the center of the Earth. Is there such a center? Is there a place where we will be able to be safe and sound, and where we will see from that moment on that we are the center of everything?

She was worrying for nothing. After the fan incident, nothing had happened, except for a few phone calls made in a very formal manner.

As far as the news from Turkey was concerned, trouble and violence prevailed. Among all the confusion, I heard that he was troubled and was the target of rumors too.

The truth of the matter is that it was the last winter of my marriage.

Turgut was buried in his job. Maybe because he was bored by my half-heartedness, we started sleeping in separate bedrooms, living in the same house like two friends, respecting each other.

We didn't let anyone know this. In fact, we didn't even let ourselves dwell on it, as if everything were normal. Now, I cannot comprehend how such a life could be possible, but in those days, we acted as if it were normal.

During the winter, a very distressful, dark, gloomy winter, I withdrew into my shell. Days passed with books, films I went to see alone, and work I did for charities.

The excitement that had started spontaneously was dying slowly. But why? To protect my marriage? Because I was afraid? Because he didn't insist enough?

To be honest, I don't remember that winter in detail. It's almost as if the heavy mist, the endless showers, the murky afternoons I spent behind the long curtained windows have become a hazy photograph in my memory.

Ayla called me during the first days of spring, and we decided that going away from this city where flowers had not yet bloomed would do me good, even if only for a few days.

The arrangements were made, and I set off on a Friday for Venice. I wore white sunglasses. Wearing a white scarf with black dots, a white shirt, black pants, and white shoes, I strolled through the cherry market. I reached the square, after freeing myself from the sympathetic young men who first tried to talk to me in Italian and then uttered a few words in broken English while trying to give me roses.

After months of gloom and boredom, I was in bright, wonderful weather. I was elated, as in the past, inhaling the smell of the sea, hearing shouts and braying, observing the colors of the marketplace, and listening to the innuendos of men to women. As I passed through the singing vendors, I was happy.

I arrived at our meeting spot. The one over there was probably the café Ayla had mentioned. There in the distance. Chairs were lined up in front of the square. She had picked the café where Proust had sipped his coffee. I scanned the lively crowd for her.

Then something unbelievable happened.

Instead of Ayla, I found Fuat in front of me.

He was dressed like a tourist. With sunglasses and a panama hat, he sat at a round table, drinking coffee.

For a moment, I thought I was dreaming. It one of those moments when you would say "Pinch me!" to the person next to you. But there was no one around to pinch me and bring me back to reality.

Unable to decide what to do, I stood there like a simpleton. I looked at him to make sure it was really him and tried to spot Ayla, helplessly. As soon as he saw me, he stood up and came toward me. He wore an azure shirt and white pants.

"I see you are surprised, young lady. It's a small world. Isn't this an interesting coincidence." Then, as always, he picked me up and kissed me on the cheek.

Speechless, I blushed. I don't remember how we went to the table and sat down or what we ordered to the waiter.

After a while, I remembered I was supposed to meet Ayla and wondered where she was, only to notice that he was grinning mischievously.

"You have a friend who truly loves you," he said, "but she's a little tough. She gave us only two hours. I promised to take you to your hotel in exactly two hours."

"How is it possible!"

"Nothing is impossible. It's part of your destiny to get on a gondola with me. You can at least tolerate such little torment."

I fired one question after another.

"I don't get it. How did you reach her? How did you find out? Who told you I would come here?"

"Wait a minute. Take a deep breath, for God's sake. Aren't you happy to see me?"

"I am, but I'm trying to understand how this happened."

"Well, I have eyes and ears everywhere, so I am quick to pick up news," he said. "I heard your friend would meet you here and wanted to surprise you."

"So even my best friend is involved in this. I'll show her!"

"Please don't treat her badly. Only God knows how I struggled to convince her."

He was always like this. The first time we met after a long time, he always addressed me formally, as if we had to get acquainted with each other from scratch.

We stood up and walked for a while.

He said, "Each time I see you, I am amazed at how you are even more beautiful than I remembered."

I was still silent as we waited in line to get on a gondola. I kept wondering how he had managed to contact Ayla, how he had come here, and how I should act.

My heart pounded violently. I felt as excited as someone who had received very good news and was eager to share it with everyone.

Wasn't it incredible that he had acted in such a mad way and come all the way here to see me? What else could such behavior be, but insanity?

Don't the crazy things, the ones that elate you, make you feel life is full of fabulous moments?

On that cool spring morning, the sun drew undulating pictures on the water, the gondolier sang sad songs with his strong voice, and Fuat held my hand as we glided through that miraculous waterland.

As if it were all natural . . . as if we had been together for years . . . as if we had both known this would happen . . . as if we were used to this kind of meeting, a meeting I could not even have imagined an hour ago.

As we passed through the narrow canals, a woman was hanging out her laundry from a window in one of the old houses lining both sides of the canal. She tried to tell us something, screaming as we passed beneath the colorful clothes. The gondolier answered her, and we waved.

"Look, there!" he said, pointing to a pier in the distance.

Women and men dressed in black and young bridesmaids in white were following a bride and groom. The entire procession got on a heavily decorated wedding boat. The guests waiting on the pier threw bunches of flowers, and two guitar players dressed in blue and white striped shirts and straw hats played songs in their honor, but we could not hear the tunes from where we were. As the black boat glided past the big poles decorated with colorful ribbons, the guests continued singing and waving.

If I hadn't seen the women at the windows with green shutters and red flowers hang out their laundry and chat with each other loudly, I wouldn't have believed this moment was a part of real life, that it was true, or that this was a real city of this world.

Yes, on that cool spring morning, the dream started again. Even a dream cannot be so beautiful.

In that ancient city on the water, it was not surprising that one could be confused and wonder if he were in a tale or reality.

I felt as if everything had been set to cause me to confuse dreams with reality.

The gondolier began singing another sad song.

With my hand locked in Fuat's, I put my head on his shoulder for a moment and let myself enter that dream for the first time.

I felt like shouting, "I don't care about anything. I love you! And it's only you I have ever loved."

Instead, I said, "I still can't believe you have done this."

"What did I do again?" he said. "Listen. This song is about a woman who waits a lifetime for the arrival of a boat from far away."

"Does the sailor have another lover on board?"

"Yes. But after traveling the entire world and coming back, he realizes he has never met anyone more breathtaking than our heroine."

"He has seen the whole world but all he saw couldn't erase the memory of her face at the window. Isn't it so?"

"Yes," he said, "I realized that not even the whole world is as big and beautiful as your eyes."

"Beautiful. So are they finally reunited?"

"Yes, but now the man broods over the lost time, all the years that can never be reclaimed."

The narrow canals looked as if they would take us to an entirely different world. Suddenly, we would pass through a secret passage in the water, travel through an unknown corridor, and arrive at a mysterious world in a fraction of time. There, we would be in a land of dreams that exists only for those who need to hide. Perhaps, if we followed one of those small corridors under that pale red house, we would get there.

At certain moments you think a miracle will happen because all the signs emerge at once.

I was overtaken by such a feeling that I thought my soul would leave my body and ascend to the sky.

I was in a dream. This man with a straw hat was singing a beautiful melody. In the city of water, in a world of tales, we had forgotten all about time, as he kept whispering something in my ear.

"I want to run away from everything," he said. "From every single thing. I don't know how I did it, but in the end, I built up a life I didn't want. Now, I'm like a prisoner in my own life."

"What a nice prison you have," I teased. But as I looked at his face, I saw a deep sadness in his eyes for the first time.

"Unfortunately, you're unable to find the key to your own prison. Besides, most of the time, you don't even realize you're the prisoner."

I couldn't grasp what he meant exactly. Maybe I hadn't quite heard his words.

The light grew dimmer. A cloud concealed the sun for a moment.

He raised my chin and took off my white sunglasses. Staring into my eyes, he said, "It's not the right time to talk about all this. I didn't come here to talk about such things."

I couldn't ask what he had come to talk about.

"We're late," was all I could say.

As we were leaving, the gondolier gave him a red rose and said something I didn't understand.

"He says that today every man has to give a red rose to the one he loves. He thinks that I have forgotten to do that. He wants me to give you this rose."

We lost our way trying to find the hotel. When we arrived at a square after passing through an alley, we came across an old merry-go-round—one of the sweetest things I've ever seen. Like a masterpiece, its pretty horses with their gilded manes swaying in the wind turned round and round to the music.

I wanted to be a child again. I wanted to flee from everything, forget everything, and start everything anew.

Forgetting the time, we got on the merry-go-round.

If a feeling called bliss exists, it was what I felt riding a smiling horse with a golden mane.

Even he, with his imposing figure, was a spectacular sight as he went up and down on his small horse.

We stepped through the hotel door and I was reminded of the glamorous life of hundreds of year ago, even though the hotel, where a noble family had once lived, looked tired and worn-out from hosting tourists from all over the world for God knows how many years. Ayla jumped up from a striped armchair in the corner. I ran to hug her, whispering in her ear, "You'll see what I'll do to you!"

"You're the one who must be punished," she replied. "It's because of you that I have had to go through this."

I can still see her confused, worried, thoughtful face.

At that moment, we were like teenagers, unable to stand still.

Fuat disappeared after saying, "Let me leave the two of you alone for a while. You seem to have missed each other. But you're my guests for lunch. I'm going to show you the best views you will ever see. Let's meet here in an hour."

I went upstairs with Ayla to our room. The cracks in the walls, the old furniture that looked as if picked up from second-hand shops, and the blue and light green carpets with bald patches here and there made me feel as if I were not at a hotel but in the living room of some good old friend.

I giggled, laughed, and screamed like a kid, wanting Ayla to tell me all that had happened right away.

As usual, she was both angry at my frenzied behavior and couldn't help being infected by my joy, no matter how much she grumbled.

"How did he find you? Quick! Tell me! What did he tell you? How did he say it?"

Without answering my questions, she said, "Look at you! You look as if you have just stepped out of a Hollywood movie! How beautiful you are! Let me look at you again!"

All she told me was that as soon as she had entered the hotel room, the phone rang, and Fuat, in a very natural tone, introduced himself and told her he wanted to surprise me. Ayla had been petrified, unable to utter a sensible word through the phone in her hand, as if she were one of those statues she dug out of the ground.

"So, what did you tell him? What answer did you give?"

"What could I say? How could I say anything before coming to my senses. I was tongue-tied. At first, like a robot, I replied that everything he wanted was impossible; then, I ended up saying yes, okay, why not."

"But how did he find out that we'd be here. How did he find you? Didn't you ask him?"

"You'll kill me! Why don't you ask him yourself? How can I know? He talked to me as if we'd been friends for ages, and I was totally dumbfounded and unable to say a word."

Yes, that was the way he was. He talked with such ease that you ended up being convinced that the most unreasonable things could happen.

"Now, you tell me what you did when you suddenly saw him in front of you."

"I almost fainted. I was in a hurry thinking I was late meeting you, and then, when I saw him just like that . . ."

"It's obvious you've sprouted wings again, but this is not a good sign. Let me tell you . . ." She suddenly stopped.

"Come on, say it," I said.

"No," she said. "I've changed my mind. It's not the right time to tell you. I've never seen you like this before. I'm not going to pull you down from the clouds."

We hugged each other again.

I was in such a good mood that I didn't question her further, and she didn't insist on telling me what haunted her mind. As the one and only witness of this extraordinary adventure, she forgot all about her own life and became immersed in mine.

I called Turgut to tell him I had arrived. Thank God, he didn't like making long calls. After learning I was safe and sound, he hung up. When I turned around, my eyes met Ayla's, but only for a moment. We were unable to look each other in the eye.

We emptied our suitcases, freshened up a bit, and then went to the lobby. The three of us went to a restaurant on a hilltop overlooking the city. As we ate, the rain began tapping on the windows. Its sound was so beautiful that we listened to it in total silence. Soon, it got dark. We talked about our journeys, Ayla's tablets, and Madame Butterfly. We chatted with the American couple at the adjacent table. Then we all sat by side, and the waiter photographed us. Fuat, calm and easy-going, behaved as if it were entirely natural for us to be here, as if we had known each other for a long time, and often met in places like this. When the Americans took a photo of us, he got closer and embraced me. The couple must have thought we were husband and wife. Who knows where that photograph is now?

The following afternoon, he left for Switzerland. He kissed us both on the cheek, as if ours had been the most usual rendezvous.

Standing by the hotel entrance, we watched him walk away.

Even after we had settled into heavy armchairs and ordered tea, my heart was still pounding. I kept asking myself whether what I experienced since the morning was real. What had happened to all that I had planned to tell him at our first possible encounter? What happened to that grave speech I had in mind? It had evaporated as soon as I saw him.

After spending just a few hours together, and still thinking about being alone on the gondola, I felt puzzled. I frowned like a young girl who wouldn't smile because she was separated from her sweetheart.

In fact, there was nothing real between us. Still, I was buried in a secret relationship, but unaware. Everything had started and advanced on its own as if we didn't need to talk about it. On its own? No, actually as he wished. I realized that until that day, none of our meetings had been planned beforehand.

"What's eating you?" asked Ayla.

I collected myself.

"Our young lady has probably forgotten that she came here to meet me," she said.

I cast a furtive glance at her. The great crystal chandeliers were lit, the waiters ran hither and thither, and the crowd in the hotel lobby was humming in different languages. I looked at her again.

"What shall I do now?" I asked.

The reflection of the city on the water illuminated by the moonlight aroused the excitement of living in a tale. I felt as if I were in my childhood again. Whatever I saw, I yearned for.

All the churches, palaces, old houses, towers, bridges, and the whole city had abandoned themselves to the water, gliding along on a serene evening.

The city and its reflection.

Nothing looked real.

After dinner that evening, Ayla and I strolled a little despite the cold. We crossed ornate bridges, walked through alleys, and returned to the square, where we sat outside a café and talked until late in the night. As if in silent agreement, neither of us spoke about him. We were like two children who happened to see a ghost and knew they were not supposed to tell anyone if they wanted to see it again.

We knew someone would hear if we talked about him.

When I asked Ayla what I should do now, I noticed a flicker of worry in her eyes.

It was because she was aware that I was sincere about wanting an answer, that I expected her to answer it, and that I knew very well there was nothing to say about it.

We spoke about the years we had spent away from each other. She had experienced certain things I didn't have a clue about.

For quite some time, her team had been digging in the middle of Anatolia—among the villages, in a land smelling of linden flowers—as if they were trying to reach the center of the earth.

Actually, they had reached the core of something. Somewhere deep in the ground, there were people waiting to be discovered at a certain spot, hoping the earth covering them for hundreds of years would be removed, anxious to expose the secrets they had been keeping for such a long time. These people had recorded everything diligently, so that someone in an unknown future would understand them. Paintings, signs, and codes. It was not more difficult than trying to understand an ordinary stranger.

Just as the archaeologists were about to read a love letter—or a love tablet—from two thousand years ago, a blue-eyed Hungarian wearing a large straw hat, with his hands in his pockets, arrived unexpectedly. He was a journalist who was at the excavation to do research for a book. The rumor was that he was a learned nobleman—a handsome man as well.

"Such things don't interest you, I know. Don't tell me stories," I blurted. Ayla blushed and looked down. "Apparently," I continued, "he's someone who knows how to make fun of life."

She laughed. "Yes, exactly. Someone who can really make fun of this life."

For the first time, I realized that my dearest friend was assuming an air different than that of the character called Jo in our favorite childhood novel *Little Women*. She was not acting like a tomboy but a woman when she talked about him.

His friendliness and amusing jokes had affected her the most. It was as if they had known each other for ages, while at the same time he flirted with her.

As they sat by the fire in the evenings, they talked about the kings they didn't know and the queens who had statues built to become immortal. Soon, however, the conversation turned to their far away homes and childhoods.

When they parted, he told Ayla he would come again, but he had not been able to tell her what was really on his mind since they were surrounded by other people in the camp. He hoped that Ayla would understand how they felt; yet, he had to go away without being able to touch upon the heart of the matter.

"I don't like handsome men, anyway," she said now. But as she spoke about him, it was impossible not to recognize how she was lost in thought as she gazed in the distance.

"Why didn't you tell him how you felt? Maybe he was afraid you would snap at him."

She stared at me, and I immediately realized I had said something wrong. I giggled. "Come on, you know what I mean. You scold people in such a way that the poor man was probably afraid of you."

"I know," she laughed. "But you know what, I never treated anyone as nicely all my life! Even when he made me crazy, I didn't scold him. Perhaps he was a womanizer. People say he has a lover in Istanbul, a belly dancer."

"Really?"

"Yes but you wouldn't expect me to question him about that, would you?"

"Don't believe everything people say. People can talk nonsense."

"Who knows," she replied. "You never know what men do. Perhaps we are wrong to hope they will fulfill our expectations. We keep expecting them to do something worthwhile all the time; in the meantime, we destroy the genuinely beautiful moments."

Night had arrived after a long and unexpected day in a faraway city washed with moonlight.

Maybe she was right. If you loved someone, did it make sense to lose time questioning how much he loved you?

"I feel I really don't know anything anymore," I said. "I don't recognize myself. I can't decide what to do. I don't know if it is him or my own life that I want to run away from. The strangest thing is that I can't grasp how all these things can change so fast."

Ayla gave me a cigarette. After eyeing indifferently the young boys who passed by saying things we didn't understand, she said, "Perhaps things we pretend not to see, or things we keep postponing, can suddenly cause something to take place in our lives at the most unexpected place and moment, making us face an amazing coincidence."

"Isn't there anything substantial in those tablets you deciphered, something we don't know, something that will give us the secret of life, or the key to what we are going through?"

"Let me tell you something," she answered, with a cigarette between the long fingers of one hand, her face supported by the other. Looking into my eyes, she said, "We still ask the same questions after thousands of years, and oddly, just like the questions, the answers have not changed much either."

I have never forgotten those two days.

The following morning, I saw a painting in a museum. A depiction of two lovers resting in a forest. I stopped as soon as I spotted it. I gazed at the scenery in the background. There was something in that picture that affected the spectator. It looked like an ordinary painting, but the light, yes, the light, in the painting was bizarre. It was a strange light, indicating that it had been painted in the autumn. You could almost smell the scent of the cool forest on an autumn afternoon in the distant past. This painting invited you to enter it, and even if just for a single moment, it made you feel that you could step into the scenery and smell the rain that would soon fall to earth.

For some time, I stood motionless in front of the painting, as if it were not of this earth.

When we returned to the hotel, I was handed a small package. I tore off the wrapping paper, excitedly. A small hand mirror emerged. A gilded, very old hand mirror. The gilding on the sides was worn away. It was beautiful. A letter accompanied it:

"One cannot help but think about life as he is dragged from one place to another. About his childhood, where he had come from, the moments he had forgotten . . . You feel you have grown up and become old. As children, how joyful we used to feel with the small things we had. Now, we have the power to do whatever we want, yet for some obscure reason, things that make us happy get fewer and fewer. Things like a dinner at a restaurant on a hilltop overlooking a city in water—a city destined to sink, the unforgettable songs of a woman, the most unexpected encounters. A sudden moment in which you long for her and wish she were by your side as you walk in an unfamiliar alley, a momentary shudder that shakes you. A very brief moment when a face that has appeared out of the blue is wiped away quickly, no matter how much you wish to preserve it.

"On one side, the indistinct, indefinable feeling of the journey you take into your past—a journey during which you remain alone, watching the lives of strangers reflected on the windows of a train as it moves forward when it actually delves into the past—and on the other, responsibilities, duties, and the people you have left behind who are waiting for you . . . Whatever object I see in everyday life, I imagine it next to you or in your hands. I want you to touch everything that I see, sharing it with you in my imagination. I looked in a tiny mirror, and it was not my face I saw, but yours.

Take good care of yourself, young lady."

How strange! We thought about almost the same things when we were apart.

"I don't know what you will do now," said Ayla, "but I think it would be wise to get rid of all these letters and notes. I hope you're not crazy enough to keep them."

"Next to all the other crazy things I do, that's nothing," I laughed.

"I wish we could return to the past," she continued. "Why did all those lovely days end so fast?"

"Yes really so fast,!"

I can remember that night, the moments I spent chatting with her, and even the way I said this sentence as if it were yesterday.

That night, we were upset thinking how our childhood had passed away so fast, so unexpectedly.

Now, childhood is far away in a distant past. Also that unforgettable night and the conversation, which we didn't know when and how we would remember.

Everything has left me alone and drifted away.

People who save everything, who collect things everywhere they go, who take photographs of everything, as if life can be preserved, amaze me. I also marvel at the way they show their pictures to others, like comic books of life. I don't have such photographs. Maybe that's why I feel this way. Even if I once had such photos, they have long been left behind, here and there. Even if they could be collected, I don't think they would have meaning. One's life has to look like something in order for its photographs to tell a story, doesn't it? My life doesn't look like anything.

Maybe that's why after coming here years later and seeing this house and garden, I cannot define my feelings.

These worn-out wooden houses leaning on each other, as if they are putting their heads onto each other's shoulders to commemorate an old friendship from the past—only when I see them, still standing after so many years, do I feel I have come to my country.

A country where houses, just like people, stand still while leaning against each other.

I have lived in so many different places that I have often asked myself which one of them is my homeland.

But this place, the strange odor the southwest wind brings, these dilapidated houses, and the feeling of having been abandoned have always reminded me I am at home here.

And these people. These timid, introverted people who lack the confident air of Europeans who think they rule the world and have solved the mystery of life. Who knows for how many years Halil Effendi has been passing along this street every morning. He still wears the same threadbare, loose jacket. His face, as worn-out as his jacket, is still illuminated with the humble smile characteristic of people who have lived a difficult life. His voice is as loud as in the past. When you hear him shout, "Sesame rolls, warm sesame rolls!" you can still smell the scent of sesame from afar.

No matter where I went, I smelled that scent. Even in cities far away. That smell is perhaps a sign that resembles a lighthouse on a dark, foggy night, showing me the way when I feel alone, destitute, and unaware of where I belong and in which direction to go.

Is it the smell of warm, crispy sesame rolls or the fragrance of my childhood? Who can tell?

The leisure hours when fastidious women pause for a Turkish coffee with a little sugar after doing the morning cleaning and preparing food for the day. Each of them conceals the secret of vast gardens, which no stranger can understand, but which we have known since childhood. The smell of giant magnolias. The idle chatter of sparrows that seem to tell each one of us apart, even if we are unable to distinguish them.

On some mornings—I began to wake up earlier as I grew older—I go to the coffeehouse at the seaside. How sad! The old coffeehouses on the shore don't exist anymore. What I call a coffeehouse is really one of those modern cafés.

A small place. Few people frequent it. Usually, authors and musicians stop by. Sometimes I take a book along to pass the time.

Sometimes I enjoy chatting with the other customers and joining their conversations.

I watch the woman sitting at another table looking at a man sitting across from her. She's in her fifties and still beautiful. As I watch her, I recognize something in her expression and gestures. But what? All at once, I realize that she is repeating the gestures of youth. The look in her eyes resembles that of a teenager. She is acting like an eighteen-year-old girl, flirting with the man.

Her glances, the way she curls her lips, the way she moves her hands in an effort to make herself attractive are things that belong to the past, but keep being repeated.

If a mirror were in front of her, she would surely be taken aback.

She would realize how her looks and gestures made her look like an out-of-focus photograph.

You cannot easily grasp how fast the years pass when you think about yourself. You always think old age and death are for others.

It is as if a sheet of thin, transparent paper that holds a new picture of us is constantly placed on an older painting drawn on a worn-out piece of paper. Each thin sheet has a small line or a barely perceptible curve, but this replacement happens so slowly that you do not realize the passing of the years as the face on the paper changes.

Now, I'm trying to peel back that photograph layer by layer in front of my eyes, hoping to return to the first face concealed under the layers.

Apparently, living life backwards is much harder than I thought. I used to believe I was strong, but now, when I recall past moments and revive a lost period in my life, details I had never noticed and feelings I thought had been obliterated descend upon me.

Wasn't this the reason why I escaped from my past for years?

One should never stop living! When you stop observing life, living becomes difficult.

Sometimes I feel a pain deep in my chest. Though I have stopped listening to my body, it's the time to worry about simple pains, expecting the worst.

I remember a book I had read years ago—a strange book that told the story of a girl who had a water lily growing on her chest, and her lover.

Can too much love kill one?

I told Ayla this the other day. Mocking as always, she said, "Don't you worry. It's not love that will kill you but those cigarettes you're addicted to."

Unfortunately, the truth is not always poetic.

A week ago, I went to the hospital because my heart began to beat faster. They put me in big machines, plugged cords all around me, and took X-rays.

Nowadays, they can even see the interior of your veins. They told me excitedly how much they could observe in the human body.

In my childhood, they used to sell stupid fake things, such as glasses that enabled you to see inside people. The boys would buy those glasses to scare the girls.

Now, they have invented giant machines that can reveal the inside of the human body.

Yet, they cannot see what happened to my heart.

They do not know when my heart began to beat faster, or since when the palpitations have been with me.

But I know.

What machine can illustrate the intricate pattern of our memory we never see but try to understand, or our past that remains hidden like a mystery somewhere inside of us?

The sky is slowly turning to white from blue, and summer is about to end. How many summers have I brought to an end—the end of this one is approaching, with the birds migrating to a distant land in a white sky. Evening is descending. The lights of the ships are already on. The sea compliments the sky as it becomes white in the mist. All the birds in the world are going away. So many of them. Like a spreading belt, they traverse the white sky painted with shades of blue. Flying far away. Far away and together. Over the blinking lighthouse; over the red roofs, minarets, and huge ships; over housewives at the beginning of an ordinary evening, worried people hastening home from work, and children unaware of worries; over the excitement of an afternoon, fights, meetings, separations, and loneliness, they fly away. To another land, to another sea, to the warm weather. Yes, to the warmth.

They fly there, and we get chilled.

I've had a recurring dream since childhood. A dream that takes place in different places, at different times, and with different plots. But the common element among all versions of this dream is the murder I commit.

I always wake up in a sweat after this nightmare. I open my eyes in incredible sorrow and pain, feeling I have committed an irrevocable crime that will follow me forever, from which I can never ever be rescued.

That morning I woke up in despair after having the same dream.

It was Saturday. A cool, misty autumn day. I went shopping early in the morning. All the shop windows were full of clothes for the new season. I tried on a few suits. I liked a black and white one that had a jacket with five buttons and that fit tightly around my waist. I didn't like the new topcoats—they were too loose for my slim figure. I dithered for quite a while looking at the hats but couldn't decide which one to buy. Finally, I bought a red scarf to wear with my new suit. Then I went to the men's section and picked out a light blue shirt and striped tie for Turgut.

If it didn't rain in the afternoon, we would probably go on a picnic.

When I came home with my arms full of packages, I found him sitting in the living room, gazing into space.

Although I had no reason, I was overcome by sudden fear. I walked into the living room with the packages still in my arms. He turned to look at me and said, "Welcome."

"I bought so many things," I said.

"Enjoy them!"

I couldn't sit, put down the packages, or say anything.

Then suddenly, I caught sight of a letter on the coffee table next to his armchair.

He saw me notice the letter, picked it up, and handed it to me.

"I was looking for the scissors, and I found this in your drawer. I thought it is a husband's right to read his wife's letters."

"Of course," I stuttered. I didn't know what else to say. Since I had first noticed it lying next to him, I had been struggling to re-member what was written in it, what was in the lines. It was the let-ter Fuat had sent me after our encounter in Venice. I had put it into my drawer and forgotten about it.

The most dangerous part of doing something in secret is when you begin to forget the rules you have been abiding by for so long and start thinking that what you're doing is simply a natural part of your life.

I had been so entranced by fantasy that I had begun feeling as if I were not married.

Many thoughts crossed my mind in those few moments. Since I felt I was about to blush, I quickly took the packages to my bedroom. What should I do? I had not considered the reaction of another person who might find this letter. I was sure the letter contained nothing explicit, yet wasn't it odd for Fuat to send me such a letter?

I put the packages on the bed and returned to the living room.

Turgut was expecting an explanation. I sat down opposite from him. My head was throbbing, but though hard to believe, I couldn't remember what was in that short letter, whose lines I can recite word by word now after so many years. In fact, I had read it many times.

"How long has this been going on?" he asked.

"What do you mean?"

"This doesn't sound like the first letter he wrote to you. You've probably been corresponding."

I realized he thought we were just writing letters to each other. Or maybe he didn't want to believe there was more to it. Or perhaps he was trying to draw information out of me.

Since my childhood, I have pretended to yawn whenever I was caught red-handed and didn't know what to do. Perhaps to gain time or look indifferent and relaxed, I forced myself to yawn.

"He sent one other letter, and I answered it, but that was quite some time ago, after he visited us here, I suppose. Now, he has sent another one."

Turgut looked calm.

"Don't you think it's a little strange that he sent it to you personally?"

"That's Mr. Fuat! You're behaving as if you don't know him! He writes whatever he wants. What's wrong with that?"

Turgut's face was expressionless. Was he nervous, upset, or

worried? Or did he know about something else that caused him to search through my things?

I was caught red-handed.

I didn't know what he knew or what was on his mind. How could I have forgotten about the letter? How could I have lost myself in a dream and neglected real life? Just like in my nightmares, I was lost and desperate. Even now, years after that day, I can still recall the same feeling of helplessness as soon as I picture that moment.

That specific moment is the only thing that still makes me feel remorse after so many other things that were experienced.

How strange!

I was sure he wouldn't be angry at me, that he wouldn't make a mountain out of a molehill, and that nothing would happen.

To tell the truth, I hadn't thought, or didn't want to think, of what I would do or how I would react if something like this happened. I hadn't planned how to deal with such a problem or how to defend myself.

It had always been natural for me to speak with everyone easily, and even flirt slightly with other men, instead of distancing myself from them. Such things didn't bother Turgut. When we went out, he enjoyed watching me dance or chat with others, and he even told me how much he admired my confident air.

Once when we had come home from a party, he had said, "You are the devil's feather. I watched you all night. Everyone, especially men, were dying to talk to you. Whoever approaches you is unable to leave, as if magnetized."

His tone when saying this was not jealous or angry. On the contrary, he was full of admiration.

He was a person who preferred to transform things he did not want to confront into a form he could accept. Without doubt, he knew my feelings about him and our marriage from the very beginning. Yet, for him, marriage was an institution that required the partners to respect each other, like each other, and participate in social life together.

He was not someone who applied pressure, became jealous, or looked for trouble because of minor things. Rather than provoking a quarrel, he preferred to sit in his cosy armchair and read his comic books.

But why did I feel this way? What was I afraid of? Of losing him? Of getting divorced? Or of being disgraced?

No, I didn't fear any of these things. I didn't care in the least. On the contrary, if he divorced me, I would probably be elated.

Was I afraid of hurting him?

No. I must confess I didn't love him enough to fear hurting him. Moreover, I didn't think losing me would hurt him anyway.

What affected me so much was that I had been caught and wasn't able to tell the truth. I was ashamed.

Until that day, I had never felt the need to lie. Neither in my childhood, nor during my school years. Whatever I did, I always told the truth, and I wasn't scared of anyone.

Once, a distant relative's daughter and I had smoked a cigarette butt we had found in our garden. Someone must have told my father. In the evening, he called me and asked, "Tell me the truth. Did you really smoke?"

"Yes."

"I'm not going to punish you since you told the truth," he said. "Now come over here."

I had recently started primary school. I went to him, and he took out a cigarette from his silver case, lit it, and placed it between my lips. "Now inhale. Take a very deep breath."

I did as he told me and immediately began coughing.

He took the cigarette and extinguished it.

"That is how cigarettes taste. Disgusting," he said. "If you are curious about something, come and ask me first. I'll tell you about it. You don't have to do anything in secret. Only cowards do things secretly. Do you understand?"

"Yes."

I really didn't do anything in secret from that moment on, and I didn't feel afraid to admit whatever was on my mind.

Now, however, for the first time in my life, I was afraid of telling the truth to Turgut. I felt ashamed and humiliated, as well as suffering a twinge of conscience.

Because he would confront me with my lie? Because horrible things would happen to me? Or because I would be exposed to public contempt?

No. I suppose because I knew I had been unfair to him.

All of a sudden, he said, "I just don't understand why you have to be so informal and intimate with him."

"I hope you did not attribute a different meaning to this, Turgut," I said, amazed at myself for saying it with such sincerity.

He studied my face. I don't think he wanted to question me further. "I'll be glad if such a letter does not come again and if you do not send him any in return."

"I won't write to him, but I can't control his actions."

Later, I would not be able to keep my word.

As I headed for the bedroom, Turgut handed me the letter. "Here, take it. Maybe you'd like to keep it."

I took the letter, paused for a moment before tearing it into four pieces, and then put it back onto the table. "It's not something to be saved," I said.

In the letter, Fuat had written: "Young Lady, I would have loved to come to your misty city on my way back after tackling all the confusion that surrounded me, but my plans didn't work out. The work dragged on. I'll be going back tomorrow. I cannot explain how tired, bored, and fed up I am. It seems that politics is not the right thing for me. You had warned me about that in Ankara, hadn't you? But I suppose everything happens as written in one's destiny. Don't let anyone know about this; it should stay between the two of us. Who knows when we'll see each other again? Maybe you'll come to visit Turkey sometime in the future. With love, as always . . ."

In those days, did I really understand what he meant by confusion? Perhaps I didn't exactly know whether he meant his life or the news from Ankara and Istanbul. Perhaps both.

Each time Turgut met people who traveled to Turkey, he tried to gather information from them. He asked them to confirm what was written in the newspapers.

İsmet İnönü's declarations and his speeches in the parliament were sharp and bitter. We heard about them. Some of the things discussed in the parliament were banned from the press, but in this way or that, the news always spread. The universities were time bombs. The army was ill at ease. Whoever came from Turkey always mentioned the army's uneasiness first. Everyone had a relative who was a major or a colonel. Turgut, who didn't like discussing such subjects openly, usually complained when we were alone. "Are they dead on their feet?" he would ask. "Even what I hear from so many miles away is enough to realize how bad the situation is. Are they asleep on their feet? It's impossible to grasp why they're acting like this!"

We spoke with my brother a few times on the phone. Each time, he told us about the new developments, none of which sounded better than the previous ones. I soon realized he was against the current government and displeased with it, even though he didn't voice his opinion. The local newspapers wrote that many journalists had been arrested and imprisoned in Turkey

Since coming to London, however, I hadn't paid much attention to the news, as if I didn't want to hear about the bad things.

Whenever someone from Turkey gave us unfavorable news, I immediately said, "No, no. It probably didn't happen like that."

Then I gave that up too and even stopped reading the newspapers Turgut brought home once a week.

I must admit, something else scared me. I was afraid something bad about Fuat would appear in the papers; they would blame or criticize him again. I had closed my eyes not only to the whole world but also to my own life. Escaping from everything, I lived in the secluded world I had created.

That's why I didn't have the slightest thought to ask Fuat about the claims against him and his party. I didn't want us to talk about anything else other than our relationship, which in fact, merely consisted of crazy encounters.

I thought that if anything about reality and the outer world surrounding us were mentioned, the spell would be broken, and we would have to provide answers we wouldn't be able to give.

Turgut opened the package I gave him, tried on the shirt and the tie, and thanked me. I was lost in my thoughts, but he looked a little upset for having started such a disturbing conversation and for perhaps having been unjust to me.

"We can go out and drive around if you like," he said. "It's so dark that we have to turn on the lights during the day. Let's not get stuck here but go out for some fresh air."

I went to my room to change. I took out a pair of trousers and a pullover, put on my new scarf, and sat at my dressing table to powder my face, while pondering the conversation Turgut and I had had a few minutes ago. When I reached for my lipstick, I saw the hand mirror Fuat had given me. I picked it up to caress it, but it suddenly slid through my hands and fell to the floor.

When I picked it up, I noticed a big crack stretching right across it.

I'm not superstitious, but perhaps we are sent signs every now and then, to which we should pay attention as we choose our direction. Perhaps sometimes when we think we are lost, or we don't know which direction to choose, we move ahead in the wrong way just because we are unaware of or unable to decipher the signs that are right in front of our eyes.

Answers we cannot give . . .

I thought the subject was sealed and wouldn't be taken up again after the day Turgut found Fuat's letter.

I had thought I could safeguard things by hiding them from everyone.

But it didn't happen that way.

Magical moments can blind you. It was as if a transformer inside caused me to misinterpret everything I touched, heard, or saw.

Besides, was it possible for a young woman with a fluttering heart to grasp what really went on during that short encounter in the mythical city where the waters diluted one's sense of reality?

I had not correctly interpreted his state of mind—though he had offered numerous hints between his words.

To be able to understand he was on the knife's edge in his life and about to break free of all bonds, I had to know him better.

Yet, I didn't know him so well.

Our conversations in Ankara in the afternoons had been too vague. In the few hours we had been alone, we had not talked about our private lives.

He had not inquired about my private life, and I had not asked about his marriage. On the contrary, we had taken pains to keep away from our private lives, even on the days we just had a chat, as if we had a secret agreement not to delve into personal matters.

We were like two secret agents who met in a distant land, far away from their own circles concealing their identities.

What we knew about each other was far less than we imagined.

I felt like I was going through an unexpected affair one could only have in extraordinary times, such as during a war.

I had failed to realize that despite the great responsibility on his shoulders those days, his ties with reality had been reduced to obligatory moments and he had lost his connection with the real world.

I mistakenly believed he was a man who always did crazy things, who didn't care what others thought, and who didn't let others influence him.

Sometimes I even told myself there was nothing bad about what we were doing. It was just a simple game of flirting. A game for grown-ups. I wasn't doing anything wrong.

Anyway, everything was so difficult that we wouldn't be able to go too far in playing our game.

I also imagined that he, too, considered our relationship a window he opened for himself among all those oppressing tasks he had to cope with. It was just an escape.

I still didn't believe such a mature man would allow himself to be overcome by such a game.

How could I have ever known?

Then the phone calls began.

After a few days, I began to stare at the phone while having my breakfast and drinking my coffee in the morning, expecting him to call.

Wherever he went, the first thing he did was to call me. "I've arrived in such and such place, now we'll have lunch, we're leaving in the afternoon," and so on. He told me every little detail.

Sometimes when we spoke on the phone, someone else came on and the line went dead suddenly. A little later he would call again.

I can never forget a certain morning when the phone rang while I was reading the magazines that had just arrived. He was somewhere else again. He told me about the weather, his journey, and that he had been thinking about me. Suddenly, the switchboard operator broke into the call, and we had to hang up. I picked up a magazine and sat down. The phone rang again, and I raced to answer it. We chatted for a while but then the line went dead. Just as I was returning to my chair, the phone rang again. This time he had to hang up after exchanging a few words because someone came into the room where he was making the call.

I sat down and picked up my magazine again. On the cover, there were three girls sitting on the stairs of a house. They looked as if they were about to leave for a ball. All three wore fashionable dresses with puffy skirts, and their shoulders were bare. Their hair was arranged nicely. The girl with a darker complexion was talking on the phone, and the other two were listening to her and chuckling. The headline read: "Young girls can't do without the phone!"

At first, I didn't understand because some part of my mind was still busy with the previous call, but then, all of a sudden, I began to laugh loudly. The article said young girls were obsessed by the phone, they talked to their lovers on the phone for hours, and their parents were annoyed by such behavior. The article offered advice to young girls and warned parents about being too harsh on the new generation.

I don't know how it happened, but after some time and a number of calls, he began saying things like, "Where were you? I called many times but you weren't there." He wanted to control me in ways not even my husband had attempted.

He felt uneasy when I didn't answer the phone. So whenever I had to go out for something, I hurried back home.

It sounds unbelievable, but yes, that was how it happened. He wasn't joking at all.

Although I thought I was setting the rules of my own game, I let things get out of hand and didn't even realize how it happened.

I got more worried with each passing day.

I didn't understand how a dream could encompass you with more passion than real life and that someone far away, someone you didn't even know very well, could determine your life more than a lover whom you saw and touched every day.

It was the first time I had experienced such a heartbeat. A heartbeat that cannot be represented in movies. Maybe in books . . . a little. We all know that sensation, more or less. Still, when we experience it for the first time, we are at a loss as to what to do. This is why, even if we try hard not to lose control, we still do crazy things that others, and even we ourselves, fail to understand.

To me, it is like becoming another person—a strange feeling that resembles waking up someone who has been sleeping inside of us secretly and switching places with her.

To be someone else, to start a new life outside of your own that has been constricted in the past, to create someone by decking her out in clothes and ornaments you take from a long-hidden secret chest.

Two different faces, two different voices, two different forms.

Two women apart.

All of a sudden I had discovered that my life was smashed in pieces.

Two different lives. It wasn't easy to learn this game. You had to pass from one life to another. And very quickly. Do you know anaglyphic images printed on cards? When you move the card back and forth slowly, the picture changes. What was happening in my life was something similar.

In those days, I thought what I felt was love, bliss, and excitement, but now I understand that it was disquiet and uneasiness.

The first thing you lose when you divide your life into pieces is tranquility.

Yet back then, I don't think I was aware of this fact, and even if I were, I don't think I cared.

When I heard his voice at the other end of the line ("So, how are you?"); when he felt like calling just to have me listen to a song ("I wait on these shores every day in sadness/the day ends, the birds leave, the long-awaited lover does not return/ in the end I understood no one has seen her"), as he moved from one place to another like a hopeless traveler, as I heard the sound of the city humming into my ears from hotels, conference halls, airports, or train stations ("tell me where you are and what the place looks like," I would say), as we attributed meanings to words in bits and pieces no one would understand, as if we knew each other for years, as if we'd been together for ages. In those moments when I wished I was with him ("I wish you were here with me, only you would know the name of those white blossoms, I wish you could smell them now, it's so beautiful here"), when he said something unexpected while saying the most ordinary things, as I stood breathless on the phone ("you little kid, I've lost my heart to you, I can't spend even a single day without hearing your voice. I'm spellbound."). Each time that inevitable, haunting question came to mind, sometimes after a long silence, and especially when I wished neither of us would ask it: What shall we do? We never voiced that question, but it crossed my mind all the time. A question I always refrained from asking, just before it was about to slip through my lips.

When you experience, you understand. Building up an entirely different life when the person you live with doesn't suspect it. Even I could hardly believe it. Sometimes when I hung up the phone, I was dumbstruck and ashamed, promising myself I would put an end to the whole thing the next time he called.

But the mind is not the master of feelings, and feelings always manage to master the mind.

Sometimes as Turgut and I strolled outside, visited a shop, drank tea in a café, or even had dinner at home, I was filled with a great desire to confess everything to him on the spot.

Once a week, usually on Fridays, we ate out. Just the two of us. He had habits he stuck to. Those evenings were the most difficult times for me. We sat face to face and had a romantic candlelit dinner. At home, we slept in different bedrooms, and when he was busy with his papers, I either read or did other things. We didn't spend much time together. Sitting like this, with our faces so close and our eyes meeting, soon became unbearable.

Once we went to a newly opened Russian restaurant—red velvet tablecloths, heavy curtains, ornate lampshades, and waiters dressed in national clothes.

Thankfully, a noisy Russian band was playing, and it was not possible to talk much.

I glanced at him as we ate our food and drank our wine. He was not interested in any of the beautiful women there, and he did not doubt me in the slightest.

Even if someone threatened to cut his throat, he wouldn't have an affair with another woman.

To have dinner with his wife in such a nice place, drink wine once a week, and have a chat: what a nice thing to be thankful for!

A voice inside me said another woman would do anything to have Turgut. It told me I had him even though I didn't deserve him.

What a low-minded woman you are, I told myself. You are trampling on your own pride, as well as his. You're not only destroying yourself but him too.

I wanted to cry. As the Russian music, which I didn't like in the least, pounded in my ears, I was filled with the urge to tell him about everything. Right there and then.

It would have been the honest thing to do.

I have fallen in love with another, I can't succeed in being the kind of wife you want, let us divorce before we have a child, you can go on with your life without getting involved in a scandal.

I wanted to say these words and then take a very deep breath.

I didn't want to imagine what would happen afterwards. I just wanted to tell him, stand up, and leave.

I was on the verge of confessing everything.

Suddenly, just as the words almost flowed out of my mouth, a loud voice struck me: "Well, well, well! Our young couple is also here!"

Turgut jumped to his feet. Mr. Mehdi was one of Fuat's closest friends. He was there with his wife and some foreigners. Fortunately, our table was too small to invite them to sit down. As Mr. Mehdi left, he said, "Such old people like us shouldn't disturb two inseparable lovebirds . . ." He smiled at me, and I blushed. I felt as if he knew something. As if he wanted to say, "you're sitting and having a romantic dinner with your husband, but we all know, young lady, with whom you mess around . . ."

I was shocked. Mute as a mackerel. I felt as if the secret land, the castle no one could enter except me and Fuat, had been captured by enemy troops. I excused myself to go to the ladies' room. I wanted to wash my face. Perhaps I had been wrong, and it was just my imagination. But wouldn't they know about us? Could all the calls he made from each and every place he went, as well as the way he went in and out of meetings to make them, have attracted attention?

Even if he hadn't been asked, wouldn't it be easy to find out? Besides, maybe Fuat had already told his friends. Would he do such a thing? No, no, he wouldn't.

I fixed my make-up and took deep breaths to calm down.

Then I returned to our table. That night, I understood the end was near. Very near, indeed.

I couldn't sleep at all that night. I knew I had to make a decision and do something. Knowing I would get upset a little but that it was best to end things since we didn't have a common future, I decided to settle it fast and for good, yet five minutes after I reached this decision, I changed my mind, feeling hopeless, as if I were lost in an endless chasm.

I immediately asked myself why it shouldn't be possible to find a solution for every problem if two people loved each other very much. Every problem had a solution. I wouldn't throw myself in front of a train just because I was in love with somebody.

Then, I decided again to confess everything to Turgut.

The worst thing was that Turgut was excited about his new plans and kept telling me about them. He wished to have a child. For him, everything was "groovy." He realized that our marriage was not the same as it used to be (he agreed to this, at least), but he thought that this was because we didn't have a child. A child changed every home, a child was the sole purpose of marriage. Of course, he was to blame, too, he said. He was overly occupied with his job. As he spoke about these things, I felt even more suffocated.

Inside, I felt deep remorse, as if I had done the worst possible thing to him.

I felt I would be able to breathe freely again if I confessed the truth.

But could I just confess? Let's suppose I did. Wouldn't he ask me who that other person was? What would I say?

Oof! I wish we had gone far away like Fuat had proposed that day in the cab! Wouldn't things have calmed down as time passed? Perhaps, it would have been the best for everyone.

I was roaming the house. It was past midnight. I prepared a cup of tea to calm myself down.

As a poet once said: "I didn't know that songs were so beautiful/ and that words were so feeble/before I was lost in this trouble."

Why didn't things go as I wished?

Supposedly, I should be able to create a future to suit myself. Had I not changed my life in the most unexpected way and at the most unexpected time?

Why can't we create a life made of simple but beautiful things for ourselves and be satisfied with it?

Were my decisions in the past wrong? Was I wrong in wishing to get married early, have children, and build a life of my own in my own home?

Was this wrong, or was the person I chose as my partner in this dream the wrong one?

Should I question all that I had, or should I believe this was a new chance given to me, or a new life expecting me?

Should I answer that call and follow it bravely, or turn my back on it, considering it a deception, a trick of the devil that would lead me astray?

I knew it was too late to think about such things. I should have considered them long before.

But at that moment, I thought I still hadn't arrived at the point of no return and could still make a decision before I reached the fork in the road.

Turgut had brought the magazines and newspapers from Turkey. I picked up a magazine. On the cover, there was a beautiful woman, and right behind her a worried looking man who sat with his head buried in his hands. The headline read: "Is your wife cheating on you?"

I couldn't hold myself back from taking a look at the related article.

Under the heading "How can you recognize an unfaithful woman?" it said:

"Essentially, it is not difficult to recognize an unfaithful woman. If a woman invents new friends all the time and goes out with excuses such as meeting an old school companion named Nermin, whom she has not seen for years and who called recently; if she looks more attractive than usual; if she applies more make-up and dresses finer; if she spends more time in the bathroom; if she flares up easily at the slightest question from her husband; if she doesn't seem content with her usual allowance; if she comes home with expensive clothes, which she says she bought at a friend's discount store; if she says she buys jewelry from a store on installments; or if she does anything similar, then her husband has reason to suspect she is cheating."

I read the whole article in disbelief. That was me! I was the woman described there! While her miserable husband brooded in a corner, she dressed in furs and jewellery and put on her make-up in front of the mirror while dreaming about the hours she would spend in her lover's arms.

I guess we both knew on those "phone-call mornings," as well as on the days when my sense of reality was erased in the mist that had covered the city for the entire winter, that what was between us could not go on and that everything would take on a different form.

But which form?

To live waiting for a voice coming from far away after crossing villages, towns, and, oceans on a cable! To wait for that voice every morning! To plan your entire life according to phone calls that lasted just a few minutes.

Was this believable?

The heavy black telephone rang loudly inside me. Each time, I jumped up in fear, excitement, joy, and trepidation.

(During that time, I could have never imagined the small mobile phones you have nowadays. Sometimes when I took a walk, sat somewhere, or chatted with women I didn't know in the park I went to on sunny days, I was filled with the desire to call and talk to him. Sometimes I desperately wanted to hear his voice. I wanted to tell him everything I saw and let him see it through my eyes.

A few days ago, I saw a telephone that can take photographs. You take a picture and then send it to anyone you wish immediately. I wish we'd had such things back then. Through pictures, I could have let him know about all the places I went to and all that I did. I wish I had been able to remove the big gaps and the unknown zone between us. But it was impossible. Only when he called me, only if I were home waiting beside the phone, only if he had a few spare minutes, only if the call went through, only if everything went right, were we able to talk for a couple of minutes. That was all!)

It is said that brave people are always honest.

Are they really?

If you ask me, being honest is easy. What requires the most courage is living a dual life as I did. To lead two different lives, to tear your life into two, to be left in the middle of a tide with a shattered soul and a broken heart.

How odd! He and I never talked about this. On the other hand, he didn't seem to be hiding anything. He hadn't even asked me not to say anything to anyone or told me that no one should hear about us.

What was he thinking? I didn't know. Sometimes I wanted to interrupt him and ask this question. Sometimes I didn't even listen to what he said. All I wanted to ask was what would happen, what we would do, and how this thing between us would go on. But each time I gathered enough courage to ask him, I got worried that I would sound like a simple, ordinary woman, and I changed my mind. Yet, at the same time, such questions accumulated and continued to spin in my head. I just couldn't get rid of them. Why didn't he repeat what he had told me in the cab? Why didn't he ask me again to run away with him to establish a life of our own? Was it too early for that? Did he think I wouldn't be able to do it yet? Or had he realized the weight of his words when he thought about them later?

In the end, one morning, I noticed that his voice on the phone didn't sound far away.

When he called, I was reading the newspapers and enjoying a cup of coffee and a cigarette.

An earthquake had occurred in Turkey. Reportedly, more than forty people had died. Even the old hotel in Abant was destroyed. On the lower part of the first page of one of the papers "Is Istanbul on a fault line?" appeared in big letters: Underneath there was a statement by a renowned seismologist and professor. "Istanbul is not located on a fault line. Earthquakes in other places, even the closest ones, will not cause any harm except for a relatively mild shaking of the city."

I had spoken with my mother the previous day. The city had shaken a little, but they weren't frightened.

I watered the flowers. The tips of their leaves looked a little dry. Dressed in my housecoat decorated with white plush fabric, I waited for him to call as usual. I picked up the newspaper again and opened the page where I always read the amusing section that included readers' letters. A young man had written, "I fell in love with a girl after many mutual signs and sighs, and although she was the one who provoked me, one day, I happened to see her with another man. I lost control. I am in misery. Now, I'm trying to forget her. But it's impossible. Years have passed, and I still have her on my mind. Can you believe I filled two notebooks with poetry just to console myself? I still can't get her out of my mind. Please tell me what I should do." The answer in the newspaper went like this: "Fill two more notebooks with your poems. We presume that by the time you finish doing that, you will have already forgotten all about her." As I was laughing out loud, the phone rang. I thought I must tell Fuat about what I had just read.

"Good morning, young lady," he said, as always. "How are you?"

"Good morning," I replied, as if my statement had a question mark at the end.

"Were you expecting a call from someone else?" His voice was teasing but joyful, and at the same time, it sounded so close and clear.

"Your voice sounds as if you were near. As if you're calling from the next room." He laughed.

"I wanted to trick you a little, but I didn't have the heart to fool you. Yes, I'm very close to you, almost in the next room."

I tried to control my excitement. "Where are you?"

"Here. I'm at the hotel on the corner, by the park."

I couldn't breathe for a moment. I couldn't utter a single word.

"I'm here for one day only. No one knows where I am."

I took a deep breath.

I knew. I knew what would happen. It was an unavoidable moment, what had been postponed until today had switched places with what was unavoidable now, and I was petrified.

"Are you still there?" he asked.

"Yes. Yes, I am. Welcome." That was all I could say.

"I'm waiting for you," he said. "I'll meet you at the door."

The game was almost over. It was not a fantasy anymore. The words, voices, glances were not designed to confuse us any longer. It was real. In contrast to how he usually acted, he had not made any jokes or allusions.

I told him I would come and hung up.

But instead of running to finally realize the long-awaited moment of getting together, which I had secretly wondered about, imagined, and repeated in my mind over and over, always dreaming of it in different settings, I remained in my chair, petrified and unable to move.

My heart was about to stop. I couldn't breathe.

I was locked up in myself.

Maybe it was this very moment that symbolized our relationship: to go or not to go. A pendulum that swung between matchless happiness and the deepest chasm of sorrow.

From that moment on, I would always feel this pendulum inside of me.

I sat there motionless, staring into space, as if my hands were tied.

At one moment I decided to stand up and go, regardless of what would happen, and at the next, I changed my mind as if a secret force had nailed me down.

I wasn't sure of anything—neither my feelings, nor what I wanted to do. Nothing.

Emotions, thoughts, the reality, and the dream had all disappeared without warning. As if I hadn't known this moment would arrive and couldn't be postponed forever, imagining that I would keep living in the realm of obscure images swirling in a foggy winter.

I don't know how long I sat there, fighting my confusing feelings. Perhaps only a few minutes.

I pulled myself together when the phone rang again.

"Are you still getting dressed?"

I studdered. "But this . . . this is most unexpected."

My voice gave away my hesitation. It sounded as if someone were choking me. Silence fell. I think I hoped that he would tell me that he was joking, but I knew it wasn't a joke.

Then he said, "Either you come here at once or I'm coming there!"

I knew he would.

"No, don't do that! I'll be there," I said.

I had realized that I was no longer at a point where I could say no. That moment, which I had thought could be postponed forever, had come at last. It was no longer a game.

In fact, I had only watched what he had done till now. I had not initiated anything. I was acting in a game and pretending. I was playing the game he had created and pretending to act involuntarily.

Yet now, I had to take a step on my own for the first time. Now, in this situation, in which I had to act my part, I wouldn't be able to feign unwillingness, for whatever I would do, I would do it by my own will. It would be my decision.

Yes or no.

I no longer had the right to roam freely in the obscure, empty place between the two options.

Was I happy? Were my feet swept off the ground? Did I feel "butterflies in my stomach," as, supposedly, always happened?

I only remember a sharp pain in my stomach, my heart beating madly in terror, and that I turned around in the room, limp, helpless, and confused. But was I also happy? I don't remember whether I was or not.

I don't think I was scared either. I was in utter confusion.

I don't think that any woman has tried on so many clothes in such a short time.

Finally, I decided on a buttoned light blue soft wool pullover, with a round neck, and a dark blue pleated skirt with a belt. My shoes had two small ornaments in the shape of cherries. I loved those shoes but had not worn them before.

Standing in front of the mirror, I put my hands on my waist, examined myself, and was surprised once again at the slimness of my waistline.

I put on cherry-colored lipstick. I looked so pale that I tried to apply some blush. I ended up making a mess and had to rub the red color off my cheeks.

Then I folded and put away the dresses, shirt, pullovers, skirts, stockings, and lingerie that had piled up on the bed.

I applied some mascara to my eyelashes, about which he had asked many times, "Are these eyelashes of yours real?"

I grabbed my dark blue topcoat and my handbag decorated with cherries and left.

It was almost 11 a.m.

Few people were on the streets. The fog blanketing the city was thinner for the first time after many months, and a barely perceptible sun pretended to warm the air, as if it wanted to proclaim that spring was finally on its way. I couldn't decide between walking or taking a cab. The hotel was at most a five-minute walk from my home. The first empty cab passed. I decided to take the next one.

Like he had said, he was waiting at the hotel door.

But how?

He was dressed in a doorman's tailed coat and derby hat. When the cab stopped in front of the building, he opened the door with an air of exaggeration as you could expect from a doorman.

"Do you have luggage, milady?" he asked, grinning.

When I saw him in those clothes, I forgot my worries. The people who saw a woman stepping out of a cab and hug the doorman must have had a shock.

Room number 114 was at the end of the downstairs corridor whose floorboards creaked under the dark red carpets. As you walked in this hotel decorated with heavy dark red drapes, antique furniture, dark wood, old landscape paintings, and wallpaper striped in the lower part and flowery in the upper part, you felt as if you were in a murky but tranquil palace.

He had made friends with everyone as soon as he had arrived. He returned the doorman's coat and hat, and the hotel staff greeted me as if I were his wife.

Once we entered the room, he sat across from me like a smiling but shy boy.

I looked at my watch. It was exactly twenty past eleven.

"This color becomes you," he said, "Why do I get surprised again each time we meet?"

"What surprises you?" I laughed. The way I started each conversation in such a formal way always made him laugh.

"Why do I get surprised? You are even more beautiful each time I see you. I dream of you, and you go beyond my imagination."

Suddenly there was a knock on the door. I quivered. A waiter in black brought a heavy silver tray on which there were embellished cups and porcelain teapots. He placed the tray on the table and asked us if we wanted him to serve the tea.

"I'll do it," I said. "Thank you."

We began to sip our tea, sitting face to face like two old friends who met every now and then. He stood up to turn on the radio.

Later I had told him, "You must have dropped something in my tea."

I remember melancholy songs. Whispers. The sound of rustling garments. Hardly visible furniture in the light filtered through the drawn curtains. An ordinary day continues outside. I have left another woman and another life outside these windows. Here, there is a different woman, in the dark. I don't know anymore who I am. The curtains are drawn now. The woman outside and I don't see each other anymore. Slowly I forget about her and remain alone. I close my eyes. The song says, "what happened to them, to those unforgettable moments?" His voice fills my ears. He says, "You can't believe how many times I have imagined this moment." I am afraid to look into his eyes. I hide under the covers and sheets. I'm drawn as if by a magnet. I lose track of where I am. My feet are no longer firm on the ground. "The summer is over, now the leaves are falling." Something is rising inside of me. Something is trying to get out. I hear the sound of breathing. "How small you are," he says. I touch him as if I'm touching a magical stone, something you see for the first time, something you don't know and wonder what will happen to it when you touch it for the first time. "Don't worry, you won't get a shock," he says. "I know," I reply, "but both of us will." It's so hot. So very hot. Shaking me. My head is turning. Colors appear only to disappear again. I open my eyes in the end. In the dark. Under the covers. I can only discern a few details. "I don't know where you are now but it's as if you have remained in my heart." Is it a beautiful song? Or is it a melancholy song? I stand on a summit and look down. I shudder. I am overwhelmed. I tremble. I close my eyes and let myself fall into the chasm. I gently glide in the air, as if I have giant wings, as if a wind fairy is carrying me in her hands. Images swirl in my mind. Colors pass by. The light changes. Whatever is trying to get out of me stops fighting. I hug him so that my trembling will stop. I hear his voice, whispering, "Are you crying?"

That day, I realized that when the bodies of two people flare up with a single touch, they either produce a pleasure like a sudden but short-lived flame or establish an incomprehensible bond that never disappears. You allow a stranger to get inside you, to touch your inner self which no one has ever touched, and explore you freely, beyond your control. It's as though you pass through a narrow gap neither you nor anyone else knew about before and enter a secret garden.

Maybe that's why I felt dizzy when I suddenly found myself in an unknown land as soon as I closed my eyes. I felt as if I had reached a matchless place, a place that had remained unused, unseen, and untouched, which didn't resemble this time and place at all, where the signs you knew were not valid, and which made you feel bewildered. Like a newborn who has opened his eyes for the first time, all you could do was cry.

Have you ever had a lost day in your life? A day that was lived but lost. A day unknown to everyone, a forgotten day, which you are no longer sure existed or not?

After we got dressed, he held my hand and had me take a seat. He sat on the floor beside me. Not letting go of my hands, he looked into my eyes for a long time, as if he were about to say something.

"Why are you looking at me like that?" I asked.

"Because I have never seen anything more beautiful than you."

I laughed.

"Don't laugh," he said and asked, "Do you really love me?

I caressed his hair. I touched his face. He held my hand and kissed it.

"Yes," I said. "I love you more than you can ever know."

"Then you should make me a promise."

A promise? As he fixed his childish eyes on mine, I could have promised him the world. I knew that I was late, but still, I didn't want to leave him. In fact, I wanted to stay there and spend my whole life in that room.

"For as long as we live and love each other this way let us come here to this room on the same day every year, come what may, and ask each other that same question. Is that alright by you?" he said.

"Come what may?" I asked.

"Come what may, no matter what we do, even if we are together or apart, promise?"

I hugged him. Tears began rolling down my cheek. I whispered in his ear, "I promise. Every year when the spring comes."

It was four-thirty when I left the hotel.

I paused at the door for a moment, looked at the big park in front of me, and took a deep breath. The woman outside was waiting for me. When I found out that she still existed, I was glad. The doorman opened the door of a cab, and both of us, that woman and me, got in.

That was it.

The most unforgettable afternoon of my life.

After that day, although he was the only person I wanted to see in my life, I refrained from answering the phone.

Many days passed during which I sat staring at the ringing phone.

I feared he would do something crazy, but I still resisted.

I was fighting against myself.

Everything had changed for me. I had crossed the threshold.

I had tasted forbidden fruit.

I no longer wondered whether I would do what I had done. It was already over. Now everything was real. I had thought that after getting physical, the game would be over, the spell would be broken, and I would leave my dreamland forever.

That was what I had believed.

Whereas, when I returned home, I realized the truth was much different. On the contrary, I was in seventh heaven. Maybe I should have writhed in pangs of remorse that night, but I didn't. I longed to go to him, walk with him on the streets hand in hand, and fall asleep in his lap. Honestly, this was all I wanted, and I didn't care about the rest.

Strange, but I was gloomy and joyous at the same time.

Those were my feelings. Bliss and wild joy instead of guilt or anxiety.

But then, I began to think. And the longer I thought, the more I began to believe that none of this had meaning, reality would never turn into the dream I had experienced, truth and fantasy were never the same, and both had to remain in their own places.

I told myself: "It was impossible to put an end to this dream be-fore I did this, before I touched him, before I let him touch me, and before I closed my eyes and felt that perfect kiss, but now I'm going to cherish its memory, keep it in my mind, and finish the whole thing."

I didn't feel weak, helpless, or indecisive like in the past. I was strong, happy, and from then on, I would never answer the phone again.

Maybe this was the defense mechanism of a woman who sensed she would really be unhappy and hurt.

I would go on living a simple, balanced, well-organized life just like I had planned years ago. I would have children. We would soon be assigned to the Far East, which we had been expecting for some time, and I would go away—so far that it would be impossible for him to reach me even by phone.

You don't believe me, do you?

I don't either.

But then, I had really believed in those plans. At least for a short while.

I began to leave home early so that I wouldn't hear the phone ringing. I went to museums and libraries. I started to call the people I had been neglecting, had lunch with them, and chatted about ordi-nary things, such as their children's education, new furniture, holi-day plans, and daily gossip.

Then one night, I had a dream.

A dream surrounded with mirrors. How should I explain this? It was as if my dream were made of mirrors. It was a weird feeling like observing the dream through the mirrors.

In my dream, I lived in an old castle in a giant forest covered with snow. The castle resembled those in horror movies, but since it was covered with snow, it didn't look very scary. I was sitting by the window of my room on the top floor. I was a little girl. A small girl with long, wavy hair who sat by the window sill and watched the snow falling incessantly outside. Did she look like me that girl in my dream? I don't know. I was wearing a light green dress with a collar and long sleeves. It resembled my favorite red dress as a child. But this one was green, and it had small faint beige spots.

As I thought in my dream that I was actually seeing my own child-hood, I suddenly recognized him in a far away place. As if he were in a different time, years away from me. He was sleeping in his bed in a room covered with white wallpaper decorated with blue stars.

But the whole thing was very strange. At the same time he was sleeping here in my dream, and I wondered if I could see the dream he was having at that very moment.

It sounds unbelievable but it seems I was actually having his dream.

He was seeing the same dream I was seeing now. In his dream, he was a puny child struggling to walk in a narrow path in a forest covered with snow. As the snowflakes stroked his face, he wondered why he was there and what he was looking for. He was freezing, and I watched him from the window. "Yes," I said, "that's him." But he was only a small child!

He was struggling to walk in the snowstorm, and I couldn't un-derstand whether he had noticed the castle or not.

I felt happy when I saw him and was very excited that he was coming towards me.

He saw the castle and came all the way to its gate. I tried to open the window, but I couldn't. I pounded on the cold glass with my tiny hands, but I was unable to attract his attention. He must have been very cold. Finally, he noticed me, but I wasn't sure whether he rec-ognized me or not. All he wanted was to get inside the castle. I could see him knocking on the door, but I didn't know what to do.

Then, as he tried to open the door, I suddenly realized door was in fact the door of the dream.

If he succeeded in opening it, he would leave the dream and enter reality. Then I would never see him again.

Everything mixed together because of the mirrors. It was snowing everywhere. Everywhere I looked, I saw his image, trying to open the door. I didn't know which image was his and which was a reflection. I called his name, but he didn't hear me. I started screaming, but my voice didn't come out.

In the morning, I woke up crying.

I relived that dream for some time. When I closed my eyes under the warm water in the shower, I kept trembling as if I was about to go back to that cold forest and the heavily falling snow. I felt as if I wanted to scream.

The phone rang, and I answered without thinking.

"I was scared," he said. "Where have you been? I couldn't reach you. I thought you would never talk to me again!"

I felt like crying again. I tried to contain myself, holding back the tears.

"You're the only one I want to talk to."

"What did I do to you?" he asked. "Tell me the truth. Did something bad happen? I can hardly keep myself from coming there."

"Nothing," I said. "Nothing happened. I don't know what to do."

Then I told him about my dream.

My voice told him I was excited. He laughed.

"What a nice dream! Now tell me, what scared you? Tell me how I looked as a child. I know your childhood, but you don't know mine. So how was it?"

"You were really cute," I said. "You were the sweetest child I've ever seen, but I was too excited to notice it."

"I wish I had such dreams," he said.

We fell silent.

"Would you like to get on a plane and come here?

"I can't," I said.

"Then I'll come next week."

"I don't know," I replied.

"I love you," he said.

It was the first time he said that. And for the first time, I began to cry openly.

How could someone be unhappy after finding her missing half, with whom she desired to be with for a lifetime, even for eternity, that precious being who caused her heart to beat like crazy every time she saw or thought about him, that dear one whom she had searched for desperately for years and whom she had lost and found again without being aware of it?

Sometimes you think you love someone. You can explain why you love him so much to another person. In words, in sentences, and with memories as examples.

Sometimes you convince yourself you're in love with someone.

You do things or wait for things just to be able to love him or to increase your love for him.

Sometimes, however, you know you really love someone madly. You feel it. Even if there is no apparent reason, you feel attracted to him because of a force outside of yourself.

Natural, like gravity. Spontaneous . . . something you cannot prevent even if you want to.

I had truly found that person, but I was still unhappy.

I spent hours sitting alone until dawn and couldn't grasp why I kept weeping instead of rejoicing and laughing.

I had found him, but I couldn't have him.

Was that why I cried?

I felt as if I had suddenly come across my lost shadow, and each time I tried to capture it, it slid through my hands and escaped. It was not far but near; I could see it, yet when I tried to touch, it ran away from me.

Should I think, years later, that he had been so precious to me because he was always impossible to get hold of?

I know they say this is the reason. But it's not.

In those days, I would have given the same answer that I give today.

If the genie that appears in tales when the lamp is rubbed asked me, "What is your wish?" I would immediately give the answer I was never able to find in my childhood: "Even an entire lifetime is worthless for me when compared to having him talk to me as I lie in his lap while he caresses my hair."

Once I had asked him why he loved me.

I wonder where we were then.

He didn't like questions. He looked away for a while and then told me in a serious tone, "I don't know."

Rain had started to fall. It was slowly getting dark, and soon, we would have to part. Who knew when we would meet again. I felt tired. It was difficult to prolong the conversation while looking into the depths of his eyes. He lifted the collar of my coat, took off his scarf, and wrapped it around my neck. Plump pigeons were running around by our feet. Red leaves covered the ground. The raindrops scattered on the surface of the lake, creating intricate patterns on the water. I stared into the distance.

"So you don't know why you love me?" I asked.

"No, I don't," he replied. "I have thought about it a lot, but I can't explain it in words. That's why it's real."

Then he turned me toward himself. Looking into my eyes, he said, "If you are not able to find any tangible reasons, then it means your love is real."

Is that true?

Many times, we only love the people who do what we want, or those who act in a way that suits us. We feel secure around them. In fact, it is easy to love someone who is suitable for us. The difficult thing is to love someone who is different from us and doesn't necessarily act according to our wishes. Loving someone not because he makes you happy but because he is the way he is and because he acts like himself is not easy.

Once I had a friend who desperately loved a man who didn't love her for years. During their youth, they had been together for a very short time. One day the man stopped calling her and left after saying he loved another. She put everything in her life on hold, even though he wasn't aware of what she did. She waited for years without demanding anything or saying the smallest thing. We all hated that man. He was a famous womanizer who lived alone and who had constant affairs with different woman. He continued his way of life without even being aware that a woman somewhere suffered distress each time she heard gossip about him and wanted to die. As time passed, their relationship turned into a strange kind of comradeship. The rumor was that the man even told her about his affairs with other women. And she, in despair, listened to his stories and seemed content with playing the role of the best friend, as if what they had shared in the past had turned to nothing.

In the end, I saw them one day at the old fish restaurant in Yeniköy. The man had grown old, and my friend, who was middle-aged, looked rather plump and not so pretty anymore. Although she hadn't married him, she had managed to move into his home and become his lover in his last years.

Everyone pitied her. She had wasted her life running after a worthless man. When I saw them there, I thought this was probably what it meant to love someone from the heart. To give up your life for the one you love. I'm sure if I had asked her why she loved that man, she wouldn't have been able to give an answer.

As I sat there in the rain, I remembered their sad story.

Suddenly, I wondered about my future. Where and with whom would I be when I got old? Was life long enough to attempt playing such dangerous games? Was it simple enough to embark on such uncertain adventures?

If you don't have any reason to love someone, it means you truly love him.

I felt a little cold. The raindrops were beating my face, and my hair blew in the harsh wind. He brushed locks of hair away from my face each time he looked at me.

"Promise me that you will never cut your hair," he said.

In those days, women had their hair cut short like boys. That morning he had read a statement by the president of the hairdressers' association and told me about it, laughing until tears came to his eyes. The president had complained that many men had longer hair than their wives.

While we sat there, not minding the rain in our faces, and he told me things with his eyes fixed on mine, I thought for the first time that he was not like the strong, grown-up man everyone thought he was.

He loved talking about the most impossible things. He thought dreams were real. He wanted everyone to love him. He had to be loved, very much loved indeed. He enjoyed teasing others, but on the other hand, he didn't want anyone to be angry with him.

"This is how it's always going to be," he said. "We will always sit hand in hand and talk through the night, we will go to places where no one knows us, we will get rid of all the people, the crowd, the rituals and rules."

He was as excited as a child. He was so elated that I was convinced. I didn't ask him any questions. That day, when the tip of my nose was almost frozen, I realized I had to give up asking him questions since his huge hands covering mine gave me warmth and since I was the happiest person on earth when he was with me. I was happy because I didn't ask questions for which there were no answers. This moment, this happiness, was not something that lasted or that you could keep forever; it was like the sun emerging only to hide behind the clouds again. That was all.

"Don't say anything anymore!" I said. He looked at me in surprise. "Don't talk. Just kiss me!"

I used to forget about everything when I was with him.

"What were you so upset about? You sounded in low spirits on the phone the other day." When he asked such a question, I always said something like, "I've already forgotten about it!"

And I really had.

I used to forget all those questions haunting me, the thoughts that kept me awake at night, the hours during which I nagged myself, the anger I felt at him, the fury I felt toward myself, and even the quandary that drained me the moment I saw him or heard his voice.

I would tell myself, no, I'm not expecting anything. I'm not planning a future for us. We don't have a future. He already has a life of his own, and I have mine. This is just a fantasy, just a dream that makes me happier than I have ever felt as soon as I close my eyes.

The reality is distorted in a dream. Sometimes it takes on forms we don't want. We cannot direct our dreams. We just observe them. No one can put together a dream.

If you find such a magical stone in your life, a stone that transports you somewhere else as soon as you touch it, a stone that makes you as joyful as a child and makes you experience the excitement of a "first time" as if you're a young girl, a stone that changes the light, the colors, and the sense of an entire life, you mustn't expect more.

Later I wondered why he had not asked me the same question. If he had, what answer could I have given him?

I learned from him that life had another room as well.

The secret room of life.

Like that secret room you come across in fairy tales, the key to which is always lost or hidden, and which requires the help of magical words, ogres, fairies or sorcerers to be opened. Yes. Exactly like that room. A room in a fairy tale.

I felt I had touched a hidden button by accident, and a door had opened wide in front of my eyes.

A corridor extended in front of me now. I had no idea where it would take me, if I would be able to return, or whom I would meet on the way.

Something that resembled the way Ayla discovered mysterious cities. The same way she found herself in underground passages or a labyrinth, the direction of which she wasn't sure, where she didn't know what she would face after lifting the heavy door decorated with stone reliefs in the ground.

Sometimes you don't even know the location of the secret doors inside of yourself and happen to discover them through coincidence or an unexpected person you come across.

You encounter illegible words engraved on the walls, unknown languages, unsolved signs whose meaning you don't understand, as if you have stepped into an ancient city or a king's temple that was meant to be concealed eternally from all evil, strangers, or unknown forces.

But maybe the real deception was that all those unforgotten words, signs, and codes were similar to the ones you already knew.

Similar but not the same.

The way words were arranged made all the difference. A sign meant something entirely different after thousands of years. The words you thought you were familiar with told a totally different story than you were able to comprehend.

But you know what, this was the best moment of all—the moment when a door touched upon for the first time after thousands of years invited you into a dream that sent a cold chill down your spine.

To walk in fear and excitement around writings, the meaning of which you didn't know. To hold a perfect little statue in your hands, to touch a past you didn't know, to look at an object you didn't understand, and to try to find a meaning in bits and pieces that used to be the inevitable parts of life. Who knows, this ring set with a brilliant precious stone which looks ordinary, maybe carried divine implications back then. To observe in admiration the chariots, terrible warriors, eagle-headed gods, dog-faced servants, priests with bright robes, and child princesses. To enter the parlor of the sun-god, who had been asleep for a thousand years, like that little girl who suddenly found herself lost in a wonderland, to stoop to pass through narrow corridors, to see someone in a mysterious room dominated by unfamiliar smells and a frightening silence getting gradually stronger, and to realize that king had been buried in peace in the heart of the earth away from fights and endless wars. To feel yourself above life as a whole, as if you had reached a fragile world you want to safeguard from everyone and everything. Exactly that moment.

Because everything is solved in the end, everything becomes familiar, and that fabulous spell, that unique moment turns to dust.

I was as excited as someone who was about to open the door to an unknown world. I wanted that moment to become infinite, to never end, and to encompass my whole life.

If only I could have found that mysterious code that would reveal the secret to me!

Just like it was in that dream, if you opened the door, you left the tale, and if you didn't open it, you couldn't live the way you wanted to.

Everything developed out of our control.

Staying inside a tale too long was impossible. After some time, you wanted to pass through that door and leave, you desired to go out and get hold of real life in the world outside of mirrors, deceptive images, the fog, and undulating emotions.

This was the dilemma that drained me.

I discovered so many things in the secret room inside myself.

It was there that I learned to view myself from different directions, to build my own statements instead of describing myself with the words of others. I learned that your body had a different life of its own other than the life you led and that life could acquire totally different shapes than the ones taught to us.

Perhaps I found a woman there who would never have let herself been seen otherwise. I was surprised to recognize her. I was scared. For a long time, I didn't know what I would do with this woman who resembled me but whom I didn't know. First I fought against her. I tried to hide her from everyone, even from myself.

I found out one could live for years without truly knowing oneself. It was even possible to believe you were a different person than you really were.

Suddenly, I realized I didn't know myself at all when I thought I knew myself so well.

If they asked me, I would have described myself as a strong person not ruled by her emotions, who said what she thought without minding others' thoughts, and who believed she could solve everything by using her intellect.

A woman who was confident, who didn't fear anything, and who knew what to do.

I believed so.

Then, on the contrary, it occurred to me that I was a foolish person who could neglect and forget about the whole world because of being ruled by her feelings.

Yes. Foolish. But don't think that I see this as a bad trait.

I was one of those people who thought she could establish and lead a life on her own. Isn't that the biggest foolishness?

I now acknowledge life is larger than us, and even a moderately strong wind can demolish without warning all those castles in the sand while taking childish joy out of it.

I could not have known that touching the body of another person or the way he touches your skin was powerful enough to carry you away to eternity.

I didn't know for all those years how and why I had concealed myself. Yet, now I knew I was full of burning passion.

I felt as if I had dug into my own soul and found a new identity, solving the obscure writings there. My own being. Who I was? That real woman whom I had not noticed for many years . . .

I continued to remember my own self as I went to that distant past and deciphered an unknown alphabet.

And I found her there.

Regardless of what others said, I really liked that woman.

Yes, maybe he was just a key in my life—a mere coincidence that opened the doors of my own life to me.

It was with him that I learned to miss.

You cannot miss something whose existence you are unaware of. You cannot feel the absence of such a thing.

You cannot feel pain because you can't have something you don't know.

If you don't have a child, you cannot know how that warmth leaning on your chest feels. Since you don't know, you cannot grasp how that warmth is worth every bit of the inevitable responsibility you are supposed to carry for a lifetime.

I learned to feel anxiety with him. The fear to lose.

I was so afraid. I feared something would happen to him. That I wouldn't be able to see him again.

If he disappeared for a few days . . . If he didn't call at the time he promised . . . Because of all the distance between us and the confusion because of the circumstances, I was immediately enveloped by deep fear. That fear prevailed no matter what I did. I used to wait in worry, unable to decide what to do, as if a knife had been thrust into my chest.

I learned to wait and to be patient with him.

I waited for so long. For the phone to ring. For a letter or a note. To see him again. Everything was so vague that regardless of what we said and what promises we gave, things always started from scratch again.

I used to try to train myself to accept that I would lose him sooner or later. I didn't know back then that when you are taken captive by an indescribable feeling, getting used to such an idea was impossible.

In fact, all life is like this.

You could have an entirely different life if only you could give up the hope of having certain things. Those things you don't have because you fear a possible pain, but that you still expect, with excitement.

With him, my whole life changed, but I couldn't manage to transform it into another form again.

They always say that life is something you are able to manipulate and that a human being can determine his fate. Don't believe a word of it! Life is controlled by destiny shaped by coincidences no one can predict.

But wait! Let me tell you everything that happened before I confuse the dates again.

I know that readers are always interested in how the story proceeds and what happens in the end.

On a morning when the entire world was discussing the Asian flu, I was in another city, for another reason. As soon as I left the doctor's office in a back street, I leaned against the door of the building and filled my lungs with fresh air.

A church was nearby. If a god who shaped my destiny existed, he would welcome me in any of his houses, even if it didn't belong to my religion, and would hear my words.

I took the road next to the statue of the fairytale character who never grew up.

The small church was empty. I sat on a bench. It was a dim and peaceful place that carried you away from the pompous turmoil of the world outside and from life taken too seriously. The rays of the sun steamed through the high, colorful stained glass windows cut into the darkness of the interior, and the statues, paintings, and old furnishings made you think you were in a different realm.

Sitting on the bench, I said, "Great God, you have probably watched all I have done, and if you have already told me in your own language what I should do, I'm not sure whether I have understood the meaning of your signs. If what's written in books is true, you have probably done your best to prevent me from committing this awful sin, but still, as an author in this land had once said, 'there is no end to the folly of the human heart.' Now I don't know what to do. Maybe this is the life I am destined to live, or maybe you have abandoned me. If so, should I then give birth to this child or commit an even a bigger sin by killing it?"

I definitely wasn't expecting an answer.

But I felt so lonely that there was nothing else I could do; I sat there alone for a quite a while, hoping to receive an answer.

On one hand, I had to plan how I would deal with this calamity, and on the other, I was beginning to realize I wouldn't be able to continue the affair in secrecy anymore.

Questions filled my head, as if I were about to take an exam.

Would I tell him?

Did he have to know about this?

How would he react?

Would he withdraw in fear or do something utterly crazy and decide to build a new life with me?

Could that happen?

Could an entire life be dismantled to build up a new one?

Why not, I told myself. We could both divorce, marry each other, go to a faraway land, and when the child was born, we could decide how to proceed.

Then all at once, the thought of Turgut haunted me. I also thought about Fuat's wife, his daughter, my mother, and my brother.

As if the problem would be resolved if we went away together.

What about the scandal? All that would be written in the newspapers. Even if he were willing, would they allow him to do it? It dawned on me that this subject would not be discussed only in Turkey but in the whole world.

I could imagine the newspaper headlines:

"The minister fathered a child by his mistress!"

"The fruit of forbidden love!"

No. It wouldn't be as easy as I thought. Everything we would have to bear, all we would have to accept unwillingly. It was not only we who had everything at stake. What would all the other people, who were not guilty, do? Did we have the right to put such a burden on them?

Wouldn't the whole country erupt?

I chuckled, thinking it would be even better since everyone constantly complained. When the government fell from power because of us, everyone would be relieved!

I would go into history as the woman who caused the downfall of a government.

I told myself to keep on laughing, and then I wondered whether I would be able to laugh in the end.

Wasn't getting rid of the child secretly without informing anyone the best thing to do?

Devilish thoughts filled my head. Who would know it was his child? For some time, Turgut had been insisting on having a child. No, I must be crazy to think about such a possibility.

At one moment, I felt like laughing. What if the baby was a boy and had Fuat's nose when he grew up!

I could call Ayla, but she wouldn't be practical in dealing with such a problem. Then I asked myself: I'm not practical about this either! You fool. How can you get pregnant like a high school girl the first time you have an affair! To tell the honest truth, I wasn't much older than a high school girl, was I?

What was done was done.

I had to make a quick decision.

Yet this was the most difficult thing for me in those days: making a decision.

That day I walked the foggy streets as if lost, found myself in a part of town I had never been before, and talked with a woman who sat at my table in a café I had entered to warm myself, is like a blurry, half-forgotten picture. But that terrible distress has stayed with me forever, even though so much was lost in the intervening years. When I remember that day, I can still feel the indescribable feeling of nausea.

There, in that café in a district I had never been before, I found myself pouring out my troubles to a total stranger, a woman who sat at my table just because there was no other place free.

I told everything to a woman I didn't know.

In return, she showed me the numbers branded on her arm, telling me how she had been rescued from a concentration camp where life and death were intertwined and about the bizarre coincidence that enabled her to survive. If it hadn't been for sheer luck that changed her fate by a few hours, she wouldn't be sitting there with me.

I couldn't comprehend how a woman of my age could look so old. Indelible grief had settled in her eyes forever. Grief that was still present even when she laughed. As I talked, I watched her devour a cream-filled cake, savoring every bit of it, as if it were the last slice of cake she would ever get.

As two strangers from different countries, we were in the same foreign town, sharing the story of our lives in broken language.

A man with a loud voice, people who seemed to frequent this place, a touching love song played at high volume, coffee and cigarettes that lost their flavor the more you consumed them . . . I felt dizzy.

I reminded myself I had to go back home, and that in reality, I had a home.

As she stood up and picked up her old handbag, she said she was happy to meet me and added, "Life is something that can end all of a sudden. Just do what you feel is right. There's not much time to spend thinking."

It was exactly then that he stopped calling in the morning.

During our last conversation, he had told me he would come in one week's time.

My head was completely in turmoil. I felt an indescribable tightness in my chest.

I still haven't forgotten a dream I saw then. In my dream, we are at my family's house. Fuat is there. My father is still alive. My brother, Turgut, and my mother-in-law are all living there. Although we are in my family home, the furniture from my own home with Turgut is also there. It feels awkward. I act as if no one knows about anything, but soon I find out everyone is informed. Nobody says a word, but I can see the expression in their eyes. I look at Fuat, hoping he will do or say something, yet he sits in silence with his head bent forward.

On some nights, I used to wake up from a nightmare—exactly

at that part of the dream when I worried everyone knew about that afternoon and the hours we spent together in the hotel.

That is the only dream that has made me very upset, even though it involved my father.

I was secluded from the rest of the world. I had withdrawn into myself.

I no longer met people. I tried to survive the hours I had to spend with Turgut, and buried myself in thought.

Fuat had disappeared just when I needed him the most. I didn't hear anything from him.

Ayla had returned to her thousand-year-old underground city again.

In her last letter, she had written that they had discovered the most important part of an epic poem that was probably the oldest love story written.

I remember sitting beside the phone for the entire day.

But the phone didn't ring.

A few times, I sat down to write him a letter. Lines written with enthusiasm, high-pitched emotions, reproach, anger and jealousy at one time and at others with unbearable longing coupled with a weary and discouraged sense of resignation.

Naturally, I tore each letter into pieces as soon as I finished writing. Who knows, maybe writing those letters gave me a little comfort and helped me to arrange my thoughts instead of talking to myself.

"I don't know where you are, why you ran away, or what you think. If you have the slightest doubt, if you regret it even a little, you should let me know. Was everything a lie? Were all those words, all those songs, all those tears feigned? I want to find you, hold you and give you a shake so that you tell me the truth as you look straight into my eyes. Or are you so scared that you ran away from me instead of admitting your true feelings? If that is the case, then you don't need to worry anymore because I don't want to see you, either. Before we destroy our lives, let us both wake up from this futile dream and do the right thing. I wish you happiness throughout your life . . ."

Of course, I immediately discarded the letter, only to write different words of despair in the evening:

"I can't describe how much I worry. Has something happened? Something I don't know or something unexpected? I'm so scared. I keep crying like a little child. I have bitten my fingernails so badly that I'm afraid you will no longer like the way my hands, which you have always adored, look now. I pray for the phone to ring and to hear your cheerful happy voice again. I don't want anything else. All I want is to know you are safe and sound. Then you can hang up. I won't mind . . ."

I kept being hurled from one feeling to another.

I didn't know what had happened. There was no one I could call to inquire about him. I wondered how I had not thought about this detail until then. I realized, for the first time, I would never be able to reach him again unless he wanted to reach me. Nobody around him knew about me. The only person who knew about us was Ayla. In the worst case, Fuat could get into contact with her, but I didn't have anyone I could call to ask. I had gotten so used to him running after me and finding me wherever I was that I hadn't thought how the opposite would work.

While buried in these thoughts, I also struggled to carry on with my daily life. I cannot relate how awkward it was to go from one place to another, shop, cook, do the dishes, or carry on an obligatory conversation with someone.

Was it really this difficult for the inner and outer world of someone to be completely different, or did I just think it was because I wasn't accustomed to this feeling?

Turgut was aware something was the matter, but he didn't know what the problem was.

All I felt with him was humiliation. Hopelessly drowned in shame, I was extremely tense and careful with my words. I suspected that I would confess everything shortly.

The dinners on Fridays and the evenings at the cinema or the theater took place as usual. I was able to bear these events at least a little, but the weekend tours with the car and the picnics were agonizing. The evenings when the embassy staff got together were a nightmare for me.

I neither wanted to see nor talk to anyone. The salespeople or waiters who tried to make small talk during shopping or when ordering food at a restaurant infuriated me.

It was then I realized you can also live with an outer shell that doesn't reflect your real self and soon create a mask, pretending it is you.

Eventually one evening, Turgut couldn't take it anymore and asked me what was going on. He said, "You have been in low spirits lately. You're constantly lost in thought."

Perhaps, that was the best moment to bring up the subject. Couldn't I have at least told him our marriage wasn't working anymore and that I wasn't happy? What did we have in common, anyway? He probably wasn't very happy with me either. We didn't talk longer than thirty minutes in the evenings.

Would we continue to share the same house like two friends until the end of our lives?

Yet, I was no longer adept at saying whatever crossed my mind. I had almost turned into an entirely different person. I had grown up. I was like other people now. The deadly secret that besieged me had taken me captive, and I was under its control now.

As if some higher power magically transformed my thoughts

into words with totally different meanings, I blurted out:

"I'm extremely bored here. I miss my mother and brother. I also miss Turkey."

He looked relived. "Alright," he said, "that was what I suspected. You don't have any friends here, so naturally, you're bored. My situation over the past months is obvious. I have so much work that I can't take you around enough. I was hoping we'd go to Turkey together, but I can't go on leave at the moment. Why don't I send you there alone so that you can rest and spend time with all the people you've been longing to see."

"Send me where?" I asked, confused.

"Where? To Istanbul, of course!"

He had said what I had been trying to decide for days.

Is willing to choose the wrong thing, although you know what's right, the worst thing that can happen to you?

Maybe it is even worse to be forced to choose what's right even though you want to do the wrong thing.

As I lay in my bed that night and closed my eyes, I was lost in thought.

Maybe this was the last sign I was sent. Besides, I still had a way out. I could get rid of the child without anyone knowing and put an end to this hopeless relationship once and for all.

Yes. I had to do that.

This love story was certain to fail sooner or later.

Don't we feel unparalleled excitement from love stories and get carried away just because they are unique, even if we don't experience them first hand?

Was it a delusion, a momentary dizziness, or magic?

Could one live such a fabulous tale for many years in real life? Just imagine yourself with a glittering halo above your head when you're stuffing lettuce and leeks into your shopping basket.

Could we live with lies forever?

No, that was out of the question.

Maybe this was the reason for all love stories to end in agony. If, one day, we wake up from a dream, we have to be content with the unequaled experience we had and move on with our life after securing its memory in the depths of our hearts.

This was impossible. You always wanted that feeling and trepidation to be with you.

Discovering that the paradise you thought was concealed in an unknown place in eternity was in fact in the most unexpected place or right there on the streets you trod every single day, and then letting it go, was not easy.

That's why all the splendid tales of love ended in despair.

Something similar to getting addicted to drugs.

I had heard nothing from him. Perhaps he was thinking the same way. He had probably realized that we had gone too far, I could get hurt in the end, or we could both get into trouble and had decided that distancing himself from me was the wisest thing to do.

Once he had told me, "I don't care about my life. My only fear is the possibility for you to become the subject of gossip and get hurt."

I had laughed at his words back then.

"Become the subject of gossip? Do you really believe I would care?"

He had caressed my face. "You're still very young. You don't know how people can hurt you."

In my life, there were only two people who calmed me down and made me forget all my worry and distress when they touched my face: my father and Fuat.

Whenever Fuat gently touched my cheek, I would slightly tilt my neck and lean onto his hand. Everything on my mind would disappear at once. I would shudder, I would have a lump in my throat, and at the same time, an immense compassion would surge inside of me. It's difficult to describe, but at such moments, I used to wish both to surrender my naked body, to make love to him and also cuddle in his arms and fall into a deep, contented sleep. Know what? I wasn't able to decide which option I yearned for more or which was my true desire.

He would remain silent in front of me with a profound look in his eyes, as if he were looking at me for the first time in his life. "Why are you staring at me like that?" I often asked.

He would say, "When I look into your eyes, I'm overcome with sudden excitement. Your eyes have such a soul-staggering glimmer that I'm overwhelmed by joy whenever I look at you."

But that happened later. I wasn't able to think about it at that moment. He hadn't said those words yet.

The only thing I thought was not what I wanted to do but what I had to do.

Whatever there was to be lived had already been experienced. What could this be but an adventure? And now, it had to end before anyone got hurt, before anyone found out, and as if the thing between us had never existed. I would wake up and think everything had been a stunning dream, and in a little while, the cloudy confusing images of that dream would slowly disappear out of sight, leaving behind only a memory.

But as I lay in the dark, I was conscious of the tears running onto my pillow. I knew I had to do this, but unfortunately, this was the last thing I wanted to do.

Can you choose whom to love?

Apparently, you can't.

As I said before, I had withdrawn into my shell so deeply that I did not know what exactly was happening.

Upon coming to Istanbul, I realized how much I was unaware of the facts.

My mother was so happy to see me that she didn't even ask why I had suddenly come. As soon as I entered the garden and saw the magnolia trees, I began to cry as if I had seen an old childhood friend.

When I rang the bell, my mother rushed out and my brother followed her.

It was impossible for my mother to hold back her tears when she saw me. As she and I hugged each other and wept in the garden, my brother complained, "Women are always like this! Can't you stop it? You're going to make me cry too." He could hardly hold back his tears.

I think everybody feels happy in places where they can smell the unexplainable smells of their childhood. I have been to so many different places in the world, but I have never seen any place as beautiful as this garden. The magnolia trees, the cobblestone street embellished with judas trees, flowers hanging from the garden walls, and the sea nearby, where magnificent mansions, which appeared humble because they were too familiar, lined the shore next to fishermen's boats.

Nowhere was I able to find the same joy I had strolling in these streets, the way I greeted the old women looking from the windows of their old homes, the joyful shouts of fishermen selling bluefish and mackerel that were carefully arranged on their bright display stands, the voice of the sesame roll seller I anticipated in afternoons when I began racing back and forth in the house like an impatient lover just because the sesame roll seller was late, the sound of the morning prayer coming as close as my grandmother's voice who checked on me during my sleep, the surprise to see the scenery change into a totally different vista with the changing light, the enormous ships that passed so close to the shore that we thought we could touch them as they traveled to a destination unknown to us, the screech of the seagulls that broke the silence and how the birds talked to each other in a mysterious language, the sea that flowed wildly touching our feet in the water, all these images, sounds and scents made me think life was a unique and an incredible joy no matter how it unfolded.

On that day, however, no one knew the real reason for my sudden sobs in the garden.

As I entered the door, I hoped for a miracle. I wished that I could become a young girl again, like on one of those long ago summer days.

There was my tea and my spinach pie and slices of cheese.

The breeze from the sea was enough to make me forget everything for a moment.

My mood had already changed on the plane. All of a sudden, I felt irritated that the whole affair was going on in such secrecy. Maybe what I experienced was something that any woman wouldn't be able to tell her husband, but all the same, it had happened. Was it better to hide everything and fool a decent man until the end of his life? Yes, I know. No one would hear about it; only a doctor or a nurse who didn't know me would find out. Yet, I would know. From now on, each time I looked at my husband's face, I would be reminded of my dishonesty and incredible deceit. Would I lead my life like a cold-hearted murderer? No, I couldn't do that.

I had loved someone. I had wanted to play a game. Perhaps, I had made a big mistake. It was not correct for a married, or even a single woman, to get so close to a married man, meet him secretly, or give him hope. I should have realized all this in Ankara during those conversations we had, putting an end to everything then. But I hadn't. Maybe the main reason was my loneliness—a feeling no one could perceive from my joyful, carefree manner. Maybe . . .

No, I suddenly realized that searching for excuses or reasons was meaningless. How could such a unique feeling have a cause? There must definitely be a reason for the human heart to beat, to stop, or to experience difficulty. But can there be a reason for whom it beats?

This was an unexpected shock, like a tremor from below the ground, or the way the earth's crust suddenly breaks. An earthquake that changes your life irrevocably, forever.

I had always believed in the superiority of reason and thought that everyone could make his own decisions and shape his own destiny.

When I had read all those romantic novels or watched love films, I had often exclaimed, "What a stupid woman!" or "Poor man, how blind he is!"

I had laughed at such things.

Though it was as unlikely as lightning striking you while you're walking in a vast desert, what I lived through was equally desperate.

It had happened. It was not possible to resist such a powerful wave. There I was, surfing on that wave, wherever it took me; yet, I still thought I was in control.

It was not anyone's fault—not my husband's, Fuat's, or mine. This was a game life had created on its own without caring for any of us.

Had I done what I had to? I don't know. I had tried to resist in my own way. I had tried to keep away from him. I had wanted this whole thing to remain a game and had wished he would make me happy from a distance, like a fantasy which slowly transformed into a pleasant memory.

But I couldn't succeed.

In fact, while I was thinking about all of this on the plane, I suddenly realized that my pregnancy, the afternoon I spent with him, and the fact that I had touched someone other than my husband did not matter. What mattered was that I was terribly in love with him.

I was in love with someone other than my husband.

Even if I did not see that someone, even if I didn't talk to him or touch him, wasn't it enough that I was in love with him? I realized that if this had been a simple affair that concerned the desires of a woman, or if we had just lived a day of lust, everything would have been much easier.

Then, we could give up everything, conceal what should be kept in secret, and even forget what had happened between us.

We could call it madness, a momentary lapse of reason, or even intoxication.

Now, however, my heart, my mind, my dreams, my happiness and my sorrow, my songs, books, and films, everything belonged to him.

Anything that was not related to him, even a single moment I spent without him, caused unbearable distress.

Can it be called a game, a fantasy, or a dream if someone chuckles to herself, or if something warm fills her heart when she hears a voice or loses herself in a distant dream, remembering his laugh, something he said, a story he told while moving his hands like a little child, his boyish smile, his eyes that look like those of a crazy lover at one moment and of a compassionate father the next?

Isn't such a thing the most beautiful truth in the world?

And what did I decide to do? I had thought I could leave this incomparable bliss aside (as if I really could) and go back to my home, lead my old life, and save my marriage without letting anyone find out about us.

But why? Just because it had to be that way? Just so that no one would get upset? Just because all marriages had to go on forever, no matter how happy or unhappy the couples were? Or was it because we were afraid of building up something new to replace what had become old and worn-out that we thought one day we would regret having acted differently?

Did we think we would not be able to cope with life on our own?

All at once, I understood that this was the real fantasy and that it could not be realized.

Besides, why would I have to act that way? For other people? Would the other people really be happy then? Could a broken-hearted woman whose lover had been so cruelly taken away be happy with any other man?

Moreover, my husband and I shared no intimacy anymore. We were just two friends—two friends who did not tell each other about their lives, who did not really know each other well, and who just shared the outwardly perceptible parts of life.

I felt sad. I knew that regardless of how I chose to act, Turgut would be unhappy. He would not be unhappy because he loved me or was losing me, but because he had not succeeded in building up the dream-life that he had always planned. Maybe letting him know about everything now, immediately, would be the best thing to do. In this way, he would at least be able to be angry at me, hate me, and start forgetting about me as soon as possible. It would be somewhat difficult for him to separate from me at first, but after some time, he would realize he had done the right thing.

This is what occupied my mind when I rang the bell, while I hugged my mother, and wept on her shoulder. I had already decided to divorce Turgut, even though no one knew about my decision yet.

Being away from my own home and in my childhood home again cleared my mind about what I should do.

I felt as if I had transcended into a different reality—away from all those foreign cities where I had always felt like a fish out of water. Now, I was in my own realm, in the garden that was so familiar to me.

As if the woman who felt so insecure and unsure last night was not me. Now I knew what I would do.

Still, I didn't want to think about how I would tell my mother about my decision.

I was lost in a world of swirling thoughts. So much had happened.

In those days, politics was the one and only subject on everyone's mind.

Listening to what people often talked about, I realized how uninformed I was. The radio was full of strangely humorous propaganda, yet just about everyone you came across complained that the situation was becoming unendurable.

Journalists were arrested, newspapers were censored, and whoever voiced his opinion was considered to be at war with the government.

Students, teachers, soldiers, state officials, everyone was full of complaints.

What I heard from the neighbors and relatives who came to visit made me realize that the end was near and something really bad was just around the corner.

As I listened to this talk, I felt pain in my chest. Although I wanted to speak favorably about the government, I couldn't find anything good to say.

Sometimes his name came up in a conversation. He was accused of misconduct, and things I knew he wouldn't do were mentioned. My face would go all shades of red, and I was unable to make a comment.

I always remembered that afternoon in Ankara when he had asked me what I thought about his going into politics and my remark, "Politics is not suitable for you."

As if I had intuitively felt what could happen.

Unfortunately, he had resented my words that day.

Now, I worried about him like a mother whose child is late from school worries.

Besides, he wasn't around.

When I had made the decision on my own, I didn't know what he was doing, if he was trying to reach me, or if he was thinking of me, and I felt both angry and hopeless.

Finally, I found out why he didn't call: he was on a trip to the Far East.

Later, he would tell me, "I was either not alone or I couldn't find a phone to call you, but you were always on my mind." Even then, however, I knew that what he said was a lie.

There was something else.

That afternoon we spent together, he had turned on the radio, and we listened to a song that had made us both cry.

It was a sorrowful tango played on the accordion, and I had told him, "Fuat, let this be our song. Let us listen to it and cherish each other's memory regardless of where we are."

He had frowned. "You always talk as if you are bidding farewell. Put that out of your mind. I'm a crazy man and will never stop following you, even if you go to the end of the world. I will come, too, because you're the only one who is on my mind all the time."

We had hugged each other while listening to that sad song, with tears rolling down our cheeks.

I could never bear to see him frown like a little child.

Before returning to Turkey, he had bought an album that included that song, and he asked his daughter to play it every night on the gramophone. He listened to that song countless times while he smoked and gazed into the distance with tears in his eyes.

I learned about this much later.

Many years later, I also found out that on that same day he had decided to tell his wife as soon as he got home that he wanted a divorce. Although he was sometimes harsh with people and never refrained from saying whatever was on his mind, even to the point of being carried away with short flashes of anger, he would not deliberately hurt people.

He just wanted everyone to understand how he felt, to guess his thoughts, and act accordingly.

Truthfully, he had no idea of what I thought. When he couldn't bring himself to tell his wife that he wanted a divorce, he made up reasons to attend state trips and buried himself in his work.

Perhaps his mind was occupied with similar thoughts. When he had returned home and met his wife and daughter who welcomed him so joyfully, he had thought he couldn't let them down for another woman and had tried in vain to forget about everything.

Lovers are always suspicious.

At that time, I had not thought such a thing could have been the case. All I had imagined was that he regretted everything, that he had decided he had gone too far, and that perhaps he had not loved me asI thought he had.

But, somewhere deep inside of me, I still knew that he would never abandon me and that we had a strong bond between us—stronger than the bond between lovers who are together night and day—and that we could never break it even if we wanted to.

While I thought about such things, I also had to spend time with relatives and acquaintances who rushed to my mother's home to see me, as well as attend tea parties and dinners. One other thing also kept my mind busy: the baby in my belly.

I had decided what to do, yet I had no idea how I would accomplish it.

As soon as I got rid of the baby, I would go back to my husband and tell him about everything. I had already taken a road of no return regardless of how Fuat would proceed with his life. Right now was the best time to make a decision because I didn't have a clue about what Fuat wanted to do. Maybe he had already changed his mind completely. Maybe only I would damage my life and end up alone. I had to do what was right for me—not by thinking about the future or of other people, but by expecting no reward and just punishment, perhaps . . .

By that time, I had realized that all I had done or thought with the aim of keeping my life unspoiled was unreal. From now on, life would show us the way.

Maybe we all must ask ourselves this question sooner or later in life: what is the right thing?

I am pretty sure that whomever we ask this question will answer it in accordance with what others think.

We all believe that "the right thing" is something determined by the approval of other people or by customary rules.

Isn't that why so many people ruin their own lives, unable to make decisions that don't harm others. They become unhappy and frustrated. They get ill because of conflicts. Sometimes they even end their own lives in deep, unbearable sorrow.

I wish they had taught us about real life in school instead of all those other things.

I wish they had showed us all those unhappy lives barely touched on in the newspapers and turned them into precious lessons.

Of course, I know that this would still be futile. We all know what others go through in life; we also learn about the lives of strangers from films and books. Even if we don't have firsthand experience, we still learn a lot from the lives of others.

Yet it's only when we actually experience something that we understand it exactly.

Most of us are not courageous enough to tear down our life and build it again. Therefore, we are unable to go after the true happiness that awaits us somewhere we do not know.

Unfortunately, a human being and the happiness he can have do not coincide as far as time and space are concerned.

It's almost as if half of you has been thrown into the distance as part of a game. Furthermore, you know neither how much time you've got left nor where and how you are supposed to look for that missing half.

Besides, even if you came accross that other half, you can only sense it through that odd feeling that comes from deep inside of you, you can never be sure about it.

Let us assume for a moment that this childish description of life is true.

Then if you happened to find that other half who completes you in this impossibly hard game, would you be prepared let go of it?

Would you be afraid of it and withdraw?

One day when I was having breakfast with my mother, I thought she had to know what was going on. However, putting everything into words was not as easy as I though it would be.

There was no point in distressing this dear old woman with my thoughts and explanations.

She thought her daughter was happily married, and all she wished for was to have a grandchild before she passed away. Each time a guest opened the subject of having children, I blushed or got angry, almost to the point of blurting out, "Here! You have your baby!"

While I was brooding and trying to find the right way to tell my mother everything, Turgut called. He said he would visit if opportunity arose. He missed me, he was bored, he was not used to eating dinner alone, he was going out with his colleagues almost every evening . . .

I didn't miss home at all. After I told him that I wanted to stay a little longer and that my mother was not willing to let me go so soon, I hung up.

"Do stay," my mother said. "He could come here if he can take some time off. We let our daughter marry him, and since then, we haven't been able to see her properly."

After my father's death, my mother had grown old quickly. She was often lost in thought, kept repeating the same old stories, and wept over insignificant things.

Living in this family house, without my father or grandmother, had caused her to enter her second childhood. She resented that I had to live so far away. She worried that my brother would go away one day too, and even though she said it was about time he married and had a family of his own, I realized that this would be possible only if his bride accepted living in this house, too.

When I had the chance to talk to my brother Nihat in private, I discovered that he was not planning to get married. He was one of those people who sacrificed themselves for the sake of others. He did not want to leave mother all alone to build a life of his own. With an air of having accepted his fate, he said, "Sorry sis, but a bachelor's life is a king's life. I'm all right this way. Let's wait and see what the future brings."

According to what my mother said, he was making good money. He had always been interested in clothes and finery. He looked quite stylish now.

I also found out that he was drinking a little more than he used to and that he gambled every now and then with his friends at the club.

My mother was aware of all this, but pretended not to be.

She lived upstairs, with Nihat on the ground floor. I thought he had quieted down a bit. He didn't look like my old, lively brother but a serious-minded man.

Yet, while speaking to him, I realized he was gazing vacantly. Silence fell over the room.

"What happened to you, Nihat?" I asked.

One's eyes never change. For a moment, I thought I saw that little boy in shorts playing with his train on the floor.

"I don't know," he said. "Sometimes life doesn't go the way you want, and all of a sudden, you find yourself in an utterly unexpected position."

"I know . . ." I smiled, "very well."

It was then that I realized how mother was showering attention on him, and that he had unwillingly taken on father's role at home.

He had brought the subject of marriage up a couple of times, but mother had criticized something in each girl he mentioned, sealing the subject.

"What would you like to do?" I asked.

Nihat laughed bitterly, as if even asking this question was futile. "The worst thing is that I don't know exactly what I want to do."

Then, he added abruptly, "It's always you who asks the questions, and you don't tell me anything about your life. Is everything okay there? Have you achieved what you wanted? Most of all, are you happy?"

Strange, but all of a sudden I was bewildered and at a loss for words, even though this was the very question that should have been asked the moment I had arrived. I shuddered as if he knew something.

If he only knew!

Would it have ever crossed his mind that I was having an affair with the man to whom he had introduced me when I was a little girl?

"I missed you all so much," I said. "I missed this place. Being away is not easy. In the beginning, you see new places, meet new people, feel amused, but as time goes by, longing descends upon you until it gets so heavy that you can no longer bear it."

We heard our mother calling: "Kids, dinner is ready! Come on, before it gets cold."

Kids! Like in the old days, we jumped up so that she would not have to call us again. Our eyes met, and we began to laugh.

As soon as I realized I wouldn't be able to solve the problem on my own, I immediately called for the help of my dear friend Ayla.

She was somewhere in the middle of the steppes in Anatolia. Her mother told me that she sent her daughter a letter once a week.

I also sent her a letter in which I wrote, "I'm in Istanbul, and I won't be staying long, but I need you more than ever . . ." Two days later she was at our front door, ringing the bell, dressed in khaki shorts and a hat.

As I jumped up from my seat, I heard my mother say, "Oh, this can only be our nutty girl ringing the bell!"

When Ayla saw how I ran to embrace her with tears rolling down my face, she quickly whispered in my ear, "I realized something had happened, and so many things crossed my mind. Tell me quickly what's going on, or I'm going to have a heart attack right this moment and you'll be shedding tears for me."

At breakfast, the poor thing couldn't talk to me since my mother kept her busy answering one question after another. Ayla must have been terribly worried after receiving my letter.

My mother just couldn't understand Ayla's job. She kept saying, "You should leave all those men who died thousands of years ago in peace in their graves, or their spirits will paralyze you!"

Finally, Ayla and I went out to take a walk by the sea.

I told her everything.

I told her what I had experienced with Fuat, the night I had to endure in my own home, the days I spent walking the streets as if I were a ghost, the conflicts I had, the shame, the excitement, and whatever else was on my mind.

Eventually, when I told her about my pregnancy, she shuddered.

"Oh, my God!" she said. "I was expecting anything but that!"

As always, she replied without taking a breath, asking one question after another, having fun, while at the same time thinking about what had to be done.

"I have made a decision," I declared. "There is not much to be done. From now on, I don't care what happens. I'm not going hide anything from anyone."

"They will make you unhappy," Ayla said. "Many people have love affairs, but they do it secretly. Does your relationship with Fuat have a future? If it doesn't, why act so crazily?"

"I don't know," I said. "I can't go on living like this. I thought I could lead my usual life, but I can't. I don't know if Fuat will always be there, but even if he isn't, my feelings won't change. They will always stay with me."

We sat on a bench.

A couple of boys with cowboy hats and water pistols were chasing another boy wearing an Indian headdress with feathers.

As soon as they spotted a candy seller, they ran towards him, screaming like crazy.

A little farther away, people were fishing in colorful rowboats bobbing on the water.

"Whatever you decide to do, I'll always be with you and support you."

I took her hand in mine. Her palms were chapped and calloused like the hands of people who till the land.

"I know," I said. "No one else will be beside me."

The sun was so bright that it hurt the eyes to look at its reflection on the water's surface. Autumn was just around the corner, but the weather was still summery: scorching, humid, and oppressive.

"How bizarre," I said. "Since leaving this country, I've only returned on distressing occasions. It's like a curse! First, I came because my father was dying, and now for this."

"Let's pray that this is the last distressing thing we will have to face. Now, forget about all this and tell me what you're planning to do after we solve this problem? Are you going to go back home to your husband?"

For a moment, I was stunned and unable to answer. At that moment, I really did not know what I would do later. I had not thought about it yet.

"I suppose I'll go back. What else can I do?" Yet his obscure future scared me. It would not be easy.

After a few minutes silence, Ayla said, "I'd like to ask you something." She sounded as if she were seeking permission. When she noticed that I looked at her curiously, she continued, "No one knows about your pregnancy. Maybe . . . How can I say it? I mean, you actually haven't spent too much time together. Right?"

"No, we haven't? Carry on."

"Why don't you continue like this for a while. Sometimes a person becomes lost in a kind of magic only to find out later that what she believed to be true was in fact totally different."

As she finished, her voice lost its strength.

"I mean . . ."

"I know what you mean. I also know that you're saying this because you want me to be alright. In fact, I have already given much thought to what you have just suggested. Who knows, maybe the whole thing will turn out to be just like you've described."

"No, I don't mean that. All I'm saying is that the relationship might turn out to be different than you think. But no one can know this now."

"You don't want me to do something I will regret later." I said. "But I cannot go on like this. You don't know how hard it is. To be honest, my marriage cannot go on, whether Fuat exists in my life or not. Perhaps you were right. I'm not the right person to lead a marriage based solely on reason. I have also understood this recently."

"At least, you should ask his opinion," Ayla said. "Maybe he will have something to say, too."

"Whose opinion? Fuat's? Whether I'll get divorced or not is none of his business. You know that I don't ask people's opinions when I make a decision."

"Oh, yes," Ayla replied, in a complaining tone. "I certainly know that." Then she added, "Alright, it's not the end of the world, is it? You can get divorced from your husband. So what! You don't have any children. It'll be easy."

"I wish I'd divorced him before all of this happened."

"What I worry about is not the divorce but the possibility of people finding about this whole complicated event. You were angry with me a few minutes ago, but did you think about what you are going to tell your husband? Will Fuat want you to tell your husband the truth? That's why I said you should ask Fuat's opinion, too."

I thought for a moment.

This was our secret. Would Fuat approve of me revealing the whole story to my husband before I asked Fuat's opinion? Was it right to make this decision on my own? Not only my life but Fuat's, too, would be affected.

"I really don't know," I said. "I don't want to think about this now. First let me solve this problem in the next few days, and then I'll think about it."

"Doesn't your mother suspect anything?"

"No. She has missed me so much that I don't think she would object even if I told her that from now on I'll stay here with her."

"If you're going to tell her, please do it after I leave. I really don't want to be around then. You know I don't enjoy dramas."

"Out of the question," I said laughing. "You are my accomplice.

If we are going to be hanged, we're going to be hanged by the same rope!"

She laughed loudly as usual.

"Since you can still amuse yourself like this, I guess you can also manage to speak with her on your own. Until the end, I will deny having known about it! I have not heard or seen anything. Have you forgotten that I was digging in the earth like a mole?"

"Has all that digging accomplished anything at all?"

"Of course it has. At least, I've discovered that what you have just told me is nothing new. The same emotions, troubles, and pains existed 2500 years ago."

"You mean the love story you mentioned in your letter?"

"Yes. It is perhaps the oldest love story ever recorded."

"Please tell me it had a happy ending."

"Well, I can't say anything at the moment because I still haven't deciphered it fully. But don't worry. Everything will be revealed soon."

"I know you are in a hurry to go back," I said, "but if I were you, I wouldn't miss the scene I will cause. Watching victims is always exciting."

She must not have liked the word "victim," because she fell silent for a few minutes, as if all her joy had vanished.

Finally, she said, "Such a long time has passed. It never occurred to us that we would leave the garden of childhood so soon?"

The children around us were sitting on the ground, enjoying colorful candy paste rolled around sticks, while listening to the candy seller singing a funny song as he played his tambourine.

After everything happened and the baby was gone, I spent the night with Ayla in her parents' summer home on one of the Princes Islands. We told our families we would spend the night together with a few friends, as we used to in the past. We left home early in the morning and returned the next day in the evening. We had lied like high school girls.

I hate to remember that day. Perhaps because it was one of the most stifling, dreary days I've ever lived.

Even if I wanted to, I wouldn't be able to remember it clearly.

Lying on a clean bed, thankfully, I closed my eyes in a room so dirty that one would not even want to touch the cracked walls, in an old apartment building in a distant district, promising myself that it would soon be over and that I would never remember this place or the people around me.

I almost forget all those details. Everything about that place, which I never saw again, was obliterated from my memory except for the heavy iron door that had welcomed me in the first place.

I was later told that I was crying when I regained consciousness. I don't know why I cried, because I had woken up from a completely confusing dream.

On one hand I felt happy and relieved, but on the other, I felt like I had been cast into indescribable gloom.

After spending almost the entire afternoon sleeping, I woke up, and Ayla and I had some fish for dinner on the balcony. We chatted for hours, and my eyes filled with tears each time I remembered the past. I guess the older I got the more I resembled my mother.

The next day, I both rested and wandered around the island, which I had missed so much. We toured the island in a horse-drawn carriage, walked in the forest, and drank tea near the shore.

We woke up the following morning, and the fabulous light of an Istanbul summer day, the chirping of the birds, the scent of flowers, and a gentle breeze in the warm sun were enough to drive away all troubles.

We were in the final days of summer.

I kept telling myself that no matter where I went, I belonged to this city and only here would I find the peace I needed.

With lollipops in our hands, we got in the horse-drawn carriage, which was decorated with tassels and words painted in poor handwriting: "neither the poet weeps, nor the lover sheds tears/ old loves have long been forgotten."

"Why didn't he use the other poem?" said Ayla. "It would have been more suitable for this carriage."

Suddenly, we were swept back to our school days. Dressed in uniforms and with our hair tied at the back, we were in Mrs. Mübeccel's class. I pictured myself in front of the blackboard reciting the other long poem I had memorized: "The first pain, the first separation resembling the first love,/The air is warm with the fire my heart has lit."

"Don't talk to me about poems. I feel awful," Ayla objected, "as if I'll have to give an oral examination. We used to feel that we would be executed if we couldn't answer the teacher's questions. How wrong!"

"Of course you felt afraid, because you dawdled around instead of studying," I teased.

"Some nights, I still dream about being called to the front of the class for an oral exam, and I wake up gasping and sweating!"

The way she knocked on wood to protect herself, as if it were really possible to become a child again and go back to the classroom, made us laugh heartily.

"You know, I really would love to go back in time and become a student again, to see your frowning face, still half-asleep, and to climb that hill together while breathing on our hands to warm them up. I really would like that."

She hugged me, and I put my head on her shoulder.

"Don't take me seriously," she said. "I also miss those days. I long for the days we rode our bikes side by side, the evenings I came to your place to study with you, the endless nights we spent chatting and giggling. Don't you know I also miss them?"

"Pray that the future does not cause us to miss this day."

The old carriage driver with a bushy moustache shouted at the horses, cracked his whip, rang the bell in his hand, and exchanged a few words with the drivers of other carriages we passed on the way.

As we rode bouncing through the pines, passing white mansions with wild vegetation in their gardens, I asked myself why we had such a hard time understanding the real meaning of what life offered us.

Later, on the evening ferry taking us back to the mainland, I was pleased and even smiled.

I was still confused, but my former distress had been replaced by indifference and a slight, sweet drowsiness.

As I gazed at the sea, I thought of him, Fuat. He was unaware of what I had gone through, and he would never find out about it. Inside me, I knew that if he had been told about my pregnancy, he would have wanted me to have the baby. Yes, he definitely would have.

He would have been very angry if he had found out what I had done.

For a moment, I caught myself imagining myself trying to choose a name for the baby with him. For some reason, it felt quite impossible. The image of him with his legs crossed, a cigarette in his hand, searching through magazines for children's clothing made me grin. He didn't fit into such a domestic picture. I had never imagined the two of us married and sharing a home.

They were selling hermit crabs on the wharf. Walking through the crowd, I inhaled the smell of Istanbul. The scents, sounds, commotion, red sky, and shimmering copper-colored sea all blended together.

On the way to my mother's house, I pretended to listen to Ayla, yet my mind was elsewhere. I was wondering where he was. Was he trying to reach me?

One part of me thought everything between us was over, whereas the other part said he would reappear in my life unexpectedly and that it was impossible for our madness to come to an abrupt end.

I had thought about many possible answers to the questions on my mind, but he surprised me once again.

When we retuned home, my mother opened the door with a queer expression on her face. For a moment, I held my breath, frightened that she had found about everything. But she was strangely joyful and happy.

When we entered the house, she said, "Come inside, girls, and see what we have here."

As we stepped into the living room, we saw a small Siamese kitten sleeping in a wicker basket, with a red ribbon around its neck—such a small little thing, covered with creamy silver hair, except on its head and tail, which had darker patches with a purplish shadow.

"Where on earth did this come from?" Ayla exclaimed.

"I don't know. I suppose my daughter can answer that question."

"Is it for me?" I asked in surprise, feeling Ayla's gaze. We had both realized at the same time who had sent it. Who else could it be but Fuat? I blushed as if I were on fire.

"A driver brought it here," my mother said, "and he left this message for you. He also mentioned a name, Sevim, or something similar."

She gave me a small, sealed envelope.

Thankfully, Nihat had not been at home. He would have asked the driver a thousand questions and wrangled information out of him.

Fuat's fearlessness had always bewildered me.

Thousands of things passed through my mind, but I was at a loss as to what to do. Ayla picked up the kitten and put it close to her chest. It woke up and struggled to get down, perhaps to its basket.

My mother scanned my face, expecting an explanation. I tried very hard to choose the right words in order not to make a mess of everything.

"Oh, so Ms. Sevim has sent this little thing. What a woman! She has always promised that when her cat gave birth one of the kittens would be mine. So she must have heard I'm in Istanbul and sent it!"

Ayla did her best not to break into laughter. She didn't respond to my helpless glances begging for help.

She even teased me secretly by saying, "I wish I could have one of the other kittens. Maybe if you asked, she would give me one, too."

I said, "I'll wash my hands and freshen up," and rushed out of the room.

In the bathroom, I opened, or rather tore open the envelope. My hands were trembling so badly that I thought I would never manage to open it.

Just to be on the safe side, probably in case my mother opened the envelope, he had written the message in English.

"Young lady, I know I'm guilty, but I suddenly found myself on the other end of the world. I was planning to run away and come to you when the delegation was going there, but it didn't work out as I had planned. We've been touring from one coast to another, and we're exhausted. When I came back to the Turkey, I learned that you were in Istanbul. You know that I'm quick to pick up news. Wherever I went or whatever I did when I was abroad, I thought of you. Even in the farthest corner of the world, you were with me. Do you remember that we once saw a woman sitting with a Siamese cat around her neck? You adored that cat. When I saw this little kitten during my trip, I couldn't help getting it. If you train it, you can also carry it around your neck. Tomorrow I'm expecting you at the Pera Palas Hotel at 11 a.m. If you don't come, I have nothing against coming over and having a cup of tea with your mother. P.S.: Don't think that it's just any Siamese cat; it was a real king who gave it to me as a gift."

After so much trouble, heartache and fear, this short note made my day and turned my world upside down.

How I had lied to myself! I had promised myself that I wouldn't care even if he didn't call me again. I would start all over again, and if our relationship was really over, I wouldn't call him again either. But all of this had evaporated. I had forgotten about everything, all my promises and decisions, as soon as I saw his scribbled handwriting and strange signature that looked like a seal.

We would go to bed and sleep tonight, and when the morning broke, I would see him; he would embrace me and tell me so many things with enthusiasm. Again, I would forget all that I wanted to tell him, and just listen with my eyes locked on the most beautiful eyes in the world.

I felt like a little child who cannot grasp that he will finally go somewhere he can't wait to see, and asks, "So we will go to sleep, wake up, and go there, right?"

Yes, it was already long-gone for me. I felt that all the bad things were over. All those horrible days that I had wanted to end were over. He would be beside me tomorrow. Suddenly, I realized again that no matter what I kept telling to myself, no matter what I thought, there was only a single place I wanted to be: beside him.

I returned to the living room to find my mother and Ayla playing with the kitten. They had a small ball of yarn, and the kitten was running from one corner to the other trying to catch it. Scurrying about, it lost its balance, and toppled over. The way it rolled on the floor, caught its tail instead of the ball, and appeared baffled was extremely cute.

"How lovable it is!" exclaimed my mother. "I have never seen a cat of this color before. Obviously, it is a pure breed."

"Of course. These used to be the holy animals of ancient Egypt," Ayla said. "The cats of the kings. Even tombs were made for them, and they were all mummified after they died."

"Cats, too?" My mother was astounded.

"Yes, Aunty. And everyone was terribly surprised when they opened the tombs and discovered thousands of cat mummies."

"Good God!" mother said. "A pharoah's mind! Ayla, dear, are you sure this one does not possess magical powers?"

"Come on, Mother!" I said. "Don't pay attention to Ayla. She's talking about ancient times. Look at this poor thing. Does it look like a magician?"

Then I winked at Ayla and said, "But, obviously it's a king's cat. Look how noble it is."

"If it is a king's cat, then it should have stayed where it was born," my mother responded. "What are we going to do with it? How are you going to take it home? Don't look at me like that! You know that I don't want any animals in my house."

"So, can't I take it home? Of course, I can. It will be my little companion. Besides, I'm bored to death back at home."

"We have to give it a name then," said Ayla. "We can't keep on calling it 'kitty, kitty.'"

The first names that came to mind were either too difficult to say, too long, or too ordinary. My mother suggested common cat names such as "Tabby" or "Misty." Ayla proposed the names of kings or queens.

In the end, my mother said, "Let's call it 'Lilac' so that its name fits its color."

A moment later, Lilac was on my lap, trying to hide herself under my arm, and licking my neck as she fell asleep and began to purr.

In fact, I wasn't very interested in animals, but I had felt a sudden affection for this kitten as soon as it made itself comfortable in my lap.

"Look at the sweet little devil!" my mother said. "How she got used to her owner as if she knows to whom she was sent—although it was I who fed it milk since it arrived!"

"Lilac thinks she is her mother," Ayla said.

For a moment our eyes met.

It was strange that Fuat had sent this little baby on that day, as if he knew of my loss.

Exactly on that day.

How incredible!

How quickly time had passed.

Now, I was walking alone in the Beyoğlu district, which used to be a fairground in my childhood fantasies, with its movie theaters, toy stores, hawkers, vivid market places, and strange crowds that resembled a conglomerate of a thousand faces; however, I was a grown-up woman now.

I felt like both a woman and a child, experiencing the different images and sounds pertaining to those two worlds of senses.

Near a movie theater, two people dressed as aliens were engaged in conversation with passers-by, trying to promote a new film.

When I entered the passageway lined with shops, I suddenly felt as if I were transported back to the old days when my mother spent hours in the hat shops, button sellers, and tailors' workshops. The coolness of the place caressed my face.

I had not been here for such a long time, but I hadn't forgotten a single detail.

I remembered the days when I used to sit and wait among the colorful buttons, thread, and cloth, with the promise of going to a gigantic toy store full of dolls where I would lose myself in joy.

In those days, they used to sell paper dolls. You could cut out various pieces of clothing from a book and put them on the paper doll. My mother would always buy one for me when we came to this district.

The slightly murky, cluttered atmosphere of the shops selling lemonade, tea, and ice-cream, where everyone inquired after each other, had not changed much.

I looked into the passageway and saw a few women wearing hats with thin veils in front of their faces. They were standing in a cobblestone courtyard and making small talk. Some women in a hairdresser's shop on the corner were reading magazines, with their heads in those enormous chimney-like dryers.

I looked at the signs on the movie theaters. I used to think the theaters were much bigger. Somebody bumped into me as he passed by. He didn't even say excuse me.

The bookshop of Mr. Artin, who was famous for his angry behavior and the way he easily found whatever you were looking for from among a huge pile of books, had unfortunately closed down.

Churches, embassies, jewelry shops with their glittering windows . . .

I couldn't seem to remember where some shops from the past were located. I couldn't find them. Perhaps their owners had handed them over to others and left. After the incidents of a few years go, when a mob destroyed and plundered properties belonging to the minorities, many had left this country.

But the old Greek man's shop, which sold the most beautiful gifts, and where a music box covered with blue velvet, a snow globe, or a porcelain doll decorated the window, was still open.

Fuat's birthday was in a few days.

I entered the gift shop. It needed much effort to find something in the fully packed shelves although the shop window was quite empty and simple. Finally, I decided to buy a black fountain pen with a green line around the body and a gold top. The shop owner, who looked chic enough to go to a ball in his tie, vest, glasses, and watch on a chain, took out a special case from underneath the counter.

"The pen must be usable as soon as it is taken out of its case," I said.

"Don't worry, madam," the old man replied, filling the pen with ink slowly and cleaning its head with a small handkerchief.

He placed the pen in the case with the utmost care, wrapped the box nicely, tied a white silk ribbon around it, and put it in a small red velvet pouch.

I wrote on a small piece of paper, "From now on you might perhaps write those unequaled letters of yours with this pen. Happy birthday." Then I slipped the paper into the pouch. The old man accompanied me to the door and bid me good-bye.

After I left the shop, I walked a little and soon found myself in front of the pastry shop I used to visit with my mother, aunt, and grandmother each time we came here.

In one corner of the shop window, there were white tulips in a crystal vase, and in the other, red ones. But what didn't leave my mind was the candied fruit. (Too bad they no longer produce the same kind today.) Shining, glacé figs and oranges in fancy paper—almost like a painting.

Thankfully, what I hoped to see in the shop was still intact. The paintings on the walls depicting the seasons had not changed. I felt excited as I opened the door and entered. I was swept into the past. Smart women, who had probably stopped in after shopping, were sitting at a table and chatting quite loudly. A man with a big belly was reading his newspaper at another table. A man and a woman were whispering to each at a table in the corner, they paused to look at me for a moment and then went back to their conversation. I listened to the music: a woman's voice singing "Moliendo Café."

I walked to the counter. The aged saleswomen did not recognize me, and I didn't tell them who I was. As they prepared my order, I took out my small black powder case and looked at myself in the mirror. I powdered my cheeks and tidied my hair.

Then I left the shop, carrying a package of candied figs.

A strapping young man whose cap was too small for his head greeted me as soon as I entered the hotel. As if sure of who I was, he said, "Here madam, the gentleman is waiting for you."

I followed him without saying a word. We climbed the marble stairs and turned right.

At a distant corner of the bar, he was talking with a short, stocky man whose back was facing me. I hesitated for a moment, but the lad had already taken the lead and was walking toward Fuat, with excitement and pride having fulfilled his duty. I followed him. When the short, stocky man saw that Fuat was looking in my direction, he turned around to look, and when I came beside them, he quickly and shyly asked for permission to leave. I thought I knew this fat bald man with a thin moustache from the past, but I couldn't remember who he was.

I thought he would extend his hand before he left, but he didn't and rushed out without shaking anyone's hand, as if he were taking pains not to look us in the eye.

Fuat turned to me and held my shoulders. He scanned my face with a smile illuminating his face.

"Finally!" he said. "So you have come all the way to this city but haven't informed me! You will certainly have to make up for it. But first, take a seat, please."

I sat on one of the light brown armchairs with dark red stripes. I was sitting near the window with my back to the door. Looking through the thin curtains, I could barely see outside. The bar was empty except for the bellboy who had brought me in and a waiter in a white uniform.

After ordering a glass of fruit juice, I said, "You never know who you will have to make excuses to. We had better leave the settling of these old scores for another time."

He was bewildered.

"By the way, who is the gentleman that left? I think I recognised him."

"Mr. Abdülhak Şinasi", Fuat said. "A man who is one of a kind. Haven't you read his books?"

"I see," I replied. "Of course I have read his books. I wish I had known who he was. I like his work. He didn't even want to shake my hand."

"He usually doesn't. He doesn't enjoy shaking hands. He's somewhat of a hypochondriac. But why are your cheeks flushed? Did you walk a long way?"

"Yes," I said. "I left home early and walked. I haven't been to Beyoğlu for such a long time. I've missed being here. I recalled the past—my childhood, my mother, my grandmother. The weather is pleasant, but when you walk too much, it becomes hot."

"So how did you like our little kitten?"

"She's very cute. She doesn't want to leave my arms. We called her Lilac. I can't believe you carried her all the way here."

"The others carried suitcases filled with useless junk, as if they had been shopping for the first time. It wasn't too much to carry a little thing like that!"

"I was shocked when I came home and my mother showed it to me. How did you know I was here?"

He laughed. Then he opened his silver cigarette case, offered me a cigarette, and took one for himself. He lit my cigarette and said, "It wasn't difficult, but I was worried when I couldn't reach you at first. You have come alone. I hope nothing bad has happened."

A long time had passed since we had last met. We hadn't even talked on the phone for a long while. Perhaps that was why we both felt a bit distant and were unable to re-establish the warmth of the past. We spoke to each other as if we were just acquaintances.

"No, nothing is wrong. I missed my mother, and I was bored. So I came to spend some time here."

I would not tell him the real reason.

What happened in my life was my own business. He had to remain outside. He shouldn't fear that my life would fall to pieces just because he was in love with me. No, I didn't want him to have such feelings.

Suddenly, everything was right before my eyes, resembling the clear weather that had enabled me to see the entire city, even the faraway Princes Islands.

Fuat had found an unexpected happiness in his life. A dream. A fantasy. A reality, perhaps, but one whose best sides alone were perceptible. Call it what you want. Now, did I have the right to mar that perfect feeling or cause it to resemble other ordinary feelings?

Was this what he wanted from me?

No, it wasn't. If I asked him this question, he would of course tell me something else, but I was sure of the real answer. At least he should be able to make the most of that happiness and excitement without the shadow of tiresome problems.

I had tried to establish a planned life for myself, but had failed.

Everything that I had thought was sound and secure was shattering.

Something I hadn't planned or was aware of in the beginning had brought him to me, and I had let myself go with the magic of this coincidence.

Now, I would forget all the rules, ideas, and opinions and words of others, in short, everything I had learned until now.

Yes, I would forget them—at least this time.

I would also do as I wished and not hesitate wondering what he was thinking. Unlike other women, I would not expect him to do things for me and become despondent when my expectations were not fulfilled. Like me, he would also follow the way of his will.

If destiny had brought us together (I had such strange mystical thoughts on my mind), and if the thing between us was as real as I thought it was, it could only bring us happiness and joy.

"You seem distracted," he said.

I really was lost in thought.

"Aren't you happy to see me?"

I was afraid that the few people around could hear me because there was no other sound in the room except our voices and very soft music from a radio.

I whispered, "Of course I'm happy. I was also worried about you. You suddenly disappeared. Bad thoughts entered my mind, but now they are gone. Now, here . . ."

"I know," he said abruptly. "Shall we go out and walk a little?"

I looked at him in disbelief, and he started laughing. Patting my knee gently, he said, "Okay, that wasn't a good idea, but I'd love to go to the movies with you."

"Sure," I said. "That's an even better idea! They're showing a film with Grace Kelly at the Saray Movie Theater."

I opened my handbag and took out his present.

"For me? It looks like something nice."

As I was taking out the case from the pouch, the note I had written fell on the table. He read it.

"So you didn't forget my birthday. Even I had forgotten it."

Then he opened the case and saw the fountain pen.

"It's very beautiful," he said. "Really beautiful."

"Test it," I said.

He picked up a small paper from the table and wrote something on it. Then he turned it around for me to read.

"Each time I see you, I forget everything else. Everything disappears but the desire to embrace you, to have you in my arms, and to kiss you. I miss you wherever I go. When I can't talk to you, I always feel as if I have forgotten something, but I don't remember what I have forgotten. I have fallen in love with you!"

When I read the words he wrote down, I couldn't help taking the pen from him and writing, "I have also fallen in love with you. This is a feeling I haven't known before. That's why I am so confused. I flutter my wings like a butterfly who doesn't care where it is going, but at the same time, I feel the urge to perch upon something. I wrote so many letters to you, but always tore them up. I don't know what I will do . . ."

As I extinguished my cigarette, he lit another one. He turned the paper on the glass table top and read it. Although I wasn't looking at his face, I felt he was trying to see the expression in my eyes. I put down the pen.

He picked it up and began writing. I was able to read what he wrote in his jumbled handwriting even though I was looking at it in reverse. "Tell me what you want, and we'll do it. I don't care about anything else anymore. If you want, we can leave this place hand in hand and walk the entire street. We can let everyone see us. Let them all know about us. Whatever will happen should happen."

He quickly turned the paper around for me to read.

As he smoked, I read his words and felt happy, but still, I realized that this was but a mere wish he lived upon.

For a moment, it also crossed my mind to tell him, "Let's leave this place and go and start a brand new life together."

But I wrote, "I am old enough to know that we can't do that. Do not ask me anything now, but I will tell you a single thing, and that is: I don't want to tell lies anymore. I'm going back home in a couple of days. After that, we can talk again."

As soon as he read these lines, he studied my face, trying to understand what I had meant.

He said, "I'm returning to Ankara tomorrow evening." Then lowering his voice and looking out of the window, he said shyly, "Will you be able to meet me tonight?"

I quickly said no as if I had been awaiting his question all the while and had already prepared the answer. In fact, this wasn't the answer I wanted to give because all I desired was to be alone with him, get rid of this oppressive, formal attitude that enveloped us, kiss his face, embrace him, and spend the night together. All the same, I said, "No. I have to leave now. We'll talk during the coming weeks. Maybe you can come to me. I don't want to talk about all the impossibilities that surround us now."

For a moment, I wished I were with him on the island where I had been the previous day. I wanted to climb into a carriage with him, walk together among the pine trees, and smell the red and blue flowers hanging over the garden walls.

Unfortunately, we were not able to do these things, that lovers do.

We couldn't even go to the movies together. We couldn't walk idly on the streets. Even though I was dying to hold his hand now, I couldn't. Just as I was about blurt out something I wanted to say, I always restrained myself. We were only comfortable in rooms behind closed doors and in places where people did not know us, as if we were besieged by enemies.

This was the reality.

Many times, I felt hopeless and told myself that I should abandon all those dreams and plans, put an end to this secrecy, and finish our clandestine relationship.

But at that moment in the hotel bar, it was not separation that occupied my thoughts. I was thinking that at least one of us (and that was I) had to be free from other bonds. We would not be able to continue this relationship when both of us were in lies up to our necks, and when we had to go back to another person at the end of the day.

He picked up the paper again and wrote, "Don't ever tell me that we should separate. Do whatever you want but don't ask this of me. Please, I'm begging you . . ."

"There will be no separation," I wrote. "We will never separate."

When I wrote those lines, we both believed that we would never be separated.

When he read my words, his face brightened. I stood up. As he kissed me on the cheeks, he thrust a small piece of paper into my hand. "Take this number," he said. "This is my private line. You can call me whenever you want. I'm there day and night. These days, I usually don't go home."

Before I left the room, I turned to look at him one last time. He waved good-bye.

When I left the hotel, I was no longer able to find that little inner child who had accompanied me here. I felt the same pain, the same wringing feeling, and a sense of emptiness mixed with a little joy.

I walked back the same way I had come. Alone.

On summer nights now—when I can hardly sleep—I sit on this terrace and look far into the distance, through the old trees that have somehow survived, and up to the bright stars in the sky above, trying to remember the past.

Memories and stars bear similarities. When you look at them, you see their past images. Just like stars, memories transmit images to us fixed in time.

I wish the opposite were also possible.

If only it were possible to "remember" the future. Then, we could see our future lives just as we could see the past. Knowing the future, we could take steps accordingly.

Would I act differently if I had the chance to live my life again? If I had known what the future would bring, would I have tried as hard as I could to change it?

Sometimes I wonder whether it was because of me that certain things happened later. If I had acted differently, would destiny have taken us to another place in life?

Who knows . . .

Human beings always suffer this conflict: to fulfill their wishes and live their lives as they like, or to remain limited with the lives of other people, the world that surrounds them, and the rules they have been taught.

Regardless of one's knowledge, courage, or life experience, it is not easy to break free from this conflict.

Neither rules nor the words and opinions of others mattered to me. None of them were of the slightest importance.

However, what if somebody else suffers because of your actions, or if your happiness causes sorrow for another?

Just like in that game played with thin wooden sticks, you can't prevent other sticks from moving when it is actually a specific stick you want to pick up. Consequently, you are eliminated from the game.

Who knows, maybe there are such people who can play skillfully, without moving any sticks, or who are not scared of being eliminated. I know that I'm not one of them.

Maybe what I am doing is the worst thing that can be done.

Once, Ayla had told me, "You are always caught between two fires. This conflict is driving you crazy. Choose one of the two options. Whether good or bad, you'll breathe freely."

I had thought she was right, then. Now, however, I know that this approach was not the one for me. I wanted to experience everything at the same time. This was the truth, and I couldn't confess it to anyone, even to myself for many years.

Perhaps we exaggerate this thing about secret affairs and acts of unfaithfulness. We expect two people, who have come together because of a somewhat meaningless coincidence, not to have affection for anybody else for a lifetime, as if their union is the most extraordinary one in the entire world.

When do we do that?

Sometimes starting from childhood.

It is true that I also thought this was possible. I didn't think that building a life for yourself had anything to do with one's feelings.

When you often cannot be completely happy with the one you love, how can you spend so many years with someone you like just a little?

Years ago, after eating dinner on this terrace, Ayla had said, "Maybe the opposite is true. Maybe we can be happy only with someone whom we are not really in love with."

Yes, maybe. She had also said that after she had her child; this was the only true love in life and other love, passion, or the crazy desires of the flesh no longer seemed important to her.

The fact that both of us had come to a point which was totally opposite to where we started had made me laugh.

When I had decided that getting married to a good man and having a happy life was the best route to follow, had she not said it was an act of madness?

Then, she had surprised all of us when she suddenly met someone and married him.

What can one do? No matter how hard I tried to convince myself, it seems that I was not the kind of woman I thought I was.

The life a person plans for himself does not necessarily coincide with what becomes of him.

Perhaps if certain coincidences had not taken place in my life, I would have pretended not to see the signs of distress and be contented to carry on in my small world and, like other women, be happy to raise children and forget about all the other ambitions one can have in life

A feeling that no one who hasn't felt it can know —the inde-scribable grief of hearing the sound of people scraping a living being off you, killing a part of you, killing the future, and changing fate mercilessly—had suddenly made me grow older in those days.

Of course I thought a lot. I thought a lot about it. What would it have been like if I had given birth to that baby? How would my life have been after that child had grown up? How would Fuat's life have been different?

After pondering these questions, I would always tell myself, "Maybe that baby was not destined to be born. This is why it all hap-pened that way."

This is how I used to console myself.

Is it possible to look into the memories of the past, as if observ-ing long-dead stars, and say something meaningful?

A few days after I walked through Beyoğlu from one end to the oth-er, I started to get ready to go home. Actually, my mother did not have any intention of letting me go. Each time Turgut phoned, she insisted that he come, while trying to prevent him from asking me to return home.

One day mother and I went to the Covered Bazaar in the old part of the city. We were sipping our morning coffee when she said, "My dear girl, you know that I don't want you to go, but this trip has already been too long. It's not good to leave a man on his own for such a long time."

I tried to break in before she could continue. I couldn't keep playing this game. "Mother . . ." I said, as I finished my coffee.

But she cut me off, saying, "Turn over your coffee cup. Let me tell your fortune."

I turned over the cup, placed it on the saucer, and slowly rotated it in my hand.

"Don't play with it too much. The figures will mix with each other," she said it as if my fate would also be upside down if I turned the cup too much.

"Mother, I want to tell you something," I said, as I put the cup and saucer on the small coffee table, adding in the most natural tone, "I've decided to divorce my husband."

She covered her mouth with her hand as if trying to prevent an involuntary scream.

"Don't worry," I continued. "It will be best for everyone. I've come to realize that our marriage cannot go on, no matter how hard I try."

"Oh, my dear! I've sensed something was going on, but . . ."

Had she really sensed it? In those days, the word "divorce" was not pronounced as easily as today. Now, I understand better how sad my poor mother was that day. Still, she didn't react the way I thought she would.

"Why don't you stay here a little longer and think everything over. What does Turgut say about this? Did you make this decision together?"

"He doesn't know about it yet, mother, but as soon as I go back, I'm going to tell him."

She was confused.

"You mean you've decided on your own?"

"Yes. Didn't I decide to get married on my own, too?"

She looked at the floor for a second, as if she felt guilty about my marriage.

"Did he do something bad to you?" she asked, and then

continued in a worried tone, "Or . . ."

"No, Mother." I said. "There's no other woman, and he didn't do anything to me. He has always been nice, always respectful, but this is not a business contract, is it? Being nice or respectful is not enough. I don't love him. I mean, of course I love him, but not as a husband. How can I explain? Please don't ask any more questions. I've been troubled for so long."

"Your behavior hinted at a problem. I thought you two might have quarreled but that it would soon be over. When he called every day, I had thought . . ."

"Yes, he calls every day, but he has no idea about my decision. I don't know how I'm going to tell him. The more I think about it, the worse I feel."

"Wouldn't it be better if you two sat down and talked about it?"

"What can we do, mother?" I said. "If it's meant to happen."

"But you're still so young," she said. "You don't have a child yet. You were always living so far away. When taking such a decision, you should look at it from all angles. Why don't you discuss it with your brother too?"

"I have made up my mind," I said. "I don't want to talk about it with too many people. I can tell my brother, but I'm not going to change my mind. Don't be unhappy. It's worse to drag something out."

"If that is how it really is, there's not much to do," mother said as she stood up. "Let's hope for the best. You know best what to do for yourself."

She must have imagined that one day I would come to visit her with little grandsons and granddaughters and that she would be able to watch them grow. Instead, she had received news that she had never wanted to hear. She was very sad, but tried hard to conceal it.

Her final words touched me deeply. My eyes filled with tears, yet I was smiling inside.

So did I really know what was best for me?

I wish I had!

Truthfully, I probably needed my fortune told the most at that moment, but the cup on the coffee table was forgotten.

That night, my brother Nihat learned about the whole thing. He was unperturbed. I suddenly realized that they either did not care about what had worn me down, or they were acting as if it wasn't important to them. Moreover, they were surprised that my marriage had lasted this long. Perhaps my father's death had caused them to see another aspect of life, making them think that a life based on strict rules was insecure.

Even without knowing the details, Nihat immediately supported me. Maybe both my mother and brother thought that an unmentionable mistake—a secret affair, or immoral behavior on Turgut's part—were possible reasons.

In fact, no one had expected me to get involved in an unpleasant situation like this.

Nihat said, "You can live here with us. If you want, we can even find you a job. A girl like you who can speak two languages can easily find work."

"Of course, she will live here," mother said. "The biggest mistake was that she left in the first place."

At that time, I still wasn't able to plan for my future. I really didn't know what would happen or what I would do. How could I turn into a child again? I had led a totally different life for years. I was used to a life of freedom, doing or saying what I wanted. I had established a home on the other side of the world, moved it many times, and reestablished it. Returning to my family and becoming a part of their life, or being confined in their small world, would not be easy. The people who visited this house, people I happened to meet, distant relatives, and old friends, all seemed like people I could not stand to spend more than a few hours with. If they stayed too long, I became bored and began to wonder when they would leave. Too bad that Ayla wasn't here all the time.

"Do you want me to go back with you?" Nihat asked later when we were alone.

"Don't worry," I said. "I can manage. It'll be a little unpleasant, but I can handle it."

He was concerned but tried to pretend it was a joke in order not upset me.

"Do you remember the night I asked how one can go to America?" I asked.

"Of course I do," he said. "You had already decided to marry before that night, hadn't you?"

I laughed.

"How angry you were with me," I said, "and now it's turned out that you were right."

"How fast the years go by. I wish I hadn't been right."

"I always wanted to grow up as fast as possible, didn't I?" I asked. "But it seems that growing up isn't that nice."

He held my hand. "Don't worry or be sad. I will always be with you no matter what happens."

"No matter what happens, Nihat?"

He studied my face as if he had sensed what had happened and what would happen in the future.

"Yes," he said. "No matter what happens."

And he kept his word. He was, and is, always with me.

When the plane landed and I saw Turgut at the airport with a huge bouquet in his hand, my self-confidence vanished.

This separation had done me good and helped me collect my thoughts. On the plane journey back, I had finished everything, at least in my head. I did not see Turgut as a husband anymore. What annoyed me the most was that he didn't even suspect my decision, and that he kept saying how much he missed me in every conversation we had.

I felt that making this decision on my own was my biggest betrayal.

Because of his kisses, I felt so bad that I couldn't tell him anything on the way home. I had never become used to the extraordinary way he showed his affection for me.

I still don't know how two people with totally opposite expectations can be together.

Besides, in my opinion, I was the guilty one, and telling a man who loved me about my decision was not easy.

When I was in Istanbul, I had thought that many things actually disturbed him.

He was not stupid. Although I tried my best not to let him suspect anything, he must have realized something was the matter from my cold behavior.

Perhaps he wasn't surprised since we had always had an inexplicable wall between us since the day we were married.

Maybe he thought my behavior was because I was bored with marriage.

It was then that I realized how he implied certain things every now and then. Once, for instance, we saw a film about an unhappy marriage. We had wanted to see it because Marlon Brando was the lead actor.

After the film, Turgut had said, "I can't understand how marriage can turn into hellish torture. If people respect each other, and love one another even a little, marriage enables them to have an orderly life."

"Yes, but perhaps some people don't want such order in their lives," I said.

"Everyone likes order," he replied. "When you're young, one can live on thrills, but when you get older, you want someone who will always be beside you. For me, loving someone is something that is within our control."

In Istanbul, I had remembered these words.

Maybe he had tried to tell me that I needed to try harder. For him, love was something earned.

I must confess that for a moment, I wanted to jump out of the car bringing us into the city and go back to Istanbul. I hardly stopped myself from doing it. I regretted not having finalized everything by writing him a letter from Istanbul, as Ayla had advised. Would it have been a vile act? In fact, what I had done in secret was vile.

We left my suitcase at home and went out to dinner. He had reserved a table in one of the fish restaurants I liked. It was a little too expensive for our budget, so we only used to go there when we had important guests or on special occasions such as anniversaries and birthdays. Even today, I still dislike New Year's Eve, birthdays, and other celebrations.

Instead of being happy, I was annoyed.

Obviously, he had worked out a plan to put our marriage into order again, thinking that we would both think about it during our time apart. He had in fact sent me to Istanbul because he sensed my unhappiness and without talking about our problems. He believed arguments, quarrels, and being too informal were things that could harm a marriage.

He accused himself of not having taken enough care of me and spending more time with me like he used to in the States, even though he had realized I was lonely.

I excused myself by saying the long way back to home from the airport had tired me and insisted that I wasn't hungry because I wanted dinner to finish as soon as possible. We only had some lobster and a glass of wine each.

Distress, fear, and a horrible pang of conscience clenched my heart, as if I were about to commit a murder.

For a moment, I even asked myself if I should change my mind, or at least postpone the discussion until the following day and create a reason to argue with him and then blurt it all out.

But it was not easy to start a fight with him. Besides, I thought that if I didn't conclude everything that evening, I would never pluck up courage to do it later.

He was so nice and sweet to me that I thought he had realized how much he loved and missed me when I was away.

The more he told me such things, the harder it would get for me. If the distance created between us by being separated for many weeks disappeared, I would never be able to talk about my decision.

I couldn't wait much longer. Whether it ended well or badly, I wanted to conclude everything once and for all.

He continuously asked about Turkey, Istanbul, and the political situation. I was almost tongue-tied. I felt like a total stranger in this wonderful square in this foreign city, in these streets and among this crowd as if I had never been there before and that it was my first visit.

He interpreted my silence and confusion as jet lag.

Although it was a little cold outside, I wanted to walk home.

When we reached our house, it looked dreary and unfamiliar. I opened the windows and turned on all the lights. The desk was covered with books and papers. Apparently, he had gone out for dinner every day and then worked upon returning home. The house was immaculate. I imagined how hard it would be for him to live alone in this place. He must have hated being alone at home while I was away.

I realized how weary I was after I took off my high-heeled shoes. I wanted to go and change first, as usual, but then I changed my mind. I just washed my hands and face and felt better immediately. I felt that if I stayed in these clothes, I would be able to talk to him more seriously.

I sat in an armchair in the living room. Newspapers had accumulated. Turgut appeared in his dressing gown and slippers. He first turned on the radio and then made himself comfortable opposite me with a drink he had prepared.

I was surprised.

"Is this a new habit of yours?" I said smiling.

"Not really," he said. "This is to honor your return."

I looked around the room.

"The place is spotless," I said.

He thought I was teasing him.

"This is all I could do when the lady of the house was away. I tried my best, but still."

"No, no. Everything is sparkling," I said. "I could never understand how you manage to be so clean and tidy."

"Don't ask," he replied. "I'm not a man who can manage to live on his own. This time, I was sure of it. I felt so bored. I didn't even want to come home in the evening."

Noticing my silence, he said, "Why don't you go to bed early tonight? You look so tired. We can talk tomorrow."

There was a live broadcast on the radio. The song "Autumn Leaves" was playing.

For a second, I wondered whether I should really go to bed, but then, plucking up courage, I said, "I want to talk about something with you."

His crossed his legs, he was making the ice cubes in his glass slowly melt away. "I'm listening," he said,

"The truth is that I went to Istanbul because of something I couldn't tell you before."

Astounded, he stared at me.

"I couldn't tell you about it. What I did is an unjust and dishonorable act."

He was even more bewildered. With a frown on his face, he tensely waited for me to continue.

I had thought about how I would tell him everything for such a long time, but now, when he was sitting right there in front of me, I couldn't decide how to start.

"You will probably never forgive me, and if you ask me, I can't forgive myself. I don't how it all started, but I couldn't hold myself back no matter how hard I tried."

He slowly put his glass on the table.

"What are you talking about!" he said.

"I had an affair with Fuat. I got pregnant and went to Istanbul to have an abortion."

The music was the only sound in the room.

I still don't remember how I managed to blurt it all out.

Yet, saying it any other way was not possible. Each part of what I told him was worse than the other, so perhaps I had tried to say everything at once to make it seem like a single big fault.

He stared at me and then looked at the floor, studying the designs on the carpet.

I wasn't sure of what would follow. I couldn't imagine his reaction after such a confession. Would he shout at me, hit me, leave the house, or just show me the door?

But he just remained sitting, motionless. A few seconds passed but the silence made it feel like an eternity.

Finally, he asked, "When did this happen?"

His eyes were still on the ground, and his voice cracked.

"A few weeks before I left for Istanbul."

"So he came here, right?"

I said, "Yes," hoping he wouldn't ask for more details.

"Were you drunk?"

It was my turn to be astonished. He knew very well that I didn't drink more than a few glasses of alcohol.

"No," I said. "I never get drunk. You know that." In the meantime, I heard many voices in my head. They were telling me to say I had been drunk, unconscious, and to make up an excuse.

Finally, he said, "Is there anything else you want to say?"

I said, "Actually, I was thinking of writing all this in a letter, but I decided to come here instead. You have a right to spit in my face."

He looked at me. His expression was not of loathing or hatred. He just looked shocked, worried, and drained.

"If anyone else had told me this, I wouldn't have believed it," he said. "What shall I tell you now?"

I said, "Fuat doesn't know about the child and what I did. He doesn't know anything at all, not even that I decided to talk to you. Let's get divorced as soon as possible. That's the right thing to do."

Now, he was really stunned, as if this was the strangest thing of all that I had said. He looked angry, as if he couldn't accept that I wanted a divorce after all my brazenness.

"So he will divorce his wife, right?"

I hadn't expected such a question.

"No," I said, "I do not know, or care, how he will proceed. I'm doing what I have to do. After all that I've done to you, I don't think you will ever want to see my face again."

He stood and began pacing the room with his hand in his pockets.

He said, "You don't really know him yet, it seems," he said. "He can't get divorced from his wife even if he wants to. I should have realized what was going on from the beginning. Unfortunately, I trusted you too much. I have always thought that in spite of your easygoing nature, you were more conservative than all the women who look so morally upright. In the end, he deceived you, too."

It was odd that he was angry with Fuat instead of me.

I was about to tell him that I was the guilty party, but kept silent. This was not what he wanted to hear. He surely didn't want to hear that I had thought of all of this on my own, that I was madly in love with Fuat, and that I had disregarded all else that mattered.

"There's nothing that can be done," I said. "I wish none of this had happened. I wish I could have contained myself. I am truly sorry to have brought shame to you, but I'm still glad that you didn't hear about it from somebody else."

He sat down again and sipped his drink.

The speaker on the radio was giving information about the Miles Davis concert that would take place the following day.

"What do you plan to do?" Turgut asked.

"I'll go and live with my mother, naturally," I said.

"Who else knows about this?"

I had to lie. "No one."

He studied my face.

"No one. Really?"

"No one except the three of us," I answered.

His low, unhappy voice, and the way he sounded devastated and astounded, proved to me that he had a weakness for me, which I had not realized until then, and which I don't understand even today.

I knew that he was afraid that his life would be shattered and he would be a failure, but I had still been unjust to him. He really loved me. I am sure that at that moment, he would have consented to anything to repair the situation. If I had apologized to him, crying and saying that what I had done was an accident, an adventure, or a crazy mistake, he would accept everything with resignation.

He was not furious with me, and he didn't yell or insult me, causing me to act more carefully than I thought I would.

"I wish we had separated before going through all this trouble," I said. "Perhaps you weren't happy with me either."

He looked at me with a bitter smile on his face.

"You think you know everything so well, don't you?" he said.

Something hurt inside me. What had he done to deserve this? Hadn't he always been the kind of husband all women would treat with respect and honor? A person who was hard-working, honest, and loving; a man who fulfilled all his wife's wishes, who didn't boss her around, and most of all, who respected her.

He was neither the kind of man who looked modern but made his wife miserable at home nor someone who acted as if he had a happy family life but secretly visited prostitutes.

Not once had he said that his way was right just because he was a man.

We had had simple disputes and had grown apart, but we never had real fights.

I tried in vain to stop such thoughts from circling in my mind.

Suddenly he said, "This is really bad."

His entire life would be ruined. This was a shame for someone like him who deemed what others said or thought about him extremely important. I had made a mess of everything.

"No one knows about anything," I repeated. "And no one has to find out. You are a good man and you definitely deserve someone better than me."

He motioned for me to stop, and I remained silent. I knew I was talking nonsense, but what would you have done if you had been in my shoes?

He said, "I've always wished that one day I would be able to tell our grandchildren about the day I first saw you.

Hearing such an uncharacteristic statement from him affected my emotions. All the distress and depression I had suppressed till that moment was set loose; I covered my face with my hands and began to sob.

At the same time, I choked, "Why aren't you angry at me? Why don't you slap me? Why don't you tell me what a lowdown person I am?"

"Let's not fool ourselves," he said. "I knew from the beginning that you were in love with him. I didn't ask because I didn't want to hear the answer. What can you tell a woman whose heart belongs to another man? No, I don't think you are low-down fallen woman."

"But I am," I said.

As he stood up, he said, "It seems that we were destined to experience such a thing. There's no escaping it."

I can still hear his depressed, upset voice every now and then.

In truth I was taken by surprise. I was pleased that we didn't have a big quarrel or exchange harsh words that I didn't want to hear. But still, there was something I didn't understand. What I had done was something unacceptable for a husband, and at the same time, it was very sad that his life would be forced to change dramatically.

I cried throughout the night.

Obviously, it wasn't easy to console your conscience just by confessing everything.

I had finally done what I had been planning for months, but still, I was very sad and distraught.

The way he accepted everything so helplessly had hurt me more. For some reason, I had only thought about myself until that time and had not cared much about his life or feelings. As if the only thing that caused me pain about him was cheating on him and deceiving him in a way that he did not deserve. Yet now, I realized for the first time that I had turned his life upside down.

Maybe he would have even preferred that all that was said had remained unsaid and a secret.

But things were said, and now he had to do something and take action. Perhaps it would have been much easier for him to pretend what he had been suspecting was not real, that everything was just an adventure, and that it would be over sooner or later.

Maybe we all think that way.

I spent the night distressed, suffering a headache, and having chaotic dreams that woke me up every now and then.

When I woke up in the morning, Turgut had already departed, but he had left a letter on my night table.

I sat upright in bed, opened the paper, and began reading while still half asleep.

"My dear girl," the letter began. It felt strange that he called me "my girl", but since I had never received a letter from him before, I wasn't sure what other word he would have used.

"I wish everyone could be able to do whatever he wanted in life and that one could choose his happiness.

"Perhaps you regard me as a cold man devoid of emotions,

someone who lives by the rules. Maybe you're right. Since the day we got married, I have always struggled to build up the home of my dreams. Isn't this the duty of a man? I fulfilled all my obligations one by one. But I neglected one thing. I didn't ask about the dreams of a beautiful, intelligent and bright girl. Because, perhaps as you can understand, I had thought that a calm and happy home was what you desired since we had married in a formal and planned way. I didn't think that you were still a young girl, that you would change as time went by, and that you could desire different things in your life.

"Yes, I am angry at you. You have demolished my dreams. But on the other hand, I realize that I had also destroyed your dreams. If it hadn't been so, then no one could have succeeded in fooling you.

"I have always seen you like a daughter rather than a lover. And when I think now that I will never be able to witness your childish sweetness again, a knife cuts into me."

At this point, a knife cut into me, too. It was very painful to cast aside so many years in one instant. In order not to start weeping again, I got out of bed and stood under cold water in the shower. As the water poured over me, I kept telling myself that I would finish the letter, that I would not make myself unhappy anymore, that I had made a decision and would stick to it, right or wrong, and that I should no longer dwell on what would happen in the future and distress myself since it was of no use to anyone if I got sad and cried all the time.

I got out of the shower, dressed, went downstairs and made myself a cup of black coffee. Then I took a painkiller for my headache, turned on the radio, and sat down to read the rest of the letter.

"I know that there is not much to be done after what you told me last night. However, I thought all night, and I decided that it would not be right to let you go on with such an obscure adventure, which apparently does not have an end. I know that no one can stop you when you decide on something. But I will not divorce you. I think that this madness is a transitory state of despair and that some time has to pass until you realize the right thing to do."

At this point I was surprised once again. What did he have in mind? Obviously, he thought that I had been blinded by love and hopelessly overcome by foolish desire. I quickly read the rest of the letter.

"It is up to you what will happen from this point on. I believe wounds can be healed. Frankly, I am not sure about myself either. But it would be a good idea for us to stay apart for some time. It is better not to make grave decisions that can change one's whole life in haste when one's going through a confusing period in his or her life. I am not sure if you will let other people know about what we are going through, but I can assure you that my mouth will be sealed. You do not love me passionately, but if you have a little respect for me, I hope that you will be able to understand what I mean in this letter. The house is yours; just feel comfortable. I will not be around for a few days.

"You should have no doubt that I have always wanted you to be happy."

The letter affected me in the most unexpected way.

I felt ashamed. I thought that I had never truly known the person who had been so close to me in daily life. I doubted myself. If I hadn't succeeded in knowing my husband, could my feelings about Fuat be true?

Or was my husband acting like this only to prevent a scandal and protect his life from being damaged?

No, I didn't think so.

Now I know very well that he really wanted the best for me, that he was sincere in his words, and that he was willing to accept all that had happened just to be able to be keep on being with me even though he was very angry.

But at that moment, I wasn't sure about anything. I was overwhelmed by doubt, emotion, and inner conflict. I did not know what to do. I also felt scared because he had written that he would not accept divorce as a solution. Earlier I had thought that the problem would be untangled all at once and that I would go on living no matter what was facing me, but nothing was that easy. Nothing was any clearer than before. I thought for a long time. I tried to come back to my senses. I struggled to get Fuat out of my mind and think only about my own life. Besides, Fuat didn't have the slightest idea about what was going on in my life.

I was at a point much different from the previous day. This letter openly told me "go and think, put an end to your desperate relationship, and if you want to come back to me, my door is always open and we can carry on from where we have left off."

I finished my coffee and went back upstairs. I changed my clothes and sat in front of the mirror. I was doing everything almost instinctively. I neither wanted to see my clothes nor the furniture in the house. Thinking that my marriage was over and that I would never be living here again would hurt me, and I wanted to prevent the pain.

Perhaps only a very few people are given such chance to go back to their good old lives once they have been forever changed and smashed to pieces.

In truth, it would have been possible to put an end to my affair, which no one knew about yet. I still couldn't even decide whether it was real or a fantasy. In spite of everything that had taken place, I could have gone on with my usual life as if nothing had happened. Furthermore, I had confessed everything to Turgut and felt "cleansed."

However, I wasn't aware that I couldn't put the chaos in my head back into order just by confessing the truth.

What mattered for me in reality was not what Turgut thought or the possibility of my affair being discovered and the harm it could bring.

I was in a strange mood because I didn't know what to do.

What would it matter if Turgut told me, "Go and do whatever you want with him, but in the end, come back here with the memory of that adventure. I'll keep this secure home ready for you."

I wasn't sure about anything. I felt I was trying to walk on shaky ground that kept sliding under my feet. Anything I tried to cling on to vanished like a dream.

Then I suddenly felt furious at Fuat. Until that day, I had never taken this feeling into consideration or found fault in anything he did, accepting everything without question.

But now, suddenly, I began to wonder why he never told me anything about his life and why he didn't care what would happen to us, imagining that he was perhaps growing weary of this flavorless adventure that consisted of few hours spent together.

During our last assignation, Fuat was not as insistent as usual.

He seemed to have forgotten that special, fabulous afternoon and disappeared out of my life. Our last meeting had not been very warm and loving.

As I considered this, I also reminded myself that I shouldn't dwell on these thoughts. In fact, I was desperately trying to reanimate a dream which perhaps did not have anything to do with reality.

But of course one could not be content with such a dream.

I went downstairs. Then I went upstairs again. I went up and down between the floors. For quite a long time, I did many in things at home while my mind was deep in thought. I did not have the energy to gather everything I had at home, so I just prepared a single suitcase.

Turgut would be away for a few days for a meeting. I flew back to Istanbul on the first flight I could book. When the cab driver put my suitcase into the car, I did not even turn back to look at my house for the last time. I clenched my teeth and for the duration of the trip to the airport, I watched the city as if seeing it for the last time, while listening to the driver make small talk.

When I arrived in Istanbul, I took a deep breath. I would definitely be dispirited, but in time, I would forget my sadness. I had done what I had to do. I would not dwell on the past.

Fuat was busy with the elections. When I returned to Turkey, I found out that his party had won the elections, but he was on bad terms with his own colleagues. They had removed him from office and wanted to send him overseas as an ambassador. I read all about this in the newspapers. We were not able to contact each other for a long time. I did not call him, and it was obvious that he was busy with his own problems. In fact, I was pleased about what was going on. In this way, I thought he would leave politics, and I felt happy. I had not realized, however, that he had been taken hostage by his political ambition.

Winter came, and I did not know how to keep busy. Turgut insisted on trying to salvage our relationship. He even came to Istanbul once, planning to talk to my family and have them convince me. However, he soon realized that all was in vain. After a rather unpleasant conversation, he finally said to me, "In the end, you will regret it, but it will be too late. There's nothing I can do anymore." Then he left.

(Now, I remember the way he looked so fed up, tired, and with stooping shoulders, and how he left me forever after he held both of my hands, unable to look me in the eye. I did not want to watch him leave. Maybe because I was afraid I would call him back just because I couldn't stand to see him that way. He called me a few years later, but we didn't meet. Many years later, I saw him in the tea salon of a hotel in Istanbul. He was sitting with a plumpish woman. He was wearing glasses and was bald. He introduced me to his wife, as he looked deep into my eyes. I wasn't able to return his look. He told me they were living in Ankara. They had two sons. They had come to Istanbul to attend the graduation ceremony of one of their sons.)

That day, when Turgut left me for good, I felt sad but also relieved. Although we weren't divorced yet, I was happy that the marriage was finally over.

Lilac had grown and become a conceited but stylish lady cat; she roamed about the house as if she were a queen.

Without recognizing the pace of time, months had passed, and I had lost weight because of stress, and had become withdrawn and taciturn. Nihat took me around the city especially in the evenings, trying hard to get me out of the house. One evening we went to the movies—Yeni Melek Movie Theater perhaps—to watch the film *War and Peace*. After the movie, we returned home and I felt a surge of excitement. Perhaps it was the approach of spring that was waking me up from a long winter sleep.

As soon as I woke up in the morning, I called Fuat's private number. He answered the phone. He was excited upon hearing my voice, but I think there were other people in the room.

"Where are you now?" he asked.

"In Istanbul."

"It's a little crowded and difficult here. When can we talk?" he asked.

"I don't know," I said. "It's also difficult here."

There was a short silence. My voice did not sound as usual.

"Are you alright?" he asked.

"I am."

"There are no problems, are there?"

He asked this question as if the fact that we had not talked to each other for such a long time was not a problem itself.

I suddenly said, "I want to ask you something." I had not thought about the question; it popped into my mind on the spur of the moment. What I asked then seems idiotic now, but I said, "Do you love me?"

He remained silent for a few seconds.

"What kind of a question is that?"

Wrong answer. What do you think? In this game, this question has but one answer, and if a man does not give that answer, the game is over.

"I just wanted to ask. Just like that." Then I said, "We'll talk later. I understand you're busy. Goodbye."

I hung up the phone.

Suddenly I felt that everything was beginning to topple all around me. I thought if I stayed any longer at home, I would go crazy. I rushed out and walked aimlessly in the streets. It couldn't go on like this. Not to upset my mother and brother, to prevent anyone from finding out about everything, not to hurt Turgut's reputation, to protect Fuat's name and position . . . To think and ponder, all by myself, all alone, to think and think. I couldn't bear this any longer. I felt like screaming and shouting and could hardly contain myself.

Perhaps I needed to go somewhere and stay on my own for

a while. But where? Suddenly I made a decision. Upon returning home, I told my mother that a friend of mine had invited me to stay with her, and prepared a small suitcase. I told Nihat what was on my mind. He booked a plane ticket for me and I set off for Paris without knowing where this idea had come from.

I had nothing specific in mind. All I thought was to go away somewhere where no one knew me and to stay alone and get rid of the past days and months, the thoughts torturing me, and be by myself.

The only hotel I knew in Paris was the one Fuat had told me once about in much detail. It was a small, three-story hotel with big windows and green shutters, where he stayed each time he visited Paris.

I went straight to that hotel. The air was bright and clear. People on the streets and in the cafés were were full of vigor and cheer, as if they were celebrating an important event.

Usually, spring didn't come to the city so early in the year. The cab driver who brought me downtown told me I was very lucky indeed.

I decided to stay in Paris for a long time. Wandering in the city like a tourist, visiting the museums and going to the theaters on my own would probably do me good.

After I unpacked my suitcase, I realized that Fuat would call me at home in Istanbul. He would be preoccupied about the strange way I had hung up the phone, and as soon as he was free, he would give me a call. If he didn't find me, he would surely do something stupid.

Suddenly it occurred to me that I had to put an end to our relationship.

Everything was getting totally out of my control.

I had the hotel make a phone connection. He was excited to

hear my voice. He said, "I was trying to reach you. What's going on? There's something strange about you."

"There's nothing going on," I said. "I decided to stay on my own for a while. Don't call me at home. I'm not in Istanbul. I'm far away." I paused and then said, "It is time that we finish this relationship. Of course, if it can be called a relationship."

"What are you saying! Are you out of your mind? Tell me right away where you are."

There was a knock on the door. A cordial young man brought in some food. He asked me whether I needed anything else. When he realized I was on the phone, he apologized and left after putting the tray on the table.

"Never mind where I am," I said to Fuat. "I am some place. I've been thinking for some time now. There's no other way. This relationship does not have a solution."

He had heard the young man talk.

He quickly said, "You're in Paris. Tell me where you're staying. I'll come there immediately."

"No, you're not coming anywhere. Can a dream last forever?"

He remained silent for some time, as if he were at a loss for words.

"When you called earlier I wasn't able to speak. The place was packed with other people," he said. "But I'd like to answer your question now. Yes, I'm in love with you. Yes, I love you. Madly. Please don't hang up. I have a few things to tell you."

I didn't say anything.

He continued, "I've told you from the very beginning that I'd do anything for you, and that I'd take any risk. But you didn't listen to me. So as not to disturb your life, I remained silent. I don't even know what you think or what you feel. You haven't told me anything. It's I who talks all the time."

In fact, he was right. I hadn't even told him that I loved him. What I felt was so natural, real, and obvious that putting it into words felt strange.

I was truly astonished. That man for whom I was crazy and had lost my heart to did not even know I loved him! He hadn't even realized the purity of the way I had given myself to him.

"Do some things always need to be put into words?" I asked.

"If not, why are you in such great doubt?" he asked in return.

"I don't know," I said. "I really do not know. It's difficult to know you exist. You appear only to disappear again so soon. I can't understand what you think, do, or feel."

In surprise, he said, "You don't know how I feel? I cannot understand this. Everyone except you has realized that I have lost my mind. It's only you who can't realize it. I can see that you're angry with me. So tell me, why?"

Yes, I was angry with him. But how could I tell him how horrible I had felt after he disappeared out of my life after that wonderful afternoon we had spent together?

"We have embarked on impossible things," I said. "Can we go on sharing a few hours in secrecy and doing everything evasively? I am always upset. I feel as if something is broken in me. No matter what I do, the pain does not go away."

"Why didn't you call me?" he said. "Wasn't it you who told me that you needed some time during our last encounter and then disappeared?"

I faltered. Had it really been like that?

He didn't allow me to think for too long, saying, "Tell me where you're staying. I'll come immediately. Let us sit down and talk. I'll answer any question you want to ask. It's only you whom I want to see in my life. It's only you with whom I want to talk and whose eyes I want to gaze into."

I said, "No. I will not tell you. I want to stay alone and think."

"But promise me one thing," he begged, "Do whatever you like, think whatever you want, but don't leave me. I'll accept all conditions. I can even do with one hour in a year, but don't talk to me about separation. Even the smallest place in your life is the best place in the world for me. Please don't forget that."

That evening I felt like a small girl who had secretly sneaked away from home to do something naughty.

Yes, just like a schoolgirl who dared to experience a forbidden adventure and bite off more than she could chew. But the odd thing was that I didn't know what to do.

I didn't know with this city. I had a few casual friends who lived here, but what could I talk to them about?

Would I spend my days crying in this hotel room all alone?

As I sat in front of the mirror, I suddenly decided what to do. Tonight was mine. Maybe for the first time in my life, when no one knew where I was, I had reached one of the biggest milestones of my life, alone in a small hotel room. I wouldn't spend my time crying.

I told myself that even if I lost everyone, I had a cat somewhere far away, and this thought made me laugh.

If we stop and think for a while, I had a husband who was at a loss as to what he should do. His life was in pieces because of me, but I knew very well that he would find a way to pull himself together again. I had a lover who did not understand what I was thinking after a strange phone call we made and who perhaps did not know what to do with his own life. I had a good friend who was far away, somewhere I had never seen, digging into the earth to find out about the kings of a distant past who had their lives inscribed on tablets to become immortal. I had a mother who was surprised about my incomprehensible behavior. I had a brother who did whatever I asked him to do, yet was worried about me although he did not ask any questions. I also had a beautiful cat.

This was my life.

I felt as if the ground was splitting in two in front of me and I was standing on the edge of a precipice that was getting slowly wider. I had to decide quickly on which side to stand, but all I did was wait, watching the gap open.

Obviously, this was not a very bright situation.

On the other hand, neither of the men in my life wanted to give me up.

When I thought about this, I began to laugh as I looked at myself in the mirror. "You're really mad, my girl," I said to myself chuckling.

At that moment, I was at the breaking point of my life, and neither of the men in my life knew where I was.

For the first time, I was totally alone, and I was laughing in a foreign city, in a small hotel room, in front of an oval-shaped mirror from the past whose gilding and silvering were chipped and worn.

No, I wouldn't sit here all alone all evening, struggling to decide what to do with my life.

Besides, whenever I would decide, hadn't I already made a complete mess of everything?

I put on my bright red lipstick, gathered my hair, put on some mascara to reveal my long eyelashes and wore violet eye shadow.

Then I put on my dark blue dress with white dots, slipped on my dark blue shoes, and picked up my matching handbag. No, I wouldn't wear a hat; my hair looked good enough.

As I was closing the door, I realized I had forgotten something. I went back in and picked up my thin blue-violet shawl.

It was still not dark when I went out. The cafés along the streets were full of people. Many people couldn't find anywhere to sit, and youngsters were either standing and waiting or sitting on the sidewalks and chatting.

Young people sitting on their small motorcycles, which were quite fashionable in those days, making remarks about the passersby; people amusing themselves; chic ladies walking their small dogs and smiling at those seated in the cafés; artists immediately distinguishable by their wrinkled clothes and shabbiness; people walking out of shops, carrying many bags and getting into cars whose doors were opened by chauffeurs; old people sitting on rattan chairs and reading their newspapers, enjoying the last bit of sunshine; waiters who realized they couldn't wait on everyone at the same time and who called out to customers and joked with them; tourists trying to squeeze an incredible holiday into a few snaps with their cameras.

It was a typical spring evening in Paris.

At least for one night in my life, I was away from all responsibilities, all attachments, all questions, everyone I knew, everyone who waited for me, and all the sights and sounds to which I was accustomed.

I went into a restaurant overlooking the street and ordered a glass of white wine. I lit a cigarette. I picked up a newspaper and began reading the "What's on tonight" column. The new movie of a new blond sex symbol had begun. Under the caption "B.B.—the new star all men are crazy about," there was a photograph of the actress wearing a bathing suit and placing one foot on a colorful beach ball.

"My wife won't let me go and see that movie," the elderly waiter complained as he filled my glass. "Can you believe it?"

I laughed. "But she's just a child," I said. "Is your wife jealous?"

"You're right, lady," he said. "I told my wife that my granddaughter was older than that girl, but who can explain it to my wife! If some girl wears a bathing suit and becomes famous, why am I to blame?"

No, I didn't want to go and watch that child's boring movie. At a jazz club within walking distance, a famous black musician would play the saxophone. I didn't know him, but the idea appealed to me. I asked the waiter, who was cross at being forced to decide between his wife and the movie, if I would be able to find a place at the club.

He said, "I don't think so. It's a small club but very popular. If you want, I can call and try to book a place for you."

While I was fiddling with some mussels swimming in a bowl, he booked a place for me.

After dinner, I wandered the streets and went to a café to have a cup of coffee. Making the most of my solitude, I lingered, letting time pass slowly.

One floor below street level, the club was a small, dark, smoky place packed with people.

I sat at a small round table next to the stage. Red velvet curtains hung on the walls, and old musical instruments were placed here and there. The walls were also decorated with black-and-white signed and framed photographs. The dark blue and red carpets were so old that they looked as if they would soon fall to pieces. The dense smoke filled place was illuminated by small lamps with red shades on the wooden tables and in wall fixtures.

Soon a heavy-set black man in a black suit and a hat, who was apparently very famous from the audience's wild applause, came on stage and took a saxophone from a worn-out case. Without saying anything, he began to play. First he played a cheerful calypso, then a rather noisy song, and then a ballad that rapidly enveloped you, leaving a melancholy feeling in your heart. It had a name, something like "Today I'll Cry."

Later, I tried to find a record of that song, but to no avail. Maybe it had never been recorded.

As the musician played that long melancholy song, I felt as if he were looking at me. There was a break after everyone had stood up and applauded, and he came up to my table as if we had always known each other. "Good evening," he said. I looked up in surprise. He pulled up a chair and sat down.

"What are you doing here all alone?" he asked.

"Is sitting together with lonely ladies part of the concert?" I asked.

He laughed with his deep, velvet-like voice.

"I feel funny if I sit on the stage during the break," he said. "When I don't have my saxophone, I don't even know how I should sit. Besides, there's nowhere else free to sit."

A waiter brought him a drink, which he gulped down in a second. He immediately asked for another.

"It seems that you're famous," I said.

He said, "My name is Dexter. Did you like the last song?"

"I loved it. Did you write it?"

"Not yet," he answered. "In fact, neither I nor the boys knew I would play it tonight."

"And I didn't know I'd be here tonight," I said. "If you ask me, you should write it down because it's beautiful."

"Don't worry. I never forget my songs." He laughed. "Is there anything you want me to play?"

I said, "No. I don't know any jazz musicians except for that good-looking trumpet player, and I only know a few songs."

Then he began playing again. Before he went on to the next song, he said, "I would like to play an old song for a young lady. I don't know where she comes from."

Later, I was able to find a record of that song: "Ev'ry Time We Say Good-Bye."

I bought two copies of that record: One for Fuat, and one for myself.

Quite odd, but a world-famous musician I didn't know had played that song for me as if he knew my story.

"Ev'ry time we say good-bye / I die a little . . ."

When it was past midnight, and while he was still playing, I wrote on a little paper: "Mr. Dexter, every time I say good-bye, I'll remember this song. I am happy to have known you. Perhaps one day, in a different part of the world, we will meet again." Before I left, I handed the note to a waiter to give to him.

With that song still in my ears, and walking on air, I went to my hotel trying to sober up in the fresh night air. For the first time in many days, I went to bed feeling better.

There, outside the little windows, a totally different life existed.

Toward dawn, I had walked alone, with my shoes in my hand, stepping barefoot on the cold stones of the boulevard.

It is only now, years after that night, that I can clearly place these memories into their proper order, as if I'm doing a deep cleaning at home. There are things to be thrown away, things to be put aside, things to be given to other people, and many other things forgotten in some hole, which we realize how much we have missed as soon as we rediscover them—let us dust them off and place them back in a place of honor!

No matter how hard you try, everything accumulates—things to be discarded are forgotten, and the leftover details of your life accumulate here and there like waste that washes up on the shore from the sea.

Now, I open the window early in the morning as if to start that spring cleaning. The thin curtains flutter in the wind, the joyful screams of children drift in from outside, and suddenly I find myself back in time, on the morning I tried to decide what to do with my life, all alone and far away from everyone in a city where nobody knew me.

The previous night had been confusing and solitary—a night enchanted by alcohol and music.

I felt as if I had been sitting in a waiting room and would soon be invited into another room to be told how my life would be from that moment on.

Did I know what I wanted?

If you ask me, all I wanted then was to stay in that imaginary waiting room forever, before finding out what would follow.

When I returned to my room late that night, after walking past a few drunkards and groups of young men and women strolling and talking and joking with each other loudly, my head was spinning slightly. Was I unhappy? No. Was I afraid? No. Today, when I try to recall that night, I realize that I was feeling as if I were far away from this world. I was feeling carefree.

I didn't want to think about anything. I was more tired than I had ever been. It was not because of the trip, or that day or night alone, but because of many long months during which I had been trying to catch a person inside me who was trying to escape.

The kind of feeling that you have when you lie down and slowly fall asleep, as if you're floating on air.

The faint sound of an accordion rather than the sunshine

streaming in through the window woke me up from my deep peaceful sleep the following morning.

I listened in surprise. Still half asleep, I tried to come to my senses and realize where I was. I was alone and in a small hotel room. But that song? How could it be that our song was playing?

No, I wasn't wrong. It was that song playing outside.

Our song.

This was not a dream. This was real. It felt as if a fairy was trying to send me a signal with her magic wand.

I have never forgotten the sound of the accordion that found me in a dream.

Even today, on some mornings in the spring, I wake up as if I'm hearing that sound, as if someone out there in front of my door is playing that song.

I cannot pass quickly from the land of dreams to the land of reality. I wake up with a start, as if a child inside me jumps up in excitement. Then I exchange places with that young girl who once woke up in a hotel room buried in distant memories, even though something in me knows that all those splendid memories have been left back in time.

This incredible experience always gives me goosebumps, as well as a mixture of indefinable bliss and melancholy that makes the years change places in time like a sweet spring breeze which is felt for a few minutes only, bringing the scents, the weather, the light and the sense of the places from which it came.

As I travel back to the past and become that young girl again, the bliss travels into the future and turns into a long-accustomed gloom.

Can you believe that today, instead of rebelling against that unfortunate reality, I feel happy that I haven't lost this wonderful feeling, that I'm still able to experience it?

I woke up in disbelief. For a moment I stopped and listened, trying to decide whether I could really hear the song or was dreaming.

Then I jumped out of bed and ran to the window. The curtains were moving with the breeze, I looked out of the window to the street below. A blind man with a red beret with a pom-pon and a striped blue shirt was playing and singing the song "everything has disappeared but you" with his small accordion in front of the hotel. His big, puffy, white dog was lying on the sidewalk beside him.

At first, I didn't understand what was happening. I felt excited. I took it as sheer coincidence. While still in a dream embellished with the fragrance and light of spring, I heard a knock on my door. Young men in hotel uniforms brought in roses of all colors, filling the small room.

On that morning, when the tulle curtains fluttered, when that song entered my room from the open window together with the scents and sounds of the city, and when my dream was full of roses, everything disappeared but Fuat.

From that moment on, I neither wanted to think about anything else nor go anywhere else.

I forgot about everything, as if I knew what was going to happen in the future, or as if I had accepted the entire future even though I didn't know what it would bring.

Things I had to think about, people I was responsible to, right and wrong, doubts, worries about my future, and the bonds of the past all vanished one by one.

Many years ago, there, on a spring morning, I released myself into the future without a single doubt and without need for words, thoughts, conflicts, reasons or conclusions. Perhaps everything has changed: cities, people, lives and even songs, but spring mornings have remained the same for me. Maybe they were stamped with a seal on that special spring morning, to be opened anew every spring.

I have always wanted to preserve that morning.

Tea served in white porcelain cups decorated with light green flowers. Ruffling thin curtains. That song the whole street had to share with me without knowing why. Pale orange, violet, yellow, white, red, and pink roses. "No matter where you go in this world, I'll follow you." The untidy bed. Clothes scattered around. The breeze of the beautiful spring morning. I wanted to laugh. I wanted to cry. I had a hard time sitting here with my huge, heavy wings no one can see.

Finally the phone rang.

"You have found me again," I said.

"I told you I would," he replied.

"You don't know what an enchanting spell you have created here," I said. "I can't describe it to you."

"It is I who am enchanted," he said. "Since that evening we danced. You don't know, but just hearing your voice makes me forget everything."

"There are so many flowers that I cannot even move in the room," I said. "They are so pretty. You can't smell them but I'd like you to hear something."

I held the receiver toward the window so that he could hear the music.

"Don't you move," he said.

"I don't want to go to anywhere else," I answered.

A feeling that cannot be described enveloped me. It can only be experienced, not explained. Yes, just like in that young Frenchman's novel, I feel as if a flower is growing in me. Will this fabulous image, this matchless moment, this room we want to stay in forever, and this fantastic picture we can't part with disintegrate and disappear?

What if the water lily inside of me grows and drags me to an incurable illness?

No, I didn't want to ponder these thoughts.

Having reclaimed my life, I was ready for everything. I was courageous and victorious, as if I had endured a war no one knew anything about.

There were things to be done before he arrived. I called my mother and told her she shouldn't worry, that I was with a friend, and that I wasn't able to make a long call but that I would call again soon.

I organized the cupboards and tidied up the room. Then I went out. First I thanked the accordion player who was sitting on the corner having lunch. I gave him some money so that he would come again the next morning at the same time and play the same music. Then I strolled around the city. I watched people painting pictures by the riverside, climbed the famous tower, and felt a chill as I observed the entire city from high above. Then I sat at a boulevard café and had something to eat.

Although I knew that I didn't have enough money, I went in and out of the shops whose windows displayed the latest fashionable clothes—they were inviting. I chatted with the sales people who let me try on the clothes one by one and examine my image in the mirror. Eventually, I couldn't help spending a little money extravagantly and bought the dress and the shoes I liked the most.

In addition, I did something I had never done before. I bought a light-yellow colored V-neck pullover with thin blue and white stripes on its neck for Fuat. The sales clerk said, "The gentleman will love this. It's perfect for the season." They made a big, fancy gift package.

I picked up city guides, magazines, and copies of all booklets and brochures for tourists. I began to choose all the places we would visit when he arrived, planning how we would fill a special photograph album that belonged only to the two of us.

The chestnut trees in the Champs Élysées were in bloom.

The weather was incredible, and I was hopping on the streets like a small girl.

In my hotel room, I heard a knock on the door. I took a deep breath, trying to calm my madly beating heart. Fuat was standing at the door dressed in a white shirt and blue sweater (reflecting on his eyes, making their tone lighter) with a small leather travel bag in his hand. His gray hair was little longer.

He entered, flung the bag on the floor, held my face in his hands, and gave me a long kiss. We sat on the floor, on the soft blue carpet with red dots. He kept saying, "Let me look at you." I wasn't able to look him in the eye.

"How beautiful you are," he said. "One look at your face lasts for a lifetime and I forget everything else."

"You have probably forgotten me." I said.

He caressed my hair, my face, and I leaned my head against his shoulder as we sat there for a long while.

"Will you tell me now what has happened?" he asked.

"No, I won't," I said. "You are with me now, and I don't want to hear or talk about anything else anymore."

I wonder if he understood.

Each time I saw him, I used to get scared that this magical reality that existed for us would shatter or become ordinary.

I guess he was aware of everything. However, he often used to put me into doubt by making a joke, laughing sarcastically like a child, or saying something unexpected that would hurl me back into reality.

I never knew whether he acted that way because he was afraid that I would get lost in the magic and become upset upon waking up one day from the dream we were able to have for a short time only.

I knew that he always regarded me as an innocent young girl.

Sometimes I used to tell him, "Don't be afraid. I know about everything, and despite 'everything' I am as happy as no other can be."

At those times, he would become thoughtful, and with a cloudy look in his eyes, would immediately change the subject to delay what was about to be discussed.

"Come on, get dressed," he said. "There are places I'd like to take you. Nobody knows where I am. I don't even have to phone anyone."

I put on a pair of dark blue tight pants with buttons just above the ankles and a white silk shirt. I wore a light blue pullover and put on a red and blue neckerchief. There were bowknots in the shape of butterflies on my recently purchased flat white shoes, representing my wild soul.

For the first time, we walked on the streets hand in hand like real lovers. We watched the sunset by the river while sitting on a wall where students usually sat swaying their legs.

He looked at me as I enjoyed the view. He took off my white sunglasses that resembled a cat's eyes, saying, "Don't wear them while I'm with you." Then he buttoned the top button of my shirt that was open.

We strolled through the back streets of the city where he had spent many years. We ate at a pub crammed with people. We went to listen to an old Cuban guitar player who sang sad songs about his faraway country and how much he missed his lover there. We went to bars that came alive in the late hours of the night and were frequented by tramps, artists, poets, and stars.

Touching him, leaning against his body as we walked arm in arm, mixing with the people, kissing in murky bars and secluded corners or against the walls, seeing the burning desire in his eyes whenever he looked at me, and listening to the things he whispered in my ears turned my head.

What did he say to me? He told me that he had missed me, that he'd been living with my memory for months, that he wanted to kiss and smell my body all over, that he wanted to undress me, that he wanted to have me sit on his lap. He said things that drove me crazy. At the same time, I felt ashamed. I couldn't tell him what was on my mind. All that had been filling up my head, all my fantasies. I just listened to him. Then, one time in a café at midnight, while sipping cognac, listening to a loud French chanson, and I was exchanging a few words with the people at the next table (they were so close that it was impossible not to chat and make friends), he leaned toward me and whispered in my ear, "I've decided what I want." As I was trying to answer the trivial questions of the woman at the adjacent table, I looked at his face, and, in Turkish, he openly said, "I want to eat you." I blushed all over. My eyes were glued on his, and I realized that he was not joking.

This is a queer memory, I know; but after all his provocative words, these drove me crazy. I still think of this as the foremost level of desire and love . . . the wish to eat someone!

Isn't it funny?

That night when we made love among the colorful roses and fell asleep at the first light of dawn, I realized that I had never thought that someone could be so close to me and that he would not only be close to me but become one with me.

There are certain things that lose their magic and glamour when you tell another person about them; consequently they turn into ordinary things.

It was with him that I learned of touch, the scent of another person's skin, the lust on one's lips, the words that are secretly whispered into one's ear, and how a man and a woman can become a united soul.

It's hard to explain that the lust we felt for each other was at the same time the most innocent and childish thing we had experienced.

It was unique because it was so pure, innocent, and childish.

Under the darkness of the soft quilts we hid like two kids, and while we were overcome with unexplainable fire, we told each other things that couples who spend a lifetime together would not be able to tell each other. Words that would have made me blush, or that I would have considered vulgar or ugly had I read them in a book, sounded entirely different, as if they had other meanings in a foreign language.

Is there anything more frequently used than words?

That is why words are old, burned-out, and contaminated.

For centuries, they have been loaded with common meanings.

Turning them into new words that carry special meanings between you and another, a meaning that only you two can understand, is almost impossible.

We were like two children, learning a new language together.

We undressed each other like two children hiding from grownups. We not only stripped off our clothes but also our skins, going on a mysterious journey within our bodies to search for something no one knew but always talked about—perhaps what was called the essence of life or the soul. The excitement of our adventure transported us to ecstasy.

What did it feel like?

Sailing on a boat that moves with a wild wind?

First you try to protect yourself, find your direction, and fight against the wind. Later, you give up and let it carry you away at fantastic speed, to the point that nothing is important anymore and the only thing left is the gradually darkening sea and the bizarre delight you feel moving in the air as if you're flying through the sky which is united with the sea.

Or did that feeling resemble the excitement of a child who suddenly finds a secret passage through the bushes in a garden?

For a moment, the child can't decide whether he should enter the passage or not. Then he decides to go in and take a look, quickly, and out again. At first he cannot see anything. Then his eyes get used to the darkness. He edges forward slowly. He forgets about time, he becomes disorientated, and he draws different meanings from every new thing he comes across. In this way, he gradually moves away from the door he had entered and reaches the point of no return.

Can lust and childishness be combined?

Yes, there, in his arms, in the moments when our faces took shapes no one had seen before, when words acquired different meanings, when even our fingers turned into staffs of pleasure, and when moans full of desire mixed with shy smiles and uncontainable laughter, I felt as if I were a small child.

Curious, shy, but fearless.

Once Ayla had asked me, "Do you really know him? In the end, how many times have you been together?"

Yes, I knew him.

But each time we were together, I realized once again that I did not know him at all.

I looked at his new image before me in awe, like the way a house looks when you first enter and how it seems different after you visit it many times and become acquainted with it.

His childish manners, his tender looks, as if telling me "my dear baby, you don't know anything, you're still so young;" the way he lost himself in passion while explaining something; the way he jumped up and waved his arms and hands; how he got carried away with his impossible dreams about us; and the way his eyes filled with tears when he said, "But I'm too old, and you're so young. What if you leave me all alone? What if you get bored with me?"

Once I caught him in front of the mirror, examining his body as he tried to pull in his belly. He felt embarrassed and angry and chased me around in the room. As I screamed while running, he became infuriated and said, "You really need a good spanking."

Sometimes he called me "young lady," sometimes "little brat," sometimes "my light," sometimes "my baby lover," and sometimes "my beautiful girl."

If someone looked at me when we were out, or if another man complimented me or asked me to dance, Fuat would foam at the mouth, saying, "Let me give him what he has coming to him!" Or his face would redden as he said harshly: "Insolent, witless idiot!"

I used to laugh at his temper and how he used to brood, even though I wasn't to blame.

He would say, "You're casual with everyone. Courtesy is one thing, and getting close to some stranger is another!" and continue muttering.

In places, where no one knew us, people used to think we were married, and this thrilled him. He would often say, "They think you're my wife! They are all jealous of me."

Seeing me frown, he would try to calm me by saying, "But isn't this the truth. Aren't you my real wife?"

I knew about his interest in women and the rumors about him. I also knew that he loved chatting to beautiful women and that he was able to store even the minutest details of a woman's clothing into his memory.

However, when he was with me, he never glanced at another woman. He would always say, "When I'm with you, I forget not only other women but the whole world." This was true. Nothing else used to interest him then.

We woke to the sound of the same accordion. I opened my eyes and saw him looking at me with his disheveled hair and his eyes slightly swollen. The same song was playing, and for the first time, I was seeing him just after he had woken up.

"Out of bed, young lady," he said. "Your song is playing."

"Our song," I said. "I told him to come today as well."

Then I caught him by the neck and pulled him back under the covers.

He kissed me but then got out of bed.

He said, "You will be angry, but we have to leave immediately. We're late. I couldn't bring myself to wake you up, but we have quite a long way to the boat."

I didn't ask what boat he was talking about, nor did I ask where we were going and how long we would stay. I didn't ask. I didn't care.

How can I forget how I packed my suitcase; how I stuck everything into it while dressing at the same time; how I insisted on taking the roses, how he made a big bouquet as I put on my clothes; how we got into a small car with a driver who never stopped talking even though we were still half-asleep; how we stopped by a big shop whose windows displayed mannequins lying on beach towels; how we hastily bought some things there; how we reached the airport after driving along twisty, tree-lined roads that passed through orderly, clean villages, and vast rural areas; and how we first got on a propeller plane for a long trip and then eventually on a rather ugly boat he called a ship?

The playful midday sun was drawing golden figures on the choppy water. Holding the bars of the deck, we looked at the coast we had just left behind. He took off his light-colored linen jacket and placed it on my shoulders. Feeling a little sleepy and a little tired, I leaned my head against his chest.

"I love you so much," I said.

Caressing my hair, he pulled me toward himself and whispered into my ear, "But I love you more."

We were leaving the coast. The sun was already up, and although I didn't know where we were going, I was beside him on a choppy unknown sea, and suddenly, I knew exactly where I was.

I was home.

I never had a home.

I lived in different places of the world and in different houses, but after my childhood home, it was with him that I found a home again.

I remember thinking one day at midnight, Maybe this is why I love him so much . . . he is my home. At the same time, I felt an indescribable commotion constantly changing places with a feeling of melancholy that could take me to the edge of death.

Now I know that after a human being leaves his childhood home, he is flung from one place to another like the adventurous traveller in popular old novels. He stays at inns, is hosted by people he doesn't know, spends the night in haunted mansions, and tries to discover life by choosing one or other fork in the road that destiny causes him to come across. Sometimes he stops for a rest and builds himself a reed hut, thinking that he is tired and can no longer travel. Then he destroys that hut to go back on the road and continue his journey.

In the end, he keeps looking for his own home, the place he really belongs to, that unique abode where he will take shelter and not do anything except be happy.

How many people have succeeded in finding that place?

How many people have been lucky enough to scream, "Land!" when they go on deck after an unparalleled adventure and look at the horizon?

In fact, how many people are even able to comprehend the real goal of such an insane journey?

In those days, the newspapers used to write about miracles. They mentioned space travel, cures for illnesses, and a vaccine for eternal youth.

But my miracle was right in front of me—it was when I looked into his eyes that day, on the afternoon of that spring day when the bright sunshine illuminated everything and when even the big sea birds whose name I didn't know let out screams in surprise.

There are things in life that we see but do not distinguish. If miracles truly exist, they are concealed among the things we see but do not understand.

He said, "Let us not part no matter what happens. Promise me. Each time I leave you, I feel as if I have forgotten myself somewhere. Please promise me."

My eyes were fixed on his. I was so happy that I didn't understand why I felt like crying.

He felt he had lost himself here. What about me?

Every time we said good-bye, I felt bewildered, like a small child who arrives at home and knocks on the door, yet no one opens it.

He and I always shared stolen hours as if we were idle lovers. We strolled through neighborhoods no one knew about; we sat and ate at restaurants in poor districts; we kissed each other under bridges; we stayed in hotels where no one recognized us; we communicated with signs whenever we went out into the open among the crowds. We wrote each other notes, which we tore up without delay.

Just as it happened in the novel he brought me one day . . .

In that strange novel in which an old man roamed secretly from town to town with a young girl he had fallen in love with. She constantly had a lollipop in her mouth, wore white socks and a short skirt, and rolled a hoop.

So he had found his home, too. But somewhere that was not appropriate. Was it really like that? Who could tell what the truth was?

I went to our next meeting wearing a school uniform and with my hair in a ponytail. He was surprised when he saw me; then he burst out laughing.

"Did you like the book?" he asked.

"I don't like unhappy endings," I answered.

He laughed again and said, "I suppose that is most interesting comment I've heard about that novel. I wish the author could have heard it too."

"I'm not a young girl," I said. "Besides, even if I were, it wouldn't matter."

In the meantime I was saying to myself that even if I were, I would still follow him everywhere.

"You are indeed a young girl," he said, "and that is exactly why I don't know what to do."

"So you don't know what to do."

The biggest bomb in the world was built—a bomb that could destroy the entire world. Now everyone was constructing shelters in their basements, thinking they would be protected if the bomb were actually dropped. (Strangely, people were not angry at the person who built the bomb but at the author who wrote a novel that was considered scandalous. People were banning books instead of bombs.)

I said, "If it means that you and I are going to stay in a shelter together till the end of time, I don't mind if the bomb is dropped."

He took my face in his hands and studied it with a sad look in his eyes. He said, "God forbid! We will not stay in shelters. One day I'll buy you the prettiest home in the world, and we will live there together. There, we will hold hands for hours, and I will look into your eyes without stirring."

He didn't know that I was already inside the prettiest home in the world. This home does not have walls, windows, curtains, a door, or a chimney, but it's still the most beautiful home in the world.

"Then I promise you," I said, "no matter what happens, even if the world turns upside down, we will not part. All that is important is that you don't get upset."

When I noticed that the same sad smile was still covering his face, I said, "I'm still very young, but I can manage everything. I can overcome all difficulties. You will see."

Then he laughed. He held my hand and made me stand up, saying, "I knew that you were Supergirl."

But this happened much later.

On that day, when a small boat took us to a lonely, green island, neither of us knew how we would proceed or how the future would unfold.

Like me, I guess he had also thought that everything could be solved with little effort once we were alone, without having to hide, without being afraid, without having to act according to the time we had, without promises or appointments, and without obscure shadows in our minds.

I did not ask him why we had come here or how he had found this place. I just asked if he had been here before. He said he hadn't. "A French friend of mine recommended this place when I told him that I was looking for a place to eat where we wouldn't have to wait for starched tablecloths."

This was a simple place, away from the busy world, and not frequented by tourists. We were hosted by a family who had turned the small shed next to their house, surrounded by a large wild garden, into a guesthouse. Their small freckled son with long hair knocked on our door every morning and brought us fresh fruit and steaming croissants. His plump blond elder sister, who had pink cheeks and braided hair, brought tea and milk. If we wanted to take a shower, we had to get under a hose in the garden.

The floor of the guesthouse was covered with reed mats. The building consisted of a small hallway and a big bedroom shaded by the leaves of the trees and wild plants. It was cool even at the hottest time of the day.

We had a very small bed, as well as a shabby armchair with broken springs to sit on. Two enormous dogs with long hair and drooping ears chased each other all day long, banging into everything in the garden. When it became too hot, they collapsed on the wooden veranda, breathing with their tongues lolling out of their mouths.

An old woman in a faded blue dress and headscarf sat in a rocking chair and talked to herself almost all day long near the entrance to the big house made of large colored stones.

The burly father of the family, who had a bushy moustache, was often away, and the plump beautiful mother managed the place together with their daughter.

In the mornings, we walked down a grassy narrow slope to the seaside, passing children on bikes, the postman in his beige short-sleeved shirt and short pants, nuns in blue dresses, and farmer women carrying vegetables on their long-haired ponies. Sometimes the small boy of the house followed us.

Old people sat idly in the coffeehouse a short distance away, fishermen washed their boats, huge seabirds came near us, as if the place belonged them, telling us things in a foreign tongue we did not understand.

We enjoyed being lazy and lost track of time under the sun on the pebbly shore. If we became too hot, we dove into the sea, whose color varied from dark blue to light green, and swam through the corals and algae, among fish we didn't recognise.

We felt as if we had found our place on a planet we had never seen before.

Half-naked, like children or natives far from civilization, we spent the whole day climbing rocks in the sea until our feet were cut and our hands hurt, swimming, playing games, watching schools of brightly colored fish gliding through the water, and collecting fabulous sea shells. Tanned, our hair smelling of the sea, and our eyes aglitter, we slowly let ourselves fall into the tranquil seclusion of sleep when we tired.

If a secret paradise really existed, it had to be this corner of the earth.

Far away from there, farther than could be seen with the naked eye, a world awaited us; however, we were rid of it for now. For the moment, we were free of that world, and from the reality that awaited us there.

We talked about many things as we lay on the beach for hours on end, from the time we closed our eyes to the warm caress of the sun until we gazed into the big smiling face of the full moon illuminating the night sky.

We told each other almost everything about our lives. So much had accumulated and remained unshared, waiting to be told some day—to someone who would understand.

I told him many things, but not everything.

Things I couldn't tell him, things that could not be put into words, how much I was in love with him—how I felt connected to him beyond love, passion, and desire . . .

We discussed memories that brought us closer, carefully selected parts of the past, unforgettable songs, our bedside books, films we never wanted to end, a street we both passed at different times but at the same age, the old white mansion on a corner, dreams, embarrassments, things hidden in the attic of childhood.

The way we observed things that were brand new to us.

The way one of us finished a sentence the other had started. The way we sometimes said the same thing at the same time.

Now, I was able to watch him communicate with other people. How he made an agreement with a boy . . . How he negotiated with the fishermen . . . What kind of a man he was when no one did anything for him and he was on his own . . . In a foreign place among people he did not know . . . He was powerful, fearless and at ease. Would it be possible to take a small boat, sail to the rocks far away in the sea, and climb on them? Why not? Why couldn't we climb all the way up the hill and observe the island from high above? It was possible to climb there. Sometimes, while we were walking waist-deep in the sea, the mouth of a cave appeared suddenly, and hand-in-hand we entered it. Inside, where we could hardly find a path and, even then, didn't know where it went, we were as serious as explorers in ages past. We discovered stalactites formed millions of years ago, and walked among corals and slippery rocks we couldn't hold on to. The sunlight filtering in created colorful designs on the water. We saw sea plants and strange fish, and heard the echo of the waves on the rocks outside. Doubtful whenever we thought we had lost our way, we laughed like children upon finding it again.

I felt like a character in the novels I used to read in my childhood. It felt as if none of this were real.

His short-sleeved white shirts with thin blue stripes . . . His long fingers . . . His ring with a big green stone . . . The veins protruding on his hands, arms, and neck . . . His watch showing lunar time, as if he might get lost on a mysterious voyage in a faraway land . . . His silvery hair glistening in the sunlight, sparse on the sides of his forehead and which lay back when it was wet . . . His eyes that reflected the blues and the greens of the sea when he swam and grew darker in the evenings . . . The wrinkles that deepened around his eyes when he smiled . . . The way he inhaled his cigarettes. The way he frowned when he was lost in thought . . . How his face got closer to mine when leaned forward to give me a kiss . . .

I felt good when I was with him.

Good and secure.

When I was with him, I didn't need to protect myself from other people. No. More importantly, I didn't need to protect myself from him.

Nothing had occupied my mind on the way here. For the first time, we were alone. What if the magic disappeared suddenly? What if an ordinary thing that couldn't be defined in words caused us to grow distant from each other?

I did not linger on such thoughts, as if I had known him for thousands of years and as if everything would flow naturally.

The strange thing was that, in spite of all this unexpected warmth and the feeling of having known each other for a long time, the excitement that overwhelmed me did not diminish.

I am relating this as it comes to mind, but perhaps back then, when I sat covered in my shawl at dusk, with my head leaning on his shoulder, watching the setting sun reflect different shades of purple,

I neither cared about anything nor did I have a single thought on my mind. You should have no doubt that even if a thought sneaked into my head every now and then, I played the games all women know from birth so that he wouldn't realize my mind was occupied.

I wondered what was going through his mind.

Did he think that I would forget all that we were experiencing, that I was going after a flashing light I saw, or that this was solely the wish of a little girl who wanted to have an adventure?

Yes, maybe that's what he was thinking, as we lay on the sand in the first strong sunshine of the year and looked at the multicolored sea stretching out far enough to make us believe that we had hidden ourselves from the entire world. Sometimes we closed our eyes to protect them from the scorching sun, on this small island where the chirps of giant locusts and crickets, the hiss of the waves gently touching the shore, the rustle of the bushes in the breeze, and the sound of a plane headed for an unknown destination tell us we could live in this distant part of the world till the end of time. Lazy and carefree. Maybe he thought that all I wanted was an adventure, just like in the movies.

But he was wrong.

He didn't know that I never forgot. I jotted down in my mind all the details, countless small things, messages, notes, letters, conversations, the way words come after another, smiles, the look in his eyes when he caressed my cheek and kissed me, his figure in the dark, clothes, scents, our belongings, furniture, and warmth. I jotted them down in my mind as if keeping a diary.

He didn't know about the decision I arrived at concerning my life.

He didn't know that people had scraped a part of him from inside of me.

He didn't know that I left home before I came here with him.

He also didn't know that on that day in the past, in a taxi on the way back from the museum, he had told me things that excited me beyond imagination. Perhaps it had been because no one else had made me excited with such words before. I forgot about my whole world for a moment and daydreamed about going to a totally different place, or maybe to an island like this one, and living in a reed hut with him until the end of our lives.

He didn't even know that I had been in love with him when I was just a child.

There were so many things he didn't know. I thought that I must tell him everything one day . . . Maybe . . . Later . . .

When I was with him, I didn't want to fall asleep. Even when he slept, I sat in the dark and watched him silently. He didn't know. There, far away from everyone but so close to each other for the first time, I wanted to stop time, and even if I couldn't do that, I wanted to make it longer, extending each and every moment as much as I could. As if I knew what was to follow. As if I was sure all those things we were living would end too soon.

When I eventually did fall asleep, I found myself back in my schooldays. In my dreams, I saw him come to our house, hide in my closet, and live there secretly in my room, so that I find him there waiting for me every day when I come home from school. Then I woke up, and we had a breakfast of fruits, croissants, and tea in the garden.

I told him, "I wish you could live in the closet in my room. When you woke up, I would bring you cookies, and every night, after everyone else went to sleep, we could play games silently and talk in whispers."

But wasn't this true? Wasn't I hiding him in a closet, or in a secret drawer in myself?

Once, while we were sitting naked in bed, he took my face in his hands, raised it, looked deep into my eyes, and asked, "Can a person fall in love with a dream?"

"Yes," I said almost instantly. "Sometimes you love a dream the most. A dream . . ."

After a few days in paradise on the tiny island away from the confusion of life, crowds, big cities, factories, and wars—making us feel that they did not exist and that our lives glided through them quietly and without effort—we left with people waving good-bye to us.

As we sailed away, the island left behind in the distance looked like a familiar place to which we would return.

On that island, where I had no chance to reach anyone by phone, I had disappeared from everyone in my life for the first time, and strangely, I did not even think about the people I had left behind.

The idea of forgetting about everything in my life and starting from scratch with just the small handbag in my hand frightened me.

"You know that I could spend my whole life here without doing anything," I said to him.

He replied, "For the first time I feel sad about leaving a place."

We had become lost in impossible dreams, and were returning home after spending the best days of our lives (at least as far as I am concerned). We were unaware of what was taking place somewhere else, which would determine the rest of our lives.

We had perhaps stopped time for ourselves but not for the world.

Fuat took a small, velvet case out of his pocket. He took out an old ring with a yellowish stone and put it on my finger.

"From now on, there will be no talk of separation," he said.

"We have not talked about separating," I replied.

"I bought this ring long time ago, but I didn't have the courage to give it to you."

"It's beautiful," I said. "I haven't seen a precious stone of this color before."

"Even if you choose not to wear it, please keep it forever."

"Why shouldn't I wear it?" I said. "I will always wear it."

In a way, we had always postponed things. Until that day, we had postponed having that conversation, during which we did not know what to say exactly or confess what we wanted to do because the reality was quite different, and we were afraid of hurting each other.

"What a strange woman you are," he said after a long silence. "You do not ask me anything."

I laughed. Should I ask him about what had occupied my mind, or all the questions that tortured me until that day?

I said, "I am not going to ask you anything. You should not tell me anything either. Because in the end nothing happens according to plan."

He studied my face, as if thinking of something . . . as if he wanted to tell me something. But he remained silent.

There were things I wanted him to say to me as we leaned against the railing on the deck, enjoying the afternoon breeze, but I didn't want to ask him anything.

A voice in me said (just like Turgut had told me earlier) that he would not succeed, that he would not be able to leave his wife and his daughter.

He would leave neither me nor his wife.

At that moment, I didn't want to consider this, but I couldn't stop thinking about it.

He was happy with me. He loved me. I knew this. But now he would go back to his old life, and with the help of the new energy, excitement and happiness this escape of a few days had given him, he would be able to continue to bear everything that depressed him and that he didn't want in his life.

But I could not act so. I could not lead a dual life. Just because I was an honest person? No, not really. Because I couldn't cope with it.

Maybe Fuat's feelings were not as strong as mine. If he loved me like he said, he wouldn't be able to glance at another woman, let alone live with another woman.

I suddenly realized that if I allowed myself to savor momentary happiness each time he appeared in front of me like a genie from a lamp, he would never be able to make a firm decision.

In a mad dash from one place to another, living a life that passed much faster than mine, facing big decisions, disputes, fights, and responsibilities, he would never be able to stop and think for a moment about starting everything all over again in a new place and with a new person.

I had made a decision. Even if I did not realize it thoroughly yet, it had become my reality. My whole life had been changed in these few days. I had thought that the dilemma I had been suffering would be over, but I was mistaken.

Once again, I found myself in great uncertainty. A little earlier, my feet had been firmly on the ground, and I felt at home where I belonged, but now, suddenly, I felt as if I had been left homeless.

Could I tell him about the tides inside of me?

Maybe if I asked him, or if I forced him, to make a decision, everything would be different. But what we were experiencing was so beautiful. Like the view of a vast area covered with snow, even the slightest touch could spoil it. Like a sleeping baby, you couldn't get enough of looking at it. It was like a sunset that changed gradually and which would never be the same, or a film you watched buried in your armchair and wished would never end, though moment by moment, its finale grew closer.

There he was, next to me, looking into the distance lost in thought. I did not look at him, but I knew. We were looking at the same thing—the horizon, as if we were waiting for a piece of land to appear. Maybe we were thinking about the same thing, yet we were unable to do anything to build up a future that was waiting for us.

I had made a promise to myself, hadn't I? I had promised myself that I would never ask or expect anything from him and that I would not build castles in the air about a shared future.

One day I realized that no matter where I went in the world, I always missed Istanbul: when I crossed clean public squares and wide boulevards in the most beautiful cities; when I visited glamorous palaces; when I was in magnificent cities with people who bumped into each other as they walked indifferently; when I was away from crowds; when I was on islands where people led secluded lives; when I was on distant continents where people maintained habits from before recorded history; when I was on cold oceans, vast plains, and even in uninhabited places where I thought I was in solitude.

I have not missed the house in Ankara where I spent my childhood but my grandmother's house in Kandilli that we used to spend summers. The small bell on the iron door that would hardly open, the garden filled with roses and magnolias, and the coolness of the stones that were dampened every afternoon.

I always heard the joyful twitter of the birds calling to each other there.

When you entered, there was a framed text on the wall, which I never forgot: "It is water that gives life to everything!"

A fat, red canary with a lovely voice lived in a huge, old cage—I have never seen a bird like that anywhere again.

A giant mirror with a gilt frame where I stood and stared at myself.

The big paintings depicting storms, illuminated by light filtered through the colored glass of the long narrow windows. My grandfather's framed photograph that was hand-colored after it was taken. Right next to it, another photograph taken on the day he and my grandmother got married.

The big soft green velvet sofa on which I tumbled and fell asleep after lunch. How I loved to nestle in it. On warm afternoons, I used to sit in an armchair in the murky hall in the entrance and read, make designs on the upholstery with my fingers, and then fall asleep studying the embellishments on the ceiling. I would sleep until teatime, when I would have my favorite cookies and sesame rolls.

Didn't I read those Turkish classics *Çalıkuşu* and *Aşk-ı Memnu* there? And what about Paul and Virginie?

How nicely Yahya Kemal had put it: "As Kandilli was swimming in its sleep/We dragged the moonlight on the waters/ It was a glimmering silvery path/ We left and never mentioned coming back."

Directly opposite the big armchair, there was a wooden grandfather clock that fascinated me. It looked like a big house, like a closed temple, and as a child, I couldn't figure out how it worked, making me even more curious. Watching the big pendulum oscillate behind the glass made me sleepy. I have always recalled the days I spent in the long room, the peace, the fresh smell of the place, and the sweet-est of all sleeps as if I were still a child.

Big rivers always go through European cities, but I missed my hometown through which giant ships pass. I have never forgotten the glitter of the sea in the morning light as it stretched as far as the eye could see.

Once my grandmother had told me in the days when she couldn't see clearly anymore and often got confused, "I hear the sound of the seagulls, and I tell myself morning has broken. I wake up, but then I am unable to see the sea. If the seagulls are here, then the sea must also be here. But why can't I see it? Come, child, take me to the sea."

The smell of the sesame rolls sold in the afternoons and the freshly baked bread came and found me wherever I went over the years.

It would always be like this. Even the images that we were used to the most would be erased in time. Hard to believe, but all the same, that's the way it was.

In those days, everything looked brilliant to me; nothing seemed as if it could be forgotten or obliterated.

Yet, how fast memories dim.

When you tell someone about your memories, no, even when you remind yourself, they get stuck behind meaningless details and nonsense. We keep forgetting them, as if they are less important than the phone number of some idiot, the names of the actors and actresses in a television series, or the political unrest in a country we have never been to.

The moment we transform things into words, the most impor-tant moments of our life, the turning points, and the images we thought would never become vague, disappear.

Remembering is something like this. All that is left is an old photo on which only the barely perceptible contours of the figures remain.

A long life and all the other lives that have intertwined with it are caught in a few feeble words. And there it ends.

There are so many things that cannot be defined—things that cannot be expressed in words or explained to another person. Perhaps this is why we sometimes cannot answer the questions people who are the closest to us ask. Even those people do not know the things that cannot be told, just as we do not know their memories that cannot be defined. How strange. We use words to talk about someone, to define someone, or to describe him.

Yet we do not know that words are useless to explain a person's essence.

Now, here, far away from my childhood home, in a totally different time and state of mind, something suddenly carries me to that faraway place. But it is not an ordinary word.

Words are not vehicles you get on to be carried from one place to another.

What is it that does this?

If words do not take us back to a long-lost feeling, a scent or a fractured image without warning and with speed, what is it?

Is it an image, a smell, a color, or another feeling?

Is it the similarities you find? Coincidences? Sounds?

None of these. In fact, we are not carried back from the place where we now stand. The only thing that is happening is that we are going to a spot in the incredible archive of our memories, consisting of countless images. We do not return to the past. The chaotic pile of images in our memories rotates on its own, dragging us at a certain point back to "that moment," as a result of a coincidence, similarity, a sound, or color.

When I was a child, I had a globe that could be illuminated.

Whenever I was alone, I sat in the dark, turned it on, and played with it for hours. First, I made it spin fast, and then I stopped it by putting my finger on a random spot. I would try to imagine the country, city, town, or island that was under my finger. In my mind, I would portray what happened in that place at that moment, whether it was cold or warm, what a girl of my age living there was doing . . .

Later, I went abroad and saw many of the countries and cities that were shown on that illuminated globe of different colors. Now I know that people there did not lead lives much different from ours, contrary to what I had imagined as a child.

There are people all over the world who resemble each other. Lives that are alike . . . The same distress, the same happiness, the same deadlocks, and the same fights . . .

When I used to play that game, I dreamed of being in different places, of escaping from the hours of my time, and of going far away. Later, however, when I went to those foreign cities, I wanted to escape from the hours of my own life.

As a child in my small, adorable room, I was able to visit the places on the illuminated globe only in my imagination. I remained in my room.

Later, during my visits to the places I had dreamed about, I used to close my eyes and imagine I was back in my room with the globe.

On the plane, which flew too close to the mountains, making me think that it would crash on them, I looked through the window and watched the propellers. When we landed, we were both a little tired, and as I walked with my head leaning against his shoulder, something unexpected happened.

As if in a Hitchcock film, I suddenly saw a familiar face turn away when we were passing by.

The eyes of that person and mine had met for a brief, barely perceptible moment.

I was so tired that I couldn't immediately interpret this encounter. After walking a few more steps, it sank in. I took away my arm from Fuat's, but it was too late. I wanted to turn around and check if that was really the person I thought it was, but I couldn't gather my courage.

"What's wrong?" Fuat asked.

I was walking faster now. He was trying to catch up with me.

"Why are you running?"

I said the name of the person who had seen us. "He saw us," I said. "Don't turn around to look. He was leaning against the wall near the corner, and he saw us."

"Maybe you mistook someone else for him. If it had been him, he would have approached us, wouldn't he?"

"Perhaps he didn't know how to react." I was out of breath. "How could you expect him to say something to us?"

"Yeah, in a way, you're right."

"What are we going to do now?"

"We'll take the first cab we see," he said, as we walked out of the gate and motioned to one of the cab drivers to pick up our luggage.

I hurled myself onto the back seat of the cab. If it were possible, I would have disappeared in my hat. How angry I was with myself! The lazy and peaceful happiness I had felt until just a few minutes ago had vanished. My mind was filled with questions. Why the hell did you take his arm in the middle of the crowd? I asked myself. Why did I lean against him like that? Then I thought that perhaps the man whom I had noticed might have been unsure that he had seen us. How could I be sure? Maybe he had been watching us as we approached the spot where he was standing. Maybe he only turned his head at the last moment? We had disembarked from a plane so it was impossible to make up lies. We were still dressed in holiday clothes. We were tanned. If the man had seen Fuat or me alone, he would have immediately come up to us; no wonder he had turned his head away—out of shock! What great news this would be for many; even the most discreet person would put aside all considerations and speak out in such a situation. The esteemed gentleman returning from a holiday with his married lover. Arm in arm . . . With eyes fixed on each other . . . Drunk with happiness . . . They were oblivious to everything. What a stupidity. Only people blinded with love can act like that.

"That fellow is a chatterbox," Fuat said after telling the driver where to take us. He was frowning now.

"I know that. Tomorrow, the whole city of Ankara will know. Besides, things will be made up and added to it."

I suddenly felt hot and suffocated. I was gradually beginning to realize the graveness of this situation. The game was over. Oh God! We had spent all that time alone and in peace, and then we were caught by some idiot here. We had messed up everything.

"I wouldn't be surprised if he's not already calling someone to give the news," I said.

"He doesn't need to embellish it much," Fuat said smiling. Then he held my hand tightly.

"Don't worry," he said. "Everything has a reason. There was a reason for him to see us at that moment."

I wasn't able to smile like Fuat.

"No, we were caught. All he lacked was a camera."

Fuat looked at me. He smiled, but it was forced. He was thoughtful but calm.

"It was a bad coincidence, but don't worry about it," he said. "People will always gossip. Sometimes you do everything, and no one believes you could have done such things; however, sometimes when you haven't done anything, they say the most unbelievable things about you."

I was annoyed. I was worried more about him than myself. His wife would surely hear about us. His friends.

I was very tense. The man who had seen us was not close to Fuat or his acquaintances. What if he went to the newspapers and told them what he had seen? Wouldn't it be a great opportunity for them? They already wrote negative things about Fuat.

He said, "I don't think he would go that far. He'd be afraid." Then he paused and smiled, adding, "Besides, the worst is the grapevine! That is the paper that has the highest sales figures!"

I panicked. I knew that Fuat was planning what to do, but I couldn't accept the way he looked indifferently out of the window, as if he didn't care.

I didn't want to go out in the evening and wished to hide where nobody could reach us, as if the whole world knew about us. Yet, he insisted on going out. We went to a small restaurant that was not well known. He raised his glass in a toast and said, "Come on, young lady, don't frown like that. I am sure such small maters will not intimidate you."

I was very uncomfortable and scared. I reproached myself. How could I have acted so irresponsibly? This situation would harm both Fuat and Turgut.

Then I realized that Fuat was worrying about me, thinking that I was concerned with myself. I told him why I was scared.

"Try not to think about it," he said. "They already say so many things about me. One more thing won't make any difference."

"How can you say that?" I objected. "This was my biggest fear

until today. When I think of what will happen to you because of me
..."

With a smile, he looked at me compassionately. Shrugging his shoulders, he said, "At least this is true. All the other things they wrote about me were lies. At least I'll be upset for something worthwhile. You can deny the whole thing. You can say the man mistook someone else for you, and everything will be solved."

Apparently, he was wondering what I would say to my husband. There was a long silence.

I said to him abruptly, "Fuat, I told my husband about everything."

I looked at his face, but he kept himself under control. He put down his glass. He took out his cigarette case from his pocket and lit a cigarette. Raising his eyebrows slightly, he glanced at me as if asking, "Really? Everything?"

"I know I did this without asking your opinion, but I could not keep on going. I couldn't live surrounded by lies. I told him that no one else knew about our affair. Now, this incident is going to be bad
..."

He listened to me quietly, perhaps astonished that I hadn't given him the news for such a long time, letting my words sink in.

"We decided to divorce, and then I left home. I told my mother, but neither she nor anybody else knows where I am now."

"I had thought that you told everyone you were on a holiday with a friend," Fuat said. "I suspected something when you stayed in Istanbul for such a long time, but that day in the Pera Palas, you didn't tell me anything, so I wasn't sure."

On one hand, I felt uneasy talking about this subject, but on the other, I felt relieved.

He was frowning. He looked worried.

"Where are you going to go now?" he asked.

"To Istanbul. To my mother's," I replied. Smiling, I added, "And of course to my cat!"

I would go back to live with my family, as if they had never changed homes, and I had never left. I would go back to my room that had been empty for so many years and to my illuminated globe.

Maybe again, I could turn it on at night. But now I wouldn't wonder about the lives of the people in the places where I put my finger.

It is not difficult for someone to fall into a dreadful pit after having soared blissfully feeling that they could almost touch the sky.

That night I realized that what I had told him about my personal life had worried him. If I were in his shoes and someone had come and told me the same things, I think I would have been happy.

But I guess he thought everything had suddenly changed, at least that was how I interpreted his silent and thoughtful behavior and the worried look on his face, even though we talked about other things and left everything to time as we had always done through a secret agreement between us.

Maybe the step I had taken was about to bring our lovely days to an end.

Fuat and I had a secret life that took place in an obscure space between reality and delusion, between dreams and truth. We were experiencing a childish adventure that was scary, wild, and perilous but exciting. At the same time, this adventure that lifted us off the ground was unique; it did not belong to the time and the world we were familiar with.

I was aware that the atmosphere of the candle-lit dinner we had at an old wooden table was disturbed by our conversation. Someone who had sat there before us had inscribed a poem on the dark table top: "I'm going to give you a big secret: You are Time."

I could not avoid reading the poem when he spoke to me, or during the long periods of pregnant silence.

The poem said: "I'm going to give you a big secret: I am afraid of you . . . / afraid of the way you move your hands and arms, afraid of the words unsaid . . ."

After the three days we spent in a place that resembled the edge of the world (I was glad I hadn't told him about my marriage on the first day), we had faced the reality at the airport (we had returned to real life) and been forced to think of what tomorrow would bring.

Then I realized that the verses inscribed on the wooden table were those of a famous French poet who wrote unparalleled poems for his lover and who said: "There is no happy love."

Was there really no happy love?

No matter how hard we tried to conceal what was going on, we were both aware of it, and we also knew that we both knew it. However, we still we didn't succeed in restoring the atmosphere, the joy, our childishly carefree attitude, and the idle ease we had enjoyed a few hours ago.

Thankfully, I was tired and still in this dazed, dreamy mood. As soon as we returned to our hotel, I undressed, went to bed, and fell into a deep sleep. It surprised me how I had quickly got used to the way he hugged me from the back as we fell asleep, as if we had been together for years.

He was thoughtful but quiet when I saw him off early in the morning.

"Wouldn't you like to eat something?" I asked.

"I'm late," he said. "I don't feel like it but I have to go now and read files and attend meetings. What can I do . . .?"

I felt like saying, "Don't worry, this is not a game, and I don't think that it's now your turn to take a step." I couldn't say it, however.

He hugged me in front of the hotel and left after saying we would meet again soon.

Under the bewildered look of the doorman, I poured a glass of water after Fuat, as always.

Yes, I pour water after a person who leaves on a journey, I knock on wood, I listen to people who say they have been to other worlds, and if I meet someone who reads coffee cups, I get excited. Just to defy Ayla, who makes fun of me saying, "Do you still stick to those beliefs that are as old as the hills?" I even drop coins into wishing wells. I'm wearing the chain my mother had given me with a protective prayer attached to it. So what? Should I be one of those people who think they will be well just because they see a doctor every year? Come on!

I went to my room to pack my suitcase. I got ready to leave the hotel and go to the airport, from which a plane would carry me to different destination than Fuat's.

Actually, everything was beginning now.

Even though I didn't know what would happen, I knew it wouldn't be easy.

Something I couldn't define, or a feeling of terrible loneliness that suddenly descended on me scared me for a moment; I even thought of calling my husband and going back to him.

Of course, I didn't do that.

I kissed the stone on the ring I now wore, as if celebrating a new start in my life.

Having to confront my mother and my brother, answering their questions, all the acquaintances and relatives who would want to interfere, other people, all the gossip . . . Oof! Just the thought of such things made me sick.

I knew that returning to Istanbul was perhaps the last thing I wanted to do, but where else could I go? I wished I could find Ayla, and that she would take me to the tombs of the old kings in the middle of the desert. I wished I could stay there, where no one would judge me or ask me questions.

But, no! I decided to be strong, to remain fearless. To endure all that would follow . . . Therefore, I would do what was hardest for me: face the truth. I knew that the first encounter would be the most difficult.

On the plane, I thought of how many journeys I had made despite my young age, how many places I had left behind, and asked myself why I felt so forlorn during each journey.

As the plane moved ahead through the clouds, I thought about the worst that could happen. I knew that I was wearing myself out to find excuses and invent lies, like a guilty school girl whose misdemeanor has been discovered. None would be of use, and everyone would eventually discover the truth.

Until that day, I had postponed and disregarded many things in my life, but I had reached the end of that road.

Eventually, I was tired of the struggle and had abandoned it. I kept telling myself that all the trouble facing me didn't matter. I am the person who created it all. I cheated on my husband, I had a relationship with a married man, I went on a holiday with him, and now I'm divorcing my husband. There's even more you don't know . . . What should I do? Die?

If you want to know, let me tell you that I would have done even more if I were sure other people would not be hurt or affected.

Unfortunately, you know that life is merely a strip of images that moves in fast forward, and a game that can end abruptly without allowing you to look back for a last time. As soon as you find the happiest coincidences among all you come across during this obscure time period, you shouldn't bother about the rest; it is impossible.

It is impossible to pick only the most beautiful images from this entangled confusion.

Even when you feel you have the most power, you cannot cope with the words of people you don't care about, the judgments of those you don't know, and the inconsiderate behavior of those closest to you.

It is not easy to demolish and rebuild a life that was established through an ordinary coincidence.

When I arrived in Istanbul and settled in my childhood room (my mother had even kept my dolls), I realized that I had not only come back to a small, familiar room but also to a world that I had grown distant from and forgotten.

I had not kept up with the news, but my old school friends, neighbors and acquaintances had devoted themselves to keeping well informed about the lives of princesses and kings, the love affairs of film stars, and all the other gossip from all around the world.

Although I had not yet been mentioned in the "community news" sections of the newly published magazines, I was a part of the gossip.

Meaningful looks . . . Innuendos . . . Stories hinting at ours . . . Some well-known ladies even left tables as soon as I arrived.

Costume balls, wild parties, American-style clubs that had popped up in the city one after another, bars, tea parties at the Hilton hotel . . .

Princes, princesses, and kings who visited the country . . . A handful of people who tried to live the life of another country . . .

The Istanbul of my childhood was being systematically demolished. New roads were being constructed, boulevards were being built, and other country's lifestyles were beginning to dominate.

I realized that these attempts were superficial. The clothes we wore, new furniture, new cars, new clubs, English and French names, self-service cafeterias, jazz clubs, seasonal balls, young people playing rock and roll, "half-naked" girls, Dior suits, Balmain shawls, and the modern hotels that were opening did not represent real life in this country.

One day, as I was reading the newspaper, a headline attracted my attention: "There are 1,771,000 donkeys in Turkey!"

I was laughing loudly when Nihat entered the room and asked, "Why are you laughing alone like a demented soul?"

"Have a look," I said. "They have counted all of the donkeys . . ."

He read the news article and also began laughing. He said, "It is impossible not to make progress with so many donkeys!"

Like many others, he thought that the new style of life was not genuine and that all the things people adopted for the sake of novelty, modernity, and being European would not take us one step forward, but would cause us to regress. The new novel by Halide Hanım with the title *Rock'n'Roll* was published serially in the newspaper, and Nihat cut each one out for me to read.

I wasn't sure of anything. In those days, everything was very confusing, just like my own life. Life had to change and evolve. But this change did not take place as fast as some people wanted it to. It was not the people, but perhaps the internal clock of this land, that resisted change.

In the end, I had settled in Istanbul, but I felt lonely.

I didn't know where I belonged. Did I belong to a glittering image that disappeared when you scratched it slightly, to the old neighborhoods you could reach by taking the tram, or to the distant foreign lands I had visited or lived in?

I would only understand later that the odd distress and tribulation, like guilt, which I felt in the beginning, were actually rooted in the fact that I had lost my point of focus.

I had not felt the need to question myself about my identity until then. I was the wife of a diplomat who lived in foreign countries—a young, married woman who knew foreign languages, who was well-cultured, and who made a good impression on other people through her vitality and the way she talked.

These acute lines of description, about which I cared the least, completed a person's image and placed him in a specific spot in society. In this way, one found themselves firmly supported, strong, and confidently advancing into the future.

But I was no longer a young, married woman or a future mother.

I did not have a profession.

I did not have a home.

I had left behind the people I knew in the places I had been.

My mother and my brother, whom I had left before I was fully grown-up, were somewhat different now.

The house where my grandmother no longer lived, and the family without my father prevented me from living in the past.

Apparently, I was one of the people I scorned, belonging to a group of women who frequented tea parties, balls, events, openings, and cocktail parties, who did not show interest in anything except clothing, jewelry, and gossip, and who passed themselves off as highly knowledgeable although they only repeated things heard from their husbands. I was one of them.

Yet, even half an hour spent with such women bored me to death, and I couldn't wait to leave as soon as possible.

In truth, they didn't like me very much either. Usually, I either remained silent when I was among them or just uttered a few brief, ordinary statements. But sometimes I couldn't hold myself back from making sharp remarks that left everyone dumbfounded.

My life was unclear, and I felt so constricted that I sometimes regretted having returned to Turkey.

In the mornings, I went for a walk after breakfast, and after strolling along the coast for a while, I returned home and read.

The summer was almost over. Everyone was expecting the arrival of the King of Iraq and the announcement that young Fazila had become a princess, but the newspapers wrote about death and the revolution. They were filled with photographs of high officials rushing from one place to another at Yeşilköy Airport, while still in their formal suits. Maybe it was after this incident that people began to talk about a possible revolution in Turkey. (What happened to beautiful Fazila who was waiting for her king in a mansion by the Bosphorus? Who knows what she did after receiving the sad news.)

Yes, the summer was nearly over—the hottest summer we had ever experienced.

Sometimes I put on a pair of pants and a casual shirt and took a boat to the other side of the city. I sat in a café in the open air, had some tea, and then returned home towards evening.

I was buried in a curious melancholy. Watching sunsets, reading poetry, strolling through the city I had forgotten helped me pass the time.

I did not want to meet relatives, old acquaintances, or neighbors. I noticed that my mother was a little angry at me because of what I had done, but I think she was also sad to see me spend my days reading books with the cat in my lap.

She didn't say anything. Maybe she thought that my love would soon end and that everything would begin to go well again.

Everyone knew about Fuat and me, but no one reproached me openly.

One night, Nihat entered my room while I was weeping.

He sat next to me.

"Why are you crying?" he asked.

"I am sick and tired of seeing myself like someone who has committed a horrible crime," I replied. "I know what I'm doing. Why is it so wrong for two people to love each other? Aren't the people who get in their way to blame?"

He hung his head. I was aware that he had been refraining from talking to me about this matter, but he wasn't able to keep silent anymore. "Is such a relationship possible?" he asked. "Do you really believe it will work?"

I was astonished by his direct observation.

"Yes, I believe it will," I said. "I love him very much. Regardless of what others think, I truly love him."

The harshness of my voice made him sorry for having asked such a question. He knew that whenever I spoke sharply, I felt like crying.

He lit himself a cigarette and gave another to me.

"Mother is very upset," he said. "What do you plan to do?"

"What do you think?" I asked, studying his face.

For a moment, he didn't know what to say and was not able to look me in the eye.

All of a sudden, he said, "I remember the day I introduced him to you."

"I was a kid," I said. "Who would have thought . . .?"

He laughed.

"You are still a kid. And I'm afraid you will always be."

Then I hugged him.

"Will you always remain my beloved good-hearted brother?"

He gulped, as if something was obstructing his throat. Trying to smile, he said, "What can I do? I promised you once that I would always care for you."

I love Saturdays.

Though unbelievable, even today, I wake up on Saturday mornings in a different mood than on other days. My heart beats with incomprehensible joy and excitement.

Not long after my return to Istanbul, Fuat began visiting me at the weekend.

Some columnists wrote things like "The cabinet meets in Istanbul now!"

The morning phone calls began again, too. I waited for him to call me as soon as I woke up. In those days, I sometimes got ill-tempered and feigned reluctance, acting in a surprisingly childish manner.

I got nervous if he didn't call, and while biting my nails, I imagined stories even though I knew where he was.

It happened like this: On Mondays, I was in a pleasant mood since I was still enjoying the memory of the weekend. I went out by myself, chatted at home with my mother, and talked merrily in the evenings. On Tuesdays, the downfall began slowly. I sat at home and read books, roaming the house in a troubled state of mind. On Wednesdays and Thursdays, no one was able to approach me. On Fridays, I became excited again, waiting for the news if he would come or not. If so, I became full of energy and jumped out of my bed at the break of dawn on Saturday.

I tried to decide what to wear, as if I hadn't already thought about it the day before, changing clothes in front of the mirror, examining my face, and gathering my hair, letting it loose, or braiding it until midday.

How strange! He never had any idea of what I did during those hours.

Maybe all men who are loved like this do not know how much time and effort women spend on such frivolous details.

He would only tell me, "Each time I see you I am attracted to you again. You look even more beautiful. You appear different. You're like a magic lantern of changing images. I have never seen anyone like this before."

As if we had a secret agreement, my mother and brother never asked me where I went on Saturday morning, where I came from in the evening, or what I did the following day.

Fuat always checked in to the newly opened hotel by the seaside in the morning, and I would meet him there about noon.

How many people remember Ariane today?

And who remembers the film *Love in the Afternoon* in which Audrey Hepburn plays a cello student?

Who remembers how she is seduced by a middle-aged playboy, and how she tries to entrap him by acting like a worldly "bon vivant?"

She cannot take her eyes off Mr. Flannagan, who has experienced the same scene with many other women before, as they dance in the moonlight to that "magical" song.

After realizing everything, her father helplessly says to the notorious womanizer, "Please give her a chance. Let the little fish go back into the water. She's not right for you."

Did I think I looked like Hepburn on those Saturday afternoons? Did I also fasten my hair with two hairpins on either side of my head?

When I talked with the air of an experienced woman, did I also open myself to him with the coy expression of a child?

Beneath my indifferent attitude, did he notice the deep pain in my eyes?

I wish I had asked him those questions.

It's impossible to see yourself in a mirror all the time. Even if you think you know how you look, you can never know how you appear on another person acting as your mirror.

After roaring and fuming at him on the phone, I turned into a pussy cat when I was with him. Sometimes I stood up and sat elsewhere when he wanted to embrace me, frowning like a child. However, I was never able to feel real rage toward him; all I wanted to do was surrender my whole being to him.

When I felt like this, I considered what I did, what would happen in the future, other people, their judgments, pain, and all the worries that consumed me and made me feel that everything was empty and meaningless.

I didn't want to spend the precious moments we had alone and the hours that passed in the blink of an eye with such nonsense. (I thought that I was the only one in the world in such deep love.)

Do you know what was strange?

Fuat thought that I was refraining from putting our life in order and asking him things any other woman would have.

Once he said, "You are so enigmatic. Do you think it would be impossible to spend your whole life with a lunatic like me? Is that why you're running away?"

Running away?

How naïve men are!

It seemed that I had made him believe what I wanted him to believe.

What did I think?

As Turgut had said, I realized that he would never be able to divorce his wife and that his family, the people around him, and even the Prime Minister, would not allow it.

If he attempted divorce, especially in those days, his family and the entire country would enter into a state of confusion.

The gossip that he was seeing a woman had started to spread, and everyone was talking about him.

One of the most important men leading the country would leave his wife and child for another woman!

His friends would surely lynch him before his enemies. Wouldn't this be an opportunity for those who were jealous of him or disliked him, as well as for those whom he had hurt?

After so much trouble, how would we ever be able to lead a happy life in this country?

We usually didn't discuss politics, but sometimes when he had them in mind or he was angry about something, he would talk about them.

Once when he was enraged, I said to him, "You told me you would abandon everything. You told me you were tired of everything. People keep attacking you, even the ones who liked you in the past . . ."

He scrutinized me, and I wasn't able to finish.

He moved his hand, as if to say that all was in vain. "I hope they all get what they deserve," he said.

"But you don't deserve what you're going through," I continued.

Then, for the first time, he didn't put an end to the topic and said, "I know. I understand everything you're saying, but I can do nothing now. I have embarked on something, and I cannot leave everyone in the lurch—especially the Prime Minister. I cannot back off just because they are putting me under pressure."

Then he stood up, lit a cigarette, went to the window, and stared into the distance. "What kind of fight is this? I don't know, but I'm sick and tired of it. Even if I do the right thing, they say I am a terrible person. Then they tell me not to worry, saying that this is politics and that I shouldn't take it personally. I wish I had listened to you from the beginning."

After that, I remained silent. I stopped telling him to give up and save himself.

I also told myself that if Fuat ever decided to do something crazy and accept the risk of what would follow, it had to be his own decision, not because I told him to do so.

I never thought that if he loved me as much as he said he did, he would do it.

Hadn't I promised myself years ago that I would never be like other women who lived their lives according to their father's, boyfriend's, husband's, and finally their children's wishes, in that order?

I knew he loved me, but he was trapped. He wanted to go back to the good old days, but he couldn't. He was not able to leave his wife and his daughter even though he was ready to come to me for good.

His life was not easy or carefree as everyone thought. He was entangled, entrapped, and struggling to survive in a life he didn't want. Perhaps he was only able to recapture his true essence during the time spent by my side.

"It's only here that I feel I can breathe . . . in this small room," he once said.

I used to wish that the world surrounding everyone's life would not enter that room.

A few times when he mentioned divorce, I quickly sealed the subject by saying, "Don't talk to me about divorce. If it's going to happen, it will. I am pleased with my life. I don't want to spend our time discussing what will happen to us or what we plan to do."

If asked, he would daydream and say how we would build our own home in a place he had visited on a trip, in a town he had been to during his youth, or in a district I liked. He would say how he would leave everything behind, how we would spend our days, and how he would be the happiest man in the world.

Perhaps he really believed his fantasies.

In a very small room . . .

I can still remember all the colors; the patterns on the dark green curtains; the lines of the wallpaper; the view from the window (ships passed in the distance and towards evening, fishermen's boats appeared); his untidy suitcase; his clothes; the dinners we had on the balcony when the weather was good; the moments of bliss when the bed, the quilt, and even the clothes were scattered; coffee and cigarettes; the songs we listened to on the "smallest record player in the world" he had found somewhere; the roses that reminded us of another hotel in a distant country; and the way we giggled like children (I wonder what made us laugh so much.).

How he said, "Stay a little longer."

How he asked, "Are you leaving me again?"

How he hid my shoes like a naughty child.

How he embraced me tightly at the door, as if we would never see each other again.

Saturday was the day of awakening—as if spring came every Saturday.

Sunday was the day of separation.

Each time he said, "The driver could take you."

"I'll go on my own."

I used to try to slip out the door without exchanging too many words, without asking if we would meet again next week, and without saying words of separation . . .

As if I were going out to shop and would return by evening.

"How bizarre," he used to say, "I start missing you even before you leave. Like a child, I can hardly stop myself from turning around and coming back as soon as I set off on the road."

A very small hotel room . . .

Our entire world.

A world that belonged just to the two of us . . .

The one and only room we were able to establish for ourselves in this world.

It was like a big cardboard box where we hid like two children, as if we were in a foreign land. Only there were we concealed and safe from all eyes, and no one could touch or reach us.

Fabrics, caresses, kisses, feelings, words, chuckles, looks, memories . . .

How much he told me . . . a great life . . . full of famous people, politicians, kings, princes, artists, poets, and crazy people.

I would sit in our room and listen to his vivid stories.

He lost himself when he told his stories, imitating people. Always finding new things to tell me, he was like a magician who kept pulling rabbits out of a hat. I had never heard anyone describe people so vividly or seen anyone express himself so dramatically, waving his hands, moving his eyes, and jumping up in joy.

I was able to imagine the places where he spent his childhood. I could see his uncle, a former captain who now repaired old clocks in a house far away from the sea just because he was angry for not being able to go to sea again; the big, burly Thracian cook; his grandfather whom everyone feared; his mother whose wishes he could still not think of going against; his brother whose death he heard about after coming home from boarding school for the summer holiday; his father who closeted himself in a ground-floor room and spent his time reading, praying, and doing religious calligraphy; and his grandmother who couldn't pronounce her "R's". It was as if they were distant acquaintances whom I visited occasionally.

Sometimes I would lose myself in thought, without being conscious of what he was telling me.

As he described all those lives, I used to delve into the depths of his dark blue eyes glittering with the light from the room's huge windows.

Then, he would stop talking all of a sudden, eyeing me doubtfully, thinking I wasn't interested in his stories.

"But I was listening to you," I would say in guilt.

He would caress my face and say, "I came to the end of my life without being aware of it. I started living again with you. All the boring things excite me again."

I would tease him, saying, "Tell me the truth. Are you really in love with me or are you just amusing yourself?"

In the film, Ariane falls crazily in love with the famous playboy at first sight. The middle-aged womanizer falls in love with her slowly, without being aware of it.

If you won't watch the film, let me tell you the finale: In the main train station in Paris, on a rainy August night, Gary Cooper embraces Audrey Hepburn who has come there to tearfully bid him farewell, pulling her onto the train that has started to move.

That scene always reminds me of another love story. Ariane succeeds in getting on the train; however, at the end of the other story, Anna hurls herself under the train.

I did not know what would happen to me.

Would I wave good-bye to him, get on the train and go far away with him, or hurl myself under the wheels.

I never found out.

The small hotel room became a home to us.

We put some of our belongings in the drawers. When we weren't there, our room was not given to anybody else. It remained empty. His small suitcase was always there. Some of his suits, shirts, and underwear were in the closet. I also brought some of my things. Slowly, the room was filled with our belongings.

Books, magazines, and small souvenirs from places he had visited—the cute family of hedgehogs from Bavaria, the small glass elephants from Italy, the small porcelain girl from Vienna (this trinket had reminded him of me immediately), and the paper house from Japan.

He used to cut clippings from the magazines he read on the way to Istanbul and keep them. I saved one of those magazines even though its cover was torn and its pages were crumpled.

I remember the day he had showed me the headline: "Why do women prefer older men?"

While he sat in the armchair across from me, I read the article aloud:

"Françoise Sagan, one of the most famous novelists of our times, recently got married to Guy Schoeller. Schoeller is twenty years older than Françoise, who is only 22.

"Like Sagan, many women enjoy being with older men. One of the most well-known is, without doubt, Sophia Loren. Although Loren is only 23, she fell in love with and married producer Carlo Ponti who is over 40.

"Princess Ira Fuerstenberg fell in love with 35-year-old prince Alphonse two years ago when she was a young girl of 15. This love affair also resulted in marriage. Audrey Hepburn married Mel Ferrer who is past 40.

"This list includes Oona O'Neill who surprisingly married Charlie Chaplin in spite of a 35-year age difference, and, of course, Odile Rodin, the French theater actress, who fell in love with the world-famous playboy Porfirio Rubirosa when she was only 19 years old. The young actress became close to Rubirosa without showing any interest in his past because the famous playboy was a mature man and he knew how to amuse her."

At this part of the article, I burst into laughter, and Fuat joined me.

"Do I know how to amuse you, young lady?" he asked laughing.

"Listen to this," I continued. "You know what Sophia Loren said? She said, 'I never feel bored when I'm with Carlo. My life unfolds peacefully and without worry. On the contrary, young men are so boring and shallow. Besides, they do not guarantee a future.'"

Fuat stopped laughing. When I perceived the meaning of what I had just read, I was startled. He was frowning.

"No, this doesn't fit you," he said. "Let aside guaranteeing your future, I cannot even promise you anything tomorrow."

Trying to change the subject, I said, "I agree with Ira."

"What did she say?"

"She says that as time goes by, an older man gives you a soul, a brain, and eventually a great desire to live."

"But psychologists think that young girls who get married to older men are in search of fatherly compassion," said Fuat.

"You have obviously not read the end of the article," I said. "The main reason is their youthful spirit and pride in being loved."

I was dressed in dark green pants with their narrow lower parts pleated and a light yellow pullover. I had fastened my hair with hairpins on both sides. Fuat said, "You really look like a child in that outfit. Thank God we are not going out. People would call me a shameless old man and might even attack me!"

"Of course, you are shameless," I replied. "You have deceived a little girl . . ."

"Let us go out and test the situation, if you want," he said.

Not getting his point, I stared at him.

It was raining heavily outside. The sea was calm. And it was slowly turning gray.

"Where to?" I asked.

"Out," he replied laughing. "You have never complained that I don't take you out, but I miss seeing you in a crowd in the blowing wind and in the pouring rain."

Suddenly I felt a deep pang of sadness. I felt both happy and sorry for us. Many times, I had yearned to walk hand in hand by the seaside or to go to the movies and lean my head on his shoulder in the dark. I would have died to do such things, but I had always refrained from mentioning it to him.

He called reception. The hotel manager would lend Fuat his car. He wore his light-colored raincoat and took his hat and umbrella; I wore my plaid jacket and put on my shawl. The wipers weren't fast enough to keep the windscreen clear. We were driving slowly on the coast road in a small car. For the first time, I was able to see him drive. I was terribly excited, as if we were two kids playing hooky who had stolen one of our fathers' cars.

It was close to three o'clock in the afternoon, but it was nearly dark. The rain had subsided. Fuat stopped the car somewhere near the lighthouse. We got out of the car and began to walk hand in hand. Then he hugged me, and I hugged him with both arms. We stood without moving or talking. Seagulls were picking things out of a garbage dump near the shore, fighting over the tastiest morsels.

Fishermen's boats with big colorful nets were passing on the water. Fuat pointed at one. It was called: "Don't make us wait".

"What a nice name," I said.

He held my head, turning it toward himself.

"I want you to promise me something," he said. "Will you?"

His raincoat was wet, and he smelled of the rain.

"A promise?"

"Yes, a promise. You must promise not to leave me even if you get extremely angry at me one day, or if something happens that I cannot foresee now."

We had promised each other many times not to separate.

Raising my head to touch his chest, I looked into his eyes.

"What if you leave me?" I asked.

"I have already promised you that I will never leave you," he replied. "But look at me. I'm an old man. What if I become old and infirm?"

"How come you've started talking about old age!" I said angrily. "Don't worry. I will take care of you."

"Promise?"

"Yes," I said without thinking further. "I promise."

After wandering around in the car that day, he dropped me at home. No one saw us. The people who did see us—the corn vendor, the people in the small teahouse where we had some tea after freezing in the cold, and the people who passed by us—didn't recognize us.

It appeared that the hotel personnel would keep our secret forever. They seemed to relate to us, so we didn't worry about them.

Whenever I entered or left the hotel, I wore sunglasses and a shawl or hat and raised the collar of my coat or jacket. In this way,

I thought, no one would recognize me. At least they didn't know who I was and probably just assumed I was his lover or mistress—a cheap woman.

One Saturday evening, we took the car and went out again. Another day, we got in a rowboat at the hotel pier and put out to sea dressed in raincoats. We tried to fish, but I got the lines tangled. Evening descended as we struggled to disentangle them. The weather changed, and freezing, exhausted, and fighting against the waves, we hardly made it to shore.

Another day, we crossed the Galata Bridge and went to an old house in Balat, after passing streetcars, crowds of pedestrians, and rowboats on the banks. I asked him where he was taking me, but he didn't give me a clue.

With the iron lion-shaped doorknocker, we rapped on the old, heavy door whose green paint was worn and cracked. An old woman wearing a headscarf and pullover opened the door. When she saw us, she was surprised and very happy. She didn't know how to welcome us. Just when she was about to call to someone inside the house, Fuat motioned for her to keep silent. We took off our shoes and entered the house. The door of the room where an iron stove was burning was shut. He opened the door, took my hand, and we entered. An old man with round glasses was sitting beside a big old wooden table covered with countless scattered objects. He wore a black waistcoat over a white shirt on which he was wearing sleevelets, like a clerk's. He was repairing a clock. He looked over the top of his glasses, noticed us, and jumped up. Fuat kissed his hand. He wanted to introduce me to the old man, but I had already recognized him: he was Fuat's uncle who used to be a captain.

We sat around the ancient porcelain stove and drank tea with the old couple. They did not ask, directly or indirectly, who I (a stranger) was. Aunt Nigar looked at Fuat and wept every now and then; she told me what a naughty boy he used to be and how she felt proud of him because he had become a great man. The captain, a wise and experienced old man, treated Fuat as if he were still his little nephew. He took out an old top that was once Fuat's from the sideboard and showed it to us. We sat and chatted for hours, as if we had all known one another for a long time. When we were leaving, Fuat's uncle took him by the arm and said, "Take care of yourself. These are not the right things for you." Then he added smiling, "And don't upset İsmet Pasha, or I'll pull your ear."

After we left, Fuat said, "He didn't scold me too much about what has been going on in the country. If you weren't here with me, he would have killed me. He will remain a supporter of the Republican People's Party until the day he dies."

On another Sunday, we had dinner in our room at the hotel. In a few hours, we would have to part. On Sundays, I usually sulked, thinking about the time I would have to leave. Fuat said, "Let us not say good-bye at the door this time. Let's go out and take a walk."

It was cold outside. Fuat wrapped his woolen scarf around my neck. Few people were on the streets. We walked in the alleys for a while. Then we entered a dead-end street that went downhill all the way to the sea. At the end of the road, I noticed a house in the middle of a garden filled with weeds. I walked toward the house, as if something familiar attracted me, and opened the old iron gate. The curtains in the windows were drawn. Obviously, the place had been uninhabited for a long time. The housekeeper of an adjacent home came out and asked us whom we were looking for.

"We're newly married," Fuat said, "and we're looking for a house to buy."

I looked at Fuat with my eyes wide open. He winked at me.

"What can I say," the man said, continuing in a low voice, as if telling a secret. "The poor woman lost her husband in an accident last year and got ill. She went to stay with her daughter who lives abroad, but I don't know where. No one knows if she will return or not. There's another house for sale over there. Maybe you should take a look at it."

"Thank you, we will," said Fuat.

Chuckling, I took his arm. We walked for some time.

"Why am I not aware that we got married recently?" I asked.

"I wanted to surprise you."

"It was a nice house, wasn't it?" I asked. "As soon as I saw it, I felt drawn to it. I wish we lived in such a tiny place hidden among the trees, near the seaside."

"Who knows," he replied. "Maybe one day we will live there."

We felt happy on the stolen weekends, buried in our world of fantasy, forgetting everything else in our lives.

Yes, forgetting everything else . . .

Until I went to that concert one evening.

One day my brother Nihat brought home an invitation to an event—perhaps to have me get out, meet people, and enjoy myself a little. İdil Biret, the celebrated child prodigy of the time, would play at the Saray Theater on a Friday evening. I felt upset for I had been informed that Fuat would not be able to come on Saturday. Although I wanted to hear the young girl play, I didn't feel like mixing with people. However, Nihat didn't accept my excuses, and we set off for the evening.

We had seats in the front row. We arrived early and immediately took our seats so that we wouldn't have to see people looking at me and whispering.

Soon, the sound of the instruments tuning up could be heard from behind the curtain, and the audience began to fill the room.

Nihat was telling me something when he suddenly stopped talking. Something had attracted his attention.

When I turned to look in the same direction, I saw Fuat.

I saw him, yet I acted as if I didn't recognize him. I looked at him as if I were looking at any person in the crowd. It was a strange feeling, and hard to describe.

A formally dressed man was showing him and his wife to their seats.

Fuat's wife was walking in front. She saw me but pretended not to notice. However, Fuat stopped as he was passing by. Nihat jumped to his feet, and I had to stand up, too. Fuat shook our hands formally and then walked to his seat without even looking at my face. The people following him smiled and greeted us with a nod of their heads and also headed to their seats.

Fuat was wearing a black suit. They sat down. There were only a few seats between us.

My legs were trembling as I sat down.

My face was red. I looked at the program in my hand. I tried to act as if nothing had happened, but my heart was beating like crazy, and I felt as if I was suffocating. Excitement, anger, having been deceived for the first time in my life, shame—I was overtaken by a mixture of all of these feelings.

That was why he had told me we wouldn't be able to meet on Saturday. He was going to spend the weekend with his wife. In Istanbul. I hadn't even been informed of his plan, and wouldn't have been aware of it if I had not come here.

What hurt the most was that he hadn't looked into my eyes when he shook my hand.

I couldn't look at Nihat, but I suspected that he had brought me here on purpose. He didn't say anything either. Maybe he had wanted me to see Fuat and his wife together.

As my mind was occupied with these thoughts, the curtain opened, and a white-haired woman in a black outfit came on stage to conduct the orchestra. Then İdil entered wearing a long red dress, acknowledged the audience, and sat at the piano to a flood of applause.

The concert began, but all I heard was ringing in my ears. I felt like I might lose control. I wanted to cry and, at the same time, stand up and kill Fuat. I couldn't decide. I kept asking myself why he had done this, why he had lied to me and kept it a secret—all those "why's."

I wish I had stood up immediately and left the hall. I wanted to leave right away, but we were sitting in the front row, and if I stood up everyone would see me. I felt as if I were naked. All of a sudden, I remembered a dream I had seen in the past—the one in which Fuat comes to our house and even though everyone knows about what's going on, no one says a word. In a way, that dream had become real. Furthermore this time it wasn't just my family in the room the world and his wife were there too

I didn't know what to do. Should I find a way to sneak out in the dark? Or should I sit and listen to the concert as if nothing had happened.

Suddenly, I realized that I had completely forgotten about the truth and the world outside since the time he and I had begun to wander about the city and visit places as if we were two young lovers skipping school. I had begun to take our dream as reality.

Now, however, I was facing reality.

I was not the heroine in this movie.

The applause caused me to pull myself together. Nihat whispered, "Let's go," and we left quickly.

After such a long time, I felt really hurt that night.

Not because I saw myself as a bad woman, the other woman in the life of a man, a mistress, or a concubine.

I didn't care the least about such things. Let me be called all those bad things. Being the other woman in his life didn't mean anything to me because I had forgotten that there was another woman in his life.

But that night, I met that woman.

For the first time, I remembered that she also had feelings and a life, that she had shared many things with him, and that she had been happy with him for a long time.

A marriage that had lasted many years . . . How much they must have shared. Loads of photographs and memories . . . Places they visited, foreign cities they went to, people they knew, photographs they cherished, the pictures of their daughter . . .

For some reason, the woman who remains in the background is always cast aside and forgotten. The audience always wants the two lovers to be united, and we never wonder what the other woman goes through.

Nihat and I arrived home without exchanging any words. We never talked about that evening again, as if nothing strange had happened, and as if we had made a silent agreement.

I cried so much that night.

I forgot all the promises I had made to myself. All the decisions I had taken became thin air.

One moment I felt rage towards Fuat, and the next moment, I told myself I didn't have the right to be angry. He had lied to me.

Is that why I was angry? Didn't he lie to his wife all the time? A reception would take place the following evening in Istanbul. A foreign leader had come to Turkey. Everyone would attend the event with his spouse. I learned about this later, yet I had thought about such possibilities that night too. Why didn't he just tell me? Didn't he think that I would find out? Wasn't he aware that I lived on the promise of our Saturday mornings? Was he afraid of my reaction, or didn't he care about my feelings?

Then I told myself that perhaps things had unfolded unexpectedly and he hadn't wanted to inform me over the phone. I kept trying to find reasons to make myself forgive his behavior. I put myself in his shoes. Truthfully, his situation was more difficult. What would happen anyway if he had told me the truth? Would I have asked him not to go with his wife? Hadn't I already accepted the situation? Didn't he go to all events in Ankara with his wife? Didn't she attend the balls with him? How naïve I was! Didn't he live in the same house with his wife?

Lost in thought, I kept remembering the moment when our eyes had met and how he had looked at the ground with an odd expression on his face. I felt terribly distressed again.

Naturally he knew everything I felt. But what did he think or feel? Why hadn't he taken any action until that day? Maybe he had. Maybe there were big fights going on in his home. I didn't know.

But both I and his wife had acted as if the other did not exist until that day. I remember our first encounter at the ball when Fuat had introduced us to each other. This was our second meeting. I was sure his wife also remembered the evening of the ball.

What if, instead of looking away, his wife had said something to me?

When I considered this possibility, I wanted to disappear.

I thought about such things until the break of dawn. I smoked

317

incessantly. With the first light of the morning, I fell asleep.

On Saturday, I woke up with different emotions than usual.

I was calmer, but felt fed up with my life.

Although I knew that the distress would soon be over, that he would persuade me again, and that I also wanted to be persuaded by him, nothing seemed the same anymore.

Sometimes when you believe you have reached a dead end, something unexpected happens and saves you, as if sent by a higher power from above. Ayla came suddenly that day.

No wonder, I always said to her, "You are my fairy: any time something bad happens, you arrive at the right time in my life."

As if we were still children, my mother forced us to have lunch at home. Then we quickly left. Ayla and I had not spoken for a long while. She wanted to learn everything, and I told her—about the previous evening most of all.

"Didn't you know that things like that would happen?" she asked.

"I knew," I said. "I thought I didn't care, but when faced with reality, meeting him and his wife in person, I became a mess."

"There are things in life that even if we know what to do or what to say, it doesn't help," she said.

I stared at her as if I didn't understand what she meant. She continued, "I have known from the beginning that no matter what you said or did, nothing would change. I knew how it would go since the evening you received that fan from him and since the morning I saw you two together, though I was scared and I wanted to warn you."

"Yes, I know," I replied. "Do you think that I didn't tell myself to be cautious? I tried hard to withdraw myself and run away."

Ayla put down her teacup. Then looking directly into my eyes, she said, "What scares me the most is something else. Do you realize you are neglecting yourself?"

Instinctively, I began to gather my hair that was falling in my face. She laughed and said, "No, I don't mean like that. You are more beautiful than ever. What I mean is that you're spending all of your time thinking about this matter."

"What do you mean?"

"Wouldn't it be better if you started working or doing something else?"

"Are you saying that I'm spending the best years of my life by running after an ambiguous adventure?" I asked.

"I don't know how it started or how it will end," Ayla said. "But it's a shame that you are doing nothing when you could do so much. You know what I thought? If you want, I can bring you books to translate. They will be of great use to us and will also keep you busy."

This was how I began to translate the books that are probably hidden away now on the dusty shelves of a few university libraries.

I realized that I had grown lazy. I didn't read books anymore. Since my mother treated me like a child, I also didn't do any chores at home. I was passing my life waiting for the weekends, rustling the pages of newspapers and magazines, and playing with my cat.

Ayla was right.

My beloved friend. My good-hearted angel. My teacher who came to my rescue with her wisdom, and my sister who held my hand and saved me when the ground slid under my feet.

She was one of the greatest gifts life had given me.

I felt as if Fuat and I were connected with a fragile tie like a telephone cord that could be cut any time. Indeed, that line was broken again. But this time, I didn't want to sit by the phone and wait for him to call.

My mother insisted that Ayla should stay for dinner but Ayla refused, saying to me, "It's always me who stays for dinner. My parents get upset. For once, you should come to our place for dinner."

I went, and her parents were delighted to see me. We had dinner on the terrace. Uncle Macit drank raki, permitting himself by saying it was in my honor. We talked about the old days and our childhood. Then Ayla's parents went to bed.

Ayla and I closed the door, threw a few pieces of wood into the oven, and placed a teapot on the stove.

I put on a pullover and went outside into the garden to smoke a cigarette.

We were in another city and in another garden, but it felt like the past. The sky, the smell of the earth, the unkempt garden, the faded chair cushions, and distant strains of music . . .

Later, we would see a shooting star and make a wish upon it.

There was nothing different from any night we had spent together over the years.

Except the years themselves.

As usual, I was the chatterbox, but there in the garden under the starry sky, I felt that there were things Ayla wanted to tell me.

Like in the old days, we were going to talk about secrets. As I said, it was all the same. She turned to see if the lights in the house were off. They were, so she began to whisper. She said, "I have some news. Are you ready?"

"Did you decipher one of those strange tablets of yours, or did you discover a new king?"

Laughing, she said, "Yes, I found a new king."

"Is he handsome, at least? How old is he? How many thousands of years?" I teased her.

I wasn't able to see her face clearly in the dim light of the garden lamp.

"He is both handsome and alive," she said. "At least for the time being."

I slowly sat upright where I was lying on the grass."

"You mean . . ."

"Yes," she said, "the Hungarian is back."

"Come on, tell me," I said. "You drive me crazy. You would have been a good spy!"

"I would have told you if only I had any chance to speak in between all your stories," she giggled.

"Stop talking about me. What did he say? What did you talk about? Why did he come back? What does he want?"

"How nosy you are!" she said. "Do I ask you so many details?"

"You should!" I protested. "What can I do if I'm nosy! You didn't put on a sour face and send him back to his country, did you?"

"No, no! I didn't. But this time he was sulking a bit."

"Why?"

When we were children, Ayla and I used to lie under the night sky in the summer, in another garden far away from here, and tell each other scary stories that made us tremble. We used to talk about the old woman who lived in a dilapidated mansion with her cats, the hunchbacked cart driver who had strange powers no one knew about, and the blue-eyed boy who believed he was living another life in another time. Everything that seemed strange to us in childhood turned into a scary story, a popular myth. Hearing those nightmarish stories used to fill us with excitement.

The old woman in the ruined mansion was put in an old people's home. I wonder if anyone except her cats missed her. The hunchbacked driver died long time ago. The blue-eyed boy who thought he was living in a different time supposedly went to a foreign country, and no one heard from him again.

Now we were old enough not to feel afraid of these stories, the rustling leaves on the trees, the dark sky, or distant strange sounds. Now, other things frightened us—things that were not far away, but our own lives and the decisions we had to make about how to act, as well as the present and the future.

"Come on, tell me," I said. "What did you do to the poor man? Why was he upset?"

"I didn't do anything," Ayla answered sharply. "He's a lunatic. He didn't come here or even write me a single line for ages; he just suddenly appeared and asked me to marry him."

I was taking slow steps in the garden and I almost fell down upon hearing this.

"What did you say! He proposed to you?"

"Don't scream!" Ayla said. "I don't know if it can be described as a proposal, but from the moment he saw me, he only talked about this subject."

"So how did you answer?"

"What could I tell him? How can one marry in such a sudden, inappropriate way? I don't even know where he lives."

"Did you say this to him?"

"Of course, I did. What's wrong with that?"

"You can kill a person, my girl. How can you say such things to a man?"

"Why not? Why shouldn't I? I really don't know where he lives."

"Stop fussing with where he lives, and tell me what's on your mind. Because of dealing with my own problem, I have been totally unaware of your life. Finding a Hungarian in the middle of nowhere is something that suits you!"

"Shhh! That's what amuses me, too. If my mother knew about this, she would have a heart attack. She already grumbles, asking what on earth I'm doing on an excavation site."

"To tell the truth, this is fate. Or maybe a curse from the ancient kings!"

"Honestly, I thought about that. We disturbed those men who had been lying in peace for thousands of years. I wouldn't be surprised if it were true."

We were trembling in the cold weather. We went inside the house and sat by the stove.

I asked, "So did he think of you all the time he was away?"

Ayla was filling our cups with tea.

"If you ask him, yes, but I don't believe him," she said.

"Why not? Maybe he was telling the truth. Maybe he fell in love with you at first sight. It was obvious, anyway."

"Come on," she said. "Don't make me laugh. Who knows how many cities he toured and how many women he had before he came to that mountain and found me."

"In two minutes, the tip of my nose almost froze," I complained. "Winter is coming. Tell me what kind of a person he is."

"Let me explain it like this," Ayla said. "If the jeep doesn't arrive, the closest place we can go to get food is two hours away. We work all day in the middle of nowhere in dust. When it rains, we struggle to walk in our boots, buried in the mud. What does he do? He comes out of his tent with his hat, his tweed jacket, golf pants, and white socks, and smells the air."

"I like him. He suits me fine."

"I bet he does," Ayla said. "I'm sure you'd like him if you met him. The gentleman comes with two big suitcases although he will just stay for a week. What's more, he brings a helper to carry them."

"What does he do there exactly?" I asked. "Except for following you."

"Didn't I tell you? They say he's writing the story of the excavation. He's preparing a book about Anatolia. With a small notebook in hand, he fires questions and talks to everyone continuously."

"Where is he now?"

"He lives in France. Even though he is Hungarian, he hasn't been to his homeland since he was a boy. His life passed on the road and on excavations. He's one of those adventure-loving people."

I laughed.

"But that's good. You can travel together. You will dig, and he will write."

"Then you will look after the kids?"

"The kids!" I exclaimed. Ayla motioned me be silent, and I whispered, "It seems that you're already in the mood. I'm telling you, it won't take long until you're married."

"Look, how she's amused," she said. "I didn't tease you like this!"

We had not laughed so much since our school days.

Without being aware of it, I had begun feeling for Fuat a kind of love not as a lover, but as someone close who has been around for years, since childhood.

If this were not the case, would he have been able to make up with flowers, gifts, and songs?

I was not able to be angry with him.

My rage was momentary like a shooting star that disappears in the night sky.

The same thing happened. But this time, flowers or gifts did not come. He came himself.

On Sunday evening, I came home by boat from the other side of the city. It had become dark early. The sea was rough and dark clouds covered the sky. It began to rain as soon as I got off the boat. I ran to find a cab. I had dressed too light again, fooled by the previous day's good weather. I was soaking wet.

I was told that no one had called me at home. This surprised me, and I became depressed. The gentleman was guilty, yet he acted as if nothing had happened. He hadn't even called after what had happened at the concert hall.

The rain didn't let up that night. I fell asleep with the roar of thunder in my ears. In the morning, my mother woke me up, whispering in my ear, "Wake up. Someone's waiting outside for you."

Still groggy, I didn't understand what she was trying to say.

Outside?

I got out of bed, went to the window, and looked outside. Sheltered under a tree, Fuat was waiting in the rain.

I put something on and rushed to the door.

"What are you doing here? Are you crazy?" I asked.

He walked toward me.

"I arrived here early. I didn't know what to do. I thought you were still sleeping."

His beige overcoat had turned brown with the rain. Water was dripping from his hat, and even the collar of his shirt was soaking wet.

"Come in," I said. "You're soaked to the skin. Why didn't you knock on the door. Thank God my mother saw you."

I took him to the living room. As if his visit was quite normal, my mother took his wet coat and hat, and I brought him some of Nihat's clothes. If he had sat down in his own clothes the armchair would have become wet. My mother brought some towels. I waited outside with my mother while Fuat changed. Without looking at me, she said, "Let me make something to eat."

I would never have believed that Fuat would come to our house and have breakfast with us wearing my brother's clothes. I was so shocked that I forgot about the last few days.

"The pants are a little short for you but never mind. We'll have your clothes dry as soon as possible," I said.

Lilac jumped on his lap, as if she remembered him.

"How much you have grown," Fuat said to the cat. While petting her, he said, "Please forgive me, but I was desperate."

I felt like grinning. He had come, but since he knew he was guilty, he hadn't found the courage to knock on the door.

My mother brought some food on a tray. Neither she nor Fuat knew what to say to each other except for "How are you?"

I served him a cup of tea. My mother left us alone, and I asked, "How long have you been waiting outside?"

"I don't know," he said. "Don't ask me. I didn't have a moment's sleep last night. I got up at dawn and came here."

It seemed that he had sent his wife back with the rest of the group last night and had managed to find an excuse to stay in the city.

"I was so worried and distressed that I went out for a walk, and I eventually ended up here," he said.

I laughed. "You must have walked quite a distance."

He sipped his tea and lit a cigarette.

"It can't go on like this," he said all of a sudden. I felt as if someone had stabbed me. He continued. "Everything is in chaos. I have pulled you into it, too. If you ask me, I can't say that I know what I'm doing."

"I am alright," I said.

"You don't say it, but I know that you're unhappy. Trying not to hurt anyone, I hurt everyone. Then I get hurt the most."

I lit a cigarette and waited in silence. Perhaps we would finally have the scary conversation that we had always postponed. What worth did it have if a conversation would not end up satisfying either of the parties? I always avoid endings. I don't like confronting endings.

"Would you come to Ankara?" he asked.

Unable to comprehend, I studied his face.

"I rented a flat," he continued, unable to look me in the eye.

"You rented a flat?"

"Yes. Even if you don't come, I will live there from now on. I have already put in some furniture. If you come, you can decorate it as you wish. It's a small garden flat in Kavaklıdere. In front of the window, there's one of those willow trees you like so much."

I didn't know what to say. We sat there for some time in silence, looking at each other. When my mother knocked on the door and asked if we wished to have more tea, I took his cup and went to the kitchen.

It had never occurred to me: going back to Ankara and becoming a part of society there. But I wouldn't be able to mix with people! I would have to stay at home all day waiting for him. My heart clenched.

He wasn't able to propose marriage. He was proposing that I be his mistress.

Unfortunately, that was the case.

Such things should have been out of the question, but all the same, they took place.

If you ask me the truth, I didn't mind being called his mistress. Whenever I hear this word, I can't help remembering the young girl who wrote unforgettable letters to the priest who was first her teacher and later her lover, in an old love story that took place hundreds of years ago. She wrote in one, "I'd rather be your mistress than the wife even of an emperor." I wasn't concerned about what other people said about me.

I headed for Ankara with only a suitcase, settling in his two-room garden flat with a fireplace.

I told my mother that I would take an exam for a translator's position, and, at the same time, meet some old friends. I would stay an extra few days or maybe a week after the exam.

I didn't know what I would tell her after that.

I told Nihat the truth. He frowned, and said helplessly, "I don't want you to go. I know you'll be upset, but I also know that you will do as you wish."

I held his hand and said, "There's no other way. It will carry on like this. In the way life wants it to be."

In truth, however, I knew that Fuat's dream of sharing the same home with me would not become real in the way he wished it would.

I was aware that his plan would not work out as desired.

But still, I had not been able to turn down his wish. He was caught in a difficult situation. He had told me, "Give me some time. Everything will turn out well. In one year at the latest, there will be elections. People can't stand the situation anymore. The Prime Minister is also tired. I will be free after the next election. Everything will be all right. We can establish a life for ourselves. We can go wherever you want."

I didn't believe him, but I also didn't want him to be torn to pieces, neglect his work, or be the object of further criticism because of me.

For me, time didn't matter. I wasn't busy anyway. I told myself that I could go to Ankara and live in his flat for some time.

Unfortunately, however, during my train ride to Ankara, I did not feel excited or happy with the thought of trying to make a broken dream come true and living in our own home.

Each time something I wished for came true, something else was destroyed.

It was a cold day. I got off at the station, and a driver took me to the flat. There were a few pieces of furniture, and, apparently, the place had been cleaned just before my arrival. Some big vases were full of roses.

The burly, grim doorman with a moustache introduced himself and asked if I needed anything. I asked him to bring some food, unpacked my suitcase, and hung up the clothes that could get wrinkled. Just as I sat down with a cup of tea, the doorbell rang. It was Fuat. He came in and hugged me with overwhelming joy, saying, "Welcome home!"

It was bliss.

I spent the first few days doing some cleaning and arranging things I bought for us.

I acted as if everything were normal. People phoned him when he was at home. He introduced me to Mr. Sami, whom he addressed as "Mr. Assistant," and who was one of the men Fuat trusted the most. If something happened and I couldn't reach Fuat, I could call Mr. Sami. When Fuat was traveling, Mr. Sami gave me information about him. This slender, short old man with a thin moustache knew all the secrets about us.

In the morning, Fuat's driver came and took my shopping orders or took me wherever I wanted to go to. Yet, I didn't go to many places.

Fuat stayed at his own home two nights a week and spent the other nights in the flat with me. Later, I found out that he also visited his other home for lunch.

What did we do at home?

I suddenly realize the details about those days have faded somewhat from my memory. We usually listened to music on the radio, played card games, and chatted until late at night. Sometimes the subject was about an article in the newspaper or a current issue. But only if he felt well. If he came home with a sour face, he didn't tell me what had happened that day, and I didn't say anything that would upset him more. Sometimes he used say to me, "If someone else told me the kind of things you sometimes say, I would go nuts. I cannot be cross with you."

I would tease him by saying, "I'm in prison anyway. They can do nothing to me. Let me at least have freedom of speech here."

"That is exactly why I put you in prison," he would joke. "Otherwise, you would have talked openly outside, causing yourself all kinds of trouble. Even I wouldn't be able to rescue you then!"

The newspapers were full of censored news, veiled articles, and the announcement of recent prohibitions. The Turkish press, as well as the foreign press, was worried. An article written by an American journalist, "Quarter to Twelve," had caused commotion and those Turkish newspapers that published it were punished severely.

One day I came across such a funny piece of news that I burst into laughter. It was after dinner, and we were reading the daily papers.

"Tell me what it is so that I can laugh too," Fuat said.

"It says here that hoop rolling is banned in Istanbul. Are these people traitors to their country? OHR, "Organization of Hoop Rollers." They should be hanged immediately!"

He grabbed the newspaper from my hand and read the article. He was furious. At that late hour of the night, he called someone in Istanbul and scolded him harshly. After returning to his seat, he looked at me and said, "Don't laugh!"

Actually, it wasn't the right time to laugh.

I became good friends with Mrs. Saadet, my neighbor in the opposite flat, as if we had known each other for a long time. She was much older than I was, but she was wise and experienced. If she didn't say things like "Don't worry about anything, my dear girl. In the end, you'll be the one who wins." One would think she didn't know anything about Fuat and I.

Naturally, everyone knew about Fuat and me.

In the end, I began acting as if I were his wife. If he came home late, I was angry. If he spent an evening playing cards at his club, I would complain. How strange! He felt timid in front of me. Sometimes he even kept his visits to the Prime Minister secret. At times, when he was with me and someone called to ask him to go out, he would reply, with a wink at me, "I can't. My wife is here. She'll be angry."

He called me from everywhere he went to inquire where I was.

I would be home, naturally. Rarely, I went out alone to do some shopping. Ayla had given me a book, and I busied myself translating it.

After my first week in Ankara, I had told my mother that I had passed the written exam and was waiting for the oral exam.

In the mornings, I sometimes played cards with Mrs. Saadet. She visited me for coffee, or I went to her place. She always read my coffee cup. Her readings were always positive news. Once, I said to her, "You only tell me good things!"

"What can I do?" she replied. "That's what your cup says. It's not my fault!"

One morning, however, she examined my coffee cup longer than usual. "My dear, it looks as if someone is going on a trip," she said finally. "It's not you but someone else. Unfortunately, you'll receive some sad news."

"My!" I exclaimed, "What news?"

"I can't tell you," she said. "This isn't an encyclopedia."

We laughed and forgot about the incident.

That week, Fuat was scheduled to go to London with a group of officials. He said to me, "Why don't you come along? We could visit the same museum again." Then, realizing the impossibility of what he just proposed, he frowned.

We would be separated for the first time since I had come to Ankara, and we were both sad, as if we were not used to being apart for long periods.

It was a Tuesday morning when I poured water after him and said good-bye. He called me when he arrived in London. His voice indicated he was in a good mood. When things went well, he always spoke in a loud voice and didn't want to end the conversation.

Every night he gave me a call before he went to bed, but we weren't able to talk in the mornings because he woke up very early and didn't want to wake me up.

I'm not sure how many days had passed—a week or maybe more. One evening, he told me on the phone, "I'm bored. I miss you so much. Tomorrow I have a free day. The main group is arriving in two days. I can come to Ankara and return in time."

"You're already tired," I said. "Let's wait two more days. There's no sense in coming here for a day."

In fact, I had said it without thinking. If I had sounded excited about his suggestion, he would have had to come.

He would have come and maybe in two days he would have been a part of the "bad news" we received from far away.

"We are very tired," he said, "but it was worth it . . . Then, I'll go out and do some shopping tomorrow. Is there anything you want?"

He always asked me this question, and I always told him not to buy anything and that all I wanted was for him to return. All the same, on his arrival, his arms would be full of packages, and I would unwrap them as joyfully as a child. At the same time, I would scold him for buying so many things. He even thought of my favorite red and white candy sticks.

"Rest and enjoy yourself tomorrow. Have some fun, but don't look at beautiful girls," I said.

"Even if I tried to look at them, I wouldn't see them. It's so foggy here that you can hardly see your hand in front of your face."

"I know that all too well," I said.

If I had told him to come for a day, and if he had listened to me, he would have been on that plane.

On the plane that got lost in the fog and crashed.

Mr. Sami visited me the next morning. He told me what had happened. He was pale. They had heard about the accident in the early morning but had received conflicting reports. All they knew was that the Prime Minister was alive but that many passengers had died.

"I talked to Mr. Fuat," he said. "He went to the hospital. He asked me to tell you not to worry."

I felt both sad and happy at the same time. Mrs. Saadet's coffee cup reading had come true. I thanked God that Fuat had not been on that plane.

As I mentioned, life gives you signs.

But only if you can read them . . .

I had talked to my mother on the phone a couple times after coming to Ankara. Although I had not been able to tell her the real reason for my prolonged visit, I had said that I had passed the exam and started working. Moreover, for the time being, I was staying in a temporary apartment. I knew that she was aware of what was going on, yet I didn't have to courage to tell her the truth.

In the end, she said to me one day, "Dear daughter, even if staying in that house does not hurt your feelings, it offends me. If you want to stay in Ankara, stop living there. That is all I'm going to say on the matter."

What hurt me the most was that my mother had told me something like this for the first time in my life. We didn't talk again for quite a long time.

Ayla visited her every now and then, and they had tea together. Ayla gave me news about my mother, and I also spoke to Nihat from time to time.

The plane crash was an unexpected incident. When the Prime Minister returned to Turkey, all hell broke loose in Ankara. A huge crowd carried him on their shoulders, animals were sacrificed, and people were trampled in the commotion. People were blessing him now as if he were immortal.

Fuat had a frown on his face when he arrived. He did not regain his good humor for a long time. Even the exaggerated demonstrations of popular support, the way it seemed that everything in the country was favorable, and the peace İnönü made with their party did not please him.

He told me about his friends who had died in the accident. He said, "We traveled so often and had many accidents, but not once did I think that our plane could crash one day." He also told me that he had often ordered the plane to depart in bad weather so that he could reach an appointment on time, and I was upset because he had done such things before.

He was worried that the early elections he was waiting for would be postponed because of the new atmosphere in the country following the accident. Things turned out the way he feared. Talk of early elections was replaced with "the public wants us, the public likes us."

During a religious holiday, Ayla visited Ankara and stayed with me for a few days. She brought along Lilac as well. She told me that she had decided to get married. Her mother, she said, was upset in the beginning that she would marry a foreigner, but then they reached an agreement in the family. Her father had bought the young couple an apartment in one of the new housing developments in Levent, in the area right behind the houses with gardens, so that Ayla could be near the family.

I had read about that area in magazines. It was a large estate resembling those in Europe. It even had a movie theater, shopping center, playground, and restaurants.

"It will be finished by New Year's Eve," Ayla said, "and then we'll move there. But I don't know how long Eric will stay here and what will happen once his book is completed. We're getting married, but how the future will unfold is unclear."

"You were saying that you'd never get married. I don't even know the groom. He should at least show his face so that we can exchange a few words," I teased.

"I really don't know how it happened," Ayla said. "Marriage was not on my mind, but he somehow managed to make me say yes. We'll see how things will go."

One evening, Ayla was sitting and reading a foreign archaeology journal.

"What are you reading?" I asked.

Raising her head, she replied, "It's strange, but three thousand years ago, misuse of authority and bribing existed just like today. Court records have been deciphered."

She paused for a moment and our eyes met. As if she had said something wrong, she was embarrassed. She tried to change the subject, and I stood up to pour some more tea into our glasses.

"Leave that aside," I said. "Tell me about the love story. You won't reveal it. You're so absorbed in your own love that you forgot about it."

"No, I didn't," Ayla replied. "It turned out to be story of a warrior who was in love with the queen. In other words—a secret affair!"

"Was it real or just legend?"

"In fact, it was recorded later, as if told by the warrior himself. We think it was real; yet, he describes the queen's beauty so wonderfully that one has doubts."

"It must be real," I said. "Only one who is truly in love can see another person in that way."

"I'll keep that in mind," Ayla said and laughed. "But unfortunately, one of the king's men found out about the secret affair."

"Don't tell me they killed him," I said.

"I don't know what they did to him, but I liked one part of the story very much. The queen's lover says: 'If you were one of the girls in that field, if you were one of the savage women living in the mountains, if you belonged to the family of my enemy, or even if you were a small child, I would kidnap you; but you are the queen. Where can I take you?'"

"I wonder if you attach any meaning to these words," she said.

The following morning, I took her to the station where we said good-bye. After returning home, I was overcome by a strange mood. The fact that she would soon be married made me feel that a period in our lives was irrevocably over.

I made myself a cup of tea, sat by the window, and thumbed

through magazines. Some cute monkeys were being prepared for space travel. They would take along eggs of sea urchins, onions, and cocoons of insects (as if they couldn't find anything else to take). The poor animals would be fastened to their seats, and people on earth would listen to the signals they sent. Those monkeys would be sent into space unable to move or to comprehend what was happening to them. For a moment, I put myself in their place and felt oppressed. I told Lilac, who whined, rubbed against me, and followed me everywhere as if she were my tail, "Thank God you are not going to be sent to an unknown place in a rocket."

As I was talking to Lilac, the doorbell rang. It could only be Mrs. Saadet at this time of day. I put down my magazine, quickly tidied some things on the table, and then opened the door.

I froze.

There she was in front of me, dressed in a plain but elegant two-piece suit and a hat decorated with feathers and with a small brown bag and gloves in her hand.

Yes, she was in front of me—Maide. This was our third encounter, and this time, we were alone.

At that moment, I wished the ground would open up and swallow me.

I could neither say nor do anything. The few moments we spent at the doorstep staring at each other felt like an eternity.

Finally, she said, "I guess I have come to the right place."

"Please come in," I said.

She entered the flat, and I noticed her glancing at the hat stand in the hallway. It was too late. She had seen Fuat's hat, coat, and umbrella. She must have recognized them.

We remained standing, unable to decide what to do. I was limp and helpless, trembling like a guilty child. Her face registered neither anger, nor pain or hatred. She looked calm but depressed. What would she say? I tried hard to look calm, masking my anxiety. I was caught red-handed when I least expected. She looked around.

"Would you like to sit down?" I asked.

Looking directly into my eyes, she said, "No. I just came to see this place. Now I can leave."

Then she turned around and left.

That was all.

If she had sat down to talk, if she had been angry, if she had said harsh thing or even slapped me, I could have forgotten that encounter. All she said, however, was a single sentence. Those words were never rubbed out of my memory:

"I just came to see this place. Now I can leave."

I didn't tell Fuat about my uninvited visitor. In fact, I didn't tell anyone about her. I don't know if Fuat found out about his wife's visit or if he just kept it to himself after hearing about it.

I spent that night alone in the house, replaying the bizarre visit in my mind a thousand times. Each time, I shuddered and got agitated again, wondering how I could have acted differently.

Why had she come? Did she want to intimidate me? Did she want to make me realize my brazenness and cause me to leave? Had she initially planned to talk to me but changed her mind?

Perhaps she had indeed "just wanted to see the place", as she had said—the place Fuat and I lived, talked, and ate together.

If she had insulted or slapped me (I would have expected that), I probably would not have been as hurt as I was now.

The way she had stood in front me in a refined manner without

338

uttering a single word before leaving abruptly had shaken me beyond description.

Maybe she had not acted this way because of her refined manner. Perhaps when she saw our home, his belongings, the table we used for dinner, and the places we sat together, she had felt helpless.

When I put myself in her shoes, I felt penetrating pain.

When Fuat came home the following evening, he was in good spirits. I tried to interpret the expression in his eyes to find out whether he knew about the previous day's visit. He looked as if he didn't know, and I didn't ask him.

He had brought fresh flowers. I placed them in a vase, and he hugged and kissed me. I got loose from his hug and set the table. When he was cheerful, he always complimented me and praised everything, from my beauty to the food I cooked.

In those days, only one place in Ankara sold my favorite apple dessert. He had brought some for me. When we were eating it after dinner, he suddenly said, "There's a lovely place near İzmir. Let's go and stay there for a few days. Would you like that?"

I was surprised, and immediately in doubt. Maybe he and his wife had quarreled at home, and, having found out about the visit, he was trying to please me. Yet, if it were so, he wouldn't be able to conceal his emotions; his face would be like an open book.

"Where did that idea come from?" I asked.

"Why don't you make some coffee?" he said.

I made him a cup of Turkish coffee without sugar and sat down next to him, while he lit a cigarette.

"It will be difficult for us to go to a resort in the summer," he said, "so I thought we should go now when there are no people. A good friend of mine has a place near İzmir. I met him today. That's when the idea occurred to me. He told me that the weather is very pleasant at this time of year. We can rest a little. Besides, you have been depressed because of staying at home all the time."

"Alright," I said. "It will do me good."

"Aren't you happy about it? Are you a little tired today? You look kind of upset."

In fact, I always smiled whenever I saw him regardless of my mood.

"Of course I'm happy about it," I said. "I just feel bored, but then I was surprised. Maybe that's why."

It would not be suitable for me to continue staying in the flat. Last night, I had decided to return to Istanbul, but I didn't tell Fuat. This game would continue until as long as we were able to play it.

We set off by car the following weekend.

The day the monkeys were sent into space, we were in Çeşme, touring the town in a covered donkey cart. Since the holiday season had not begun yet, the villas, hotels, and pensions were all empty. There were only a few Greek tourists.

Fuat had rented a house that belonged to an acquaintance. The old faithful servants of the house prepared fish and jumbo shrimp, Fuat's favorite dish.

I picked lettuce and tomatoes in the garden. We bathed in hot springs, and in the evenings, we walked on the seashore. Walking hand in hand in the moonlight, we reminded ourselves of our story from the beginning: our first dance, the day we first held hands, his first embrace, the shudder of the first kiss, the distant island, and our astonishing meeting in the city of waters.

We remembered everything, we laughed, we trembled with excitement, we felt afraid, we lived each moment again—in a way, we fell in love again.

We realized that in a relatively short time—what are a few years in a lifetime—we had experienced and shared a myriad of things, hiding in small rooms. Time had passed so fast that we had already forgotten some details.

At night, we turned up our trousers and walked barefoot on the shore. We sat on the sand and inhaled the scent of the sea washing over our feet. We thought that the lighthouse blinking in the distance was winking at us. We sang songs softly, and we kissed, embracing each other on the beach until we were covered all over with sand.

We listened to the sound of small creatures stirring in the bushes.

Then there was a long, profound silence, as if the whole world were waiting for something very important.

"Would you like to be somewhere else?" Fuat asked.

"No, I wouldn't," I replied. "As long as I'm with you, I don't care where I am."

He said, "I have never loved anyone or anything the way I love you. I don't yearn for anything in life, but I wish I were ten years younger and that I had met you ten years earlier."

That winter had been rough. We had learned about each other in depth. We had spent long hours together. We had fallen asleep and woken up together. We had talked about this and that. Sometimes we had sat side by side and read our books in silence. We had played card games and sung to the music on the radio. We had amused ourselves by playing with Lilac.

We had experienced nights when he talked in his sleep, or when I suddenly woke up after a nightmare. We had shared evenings in silence because of his distress.

We had spent nights together as if we were already married, and starting a life together. Months had passed with days full of shopping, having evening snacks while listening to the radio, and chatting about whatever came to mind.

If his wife's visit had not taken place, I would have been satisfied with this pretend system.

Maybe these coincidences, the shore, the gardens, the silences, the twilight, and the stars illuminating the sky were all trying to give us a message.

Perhaps they were telling us to enjoy the scents hidden in the chaotic world surrounding us; to enjoy the delicious food; to touch the earth, the water, and the grass; to lose ourselves among the honeysuckles and the roses; to dream while watching a boat sail by; or to abandon ourselves to a peaceful world, caressed by the sea breeze drifting in through the open window at night.

Perhaps the world was trying to show us its unique nature compared with the world we were struggling to build for ourselves, which, in fact, did not amount to very much.

Memories and images.

They were what I had built my life upon unconsciously.

When I look back on the past now, I realize that I have been dragged by an irresistible wind.

I have failed in anything I have tried to resist, abandon, change, or plan.

It is no use getting upset today and wondering whether everything would have been different if I could have changed a Tuesday with a Thursday, if I had said one thing instead of another, or if I had told him what I really wanted instead of remaining silent.

Besides, what did I want?

All I knew was that each time I felt happy and as if I were in the clouds, my life was shadowed with vague but deep distress and anxiety, like a pain one gets used to living with.

I felt as if everything was half. Everything was broken.

When the painting was just about finished, a wrong stroke of the brush turned it into a mess, spoiling its perfect unity.

Many years later, I visited the same museum where we had seen the angels, and where I had felt hurt for the first time, as well as incredible happiness and fear.

There was an exhibition of that famous Spanish painter.

I stood in front of a single painting hanging on a big empty wall.

It was a woman's portrait.

She wore a red hat with flowers. Her eyes looked as if they had moved from their sockets. Her mouth and nose were also in the wrong place.

I had seen that painting before. I like paintings that portray reality like an old photograph, so I remember having disliked that picture. I had not understood why the woman had to look so ugly.

Later, in the museum, however, with the painting in front of me, I realized why she looked like that.

The painting was called *Weeping Woman*. The woman was weeping in indescribable despair, and there was no other way to reflect such pain on a canvas, because our faces never reflect that kind of cutting sorrow in everyday life.

When I looked at her contorted, torn face—on which the eyes, mouth and nose had changed places—and the colors that were mixed in such a way that made the painting appear to be the work of a child, I realized that I also felt torn and shredded.

Does integrity in life, which makes us strong, happy, and at peace, really exist? If so, I have never found it.

My life was full of snapped moments and short, transitory time fragments.

As I traveled from one beautiful moment to another, the time between them broke the fragments apart.

Everything in my life was shaped automatically according to the rarest moments.

Strangely, I didn't complain.

Sometimes, like many other people, I wondered how long this could continue. At other times, I asked myself why it shouldn't go on as it was.

Life does not have a single form!

You can spend your life sitting in a chair waiting for the day to end, waste it for a loved one, or have one adventure after another.

Don't many people spend their lives working all day long?

What about those who are not able to make a choice? What about people who have to spend their whole life in a cell? What about those who cannot move from their chair or their bed?

What about the ones who have to give up their own life for someone else's?

So many people have died without experiencing so many emotions, the state of being blinded or uplifted by excitement.

I used to think about such things and be thankful for the extraordinary, stunning characteristic of everything I experienced, even if I couldn't comprehend the reasons as clearly as now.

I used to ask myself if it would have been better if Fuat and I had made the home he always dreamed of, if our children had played in our garden, and if we had been assured that we would always be together. Yet, the cost of having this would have meant the loss of the feeling that enveloped my whole body as soon as I saw him.

No, I didn't want that.

We love having adventurous voyages full of fear and excitement, but only if we know that we will eventually reach a safe harbor.

But I didn't want to spend the rest of my life in the harbor buried in the memories of the tempestuous voyage, telling everyone about it and mourning as I gazed into the distance trying to recall the excitement of the moments that belonged to the past.

My excitement and the spasm-like feeling in my belly never disappeared, perhaps because Fuat and I were constantly fighting with the waves that lifted and lowered us.

Maybe this was the reason that allowed me to feel so happy in spite of the ups and downs we had to go through, that prevented me from choosing another style of life, and that stopped me from making a different decision.

To be able to organize time as you wish . . . To disregard other people's rules . . . Not to be one of those people who felt afraid with the thought of being the loser . . . To lose and yet not care about it . . . To live as if soaring above everything . . . Moments . . . Pursuing the moments . . . Moments that do not resemble the novels whose ending one wonders about but poems you put away after reading the first line, feeling that you can extract a different meaning each time you read it.

When I recall those days, for the first time after many years, I do not compare myself with a lady in a portrait, looking calm and tranquil, indicating that she has accepted life in a simple way, but with the tattered face of the woman in the painting at the museum.

I know that life always disintegrates, even if we want to keep it in order or reconstruct it according to our liking.

I wanted to go to Istanbul after our short holiday, but I couldn't help returning to Ankara with Fuat. Everything was so lovely that I didn't want to spoil it.

I stayed alone at home for a couple of days. Everyone in parliament was fighting again. On one side were the trips to other countries, and on the other, foreign guests and never-ending disputes.

Sometimes Fuat even forgot to call me.

One evening, while I was waiting for him at the dinner table, I suddenly began to cry.

I had made myself beautiful, cooked a lot of food, and decorated the table with candles, yet I was sitting there alone, waiting.

I was listening to the radio. Şükran Özer was singing "A Spring Evening," a song whose lyrics were written by a 50-year-old teacher who came across the love of his life at a school prom. The teacher fell in love with a young girl who was 15 or 16 at first sight. Thinking it was too late for anything, he "humbly" asked her "where she had been until that time."

As I sat alone listening to that melancholy song, I suddenly asked myself what I was doing.

I stood up, blew out the candles, and cleared the table.

I went to the bedroom, changed my clothes, put a few belongings into my travel bag, picked up my cat, and called a cab. I wrote a message on a scrap of paper, saying that my mother had fallen ill and I had to leave immediately. Then, I boarded the first bus to Istanbul.

My mother was surprised when she opened the door and saw me so early in the day. We hugged each other and forgot about the chill between us.

I had made this decision without much thinking—like all my decisions.

I would never return to the house in Ankara again.

But Fuat didn't know this yet.

The lie about my mother's illness continued for some time. Then I told him that Ayla would visit us together with her future husband.

Fuat was so busy with his work that he couldn't come to Istanbul. Unable to grasp our situation thoroughly on the phone, he felt angry and helpless and muttered all the time.

Time passed. We had a dark, rainy autumn, then a depressing winter.

He finally came to Istanbul before going abroad on an official trip, on a day when it was thundering and raining terribly. We saw each other for a few days. He hugged me and said, "I know you aren't coming back. I realized it. I cannot give you any promises at the moment. There is so little time left. You'll see that everything will be different soon. I will come and collect you."

"I made a promise," I replied. "Don't worry, I'll wait for you."

Ayla had finally completed the mythical love story she had been working on. Many parts were illegible or indecipherable, but Ayla had discovered that the public had protested when their beloved queen was accused of immorality and when they found out she would be stoned to death and burned in the city square together with her lover, and eventually, they had forced the king to set the lovers free. The queen abandoned her crown and palace and went to a small distant village with her beloved, where they began a new life.

Perhaps I established connection between this story and ours. I was so happy that the mythical story had a happy ending that I forgot what Ayla had accomplished. Her work was a great success worldwide. The publication of the text was something that would take its place in history.

My beloved friend got married in a small family ceremony. Her professors and a few family friends also attended. She resembled the brides of olden times with her simple white dress and flowers crowning her hair. A colorful necklace of huge stones decorated her neck. She had insisted on walking barefoot, and we were not able to make her change her mind. She looked so beautiful that even her mother, who complained about Ayla's refusal to wear a classic wedding gown, admired her. Apparently, the groom had not been informed about our marriage customs. He wore an attractive black tuxedo and a huge, white bowtie. When it was time to kiss the bride, he not only kissed Ayla but picked her up, held her in his arms, and began to turn around crazily, watched by the bewildered guests.

Their home in Istanbul was still not ready so they decided to go Paris and spend a few months in Erik's flat in a suburban district.

We saw them off. My loneliness grew. Later, towards April, we received some good news: my dear friend would soon become a mother. I felt happy beyond description.

I met Fuat a few more times. Every now and then, when he was heading for some destination, he stopped for a rest in Istanbul, trying to stay at least a night. We again took refuge in our small hotel room during these stolen hours.

I felt distressed and tired, but what worried me most was his situation. He was extremely agitated, angry, and ill at ease. He constantly complained and shouted.

Maybe I haven't mentioned it before, but until that time, he and I had never had a fight. We had not even had a serious quarrel. Not once had he raised his voice to me or said harsh words.

He usually accepted my criticism and warnings with humor, joking with me by saying, "It seems that I've been nourishing a viper in my bosom."

During one of our meetings, he talked to someone on the phone when he was beside me. He complained to the person on the other end of the line about the opposition. While saying that he and his party were being accused unjustly, he accused everyone else. Apparently, the person he was speaking with could not keep his opinion to himself, was scared of him, or, like many others around Fuat, wanted to believe his words.

As I overheard the conversation, I was overcome with anger.

As if it were not enough that all of this nonsense had taken him away from me, he had lost himself in these matters and was unable to perceive the impending disaster.

When he hung up the phone, I couldn't help saying irritably, "Fuat, do you really believe all those things you're saying? Aren't you aware of what's been going on?"

He looked at me in astonishment.

"So let us hear your point of view, young lady," he replied mockingly.

"What can be worse than this?" I said. "All of you have withdrawn yourselves, and you are not aware of the reality around you. You don't listen to anyone except those who flatter you. Everyone's complaining. Everyone's angry."

"Who is angry?" he roared, jumping up from his seat. "Who are they angry at? At me? What have I done to them?"

"Not just you, all of you," I answered. "If a person starts seeing all criticism as hostility and sees everyone who reveals his opinion as his enemy, then that person is headed for despair."

He was silent. The expression on his face told me that he was furious at me for the first time, but it was too late to do anything about it now.

"So you think like the others too," he said. "You believe that people who insult us or swear at us, the ones who slander us, are right!"

"I'm not saying anyone's right. All I'm saying is that the way things are going is not good."

Suddenly, he started to shout.

"The way things are going is not good! Enough! I don't want to hear this nonsense anymore. At least, I don't want to hear it from you!"

Now it was my turn to be furious.

"I know you don't believe any of those things you say! You cannot be so blind! You know it better than anyone else that a dictatorship is not the way to achieve things. Are you putting on an act for me too?"

He became even more angry when he heard the word "dictatorship."

"I thought you supported me! But you were in fact against me. Shame on you! I would expect this behavior from anyone but you!" he screamed.

I took a deep breath. I was red with rage. In his mind, he separated everyone into two groups, "us" and "them." He thought anyone who had a different opinion was an enemy. I wanted to slap his face. For a moment, I couldn't decide what to do. I stood there squeezing my fists. Then I picked up my bag and coat and left the room.

All that time we had been together, we had never had a serious argument about a personal matter. Now, unexpectedly, he had shouted at me for a totally different reason.

The words "Shame on you!" had offended me so much that I couldn't stop crying in the cab all the way home.

He would go on a trip the following day. I didn't want to part with him without us talking again or in disagreement, but he didn't call me at home. I didn't call him either.

I was very angry. I felt rage toward everything and everyone.

I made a sudden decision without thinking in detail.

I called Ayla, bought a flight ticket, and prepared to visit her.

It was perhaps the day of my departure. At breakfast, Nihat told me about the discussions and disputes in parliament, which everyone was talking about. İsmet İnönü had given his famous speech, saying, "Not even I can rescue you!" But I became stuck on something else he had said: "Now a coup is legitimate."

"Did he really use those words?" I asked Nihat.

"He said that exactly. The newspapers were prohibited from reporting it, but all the same, everyone has been talking about it since yesterday."

"What's going on, Nihat?" I asked.

"I really don't know," he replied. "But it seems this will have an unfortunate end. Fuat's party will start playing rougher now. I'm glad you're leaving. Rest a little. Stay away from here. It will do you good."

Before I left Turkey, I called Mr. Sami to tell him about my trip.

"How long will you stay? What should I tell Mr. Fuat if he asks?"

"You can tell him I'll be there for a week or ten days," I said. "I'll give him a call from there. He shouldn't worry."

"Yes, Madam," the old man replied. "Have a nice trip. I'll inform him immediately. But you know, if he cannot reach you . . ."

"OK," I said, "I'll call him as soon as I arrive."

I didn't have a specific plan in mind. I thought I would stay a week, maybe two, and then return. All I had taken along was a single suitcase.

How could I have known?

I was distressed and worried but unsure of the reason for my mood. I thought it was because of our fight and that we didn't talk to each other before I left.

Ayla and Erik picked me up at the airport. I immediately looked at Ayla's belly, but her pregnancy was not noticeable yet. After seeing her and the trees and grassy plains of the countryside, I felt better. In the car, I asked Ayla about her new life, and she also questioned me.

Whenever I have more than I can handle, find myself in an impossible situation, or start tossing and turning in bed at night, I want to go somewhere. The place doesn't matter. When I can do that, I feel as if I have been rescued. Other people, other lives, and different images make me forget my trouble, even if only for a while.

As soon as I arrived at Ayla's house, I called Mr. Sami. Then I settled into the attic flat prepared for me. I changed my clothes. Ayla's home was in an adorable small town with old stone houses in the forest. There was a big church and a castle from the Middle Ages. We drank tea and ate raisin cookies as we chatted. A few hours later when we were about to go out, the phone rang. It was Fuat. Ayla gave me the receiver. He shouted, "What are you doing there?"

Like a scared child I blushed and wasn't able to answer. Then I said slowly, "Ayla asked me to come, and I couldn't turn down her invitation."

Fuat began to laugh. "Don't worry," he said. "I was just joking. I haven't been getting any sleep in the last days because of my sorrow. I know you're angry at me. I was so nervous. I didn't know what I was saying. Will you forgive me?"

I was relieved.

"I know," I said in a low voice. "I also said unnecessary things.

Now I feel better."

"Me, too," he said. "I'm going to Tehran. You should rest a little. The change will do you good. Who knows, maybe I can come there too. How long will you stay?"

"I don't know," I replied. "Perhaps one week only. We'll talk later."

I hung up the phone. Ayla, with her hands on her waist, eyed me menacingly. "Stop talking about a week," she said. "You have just arrived and you're already talking about going back!"

"Were you eavesdropping?" I asked jokingly.

She said, "One week is not enough even to show you the area. We'll also go downtown, to concerts, plays, and exhibitions. Give up the thought of going back soon." Since Erik didn't understand Turkish, I said, "One should not be the guest of newlyweds for too long. Your husband will get angry with me!"

Surprisingly, Erik looked at us and smiled.

He was an attractive man. He looked like a playboy, but when you got to know him, you realized he was friendly and relaxed. He had been to so many different places that he always had interesting stories to tell. Not too many people can effortlessly combine what they have read and what they experience. It was impossible to be bored around him. He knew many languages. He had already begun to learn Turkish and felt happy when he understood a few words of our conversation.

Thanks to Ayla, we went to all of the important events and visited all the places worth seeing, as if I were on an official visit. After returning home tired in the evening, we talked until the late hours of the night.

Days passed and the initially planned one-week vacation got longer and longer as I postponed returning to Turkey. One month passed. Each time I mentioned departing, Ayla told me know how much she wanted me to stay.

Anarchist incidents had begun in the universities in Turkey again. We heard on the news that a big demonstration had taken place in Ankara. Some soldiers had even taken part in it, and the Prime Minister had been treated roughly.

I sulked most of the time. Yet I tried my best not to show my worry to Ayla and Erik since I didn't want to upset them during their happiest days.

Ayla constantly invented things to amuse me, and we continued to go out to eat and to concerts and the cinema. They had recently purchased a small white car. Erik chuckled all the time, and asked us questions. He was curious about everything and made us tell him about our childhood days, friendship, and Turkey.

"I have traveled to so many places. It seems that I had been searching for the love of my life, and I have finally found her. Now it's time to have children. After the first, we shall have more," he said, teasing Ayla.

"Did you marry me because you loved me or to have me as a brood-mare," Ayla replied angrily. "I will not have ten children. I already have too much do."

Erik generally worked on his book late into the night. During the daytime, he took us to the historical towns and medieval castles in the region.

He was a man who could calm you as soon as you started talking to him. He had thought hard about what to name their baby and had come up with strange historical names for both a boy and a girl.

Their tiny two-storey house, whose staircase was even too narrow for two people to climb at the same time, was in the middle of a small garden. The old furniture left from Erik's family was heavy, either bare wood or covered with dark upholstery.

Seeing their happiness made me happy, too. For some reason,

I had always thought that Ayla would never marry. Now, when I watched her doing housework (which she was not very good at), making preparations for the baby, or taking her husband's arm, I was bewildered, yet laughing at the same time.

I teased her, saying, "Erik probably takes us out to dinner every evening because he is trying to find a way not to eat your food!"

Ayla often complained, "Supposedly I have a foreign husband, but he's no different from Turkish men who act as if they are the sultan's grandson. He doesn't even know how to fry an egg. As if I have nothing else to do, I have to learn to cook."

One evening, Fuat called me and said, "I'll be there tomorrow. I'm coming with a group of officials. We can only see each other in the evening. I have booked a room at our old hotel. You can go there anytime you like. I'll be there as soon as I can. Please come."

The jewelry store across the street rolled down its shutters noisily. The lights of the houses were lit one by one. In the café opposite the hotel entrance, I sat at a small table on the sidewalk, buried in thought. I contemplated beginnings, waiting, and the hours flew on wings of joy. I heard the old accordion player's tunes, as if he were here now. Such a long time had passed, but those years seemed as if they had passed in the blink of an eye. Didn't everything resemble our first encounter? Riding like mad on my bike, I had fallen to the ground in front of him. It felt as if my excitement racing down the hill, as well as my fear and shame after falling, had lasted until today.

In a secret corridor hidden in life . . . In a dark room illuminated with a red lamp . . . Like a child in a tale who is chasing a dream .

. . Without minding that it was too late, without caring about the things taught to us, forgetting that dreams suddenly end when we least expect, and that we can never predict what happens next in a dream . . . I didn't know if I saw a child in my dream or if was having the dream of a child. Pain gripped my heart . . . Meetings no one knew about . . . Lives that continued engulfed in a secret . . . People who told me to let matters take their course . . . Others who told me to choose how to live my own life, saying I had the right to make my own decisions . . . People who didn't know what it meant to hide a secret . . . Hours that passed looking into the most beautiful eyes in the world.

I was waiting for him again—who knows how many times I had done it—with a throbbing heart. The same old feeling, as if "something is rising inside of me."

I smiled as I sipped my coffee, saying to myself, I have waited for you to arrive so often. But I wasn't complaining. I remembered all the times I had waited for him—a kaleidoscope of images. Like rain, the memory of all those places, dates, and feelings showered down on me.

Life had hurled me around so many times, but still, I had returned to the same center of attraction.

There was a light breeze. As I sat and drank my coffee, I did not ponder doubts, worries, or the future. All I thought of was that very moment, that he would soon be there, and that while embracing each other, we would forget everything.

All at once, I realized that this feeling was strong enough to obliterate the entire truth and its unfavorable dimensions. This only happened when I saw him, when I looked into his eyes, when he held my hand, when he hugged and kissed me, and when he told me how much he loved me.

Is this believable?

Fuat was late. He was only able to free himself from the others and come after dinner. From the café, I watched him get out of the car in front of the hotel. I called out to him before he went into the building. We hugged each other warmly, without caring about the passersby.

"You look tired," I said.

"Yes, but I feel perfect as soon as I see you," he said. "What would I do if I didn't have you?"

"We have so little time, don't we?" I asked frowning.

"Quite the opposite," he laughed. "We have till the morning."

That evening, the streets were packed, as if a celebration was going on. Just like at a festival, the streets were full. Young couples roamed the banks of the river, arm in arm.

Fuat said, "I can't tell you how much I miss my school days. We don't realize the value of those carefree days. I would give anything to go back in time."

"Wouldn't it be nice if you and I were young students in this city?" I asked.

We jumped into a boat for tourists at the last moment, and watched the city from the river in the moonlight.

"Would you have been able to imagine this day when you were a student?" I said.

"I'm not sure," he replied. "Actually, I never imagined my life would be like this. I had always thought that I would lead an easygoing, comfortable life. In those days, being in politics never occurred to me."

He held my face and looked into my eyes. "I never would have thought that I would meet someone like you when my life was totally established—not even in my dreams."

I thought that if this seemingly unbelievable coincidence could come true, if we were experiencing an impossible love, and if our feelings persisted even though we postponed things and stayed apart for long periods, then it probably had a profound meaning. Perhaps what was between us was not temporary.

Years had passed. I thought about the journey we had shared during that time.

We had done so many things together—from making secret phone calls and sending small notes and letters like encoded messages to sharing the same home, spending nights together, traveling to distant islands, and strolling hand-in-hand.

In fact, everything I had dreamed of had come true. Though it had happened slowly, I had realized my dream.

In the beginning, I had dreamed of spending a single night with him—a night only the two of us shared. Then I had wished to walk with him hand-in-hand in the moonlight . . . Chatting with him for hours without thinking about anything else, without counting the hours, without being afraid . . . Falling asleep and waking up together.

We had lived everything.

Years ago, he had once asked me, "What is it that you want?"

"To be closer to you," I had answered.

Now I was closer to him than I had ever dreamed of.

Eventually, he asked me, "What are you thinking about?"

"Do you know that it was three years ago that you came to the hotel in London and called me?"

He was bewildered for a moment, realizing how much time had passed.

He said, "We had promised each other that we would go there once every year, but we couldn't keep that promise."

I felt gloom descend over him.

"But we met each other every year," I said. "We went to that same hotel two years ago. Have you forgotten?"

"How can I forget? Everything starts all over again each time I meet you. Maybe that's why it didn't dawn on me how many years have passed."

We got off the boat. Like idle lovers, we walked the streets, locked in a close embrace. I felt like saying to him, "Please stay here. Please don't ever go back. Let us start a new life here for ourselves." I felt so happy.

As if he read my mind, he said, "I know you're afraid. You're worried about me, but don't worry. I have thought about everything in detail. You were always on my mind when we were apart. I've already decided. I won't stand in the next elections. I'll quit. My daughter has grown up. She's at an age to understand my decision. I'll do what I told you I would. You will see."

I covered his mouth with my hand, but he pulled it away.

He said, "I know that you've heard similar words from me many times, but the time was not right before. Now, it has come. No one can say that I was afraid or that I ran away. I will tell them I won't be with them from now on. After that, we can do whatever you want and go wherever you wish."

Wasn't it really true that everything started over again each time we met?

"Will those things come true, Fuat?" I asked as we passed under a street lamp.

"Each one of them will happen," he answered. "Besides, I have a surprise for you. You'll see it when you return to Turkey."

"Please tell me now," I insisted like a child, but he didn't give me a clue. "Do you know what?" I asked then. "I don't care about anything at all. I wouldn't even care if I had to spend my whole life like this."

He hugged and kissed me crazily in the middle of the street. I could hardly rescue myself from his embrace.

We fell asleep toward the morning. Fuat constantly talked in his sleep. He said incomprehensible things, ground his teeth, and tossed and turned in bed. I tried to wake him up but I couldn't. After a short, insufficient sleep, we got up, and went to the airport.

I fretted, as if something bad was imminent. The closer we got to the airport, the more I felt agitated and wanted to stop him from leaving.

I prayed that something to stop him from going back would happen. I wished that we would have a car accident and be saved, so that he would have to stay.

"Why are you frowning, young lady?" he asked. "You look as if you're going to burst into tears. How can I leave with a relaxed mind if you act this way? I won't be able to think straight."

I told him exactly what was on my mind.

He laughed, and holding my hand, said, "I'm not going to war! Don't worry. Everything will get better. Nothing will happen to me. I won't die!"

So that was how he left. Before going through the main gate, he turned to look at me. I opened the window and waved good-bye. He smiled and disappeared in the crowd.

I returned to Ayla's house with a terrible weight on my heart. Ayla met me at the door. Then suddenly I exclaimed, "Oh no! I forgot to pour water after him to wish him a safe trip!"

The feeling I had was indescribable.

I missed him constantly. Even if he was with me or far away from me. I felt as if my longing for him would never end, even if we spent a lifetime together, shared the same house, or slept together every night.

On his last visit, he had brought me a very old music box with blue and green enamel. It was beautiful. (It stands by my bedside today. For many years, every night before falling asleep, I have opened its lid and listened to that wonderful song.)

When he gave it to me, I had kissed him.

I had said, "You always think of the prettiest and kindest things."

"Whatever I do for you isn't enough," he replied. "When I see something, I ask myself if it would become you and how you would look in it. Usually, I end up thinking nothing is good enough for you."

I can remember now. He had given me so many presents, but the only thing I got for him, in addition to the small things I gave him as gifts, was an embellished blue watch on a chain. I had found it in an antique shop in London. There was a star and crescent on its dial. Fuat had always carried from that time on.

He used to laugh and say to me, "I look at my watch constantly because of you, and everyone asks if I'm late for an appointment.

I was so exhausted that I took a nap after arriving at Ayla's home, and I dreamed about a strange place. I was on a riverbank. Behind the clouds that slowly dispersed in front me were dark blue mountains and colorful trees. I begged a silent fisherman to take me there. We got in his boat, but he always changed direction, as if he didn't want to take me to that place, and I got angry at him. The scenery in front of me was incredibly beautiful. I had never seen anything similar. It was so perfect that it aroused awe. Just as I thought we had finally reached our destination, the entire coastline in front of us suddenly sank, leaving us high up on the edge of a huge, churning waterfall, over which we fell.

I woke up screaming. Ayla came running. I told her about my dream. She laughed and said, "It's alright now. We will send you back immediately. Don't worry."

"I'll come back for the birth," I said, trying to please her. I also told her about the previous night and everything Fuat had told me. "Finally!" she said. "Don't get me wrong, but I've been waiting a long time for him to say those things."

I was still under the influence of my dream while we drank tea.

"Know what?" I asked. "I wasn't expecting him to decide. I still don't expect it. It's hard to believe that what he said will come true."

"Come on," Ayla said. "Your relationship will surely begin to go smoothly. Or else, how can you people go on living?"

I studied her face, and then said, "Why shouldn't we?"

"You really do have a few screws loose!" she replied.

We finished our tea and went out for a stroll. We did some shopping at the small town market and then came back home to cook. I didn't want to go out again because Fuat would call.

He called in the evening. He had realized that I was worried and scared. He kept saying things to calm me down. "Now that I've seen you, I feel fine," he said. Yet my mind was focused on the elections. I asked what would happen. "Don't worry," he answered. "The elections will take place soon, perhaps in the fall."

Not much time was left. Just the summer. After enduring so many seasons, so much rain, so many storms, snow, the warm breeze from the sea, and the hot winds, a single summer was left to endure. The time would pass in the blink of an eye.

The following winter would be ours. Perhaps we would go to a place where we could wear our thick sweaters, coats, and hats, and roll in the snow. In such a place, we could talk about the fabulous days we had spent together. We would tell each other about the missing parts of our own version of our unique story, bringing it to completion.

Erik went to bed early that night. Ayla and I stayed up late and discussed the same matters, dreaming about the future trips we would make together. Ayla had already begun imagining us all living in the same area.

The next day we booked my ticket, and I started to prepare to return to Turkey in a few days. I did some shopping. The time spent abroad had done me good, but I missed my family and my cat.

I felt very happy, as if my life had suddenly begun to settle into shape.

Ayla was confused a little. She couldn't decide whether she should give birth to the baby here or in Istanbul.

It was a cool, pleasant day. As we were getting ready to go out for dinner, the phone rang. Ayla answered it. After exchanging a few words, she gave the receiver to me. It was Fuat. His voice had an echo.

"I'm still working in my office. I'm terribly tired. I just wanted to hear your voice," he said.

He sounded weary. To cheer him up, I said, "Don't strain yourself. I need you. I don't want a weary old man! Okay?"

He laughed. "At least tell me beforehand if you're going to get rid of me when I get senile!"

My heart sizzled.

"Nothing will happen to you," I said. "Even if something does, don't worry because I will take care of you."

"I would never leave you even if I died," he said.

"Heaven forbid! You shouldn't say that!" I scolded.

He asked about my departure date.

"We'll talk tomorrow morning," he said.

"We'll talk in the morning," I said.

Then we hung up.

We had promised to talk again the next day. However, the following morning, I didn't wake up to his call but to Ayla's anxious face.

"There's been a coup in Turkey," she said. "The army has taken control."

I jumped out of bed and got dressed.

We didn't know what to do or whom to call.

It was impossible to reach anyone in Turkey by phone.

All flights had been cancelled.

I wanted to go there even if I had to walk. That was all I could think of. "Let's wait for a while," Ayla said. "Let's first find out what happened. They say that no one is dead or injured. If the situation were really grave, we would have heard." Yet her face reflected her anxiety.

Just like me, Ayla scurried around the house, listening to the radio helplessly. However, we were unable to get more information than the few sentences the announcer on the radio had been given to read. According to the radio reports, tanks were in the city centers, but the public was calm and even pleased. Some people had been arrested, but no one knew any details yet.

Erik stayed at home that day, and both he and Ayla kept telling me things to cheer me up, insisting that the army would not risk opposing the whole world and would not harm Fuat or the others.

Yet, nothing except hearing his voice and knowing that he was safe would relieve me.

Finally, Mr. Sami came to my rescue. He had managed to contact the embassy and give information to someone he knew there personally. When the phone rang, we all jumped out of our seats. The embassy official was utterly confused because of my rapid, never-ending questions. All he could say was that Mr. Fuat was safe and sound, that I should not worry about him, and that I was supposed to stay where I was. The man was not able to provide with further details. That was all he knew.

Don't ask me how I spent that day and night.

The next day, an acquaintance of Fuat who worked in Paris called me. I met him in the city. Ayla and Erik also came along, but they sat at another table.

The gentleman, who had the expressionless face of a diplomat, sipped his coffee.

"I would like to tell you everything," he said.

I asked, "What's going on? Have you received any news from him? Were you able to talk to him?"

"No, they won't allow him to talk to anyone. He's under arrest."

I tried to keep calm, but it was nearly impossible.

I finally managed to say, "What is going to happen? What will they do to him? Please tell me. I want to know."

He stretched out his arms and said, "At this moment, no one knows anything. But if you ask me, I don't think they will do anything bad to them, at least for the time being."

He occasionally frowned and looked somewhat sad, yet he didn't show any sign of agitation. Obviously, he wasn't surprised at what had happened. Didn't we all know that everything would end like this? Haven't we all talked about this possibility?

"So you didn't get any news from him," I insisted.

"Many things are being said," he explained. "In such times, it is difficult to tell rumor and truth apart. I understand how you feel.

However, there's nothing we can do except wait a couple of days. It is rumored that the president attempted suicide, but was prevented. The Prime Minister was seized in Eskişehir and brought to where the others are being held. There has been no resistance or chaos in the streets."

"What do you think they will do to them?" I asked.

"I guess they will all be put on trial . . . At least, that's what I think."

"Are you sure nothing else will happen?"

"I don't think so. If the soldiers wanted to follow a different route, they would have done it by now."

"I hope it happens like you say," I said.

"I wanted to meet you here for another reason too."

I waited for him to explain.

"No matter what happens, please don't go back to our country. If you do, you will be pulled into the problem."

"I don't care," I said. "I'm not afraid of such things. It doesn't matter to me."

Trying hard to choose his words correctly, he finally said, "Yes, perhaps, but if you went there, it would be worse for him than for you."

At that moment, I realized what he was trying to tell me.

He would return to Turkey the following day. Would he be able to give Fuat a note from me?

"I'll try my best," he said.

I scribbled a short note on a piece of paper on the table: "Everything passes. You should just keep alive." He took an envelope out of his briefcase and gave it to me. I placed the note in the envelope and handed it to him.

As he was leaving, he said, "Please keep in mind what I told you. I will try my best to keep you informed. Don't worry, everything will be alright."

He shook my hand and left.

It was unbelievable.

What was I thinking one day ago and where was I now?

Only a day ago he and I were chatting and laughing together. Now, I didn't even know when I would hear his voice again.

I hugged Ayla and began to cry.

Time makes everything meaningful.

If we had the power to speed up time or prolong it as much as we wished, life would be marvelous.

Some people find out about this through sorrow.

Maybe that was how I learned—by enduring passing time.

I had gone to Paris for a short holiday, which I extended. Since I couldn't return to Turkey, Ayla decided to stay in Paris and give birth to her child there.

Through a connection Erik had, I even found a job in an institute. I went to my part-time work every day.

Those days have faded in my memory: the colors, sounds, and voices seem as if they belong to an old film. But this did not happen later. Even then, I perceived them in this manner.

I can see myself there, sitting on a bench in a small town full of trees, with the river flowing in front of me, trying to convince myself that such a wonderful love story cannot have a sad ending.

That hot summer, which I thought would end in an instant, did not cease.

Ayla's belly grew rapidly. She looked cute, but her temperament changed. She complained about everything, kept tormenting her husband, as if she wanted to make him suffer for the distress of the past months.

At night (just like now), I put my small music box on my bedside table and fall asleep listening to that song.

It is an odd, stifling period, during which I wait for time to pass, counting the days as if I am imprisoned with him. I do nothing at all, feel suffocated, weep all of a sudden, and let my mind wander in the middle of conversations.

I went to work, and in the evenings, we went out as usual, met with Ayla and Erik's acquaintances. I followed up with the latest movies, plays, and exhibitions thanks to my dear friend, who arranged everything in between all her other work. Life went on, yet I did those things as if they were my duties. I didn't put my heart into anything. I felt as if I were out of my body, watching myself from the outside and wondering how I—a stranger—survived and kept abreast of daily life.

All I wanted was for time to pass.

Now, saying this, it has suddenly occurred to me that although it sounds strange, I have spent my entire life by wishing for one thing: to go beyond time and to stop it, since the day I met Fuat.

I wonder if there really is a way to achieve this.

I have never found out.

All I learned in this process was to find small things that enlivened my life and kept me busy (because it was early, always too early) and made me forget what time of day it was (that's when I took off my wristwatch and never wore it again).

Don't we always try to keep small babies, who must lie down until the day they can run and talk, busy with colorful toys that emit strange sounds?

Like a baby, I waited for time to pass and felt grateful for any distraction.

You get used to everything as time goes by.

I was constantly expecting news, but the news I hoped for didn't arrive.

I found out about some things from Mr. Sami, who, in fact, kept the truth a secret, from Nihat, a few acquaintances, and the newspapers.

As time passed, I became more relaxed. I knew that Fuat and his colleagues were together and that they would be taken to court. Although they were not allowed to talk to anyone, we received news. Whomever we talked to in Ankara said that the court cases would turn out okay and that they would eventually be released.

We found out that a film had been shot and shown in cinemas. In it, Fuat appeared reading a book. (I never saw the film, but I realized later that it had been made under duress. They had been forced to act. Among many things, this hurt me the most. I still cannot accept that they were forced to act in such a situation.)

In those days, however, I readily accepted the favorable news we received. I wanted to believe it.

I even began thinking that this was our destiny and perhaps a chance for us to be reunited.

All the same, I fretted, telling myself that I should never have come to Paris. Whenever I went crazy and wanted to go back to Turkey, Ayla convinced me to stay. She said, "As long as I'm alive, you are not allowed to go anywhere. It will not help anything but will only cause him more trouble. Wait a little longer. Soon the court case will start."

Sometimes I would tell Fuat, "You are upset about something."

He would reply laughing, "Yes I was, but when I saw you, I forgot about it."

If I then asked, "Why don't you share with me the things that upset you?" he would say, "I want to see you in good times. I want to spend them all with you. I don't want to bring trouble and distress. I want you to smile all the time. I want your smiles to infect me, too."

Now we were experiencing bad times, and I was not beside him.

Maybe this was what he wanted. I knew that if I had been able to ask him, he would not have wanted me to be near him or see him in handcuffs between soldiers, with his shirt wrinkled, his face unshaven, and perhaps being pushed around.

No, he would not have wanted that.

But still, if I accepted the risks and returned to the country, found someone, begged everyone . . .

But wouldn't they ask who I was?

What could I tell them?

At that moment, I realized that I was just a rumor in his life. Even at the time when he needed me the most, I wasn't able to be with him.

It hurt to think about such things. I felt like I was in exile, dreaming that everything would be over soon and that our life would begin anew, just as we had dreamed of.

This dream alone calmed me down, enabling me to endure another day.

Finally, the hot summer ended. The leaves turned red and yellow. Uninterrupted rain began. We had a lovely baby girl on the same day the handsome man who was later shot in a convertible was elected president. We called her "our baby" because Ayla and Erik gave her my name; I also became a mother, like Ayla. This beautiful baby became my new, bright light. On mornings when she looked up at me with her blue eyes, I thought there was a reason to stay alive.

After we came back home from the hospital, the same man, Fuat's acquaintance, gave me a call. He said that he had a letter for me, and I went downtown to pick it up. I opened it with trembling hands and began reading it in the street.

"My light, my mornings, my Bosphorus, my love,

"I wonder if this letter will ever reach you. I wish we could talk, even if only once, on the phone so that I could ask you not to worry about me. Even if my life is taken away, your image is here beside me. No matter what happens, no one can take that from me. Here, I can feel that you're thinking about me, far away. Don't forget that if you do not get enough sleep, I also feel sleepless; if you cry, I cry too. Wouldn't they then reproach me, saying how can a grown-up man cry like a little child without being ashamed? I exercise in the morning. I read a lot. The food is good. When you see me, I will have become a young and slender man! It seems that history was fated to unfold like this. Perhaps one day, the truth will be revealed and everything will fit into its correct place. Don't worry about me; I'm alright here. I caress your beautiful cheeks and kiss your eyes."

That was all.

There, in the street, I was reading his letter with tears rolling down my cheeks. He was there. He was alive. He had been able to write a letter to me. I should be happy instead of weeping.

I stood up and dried my eyes. Feeling dizzy, I slipped the letter into my coat pocket. On the way home, I read it again and again until I had memorized Fuat's words.

Sometimes the biggest of all dreams comes true.

I have had such a dream. When I was a little girl, when I did not know what life was like (do I know it now?), and when I was still unaware of real fears, I had had a dream, and it had come true.

Like a child in a tale who finds a secret passage while playing in a garden one quiet afternoon, I had opened the door of my dream and gone out into reality. Everything had continued in the real world as well.

Perhaps only a few people can experience a dream while they are surrounded by reality.

A world where people grow up and forget about their dreams, considering them to belong to a child's world, is not a place worth living.

Isn't this why the world is full of so much destruction!

Yes, sometimes the biggest of all dreams comes true.

Sometimes, however, the biggest of all frustrations comes along too.

Seasons passed, and the little baby girl began to smile and tell us things in her own special language, even if we didn't understand what she was trying to say.

People were saying that the trials were about to end and that a verdict was just around the corner. I began to pack my suitcase. My friend and her family would also return to Turkey soon. In those days, I developed the habit of embracing the baby and inhaling her wonderful scent.

It was autumn in Paris. The trees were slowly shedding their leaves, the rain was drizzling, and when I looked out from the window of my office, a layer of moving umbrellas covered the street.

Erik had gone somewhere for two days.

That morning, the little girl didn't stop crying no matter how we tried to calm her, and her face turned completely red.

"What's happened to this child of mine?" Ayla asked. "Maybe she realizes her father has left. She's never cried so much before."

We were helpless. Finally, we put the baby in a blanket, wrapped the ends tightly, and began to rock her. It was all in vain.

A man on the radio was singing a melancholy song about his homeland, which he missed while in exile.

The rain was pounding on the windows.

When the telephone began to ring, mixing with the baby's cries and the sound of the rain, Ayla and I looked at each other and began to laugh. We put the baby in her crib. Ayla turned down the volume of the radio, and I answered the phone.

Nihat was on the line. The baby was yelling so much that I could hardly hear him. "Talk louder," I said. "This little girl has been bringing down the whole world since this morning. We've been trying hard to calm her, but it's impossible. We're two grown women, but we're unable to cope with one baby."

I was rattling on, but Nihat was silent.

"How are you?" I asked. "How's mother? What about Lilac?" I kept talking. He was still quiet.

"Are you on the line? Are you there? I asked.

"I am here," he said.

I paused and then asked, "What's happened?" Ayla was standing in front of me and studying my face.

"I had hoped that I wouldn't be the one to tell you . . ."

I suddenly felt dizzy and stopped talking. I was holding the telephone receiver tightly.

I remember screaming "What's happened Nihat? Tell me! Quick!" as Ayla's face blanched and she groped for something to hold on to.

With a muffled voice, Nihat said, "They executed him. It's over . . . Don't ask any more."

I dropped the receiver and collapsed. A song was playing on the radio: "I am banished from the sunshine of my land, the gardens of my childhood, and your fair face."

I felt as if I were in a world made of glass, the dome over me had shattered, and all the pieces were raining down. The hum in my ears rose so much that I could no longer hear the song, the voices around me, the cries of the baby, or the driving rain outside.

It was a Saturday morning.

These are the images from my "camera obscura," reflecting on the walls.

I couldn't come to this country for a long time. I neither wanted to receive news, nor see any photos. I didn't read what was written and I didn't listen to what people said. I still don't want to hear anything about that incident. I've told you before: I have never liked the sheer truth. The truth about life. The reality of others. Not mine . . .

I didn't want to collect memories either. No one asked me anything, and I didn't tell anyone anything.

What are memories worth, anyway? Do they help us realize that what has been lived is now over and that it can never be experienced again, since it is lost somewhere unreachable in the past?

I went back to those places we had gone together: the museum, the hotel where he had met me wearing a derby hat, the streets of a foreign land where we had walked quickly under the drizzle with our collars up for fear of being recognized, the hotel room where I awoke to the music of the blind accordion player whom I never saw again, the bench where I had sat under the moonlight and leaned against his chest, and the bar where I had read a poem engraved on a table.

Didn't it always happen that way?

Hadn't he always appeared suddenly in front of me?

Wouldn't he always surprise me by appearing at the most

unexpected moment like a hero in a tale?

It is hard to believe, but even today, when I wake up and water my plants, when I'm walking on a street, when I see someone who resembles him in a concert hall, when I hear the telephone ring, or when a certain song is playing, I instinctively lift my head to look for him.

Our correspondence remains only in my memory now. The day they took him to prison, they also confiscated our letters in our home, just like many other things that belonged to us.

Much later, I learned that the surprise he had told me about was the house with drawn curtains hidden among the trees and plants— the house I cherished each time we passed it.

How much he loved surprises.

Once, he had told me, "One day, I will buy you the prettiest house in the world, and we will live there together."

I am not sad because I couldn't see that house again and wasn't able to live there, but because I think of how much he must have dreamed of picking me up upon my return to Turkey and taking me to that house to surprise me.

Over these many years, I haven't felt pain by dwelling on the things we couldn't do together but excitement for the wonderful times we spent together. If we had not experienced that morning when he entered my life by coincidence, I would not have had the glitter in my eyes, which still exists today, though you may not notice it, or the flutter in my heart.

For a moment, I feel as if I'm living in a totally different period on this tired, slightly drowsy afternoon, listening to the distant voices of children playing outside and the screams of seagulls in this magnificent city that stretches effortlessly to the seashore through old brick-roofed houses scattered among the trees.

When I was a little girl, while everyone else slept, I used to hide among the trees in the garden, where the cicadas never ceased chirping.

I must have forgotten this image for a long time. Now, suddenly, I feel as if I am in the garden now, and that if I held out my hand I could touch the shoulder of that little girl, that if I turned back and called out toward the house, my mother would come and play our usual game, pretending to be surprised that she couldn't find me.

The days when we were lazy and indifferent and unaware, that time is something that can never be retrieved regardless of how hard you try, and that it is the most valuable thing in the world, we did not care about how quickly it passed. We never needed to make a plan or a decision since we were free of worries, sleeping long and deeply and waking to mornings when reality and dreams mingled, to the comforting scent of a glass of warm milk. Maybe because I felt like that and because I was such a child (or are all children similar?), I still confuse reality and dreams today, when I have already left behind most of my life.

That music playing on the big radio with lights—the music I haven't heard for years, though I have tried to remember it many times in vain, suddenly comes to my ears, sounding as lovely as in the past.

Tales that talk about giant gardens . . . Princesses . . . The most beautiful young girls with long hair and emerald eyes whose long skirts rustle as they walk . . . Goodhearted knights . . . Wizards who turn people into other things . . . Palaces of ice . . . Talking animals . . . The flower of bliss beyond the mountains . . . Talismans and gems that are obtained with difficulty but can be lost easily . . . Secret codes that open doors, unfasten sealed mouths, and help heroes traverse long distances . . . Secret passageways . . . Tears that melt hearts of ice . . . Magic potions that suddenly appear in front of you in a cave or in a hollow everyone speaks of but no one can find . . . Mysterious languages no one is able to understand . . . Castles of fear . . . Beauties and the beasts . . . The good and the bad . . . The right and the wrong . . . Happiness and sorrow . . . Reunion and separation . . . Unforgotten kisses . . . Love.

Love?

Was the grandmother telling a small child about love?

In fact, it was the only thing she was telling the child about. Love was the only thing that all the potions, talismans, birds that guided humans, the bad people who blocked roads, wizards seen through smoke, magic, secret codes, dazzling emeralds and rubies . . .

Love and the adventures it brings along . . . Imperceptible journeys, people you come across unexpectedly, coincidences, and stories that are not content with an enormous world but unite dreams, fantasies, and imagination hidden in the most secluded corners of the mind . . .

But life is different.

Or did we not learn the lessons we were supposed to learn from those tales? Didn't those tales tell us that many other things exist besides the lives we wedge into small rooms, houses, worries, or fear?

Didn't they change the locations of the ordinary pictures of life, rearrange them, and display them to us in a new way?

Yes, a wooden puppet can come alive . . . Tin soldiers can walk . . . Houses and cities can be built in the sky . . . With the help of an intricate machine, you can go anywhere you want in time or space, and find missing people and lost moments again . . . Everything can take on a different color with the touch of a magic wand, rescuing you from the pictures that frighten you. The genie of the lamp can bring everything back to you in those moments of grief when you cannot stop the tears.

But only if you know what you want and you can dream.

How strange! I can comprehend all of this and a long-forgotten song after so many years.

Not everyone has the power to gather the courage of the knight who mistook windmills for giants and priests for bandits who kidnapped the princess.

Something hurts inside of me. If I go back and call for my mother, will she not come? Won't a little girl with white socks appear from a corner as well—a small girl playing hopscotch, who thinks that everything that exists can suddenly turn into something else, believing firmly that we can reach things that will make us happy just because we want them.

Or are the cookies and tea not ready yet?

No. Unfortunately not.

I am here now. I am far away from the cookies and tea, from the most fabulous afternoons of the world, and from songs and tales that invigorate one unexpectedly. So far away . . . So far that I cannot return.

Why is it so? Why can we reach all parts of the world by traversing long roads, yet we can only travel back in time in our memory?

Wouldn't it be better if time extended in front of us like space, and if we had the ability to travel in it whenever we wanted?

If only we could relive all those splendid moments we have lost, the days that quietly slipped through our hands, the unforgettable voices of loved ones, touches, embraces, kisses, the shudders of youth, and the enthusiasm again . . . If only those familiar smells welcomed us as soon as we went through the door.

If only we had one last chance to ask everything we have ever wanted to ask, to say the words we often decided not to say, to live the dreams we always postponed, and to experience the kind of things we couldn't accomplish just because something got in our way.

To change a decision we made and start all over again . . . To change the chain of events . . . To rewrite the life stories of others whose lives we have influenced . . . To put together the strange pieces of an enormous and daunting puzzle, creating an entirely different picture.

Oh, I know. They weren't able to build that time machine . . .

NOTES

The notes that follow are meant to be an informal guide to some of the references—people, places, events, and phrases—to the history and culture of modern Turkey in this novel.

p. 13   *cold mausoleum on Rasattepe:* The burial place, in Ankara, of Mustafa Kemal Atatürk (1881–1938), the founder of modern Turkey; curiously, the word "mausoleum" itself comes from the tomb of King Mausolus (c. 350 BCE) in what was then Greek Halicarnassus, and is now the Turkish city of Bodrum.

p. 21   *İsmet İnönü:* Greatly respected Army general (1884–1973) who became Prime Minister and the second president of Turkey, after Atatürk. His mausoleum is across the street from Atatürk's.

p. 21   *I'm going to enroll in Türk Kuşu:* Flight school of the Turkish Aeronautical Association, opened 1935. Atatürk's adopted daughter Sahina was its first female trainee and Turkey's first female military pilot.

p. 46   *Kandılli:* Neighborhood in Istanbul.

p. 87   *Filiz Akın or Fatma Girik:* Turkish film stars (b. 1943, 1942) in Yesilçan, the Istanbul Hollywood.

p. 137   *You are the devil's feather:* Turkish proverb, a woman who draws men to her without being aware of her seductive power.

p. 210   *Pera Palas:* A grand hotel in the European district of Istanbul; Atatürk made it his headquarters.

p. 215   *Moliendo Café:* Popular song (1958) written by Venezuelan Hugo Blanco.

p. 218   *Princes Islands:* Islands near Istanbul where many wealthy Istanbullu have summer homes; the largest island, Büyükada, has horse-drawn carriages and large villas.

p. 282   *Çalıkuşu:* Reşat Nur's novel (*The Wren*, 1922) about a young woman living in Anatolia during the dissolution of the old Ottoman Empire, told partly in diary and first-person narrative.

p. 282   *Aşk-ı Memnu:* Halit Ziya Uşaklıgil's 1899 novel (*Forbidden Love*).

p. 282   *Yahya Kemal:* Turkish poet (1884–1958) Ahmet Âgâh, involved in protests against the Ottoman rule, but later prominent in the Republican Party government following independence.

p. 290   *There is no happy love:* Louis Aragon (1897–1982) "Il n'y a pas d'amour heureux."

p. 295   *Halide Hanım:* Halide Edip Advar (1884–1964) Early feminist, writer, professor and intellectual, active in politics.

p. 297   *death and the revolution:* 1958 coup in Iraq that removed and executed King Faisal II and members of his family, and established the Iraqi Republic.

p. 312   *Republican People's Party:* Çumhurıyet Halk Partisi (CHP), founded by Atatürk. Originally founded in 1919 as a resistance movement; formalized in 1923 as the "People's Party," changed to CHP, 1924.

p. 327   *Kavaklıdere:* Neighborhood in Ankara.

p. 332   *I poured water after him . . . :* Turkish custom when saying
good-bye: "Go like the wave, come back like the wave."

p. 333   *On the plane that got lost in the fog . . . :* On 17 February
1959, a plane crash at Gatwick Airport outside London
killed fifteen members of the Turkish government; Prime
Minister Menderes survived.

p. 335   *Levent:* Istanbul neighborhood, on the European side.

p. 340   *Çesme:* Turkish resort city on the Aegean coast.

p. 351   *Not even I can rescue you!:* İnönü's famous warning speech
(April 1959) to Prime Minister Menderes and the Demo-
cratic Party after Menderes's imposition of extreme repres-
sive measures.

p. 354   *Anarchist incidents had begun in the universities:* In April,
1960, a series of student demonstrations escalated into vio-
lent confrontations with police, followed by the imposition
of martial law on 1 May 1960.

p. 364   *There's been a coup in Turkey:* On 27 May 1960 the government was overthrown by the military, who saw themselves
as the keepers of Kemal Atatürk's vision. The trial of Prime
Minister Menderes and over four hundred of his government staff began on 14 October 1960. Although world
leaders tried to intercede, three ministers were hanged on
16 September 1961; Menderes, who had attempted suicide
on 16 September, was resuscitated and hanged on 17 September.

KÜRŞAT BAŞAR was born in Istanbul in 1963. He graduated from the Department of Philosophy at Istanbul University, and has worked as a writer and editor for several daily newspapers, as well as a consultant for local television. He has published numerous novels, including bestsellers, in Turkey.

ÇIĞDEM AKSOY FROMM was born in 1969 in Turkey and studied Tourism and Hotel Management in Bilkent University in Ankara, Turkey. She translates from Turkish to English and from English to Turkish. Among her English translations are *The Traveler* by Sadık Yalsızuçanlar (Timas) and *Bliss* by O.Z. Livaneli (St. Martin's).

SELECTED DALKEY ARCHIVE TITLES

MICHAL AJVAZ, *The Golden Age.*
The Other City.
PIERRE ALBERT-BIROT, *Grabinoulor.*
YUZ ALESHKOVSKY, *Kangaroo.*
FELIPE ALFAU, *Chromos.*
Locos.
IVAN ÂNGELO, *The Celebration.*
The Tower of Glass.
ANTÓNIO LOBO ANTUNES, *Knowledge of Hell.*
The Splendor of Portugal.
ALAIN ARIAS-MISSON, *Theatre of Incest.*
JOHN ASHBERY AND JAMES SCHUYLER,
A Nest of Ninnies.
ROBERT ASHLEY, *Perfect Lives.*
GABRIELA AVIGUR-ROTEM, *Heatwave
and Crazy Birds.*
DJUNA BARNES, *Ladies Almanack.*
Ryder.
JOHN BARTH, *LETTERS.*
Sabbatical.
DONALD BARTHELME, *The King.*
Paradise.
SVETISLAV BASARA, *Chinese Letter.*
MIQUEL BAUÇÀ, *The Siege in the Room.*
RENÉ BELLETTO, *Dying.*
MAREK BIEŃCZYK, *Transparency.*
ANDREI BITOV, *Pushkin House.*
ANDREJ BLATNIK, *You Do Understand.*
LOUIS PAUL BOON, *Chapel Road.*
My Little War.
Summer in Termuren.
ROGER BOYLAN, *Killoyle.*
IGNÁCIO DE LOYOLA BRANDÃO,
Anonymous Celebrity.
Zero.
BONNIE BREMSER, *Troia: Mexican Memoirs.*
CHRISTINE BROOKE-ROSE, *Amalgamemnon.*
BRIGID BROPHY, *In Transit.*
GERALD L. BRUNS, *Modern Poetry and
the Idea of Language.*
GABRIELLE BURTON, *Heartbreak Hotel.*
MICHEL BUTOR, *Degrees.*
Mobile.
G. CABRERA INFANTE, *Infante's Inferno.*
Three Trapped Tigers.
JULIETA CAMPOS,
The Fear of Losing Eurydice.
ANNE CARSON, *Eros the Bittersweet.*
ORLY CASTEL-BLOOM, *Dolly City.*
LOUIS-FERDINAND CÉLINE, *Castle to Castle.*
Conversations with Professor Y.
London Bridge.
Normance.
North.
Rigadoon.
MARIE CHAIX, *The Laurels of Lake Constance.*
HUGO CHARTERIS, *The Tide Is Right.*
ERIC CHEVILLARD, *Demolishing Nisard.*
MARC CHOLODENKO, *Mordechai Schamz.*
JOSHUA COHEN, *Witz.*
EMILY HOLMES COLEMAN, *The Shutter
of Snow.*
ROBERT COOVER, *A Night at the Movies.*
STANLEY CRAWFORD, *Log of the S.S. The
Mrs Unguentine.*
Some Instructions to My Wife.
RENÉ CREVEL, *Putting My Foot in It.*
RALPH CUSACK, *Cadenza.*
NICHOLAS DELBANCO, *The Count of Concord.*
Sherbrookes.
NIGEL DENNIS, *Cards of Identity.*

PETER DIMOCK, *A Short Rhetoric for
Leaving the Family.*
ARIEL DORFMAN, *Konfidenz.*
COLEMAN DOWELL,
Island People.
Too Much Flesh and Jabez.
ARKADII DRAGOMOSHCHENKO, *Dust.*
RIKKI DUCORNET, *The Complete
Butcher's Tales.*
The Fountains of Neptune.
The Jade Cabinet.
Phosphor in Dreamland.
WILLIAM EASTLAKE, *The Bamboo Bed.*
Castle Keep.
Lyric of the Circle Heart.
JEAN ECHENOZ, *Chopin's Move.*
STANLEY ELKIN, *A Bad Man.*
*Criers and Kibitzers, Kibitzers
and Criers.*
The Dick Gibson Show.
The Franchiser.
The Living End.
Mrs. Ted Bliss.
FRANÇOIS EMMANUEL, *Invitation to a
Voyage.*
SALVADOR ESPRIU, *Ariadne in the
Grotesque Labyrinth.*
LESLIE A. FIEDLER, *Love and Death in
the American Novel.*
JUAN FILLOY, *Op Oloop.*
ANDY FITCH, *Pop Poetics.*
GUSTAVE FLAUBERT, *Bouvard and Pécuchet.*
KASS FLEISHER, *Talking out of School.*
FORD MADOX FORD,
The March of Literature.
JON FOSSE, *Aliss at the Fire.*
Melancholy.
MAX FRISCH, *I'm Not Stiller.*
Man in the Holocene.
CARLOS FUENTES, *Christopher Unborn.*
Distant Relations.
Terra Nostra.
Where the Air Is Clear.
TAKEHIKO FUKUNAGA, *Flowers of Grass.*
WILLIAM GADDIS, *J R.*
The Recognitions.
JANICE GALLOWAY, *Foreign Parts.*
The Trick Is to Keep Breathing.
WILLIAM H. GASS, *Cartesian Sonata
and Other Novellas.*
Finding a Form.
A Temple of Texts.
The Tunnel.
Willie Masters' Lonesome Wife.
GÉRARD GAVARRY, *Hoppla! 1 2 3.*
ETIENNE GILSON,
The Arts of the Beautiful.
Forms and Substances in the Arts.
C. S. GISCOMBE, *Giscome Road.*
Here.
DOUGLAS GLOVER, *Bad News of the Heart.*
WITOLD GOMBROWICZ,
A Kind of Testament.
PAULO EMÍLIO SALES GOMES, *P's Three
Women.*
GEORGI GOSPODINOV, *Natural Novel.*
JUAN GOYTISOLO, *Count Julian.*
Juan the Landless.
Makbara.
Marks of Identity.

FOR A FULL LIST OF PUBLICATIONS, VISIT:
www.dalkeyarchive.com

SELECTED DALKEY ARCHIVE TITLES

HENRY GREEN, *Back.*
Blindness.
Concluding.
Doting.
Nothing.
JACK GREEN, *Fire the Bastards!*
JIŘÍ GRUŠA, *The Questionnaire.*
MELA HARTWIG, *Am I a Redundant Human Being?*
JOHN HAWKES, *The Passion Artist.*
Whistlejacket.
ELIZABETH HEIGHWAY, ED., *Contemporary Georgian Fiction.*
ALEKSANDAR HEMON, ED., *Best European Fiction.*
AIDAN HIGGINS, *Balcony of Europe.*
Blind Man's Bluff.
Bornholm Night-Ferry.
Flotsam and Jetsam.
Langrishe, Go Down.
Scenes from a Receding Past.
KEIZO HINO, *Isle of Dreams.*
KAZUSHI HOSAKA, *Plainsong.*
ALDOUS HUXLEY, *Antic Hay.*
Crome Yellow.
Point Counter Point.
Those Barren Leaves.
Time Must Have a Stop.
NAOYUKI II, *The Shadow of a Blue Cat.*
GERT JONKE, *The Distant Sound.*
Geometric Regional Novel.
Homage to Czerny.
The System of Vienna.
JACQUES JOUET, *Mountain R.*
Savage.
Upstaged.
MIEKO KANAI, *The Word Book.*
YORAM KANIUK, *Life on Sandpaper.*
HUGH KENNER, *Flaubert.*
Joyce and Beckett: The Stoic Comedians.
Joyce's Voices.
DANILO KIŠ, *The Attic.*
Garden, Ashes.
The Lute and the Scars
Psalm 44.
A Tomb for Boris Davidovich.
ANITA KONKKA, *A Fool's Paradise.*
GEORGE KONRÁD, *The City Builder.*
TADEUSZ KONWICKI, *A Minor Apocalypse.*
The Polish Complex.
MENIS KOUMANDAREAS, *Koula.*
ELAINE KRAF, *The Princess of 72nd Street.*
JIM KRUSOE, *Iceland.*
AYŞE KULIN, *Farewell: A Mansion in Occupied Istanbul.*
EMILIO LASCANO TEGUI, *On Elegance While Sleeping.*
ERIC LAURRENT, *Do Not Touch.*
VIOLETTE LEDUC, *La Bâtarde.*
EDOUARD LEVÉ, *Autoportrait.*
Suicide.
MARIO LEVI, *Istanbul Was a Fairy Tale.*
DEBORAH LEVY, *Billy and Girl.*
JOSÉ LEZAMA LIMA, *Paradiso.*
ROSA LIKSOM, *Dark Paradise.*
OSMAN LINS, *Avalovara.*
The Queen of the Prisons of Greece.
ALF MAC LOCHLAINN, *The Corpus in the Library.*
Out of Focus.
RON LOEWINSOHN, *Magnetic Field(s).*
MINA LOY, *Stories and Essays of Mina Loy.*

D. KEITH MANO, *Take Five.*
MICHELINE AHARONIAN MARCOM, *The Mirror in the Well.*
BEN MARCUS, *The Age of Wire and String.*
WALLACE MARKFIELD, *Teitlebaum's Window.*
To an Early Grave.
DAVID MARKSON, *Reader's Block.*
Wittgenstein's Mistress.
CAROLE MASO, *AVA.*
LADISLAV MATEJKA AND KRYSTYNA POMORSKA, EDS., *Readings in Russian Poetics: Formalist and Structuralist Views.*
HARRY MATHEWS, *Cigarettes.*
The Conversions.
The Human Country: New and Collected Stories.
The Journalist.
My Life in CIA.
Singular Pleasures.
The Sinking of the Odradek Stadium.
Tlooth.
JOSEPH MCELROY, *Night Soul and Other Stories.*
ABDELWAHAB MEDDEB, *Talismano.*
GERHARD MEIER, *Isle of the Dead.*
HERMAN MELVILLE, *The Confidence-Man.*
AMANDA MICHALOPOULOU, *I'd Like.*
STEVEN MILLHAUSER, *The Barnum Museum.*
In the Penny Arcade.
RALPH J. MILLS, JR., *Essays on Poetry.*
MOMUS, *The Book of Jokes.*
CHRISTINE MONTALBETTI, *The Origin of Man.*
Western.
OLIVE MOORE, *Spleen.*
NICHOLAS MOSLEY, *Accident.*
Assassins.
Catastrophe Practice.
Experience and Religion.
A Garden of Trees.
Hopeful Monsters.
Imago Bird.
Impossible Object.
Inventing God.
Judith.
Look at the Dark.
Natalie Natalia.
Serpent.
Time at War.
WARREN MOTTE, *Fables of the Novel: French Fiction since 1990.*
Fiction Now: The French Novel in the 21st Century.
Oulipo: A Primer of Potential Literature.
GERALD MURNANE, *Barley Patch.*
Inland.
YVES NAVARRE, *Our Share of Time.*
Sweet Tooth.
DOROTHY NELSON, *In Night's City.*
Tar and Feathers.
ESHKOL NEVO, *Homesick.*
WILFRIDO D. NOLLEDO, *But for the Lovers.*
FLANN O'BRIEN, *At Swim-Two-Birds.*
The Best of Myles.
The Dalkey Archive.
The Hard Life.
The Poor Mouth.

FOR A FULL LIST OF PUBLICATIONS, VISIT:
www.dalkeyarchive.com

SELECTED DALKEY ARCHIVE TITLES

FOR A FULL LIST OF PUBLICATIONS, VISIT:
www.dalkeyarchive.com

SELECTED DALKEY ARCHIVE TITLES